KATHRYN WILLIAMS PLATT

BRYANT AND DILLON PUBLISHERS
ORANGE, NEW JERSEY

Requests to make copies of any part of the work should be mailed to:
Bryant and Dillon Publishers, Inc.
P.O. Box 39
Orange, New Jersey 07050

Library of Congress Cataloging-in-Publication Data
Williams-Platt, Kathryn
1. Forever Mine 2. Afro-American Literature 3.Fiction 4. Civil War 5. Indians
(A Bryant and Dillon Book)

Publisher's Note:
This work is a work of fiction. Names, characters, places and incidents either
are the product of the author's imagination or are used
fictitiously, and any resemblance to actual persons, living or dead, events, or
locales is entirely coincidental.

Printed in the United States of America.

10 9 8 7 6 5 4 3 2 1

This book is dedicated to my parents, Helen and Walter, for their love and patience. To my family, Amber and Jeffrey, for their endurance through it all. To my ninth-period class of 1990–91: Isis, LaToya, Simone, Desiree, and Dwayne, who encouraged me to continue writing when it seemed impossible. And let's not forget Diane, Michele, Mrs. Gibson, and Mrs. Bowie, who all maintained a steady vigil of inspiration. I love you all.

Dedicated to the memory of my grandparents: Bertha, who inspired the story; Hazel; George; and Walter I; and to Aunt Marva. May I always remember and keep in me the values they instilled in me. God Bless!

WILMOT, OHIO
JUNE 29, 1859

CHAPTER ONE

SUMMER WAS JUST COMING into full bloom, and it was a beautiful day for a wedding. At least a hundred guests, friends of the bride and her family, filled the ballroom waiting patiently for the bride to make her entrance.

René Bainbridge was quite beside herself. She projected a state of calm, although she was thoroughly nervous about the approaching nuptials, which were only minutes away. The thought of her wedding taking place on this very day caused her to feel closed in. René knew that she wasn't ready for the role of being the wife of an army captain. She questioned whether she wanted to be part of such a group of people, so disciplined and so orderly.

She recalled the very day she met Captain James Courtland. It was at the annual ball, which was a fund-raiser for the new schoolhouse. He was in his formal uniform, standing among a few of his fellow officers comparing stories of strength and wit. He was very much a man about the time and very well-schooled.

From first glance James Courtland had already made up his mind that she would be his. He made it clear to all that he was taken by her beauty. He was enticed by her narrow waist and by the way she held her head as she walked. Then there was the promise of the Bainbridge fortune: the land, the horses, and, of course, the money. The other officers were warded off and coarsely reprimanded if they even considered becoming one of his rivals.

His dashing manner and gift for gab made it easy for René to accept his courtship. Her parents were thrilled when he asked for her hand, although the suddenness of his proposal made them a bit wary. He was, after all, her first and only courtship.

Then again, why should she worry? She was content with his company. Content? *was and is in all respects, the ideal man,* she kept telling herself. He is handsome, charming . . .

Lily entered René's room without knocking and disturbed her train of thought. She seemed to have a knack for intruding at the worst of moments. Lily had served the Bainbridge family for only a short while. All she knew of the family was that they had come to Ohio years ago when René and her brother, Robert, were only babies.

Life had not been easy for Lily, who was twenty years old and widowed. She had lost her husband of five years in a gunfight over a card game. It had happened more than nine months ago, and she was grateful for the opportunity to work.

"There is a messenger in the lobby waiting for you, Miss René," Lily said softly. She knew that this was probably the wrong time to interrupt René, but the messenger seemed as though he couldn't wait any longer.

"He seems quite anxious to see you, Miss René . I told him it was your wedding day, but he said it was urgent and that he must give a letter to you personally," Lily continued.

René wasn't ready to see anyone. She really wasn't sure if she could go through with the wedding her parents had put so much effort into. "This cannot be happening. Not now! Just take the letter and give him two bits. I will read it later!" René scoffed as she handed Lily the money.

"But he said that he had to give it to *you!* He was very clear about that. And he has some mean eyes. He kinda scares me, a little." Lily's voice trembled.

"Oh, never mind!" René flushed. Then apologized. "I'm sorry, Lily. I'm just nervous about my wedding. Tell him I will be down soon. Oh . . . and Lily, please close the door to the ballroom. It would bring bad luck if the groom should see me before the wedding," she added, while trying to put herself at ease. Lily rushed out of the door to do as she was asked. She wondered what could be so important that it couldn't wait until after the wedding.

René sighed and rested her head in her hands. Then she looked at her reflection in the mirror. The signs of worry were etched across her face.

She applied a small amount of powder to her forehead and neck, where tiny beads of perspiration had formed. Then she pinched her cheeks and brought back some color in her face. She smiled at the reflection, hoping that what she saw would change to her satisfaction. But the signs were still there. Frustrated with everything, she headed for the door, thinking that the next time she entered this room she would be a married woman.

The banister in the hallway and the ballroom had been decorated with assorted flowers, from roses to buttercups. Rachel Bainbridge had made sure that all of her daughter's favorite flowers were everywhere for her to see. The house had a glorious smell, as well as a wonderful appearance. The guests were all seated and waiting patiently for the bride to make her entrance. Only a few noticed Lily as she quickly closed the door to allow her mistress a little privacy.

The messenger, however, wasn't much into waiting. He impatiently asked Lily, "When is this grand lady of yours planning to make her way here?"

Lily turned to look at the man and then decided that he wasn't as scary as she had perceived moments before. She also decided that she didn't like him or his manner. Lily could tell by his tone that he was anxious to leave, especially since he had continued to pace the lobby floor and seemed to be under a great deal of pressure. Then Lily tried to lead him to the kitchen. He was about to argue with her when René descended the steps. He was quite taken with her, so much so that he almost forgot his purpose for being there.

The messenger addressed her directly. "Miss Bainbridge? Miss René Bainbridge? I have a letter for you." He paused briefly before he gently placed the letter in her hands. He had to focus on his task and nothing else. He had been hired anonymously and paid in the same manner. But the colonel had coached him on everything, from what to say and to whom he should direct his attention. Therefore his task would be complete only when the young lady replied to the letter.

At that moment, Devon Bainbridge, owner of the Bainbridge Estates, had just entered the lobby to find his daughter. "Well, well, it's about time you came down," he said endearingly to his daughter.

Devon Bainbridge was a handsome man in his late fifties. He was tall and very much the horseman. He had taught his children to ride and had helped them to learn the family business. He felt that ignorance in any gender was the fault of the head of the family. His constant care and love had developed two beautiful children into loving and responsible adults.

Everyone considered him the doting father, and he was forever showing how proud he was of his children.

He briskly walked up to the messenger. "What's going on here? What business do you have that can't wait until after my daughter's wedding?" Devon demanded.

"I . . . uh . . . I was hired to deliver this letter to your daughter, sir. I am very sorry if I have intruded on this happy occasion. But my orders were specific. Now that I have delivered the letter, I must wait for her response as ordered, sir," the messenger said distinctively.

Devon was puzzled by the urgency of the letter, but prompted René to hurry. "Well, girl, get on with it. Read the darn letter, so we can get on with the marriage. This *is* your wedding party, you know!" Then he smiled. "So darling, what is keeping you from your guests? James is wondering whether you have changed your mind. Have you?" He raised a brow, half flirting with the idea that she had, in fact, changed her mind.

The question was pressing on her, for she still had doubts. Then she realized that she had not yet opened the letter, and the courier was still waiting for her to respond.

René didn't want to raise any more concern, and said, "Father, you know that there is nothing on this earth to keep me from marrying James Courtland. Both you and mother saw fit to make sure he was a true match for me. How can I let either of you down, especially now?"

"There's one thing you have not said, my child. Your words do not include 'love.' Do you love him?" he asked finally.

The messenger began to twitch with impatience as he listened in on their conversation. Without any consideration, he blurted, "Miss Bainbridge, I must have your answer before I leave."

"All right . . . just be patient," René said as she quickly read the letter. Then her eyes widened as she read the heavy print for the second time. The penmanship was crude. It was as though a child had scribbled the message, which read:

Dear Miss Bainbridge,

Urgent. You must cancel your wedding.
There is information in my possession that will
prove you a fraud. You are not whom you claim to be.
If you choose to marry Captain Courtland, he will

lose his rank and position. I think you should take
this very seriously. Your livelihood and his are at stake.
Your father knows the truth.

There was no signature. René examined the note in disbelief. The very thought of someone making such a statement was beyond her comprehension.

Devon took it from her and read it. "Who sent this letter to my daughter?" he demanded. His anger would not be silenced. "I demand to know who sent you here and why, young man!"

The courier couldn't answer Devon, because he didn't know the answer. All he was supposed to do was deliver the letter and wait for a reply. He never bargained on having to deal with anyone else but the girl. Devon's demeanor had cracked. He could no longer hold his temper, and an explosion erupted when the courier asked for the response to the letter again. Devon grabbed the man by the back of his trousers and collar and ran him squarely out of the front door. The courier yelled for help as his feet left the ground and he found himself sailing through the air, then crashing to the ground.

"There will be no answer. Whoever contacted you with this filth . . . is a coward! You tell him that!" Devon ordered, slamming the door behind him.

Devon rushed to his daughter's side. She was apparently in a state of shock. The letter had slipped from her hand and floated like a feather to the floor and landed just under the table. Finally René spoke. "The letter said that I am a fraud. That I am not whom I claim to be! What does that mean . . . Father? What . . . does it mean?"

She became weak in the knees and needed to find a place to sit down. Devon gave her the support she needed. Then she looked into his eyes in wonder and bewilderment. She always thought that her life was based upon the truth. She never found a cause to lie about anything. So, how was she a fraud?

"Father . . . the letter says that I am not whom I claim to be. So who am I?" she asked simply.

Devon was at a loss for words. He couldn't answer her, for he feared the knowledge of her birth would destroy her. He planned long ago to cover all indications of her origin. He also knew, or at least thought, that he was the only one who knew of her birth, besides Sarah Josephine, her mother, and the old slave who helped with her delivery. But they were dead . . . long dead.

Without a word, René slowly walked back to her room. The violinist had started to play the wedding march, but René didn't hear it. She could only hear her heart pounding in her ears. She didn't even hear her father calling after her. Her path was set. Devon was forced to run up the stairs behind her. For too many years he'd kept this secret and he knew it was time to explain. Just as René was about to close the door behind her, Devon slipped his hand through to prevent her from locking him out.

Devon entered and closed the door behind him. He slowly turned to look upon his child. His eyes had reddened from holding back the tears he knew would fall no matter how hard he tried to hold them back. In a whisper he spoke, in a manner that had always calmed her. "I never wanted you to be hurt, René. I always thought that the matter was far from touching you and our family. But now I see that I was wrong . . . very wrong," he said gently.

René started to speak , but he stopped her by placing his finger to her lips. "When you were born, my wife . . . Rachel, had delivered twins . . . a boy and a girl."

"You mean Robert and me?" she asked painfully.

"No, my dear. I am talking about the two who were born the same day you were. As a matter of fact, you were born almost at the same time as the baby girl, almost to the same minute," he continued.

"Father . . . I don't understand," René said cautiously.

Devon interrupted before she could continue. "You want to know why, don't you?" he asked solemnly.

René could only nod her head. And Devon began his tale. "Well, my child, I still feel her in my heart. The memory of that tiny child lives and thrives through you. You see, your mothe—I mean Rachel—had had a difficult delivery. The doctor didn't come until after the babies were born. The little one . . . oh, my God . . . she had trouble breathing. She became so cold, and her tiny body trembled in my arms. I tried in vain to keep her warm. I . . . tried. I tried," Devon cried. "She died in my arms. When she died, a part of me died, too." He paused for a moment, and then continued, "I could not bring myself to tell your mother—I mean, Rachel— that our daughter had died. She wanted a girl so much. So I decided to put you in her place. I had no other choice in the matter, for I loved you, too. I . . . I never thought anyone would find out what I had done twenty years ago," Devon admitted, his voice cracking.

"What would you have done with me had the child lived?" René asked.

She seemed bewildered and betrayed at the same time.

"I had every intention of protecting you even if the baby hadn't died. I wanted you the very moment I saw you," he said hesitantly. "You are my real daughter, too. You must believe that! You must!"

René's heart was pounding so hard and fast, she thought she would die from the pain. And her lungs had tightened to a point where she was nearly unable to breathe. Devon could see that his daughter was in distress and he cradled her head on his broad shoulders. His only thought was to protect her. If he only knew who it was, who threatened to destroy any sense of peace and happiness she knew.

"I love you, my child. All I have ever wanted was your happiness," Devon said as he gently eased her into a lounge chair.

Devon glanced around his daughter's room. He always felt that René had a good eye for color. She spent many hours decorating her room in soft pastels and floral prints. He could smell the gentle perfumes she used, and he immediately remembered her mother. What a beautiful woman she had been. Her memory brought both pain and joy. A memory he knew he would treasure till his dying day.

"You still haven't told me who my mother was. Is she still alive? Where is she?" René asked, her nerves shattered beyond repair.

"Your mother was someone very close to me. She was a beauty that could not be compared to any other. You see . . . my dear, I fell in love with her the instant I saw her. But because of her mixed heritage, we were destined to remain apart. She made every day a blessing and every blessing was cherished until the very end," Devon said as he tried to put his thoughts in order. Then he continued. "Twenty-two years ago I purchased several slaves. Your mother was one of them. I paid a tidy sum for her, and she was worth it all . . . and more. At that time I owned a cotton plantation, so slave ownership was appropriate for my needs. I later found I could no longer own another human being. Your mother had a lot to do with that decision. So, because I took that route and freed all of my slaves, I was forced to sell my plantation."

Devon could feel a sob well up in his throat. And even though René sympathized with her father's pain, she waited in silence. Devon walked toward the window that faced the afternoon sun and continued. "Your mother was born a free woman—somewhere in New York. One day she found herself on a boat heading south for Louisiana. She tried to tell them that they had made a mistake, but they only laughed at her. She was kept away from the others who were captured along with her. I purchased her through a private auction. That was the first time I ever set eyes on her. She was fair of skin with long black hair. She intrigued me more than I ever thought any woman would. So, I kept her close to me. Instead of having her work in the fields, she ran my household. She managed my ledgers whenever I had to leave for business. I always thought she was happy being with me. But she wasn't. It was my constant visits with her that pushed her further away from me."

All of a sudden the room seemed gray. René felt lost and . . . dead to him. She could see his mouth move, but no sound beaconed her ears to awaken. Then she heard him say, "On one of my major business trips, I met and married Rachel Corday. I married her out of convenience . . . at first. I couldn't be with Sarah Josephine and I couldn't let her go. I know I was wrong to continue with such a relationship . . . such that it was. But there was no comparing the two of them. Rachel was beautiful, but she was not my true love."

René could only stare at the floor in disbelief, for what she heard from her father's own lips wasn't possible. She couldn't look at him any longer and wanted to run. A sudden staleness seemed to surround her. She wanted air. She wanted the light of the outdoors. She wanted to run away from all of this. Just then Robert burst in, startling both of them half out of their wits. Devon cleared his throat and wiped the tears from his eyes, while René turned away from both of them. The silence in the room was unbearable, yet, Robert tried to bring some light into their dark and sullen faces.

"I hope I haven't interrupted anything important, but mother is getting worried. We can't keep your guests happy much longer," Robert said hurriedly. "The people are here for a wedding. Well! How about it?"

René couldn't contain her emotions much longer. She turned to her father and asked, "Shall I tell him—or will you? I . . . I know the moment he hears the truth, he will certainly hate me! He will!"

Robert quickly surmised that he had walked into something that was far more serious than he had imagined. He approached his father for an answer as to what ailed his sister. Devon, however, seemed unwilling to disclose the problem. Robert turned and joined his sister on the lounge chair and asked, "What could possibly make me hate you, René? You are not only my sister, you are my best friend!"

Robert was getting nowhere. His words could not penetrate the wall that was obviously growing between them. Then without any warning,

René blurted, "The wedding is off! I can't marry James now. I may have been uncertain about marrying him before the letter came, but now I am very certain. He would never marry into a family whose lives and fortunes are built on lies. And besides—with my past—he wouldn't want to take a chance. You agree with me, don't you?"

There was no dispute from her father, who offered little to Robert's understanding of the crisis his sister was enduring. However, Robert was thrilled that she had called it off. He was glad that she had finally come to her senses.

As though shot out of a pistol, René bolted for the door and stormed out of her room. She left both men to handle the mess that had been created by the deceit of her own father. She ran as far as her legs would carry her until she reached the stables at the east end of the house. She wanted to be alone with the pain that consumed her.

Meanwhile, Devon cleared his throat and headed for the open door. It was apparent that the wedding was definitely off. He tried to hide his disappointment when he said, "Bring James to my study. It wouldn't help your sister any if he were told by someone else."

Robert hurried out, for he had every intention of learning what had happened and why his sister was in so much distress. Rest assured he would find out. Robert walked into the ballroom drawing some unwanted attention. The musicians continued to play a gentle tune to keep the crowd at ease. The ladies sat fanning themselves, putting on airs, making excuses, and of course gossiping about the bride and her family. The men, however, wagered whether the wedding would go off without a hitch. Robert ignored everything he heard, for his goal was straight ahead of him and looking very worried.

James Courtland stood tall and erect, just as if he were standing at attention. His commanding officer, Colonel Sheridan, kept him from losing his patience and managed to help him maintain his honor.

There was something about James that made Robert feel his sister would be in danger while in his care. By the look on his face, James most certainly wasn't happy about the delay.

Robert quickly got James's attention and summoned him in his direction. He was trying not to rouse any more attention his way. James, a gentleman to every extent, followed Robert's lead and joined him by the door. After clearing his throat, Robert said calmly, "There's been a delay. Father wants you to come to his study."

James was puzzled at the ease with which Robert spoke. He knew that Robert didn't care for him. And he knew it all stemmed from the day that he had intercepted a letter of recommendation for the academy meant for Robert. With a little ink and the penmanship of a good forger, James took the only open seat. Robert was the only one who knew of this farce. Since then, the two men were rarely found in each other's company.

No words were shared between the two as they reached the study. There was tension in the air, and James began to realize that something was amiss. Both men entered the study simultaneously. Then Devon asked that the doors be closed. Once they were closed, Devon spoke clearly, but also very blandly. "James, I am sorry to tell you, my boy, that René has had a change of heart. She has decided . . . not to wed." Devon wasn't sure how well James would accept the news. But, he knew he had to plead René's case and justify it. Devon paused for a moment, then said, "Something has happened, and she discovered that she wasn't quite ready to settle down."

Devon would do anything necessary to protect his daughter, even if it meant lying. But he faced a man whose honor was at stake and who faced being the laughingstock. Devon considered all options as he watched James pace the floor like a caged animal. He swallowed and then cleared the lump in his dry throat. He had so much ground to cover, but his offering would be sparse and unattractive compared to his daughter. He wondered whether to compensate the boy for his trouble, but that was thrown out when James refuted René's decision.

"It seems that someone has turned her against me," he said as he eyed Robert with contempt.

"No . . . that's not true! She's just not ready. I know you were looking forward to making a life with her, but . . . " he was interrupted before he could say another word.

James had reached his boiling point. He was definitely not happy about the prospects of losing a family fortune in this manner. He had already written a letter to the head of state to resign his commission. Everything was ruined. He wanted to hit someone, anyone, but he held back. He eyed the elder Bainbridge like a wolf about to attack. The Bainbridge land, the money, and the assets well into the millions were slipping through his fingers. He looked around the study, thinking this was supposed to be his. *His fortune! His money!*

"So, I'm not good enough for your precious daughter. Well, we *will* see about that!" James snarled. "But I have reason to believe that there is something you are not telling me. Is that correct sir?"

James's anger was more profound than ever, for he was now standing toe to toe with the elder Bainbridge. Each time he spoke, his sarcasm and dislike became more noticeable. There was no turning back now that the wound had been opened. Both men were about to engage in a major confrontation. Robert was about to jump in when Colonel Sheridan entered and managed to draw the attention to himself. "Gentlemen! *Gentlemen!* I could hear you both clear out in the lobby. I came to make sure everything was in order for the wedding, but it seems that there is another matter to be considered here," he said with great authority and ease.

Colonel Sheridan, known by his men as Colonel Sherry, was very aware of the problem brewing between the intended groom and his future father-in-law. Pandora 's box had been opened, and he was secretly glad he would be there to reap over the end results.

"Well, son, it seems you have been left standing at the alter. I expect you to conduct yourself in the manner that will not shame the uniform you wear," Sheridan stated firmly. "You host has shown you every courtesy by not announcing this news in front of your company. I do believe an apology is in order."

"Yes . . . quite true! An apology is definitely in order. *But it will not be coming from me!*" James said insubordinately.

Robert waited and watched for any indication of James's volatile nature. Before another word could be spewed, the jilted groom left the room. James was planning to find René himself. She would not be able to put him off, not like this.

"Wait a minute . . . James . . . wait! You can't force her to marry you," Robert called after her.

"And who's going to stop me? You? Don't make me laugh"! James retorted.

"Now wait a minute! If you think I'm going to let you . . . " Robert was cut off. James waved him off and walked away. Robert turned to his father, who seemed at wit's end. He knew that James would stop at nothing until he spoke to René face to face. That was the one thing she didn't need. But, Devon was tired of trying to reason with James. He was a clever man. No matter what was said, James would twist it to suit his needs. Through it all, he never once said he loved René. Those few words would have made all the difference.

Robert and Devon were not far behind James as he headed toward the door. Devon took one more try at convincing him to give René some time, "René is very upset right now. She didn't want to hurt you. But at the present time she is unable to fulfill her promise to marry you."

"You won't mind if I find this out for myself . . . will you?" James asked. There was no turning back now. He had already shown that he didn't care for René and it was more than apparent that he had other plans for her and her share of the Bainbridge Estates. He, in other words, intended to have it all.

There were very few places for René to go in such a short period of time. She had to be nearby from what James had surmised. He turned away from the front door, climbed the stairs, and paid a visit to her rooms, which were forbidden to him until after the wedding. They were empty. Then he ran down the stairs and into the dining hall, where he ran into Lily, who had just finished setting the large table. *She would know where to find René*, he thought.

James's sudden entry caused Lily to drop a crystal goblet on the floor. She cried out, since she knew that every broken glass or dish would be a week's worth of lectures from the matriarch of the house. She surely wasn't looking forward to that session.

"Lily!" James said in a commanding voice. "Where is Miss René ?"

"I don't know, sir. I have been here for a spell," she answered slowly.

But that wasn't a good enough answer for him. He grabbed her by her upper arms and shook her violently. The glare in his steel-blue eyes made Lily's feet too frightened to move and her mouth too horrified to speak. He roared his demands down her throat. Then he shook her again, painfully.

"*Where is she? . . . Where is she?*" he demanded again and again.

Frightened and terrified of the man abusing her, Lily cried out tearfully, "*I don't know! Please ! Please! I have been here since I told her about the messenger. Honestly! I don't know where she is!*"

Robert walked in just in time to catch James in the act. In his fury to find René, he had left a trail that was easy to follow. All the servants, including the one preparing René's room, were able to tell in detail what had transpired.

"Why don't you leave her alone?" Robert stated calmly, but not for the benefit of James Courtland. "She *doesn't* know where René is! I, *however, do!*" He continued, knowing that he had his nemesis's attention. "You know . . . I'm glad things turned out the way they did. You have cheated this family once too often. Now it's time to get what you deserve," he smirked.

James responded quickly, knowing that the Bainbridge heir had the upper hand. "And what do I deserve, little boy? Do you think you can stop me? Hmmm?" he asked as he pushed Lily aside like a rag doll.

"Would you really like to find out? It seems you like abusing women. René is not the kind of woman who would tolerate abuse of any kind. And you, *my friend* are just a black-hearted fool," Robert pressed, knowing how to ignite James's fiery temper.

The remark stung as Robert hoped it would. He used it like a whip and struck again. The result ended with the two charging each other like young bulls. They crashed to the floor in a clinch. They rolled into the legs of the table and chairs that were in their path. A punch bowl tilted over and spilled its contents to the floor.

Robert had speed on his side and he used his wits to put James in his place. He managed to free himself and had gotten to his feet before James could catch his breath. He glared at James, who could barely stand on his own. Lily was still cowering in the corner of the room. She was the only distraction James needed to wrestle Robert back down to the floor.

"Robert yelled out, his voice very anxious, "Get out of here, Lily! Make sure René . . . keep her out!"

Lily couldn't move fast enough to suit herself. She fretted all the way through the kitchen, wondering where she should go first. She headed down the path that led to the gardens, but René was nowhere in sight. As she passed the hedges that surrounded the gardens, she said aloud, "The stables . . . René goes to the stables to visit Star Fire when she has a lot on her mind."

Lily hurried along, knowing that eventually René would be coming back to the house. How would she be able to keep René from doing what she wanted? She was a paid servant. Although René never at any time made her her feel like a servant, Lily's own pride kept them from becoming friends.

As Lily neared the stables, she heard the loud crash come from within the house. She ascertained that it was glass being shattered. And she was correct. The punch bowl, the matching cups, and almost all of the china lay in broken shards all over the floor. The large dining table had been pushed so far and so hard that it put a hole into the wall. A few chairs were broken and were now being used as weapons. Food and glass everywhere.

All of the guests filed in one by one to see who would be the victor. They watched in amazement as Robert landed another right cross to James's jaw, sending him across the table. James, thoroughly shaken by the blow, finally realized that this was not an old man punching him. He was faced with a twenty-year-old whose blood was just as hot as his. He had rethink, to reorganize his thoughts against such a worthy opponent. No one had ever been able to get the best of him, but Robert proved otherwise. Now, in front of all his guests, he had to regain his respect.

James spied a wine bottle on the floor just within reach. He flung himself toward it, avoiding the fist that most certainly would have knocked him out. He grabbed the bottle, then stood on his shaky legs. With a smile—a smile of cunning—James broke the bottle, sending glass in all directions. A woman's scream made him hesitate momentarily. That moment cost him, allowing Robert time to recuperate from the volley of blows he had given and received.

James lunged at Robert, but he slipped on the the food that covered the floor, giving Robert the edge he needed. He reached for the tablecloth and threw it over James's head as he made another pass. He wrapped James up like a fine package. Though tired and weary of the fight, Robert couldn't resist giving James one final blow, leaving him sprawled under the table. He heard the women voice strong opinions about his treatment of the groom, and each of the men were more than happy that it was Robert rather than them facing the tough man from Fort Wayne.

"Get him out of here!" Robert ordered as he leaned against the wall for support.

Devon quickly echoed his son's words. Lieutenant Gantry, one of the new officers of the fort, offered to assist. Colonel Sheridan apologized to his host for the shameful behavior of his junior officer. He had to maintain a margin of control, even though he secretly hoped James would be the victor of the ruckus.

The noises in the house prompted Lily to quicken her pace to the stables. She rounded the bend only to find the stable empty. René had taken Star Fire from his stall, and there was no telling where she could be or when she would return. After pondering over where her mistress might be, Lily decided to wait for her to return. She made herself comfortable on the cot in the stable boy's room. At least she wouldn't have to go back to the house, not just yet.

Lily didn't look forward to cleaning up the mess after such a fight. Then she wondered why Robert had defended her from the monstrous James Courtland. It wasn't the first time she felt her heart flutter over his nearness. There were many days she found herself blushing when he would ask for the smallest thing. She knew that she would never have a chance with him, except in her most private thoughts and dreams.

A half hour later René approached the stables on Star Fire in full gallop. The horse must have run for miles, for the foam on his back was thick, and his body was quaking. René quickly dismounted and rushed to the trough to wet down the rags and wipe him off. She had just started to cool him down when she noticed the door to the stable boy's room was ajar.

"That's strange! It was closed when I left," she said as she continued to wipe the sweat from Star Fire's back.

She knew that the stable boy always closed his room off when he was scheduled to be away. She shrugged her shoulders and proceeded to administer the cool cloth behind Star Fire's ears. The horse snorted with content as the water splashed all over him. He seemed to sigh with relief, because his eyes sparkled when she allowed him to drink from her hands.

René's wedding dress was ruined, saturated with the water spilling from her hands. She didn't care; after all, she wasn't getting married today—or maybe ever. She couldn't think that far ahead. The prospects of marrying anyone at this time caused a dull ache in her head.

"I will be better off alone, anyway," she said in Star Fire's ear. "And besides, I have a lot to be . . . " She had a loss of words. Nothing . . . nothing in this entire matter made any sense to her.

She took time to remove Star Fire's saddle and then propped it up against the wall. Then she burst into tears and cried out, "How could he? How could he do such a thing to me?"

René realized now that the ride had only helped her to focus in on She felt naked and vulnerable after hearing her father's account of her birth. She wouldn't be able to live the same lie that her father had lived for all these years. She wanted to hate him, to hate Sarah Josephine—her mother—a woman she'd never had the chance to know.

With that settled into her head, René continued to administer cool water to Star Fire's back. He suddenly whinnied to let her know he was feeling better. He brushed his nose against her playfully, knocking over the pail of water. But she wasn't in a mind to play. Scornfully, René picked up the pail and threw it against the wall. For the first time in her life things were out of control with no chance of getting better.

CHAPTER

TWO

THE BAINBRIDGE DINING HALL had taken on a new decor. The walls were covered with food and debris was strewn in all directions, covering the walls and dripping from the shattered dinnerware. Devon stood back and took in what was left of his daughter's wedding and just sighed. There was nothing to do but send their guests home with any excuse he could make. And yet, in all the excitement, he had forgotten that there was another person involved.

"Rachel, my God, my poor Rachel!" he exclaimed as he pushed through the stragglers who still wanted to see more. "How do I explain this to you?"

Rachel, overwhelmed with grief, felt weak and helpless. She had just watched her son and intended son-in-law try to kill each other. "Why? Why is this happening?!" she begged. "There was supposed to be a wedding—a glorious wedding—but look what they've done to my poor baby's beautiful wedding day." She seemed weary and unable to handle any more excitement. Yet, she wanted answers. She looked at her husband, her son, and then Colonel Sheridan, hoping one of them would shed some light on the matter.

Devon's family and his way of life were being torn apart. He could only wonder who was behind it all. He finally bid farewell to the last of the guests, or so he thought, when he happened to see that Colonel Sheridan hadn't departed with Captain Courtland. The Colonel didn't seem to be in a hurry to assist or comfort his fallen junior officer. But there he was, comforting Devon's beloved Rachel with soothing words and gently stroking her hands with his. Devon was suddenly jolted with jealousy, and his angry presence was noticed immediately. The last thing he needed was the meddling hand of George Sheridan interfering with his family.

Robert stayed by the door, torn between wanting to stay with his parents and searching for his sister. He, too, felt a twinge of anger seeing the colonel so close to his mother, as if they couldn't come to her aid. Devon, however, put his anger aside and spoke calmly to his wife. "Rachel . . . dear . . . I know this has upset you, but we will have to talk when all the guests have gone," he added for Colonel Sheridan's benefit.

Rachel hadn't been well for many months, and she had put all her energy into making René's wedding day a special one. There wasn't a day that went by when she hadn't issued orders for the furniture to be moved, for the best flowers to be picked from the garden, or for the food to be prepared just right for the wedding feast. She was relentless. She wanted her daughter to be happy. And besides, the whole town was waiting for the event with great expectations.

Even with all the concern centering around the wedding, Rachel was unaware of what was happening in her family. She felt certain that the escapade that had just taken place would definitely affect René most horribly. She was about to ask more of her husband, when Devon quickly put his finger to her lips to silence her. He knew what she wanted.

Then he gave his full undivided attention to Colonel Sheridan. Without giving the colonel a chance to argue, he gave him leave. "Now, Colonel Sheridan—George—if you don't mind, I would like to have some time with my wife . . . alone," he said directly.

It was an abrupt indication to leave. As much as he wanted to, George couldn't put up a fuss. The tone in Devon's voice was enough to let him know that he had no choice in the matter. The Bainbridge Estates wasn't his home, even though there were times he imagined it to be. Without a word to his host, George quickly snatched his hat from the mantle and barged his way through the large hall. As he passed the center table in the lobby, he spied the neatly folded letter on the floor. Swiftly he picked it up and placed it in his sash. Finally, as though he had won a round, he gave a wry smile as he adjusted his hat and made his way out of the door.

"The Bainbridge family will feel what it's like to be cut off," he said under his breath. His plans to ruin Devon's name had taken root. Then he dignified himself, standing tall and proud. "Hey, you, over there . . . get my horse. And be quick about it!" He was ready to play his trump card, only Devon wouldn't know that he was playing his game. He felt quite sure that no one suspected him, since he had covered all possible areas that would lead back to him.

"Your horse, sir," young Jonas said, almost whispering. If he seemed shy, he had good reason. The colonel always frightened him. He usually overheard the colonel plotting to do away with Devon Bainbridge, but never really took him seriously. Now, the colonel had the look of a mad dog. He was up to something.

As George Sheridan rode back to the fort, he remembered the time he spent courting Rachel. She was the beautiful Rachel Corday of Hamilton County twenty-two years ago. "Two long years I courted her," he said. He remembered the day he proposed to her. He presented her with a small ruby ring to seal their promise, and she refused him. Rather, her father refused to allow a mere cadet to marry his daughter. "Then that bastard . . . Devon Bainbridge came to Hamilton County and stole my Rachel . . . *my Rachel!*" he fussed. To this day, George Sheridan hadn't forgiven Devon. He pined over her, still dreaming of the day when she would be his. But he had nothing but his rank to give. And Rachel, the beauty that she was and still remained, kept putting him off. She never gave him a chance to make good on his word to her. "Now I hold the rank of colonel," he said with great esteem. "That . . . should account for something."

He snorted with anger when her wedding announcement flashed before him. It took Devon less than a month to marry her. Those memories made his blood boil to a point where he made his horse move into full gallop. His mind, still focused on the past, recalled how little anyone knew about Devon Bainbridge: a man who presented himself with letters of introduction and put himself among the ranks of the rich. However, they only knew that he once owned land in Louisiana and was now a successful businessman who planned to buy horses and breed them for the government. That appealed to Rachel's parents, who quickly gave their blessings for the two to wed. Devon had everything. He was handsome, wealthy, and ambitious . . . and he had Rachel. George lacked all these qualities. That alone put another bitter taste in his mouth. Again he pushed his horse into full gallop, pressing his spurs into its sides and drawing blood.

Meanwhile, George Sheridan raced back to the fort, and Rachel waited patiently for her husband to explain the day's events. There was a problem, and it was focused on their missing daughter. She slowly rose from her chair and walked toward her son. She could see that he was in pain, most of which was caused by the brawl. Yet, she could see there was more. She wanted to console him, but turned to face Devon, who could barely look her in the eye.

Puzzled by his reaction, she decided to fuss about the obvious. "This is disgraceful! Both you and James should be ashamed of yourselves," she said as she turned to face Robert again. "Did you even think how this would affect your sister?" she continued as she crossed the floor, moving broken glass and debris out of her path. Then she blustered,"Look at this mess! My favorite china . . . broken into thousands of pieces!" Both men couldn't help but look at the shambles. There was immeasurable damage to the dining hall, but to make matters worse, the truth of why it had occurred still hadn't surfaced. Without a word, Devon signaled Robert to leave the room.

Lily awoke to the sound of René's voice and to water splashing. Without thinking of how she would be received, she rushed out of stable boy's room in such a manner that startled everything breathing. It took a while to calm the horses with the commotion she brought in. René was still shaken by the news she had received earlier, but still managed to bring everything under control. "Are you out of your mind?" she asked. "Whoa . . . whoa Star Fire. It's all right," she tried to say in a gentler tone. Her heart was throbbing like a drum. "You can't just burst in here like that! You and I could have been killed!" she said angrily, even though she knew it was misplaced anger.

"I'm sorry, Miss René !" Lily flushed as she tried to hold back her tears. "But I was told to keep you from the house. Your brother and . . . Captain Courtland . . . well . . . I was told to keep you from the house," she stammered.

"What do you mean 'keep me from the house'?" René asked.

But Lily couldn't bring herself to tell what had happened in René's absence. She could still feel the imprints of the captain's hands on her shoulders, a moment she wouldn't want to relive. She was frightened and began to wring her apron while she looked from the door to the window and then back to the door again.

René could see that Lily was in distress and managed to change her demeanor toward her. Then she asked calmly, "Has something happened back at the house?"

Lily nodded quickly and continued to watch the door as though it were about to explode. René's nerves were already at their peak. She didn't want to think of anything, not even her present situation. However, she knew something was bothering Lily or else the poor girl wouldn't be acting so weird. "Is Robert all right? My parents . . . are they . . . ?"

"I don't know, Miss René ," Lily interrupted with respect. "I don't know what happened after I left them fighting . . . . "

"Fighting? Who, and over what, may I ask?" René continued as she used her wedding dress to wipe the dirt from her hands.

Lily bit her lip. She only knew what she had seen, and she was sure that Robert didn't want his sister to hear of it secondhand. So she quickly changed the subject. "Oh, Miss René ! Your lovely dress—it's ruined! " she exclaimed, hoping in vain that René wouldn't try to press her for more information. At least this way she was sure that what ever the problem, Robert would handle it well.

René knew then what had occurred. She knew that James wasn't the sort of man to take "no" for an answer. She also knew her brother only tolerated James, just for her, and that Robert would only take so much before he would take James on. "Then it's all over," she said dryly.

Without another word to Lily, René dropped everything she was doing and headed out of the stables. "I need some time to myself, Lily," she said as she made her exit. She had had more than her share of anguish . . . enough to last a lifetime. James would never understand her plight, because she didn't understand it herself. With the wedding called off, she would have more time on her hands, time to find the truth. Yet, she wondered, what truth? For now, she was better off alone.

Robert suddenly burst through the door just in time to see his sister making her way to the open field. He called to her, but she didn't or wouldn't hear him . "I'd better get out there before she decides to run off," he said as he jumped the porch railing. His shirt was torn and practically falling of his shoulders. When he reached René's side, he was puffing and blowing, completely out of breath. "René . . . René, stop!" he gasped.

She turned to face him, her mind set on telling him to leave her alone, but she stopped short of crying when she saw him. "Oh my God! Robert, are you hurt?"

"It doesn't bother me any," he said playfully.

"But your face—look at you—your clothes, Robert," she said softly as she touched his cheek.

"This is nothing!" he responded quickly while taking her hand. "James looks far worse than I do."A smile etched across his face, but changed instantly to concern toward her. "Now, dear sister, don't you think it's time you told me what's really going on?" He was determined to learn the truth.

"I can't!" she exclaimed. "I can't bring myself to talk about it."

"It can't be that bad," he said soothingly. "No matter what you say, I don't think it will change the way I feel about you. You are my sister, remember? My twin sister."

His words only brought her pain to the surface. He could see it in her eyes just how much she suffered. "*Sister!*" René exclaimed. "I'm not you sister or anyone else's for that matter."

Shocked at what had passed from his sister's lips, he snapped. "What on earth are you babbling about? Don't be ridiculous!" he said sharply as he grabbed her wrist. He was just as confused then as he had been when she had run out of the house earlier. His father didn't even give him a clue. And René . . . well, she just wasn't making any sense.

But, René was quite serious, and everything she had said up to that moment made sense to her. Her pain was far greater than even he could imagine. And she seemed to look through him as though he weren't there. She was trying to put what little she had left of herself back into some means of control. She needed more than a brother; she needed a friend.

"Can you stand being the laughingstock of Wilmot?" she asked coldly. "Well . . . can you?"

Without giving it much thought, he replied, "It doesn't matter what the people of Wilmot think. Nothing matters except you, our mother, and our father. Anyway, what's that got to do with anything?" he pressed. He had lost all patience in waiting for her to respond. He wanted her to tell everything. If he could, he would fix it, just for her.

Seeing that she wasn't going to get out of answering him, she blurted, "I'm not your twin sister. I'm . . . just your half-sister . . . your half sis——."

"That's silly and you know it," he said, somewhat shocked that she would consider saying such a foolish thing. "Are you trying to play a joke on me?" he asked finally, but he could see that she wasn't laughing. The wedding being called off so abruptly and the strange way their father was acting made him wonder if there was some truth in what she was saying.

"You can't believe it. That's just the way I felt. In these past few minutes—or just after I learned about myself—I wondered why. I even tried to understand, but I'm too overwhelmed with it all," she said as she brushed at her dress. Then she decided to put the rest in his hands, almost without mercy.

"Stop!" he yelled. "Just stop! Don't say anymore!" He turned away from her briefly, saying in a manner that was somewhat ragged and anguished, "I would've known . . . even you would've known the difference." But his bantering landed on deaf ears. He was truly astonished. "René . . . *René* . . . this can't be true," he said, almost pleading. But René said nothing to change her story. He paced the grassy meadow where they had played as children and where now as adults they were trying to salvage what they could of their lives.

"Now you know just as much as I do," René added. Then there was silence between them, more silence than either of them were used to. "I've been living a lie, Robert. The only difference is, I didn't know it," she said finally. René withdrew again, trying to escape into her own world. She wanted to die, and he knew it. At least in death, she would be René Alexandra Bainbridge.

Robert held René at arm's length and said, "I don't care about your past, it's your future that I'm concerned with. And, as far as I'm concerned, you are and will always be my twin sister."

Without another word, they watched the sky as the clouds covered the sun and brought shade to the field. A light breeze cooled Robert's brow, even though his heart was angry and full of rage. He admired the calm, distinctive guise that his sister portrayed. Her hair was still in place, and her dress had dried without leaving a wrinkle, though it was a bit soiled. The only wrinkle was on her forehead, one of worry. He had to wonder who could have written the letter in the first place. How could this person know so much about her birth and, of course, make threats? There were only a few people involved that day: his father, the midwife, and Sarah Josephine, René's real mother. None of it made any sense. René had no enemies. She was, however, envied by many women who wanted the attention of the dapper young captain. But that wasn't enough to bring René so much pain. Whoever he is, he posed a threat not only to René but to the entire family. They would have to wait for him to play his next hand. "When I find out who he is . . . he's dead," Robert said under his breath.

Then he hugged his sister, letting her know he loved her regardless. They walked back to the house together to face their parents.

In the northern territory, nearly 450 miles north of Wilmot, a small band of Ojibwa Indians were heading for the trading post with their bounty. They were traveling south along the Canadian border into Michigan, keeping Lake Erie to the left. This vast land hadn't been charted or mapped since the early 1800s by the French. The only ones to travel these lands, other than those native to it, happened to be the French trappers and several black-robed priests who traveled from village to village teaching the word of God.

The young Ojibwa band had planned to trade for horses and supplies for the winter. The leader was a strong young man of twenty-four summers, who held a great sense of dedication for his people, always putting their needs before his own. But, on this trip, he planned to bring something home that would only belong to him.

Two days prior to leaving his home, he had paid a visit to the shaman. His dream revealed that the trade would be the best it had ever been in years. They would have meat in their cache, and rice would be plenty even through the cold of winter. However, the best his vision had come last. He would not spend the winter months alone. He would have the woman of his dreams cooking his meals and making his home a place for the living again.

He knew that the woman he sought would be coming to the trading post. The only thing he had to do was wait. *She will come*, he said to himself as they walked through the forest. They had several miles to go, and he didn't want to rush. The sun was setting—a signal for the new camp to be set. They would stay here for the day, hunting and fishing and digging another cache for their supplies. All would be well when they arrived at the trading post. All would be well.

All was not well on the Bainbridge Estates. René hadn't spent any time with her mother or father since that ill-fated day. Rachel wanted to comfort her daughter, hoping in vain that she would finally come and confide in her. But René kept to herself and stayed locked in her room, content to wallow in her own tears. She hadn't eaten or slept in two days. She avoided Robert, who pleaded with her to go riding with him. She refused to allow Lily to enter her room, not even to change her linen.

René sat in her window seat and pondered her life. There was little she could do. She thought about going east, but she had no family there to speak of. She even considered Europe, but was she planning to live a lie there as well? What could she do?

CHAPTER

THREE

JUST AS RENÉ PONDERED her future and what was to become of her, minds were at work plotting to destroy the peaceful existence her parents had given for so many years.

The evening breeze was dry and hot. Colonel Sheridan sat calmly at his desk, smiling and feeling that he had reached a pinnacle that would make him great in the eyes of his lost love. He was quite satisfied with the events of the fumbled wedding and with Courtland's feeble attempts to regain respect from the Bainbridge clan. He had to make sure Courtland took the blame for whatever transpired after his altercation with the brash Bainbridge heir.

"No one will know that I orchestrated the whole thing. I especially enjoyed the look on the young René's face when she read the letter. She honestly believed what was in the letter. Poor thing. She is a lovely young woman, but she and her scheming father are in my way. The whole lot of them are going to get everything that's coming to them," he said as he pulled the letter from the drawer. "If God wills it, I will have Rachel with me by the end of the week. Devon's name will be smeared, and he and his children will be forced to leave Wilmot." He felt he had concocted an ideal plan. The fate of five lives were hanging on the fringes. With satisfaction, he poured himself a generous glass of whiskey and made a toast to the fall of the Bainbridge empire.

Meanwhile, the fort was being readied for inspection. Sergeant Wills, who had escorted Captain Courtland back to the fort, had also been given the duty of preparing the colonel's new quarters. Fresh bedding and new linen had been brought in from town. Even a new mirror with beveled edges was gently transported to the fort.

"I wonder who the colonel is expecting with all this finery?" Young Private Smith asked.

"That is none of your concern, boy," Wills said sharply. "Just bring it in and don't break anything. You hear me, boy?" he demanded.

"Yes, sir!" the private answered quickly. Smith was used to being put in his place and made no further mention of the delicate pieces he and Wills placed in the inner room. He was a boy, no more than seventeen, whose father thought it necessary to put his bungling son in the army to make a man out of him. He was a little slow at following orders, yet he always seemed to try harder than the others. "Yes, sir!" he said again.

Even Wills wondered what was going on. The colonel had been acting strange lately. He had ordered several men to go on patrol when they had only just returned. He had them clean the stables twice in a single day, never accounting for the first order he had given. He repeatedly yelled at the men; mostly, however, at Private Smith, who jumped every time he came near. It was clear that something was bothering the man, but no one dared to inquire.

Smith went out to gather up the last piece of the furniture when he was summoned to report to Colonel Sheridan. He began to tremble in his boots, because only a fortnight ago he had caused a stampede when he burned down a section of the stables. The colonel's horse was injured in that fiasco, and Smith began to wonder whether he had done something else wrong. If he had, he knew that he didn't want to have another run-in with the old man, especially when he was in such a bad mood. When he reached the colonel's quarters, his knees began to buckle. He wiped the sweat from his forehead and took a deep breath before knocking. How was he to know that he wasn't in trouble this time?

Colonel Sheridan was thoroughly irritated and becoming more so waiting for the addlebrained youth to get there. He had waited long enough and he abruptly snatched the door open. Smith's hand was still clutching the doorknob, and he was yanked into the room practically falling over his feet. He could barely bring himself to attention when the colonel cleared his throat and said, "It took you long enough, boy!"

"I'm sorry, Colonel Sherry," Smith squeaked. "I mean, sir!" The boy knew full well he had made another error by using his superior officer's name in a familiar manner. He knew that it meant extra duty, probably cleaning the mess hall, or was it back to the stables again? He was still serving extra duty for mis-addressing Captain Courtland.

"Boy . . . you haven't learned how to act like a soldier! You are a sad excuse, " he tried to say sympathetically. It was as though he had patted Smith on the back. "Now, have you and Sergeant Wills finished putting the furniture in my new quarters?" he asked.

Private Smith snapped to attention. "Yes, sir, yes, sir! Everything is in order."

"Very well, Private, and has the captain completed his inspection of the grounds yet?" he asked, knowing very well that the captain was still incapacitated.

Confused that the colonel would ask him, a private of all people, about Captain Courtland, the boy began to babble. He hadn't seen the captain in two days and was quite glad of it. The last time he saw the captain, he was being helped from his horse, bruised and battered, and taken to his quarters. From what he had seen of him, he was worse for wear. The colonel's tone changed again. This time Private Smith heard the familiar sounds of anger. The only thing he could do was tell what he knew. "I haven't seen the captain for two days, sir."

"*Two days!*" Sheridan roared. "*What the hell is going on here?!*"

Smith nearly jumped out of his skin. He didn't know any more than what he had seen. Then again, he did take a peek just to see how bad the captain had fared. He even remembered how he had laughed at the way the captain had fallen from his horse and had wondered who had done this to the almighty Captain Courtland.

Seeing that the private wasn't going to be any help, Sheridan demanded, "Well, who knows, boy? Make it quick!"

"I think Sergeant Wills saw him last as far as I know, sir. I don't . . . know any . . . more, sir!" Smith exclaimed. He was shaking again. "Get out! You're no help to me, boy! Send me someone with more wits than you! Send me Wills now, boy!" he demanded.

"Yes sir! . . . Yes, sir!" Smith said as he ran through the door. He had forgotten to salute again. The colonel was anxious for him to leave and didn't bother to call him back. Maybe it didn't matter that he hadn't paid his respects—not this time, at least.

Wills had just left Captain Courtland's quarters. He didn't relish having to put a grown man to bed, much less clean up after him. But the man was in a drunken stupor and had been that way since his return from the Bainbridge Estates without his bride. He hadn't completed his rounds in the fort, nor had he compiled the new orders from Washington. If it hadn't been for Lieutenant Gantry and Lieutenant Birney, he would have lost his rank for sure.

Wills grumbled under his breath, "I always manage to get the dirty jobs. If there's one thing I can't stand . . . " He stopped short of mumbling his last outburst, when he saw Smith rushing toward him. He wondered how much the youngster had heard.

"Private, you'd better have a good reason for being here!" he bellowed. Then he lowered his voice, being mindful of the occupant behind the door.

Before he could utter another word, the boy said anxiously, "The colonel wants you . . . he's awful mad . . . I mean, he's not . . . "

"All right, all right, already!" he scoffed. "In the meantime, you still have to finish cleaning out the stables, or have you forgotten?" Wills asked sarcastically.

"No sir! No sir, I haven't forgotten," he answered reluctantly. But he was glad that he didn't have to face the colonel again.

Wills sighed and rounded his shoulders. This was going to be a long evening. It never failed: The colonel would call on him to do the work he couldn't do or wouldn't do for himself. In the twenty years of his serving in the United States Army, he had served under the best officers that the academy had produced. Now, he was serving under a lout and an arrogant son of a bitch, who could drain the very soul of you.

In his mind he rehearsed the words that the colonel had ordered him to say to René Bainbridge. He wondered why he had to deliver a message to her in the first place. Why did he have to put the letter in her hand directly? When he looked up to see her descend the stairs, he could hardly keep his nerve. There she was, standing there before him, beautiful and innocent. When she touched his hand to take the letter, he thought of how lucky Captain Courtland was. He could still smell the soft scent of the rose water she wore that day.

He hadn't read the letter. He didn't know that it would hurt anyone, especially her. Even in her pain, her beauty remained unscathed. In his mind's eye her could still see her bright green eyes, her shapely fingers, and the lovely way she walked. "Why was the colonel so interested in the Bainbridge family? What did the young woman have to do with it?" Wills asked as he reached the colonel's office. "To have a woman like that is any man's dream."

The moon seemed to create a reflection of water across the grounds. The fort was always well-kept, even after the detailed maneuvers on horseback. Yet, the grass was turning brown from lack of rain. The well was low, and the horses needed watering daily. The men would have to ration what water they had left now that the water shipment from the Bainbridge Estates might not be coming. The smell of sweat and hay filled the air. The night air delivered no breeze to touch the brows of the men on duty. The stillness of the night changed briefly with the low rapping sound on a door frame and a door slowly creaking open and then closing. A new plan was about to be put into action, and the players were about to pay their dues.

James Courtland finally came to life in the wee hours of the following morning. He sat up slowly, moaning as he tried to stretch the stiffness out of his neck. He winced from the pain in his jaw and then cursed the Bainbridge name in silence. His head felt as heavy as an anvil, and his throat was dry and sore from drinking.

"I'll make them pay . . . all of them," he said in a fury. He suddenly glanced at the window, thinking that someone was spying on him. However, he only imagined seeing a shadow. When he felt sure that he could stand, he moved toward his desk and gently lit the oil lamp. The light hurt his eyes, and he could hardly focus. Finally, James got a look at what two days of a drunken spree had done to his room. Empty bottles and clothing were strewn around the room. His desk was piled with paper . . . orders from the colonel and from Washington. Some of them were wet, and others were crumpled. The room look the way he felt. Again he stated, "*I want satisfaction!* I've lost everything: the money, the prestige, and the property. It was supposed to be mine. It's all her fault," he said while placing his hands on his head. "All I need to do is get her alone. I'll make her change her mind."

He winced again, but the pain in his head was generated by his own voice. He didn't care what it took, he wanted revenge. "Just let me get my hands on her. If she refuses, I'll snap that lovely little neck of hers," he continued. His greed was shone like a beacon. He had suffered greatly at the hands of the Bainbridges. He had lost his dignity and his honor all in one moment. "They never intended for the wedding to take place. That's right!" They had played on his greed and then pulled the rug out from under him. "They're going to pay dearly, especially *you*, René," he added.

Then he turned his attention to the unopened letters on his desk. The first letter was an answer to his request for resignation, which he had posted nearly five weeks before. He laughed sharply as he read it. His resignation had been denied. He would have been upset had the wedding proceeded as planned. But since his plans were changed indefinitely, it was the best news in the world.

James had been ordered to explore the northern region beyond the Ohio Valley and the western territory beyond the Dakotas. He was happy that this would keep him away from the probing eyes of the townspeople. But, he didn't really want to leave with these matters unsettled, especially when he hadn't acted on his revenge. His orders were explicit. He had to leave in a few days. "Not enough time," he muttered. He fiddled with the thought of kidnapping René, possibly taking her away when he left. "I could get away with it," he said as he walked away from his desk to the water basin. He needed to wash the cobwebs from his eyes and, if possible, rinse his brain free of the aching pain that throbbed as he moved.

His hand still held another letter. The letter wasn't marked or stamped with government business. But he opened it just the same. "What the hell is this?" he asked, and then suddenly burst into uncontrollable laughter. It was worth it. It was worth all the pain he had suffered. Finally he had something that would bring the walls down around the Bainbridges. "So . . . she thought she could hide her secret from me," he said slyly. With that, he knew he had an advantage.

That same morning, James set out for Wilmot with treachery in mind. He decided to use the letter as a tool of getting his revenge. What an advantage it was that the unsuspecting Bainbridge family would get their comeuppance. He considered the townspeople a weak sort, anyway. They were the type who were easily led, and with the right fuel, they would riot. He knew one man in particular was good for starting up trouble: Old Cap, the town drunk. He was the cause of an innocent man being hung less than a year ago. No trial, just a mob ready to kill a horse thief. He was also the cause of a feud between two families, which ended in a shoot-out in the middle of town. Old Cap had a way of twisting the most innocent act into a hanging offense. A gleam of cunning and ruthlessness came through as James would be able to act out his revenge without tarnishing his own good reputation—or what was left of it. "I'll use enough truth filtered with a lie or two and feed it to Old Cap," he said as he pressed his horse into full canter. If need be, he would spread the vicious lie himself. Yet, he needed a catalyst, and Old Cap was the perfect man for the job. The long ride to town gave him time to plan his next move. It was hot and unbearable, but James put up with it knowing that he had a job to do.

Upon his arrival into town, he noticed the town's busybodies were whispering and spying on him. They quickly turned away from him as he passed. The whole town had heard about the fiasco on his botched wedding day. All turned away from him, all except Old Cap, who greeted him with open arms. There was nothing he wouldn't do for a drink. Yet, it was Old Cap who broke the silence, saying, while James dismounted and then tethered his horse, *"Well, well, well, I do declare . . . it's my young friend Captain Courtland!"*

"And greetings to you, Old Cap," James said while trying to hold his breath. Old Cap had drawn too near and his odor was far too great. He hadn't seen a bath in years. No wonder people gave him whatever he wanted. It was their way of getting rid of him. However, James had business to conduct with him and if he had to endure an unsavory odor for a few minutes, he would do it.

James, followed by Old Cap, entered the saloon. The men at the bar turned their backs on him. He usually received a huge welcome when he would come to enjoy a drink or two. Now they were acting as though he didn't exist. Old Cap was above all the formalities of snobbery. He knew he could get at least two bits or even a bottle from the captain when he was at his best.

Old Cap staggered behind, but followed the young captain to a table in the center of the large saloon. It was a slow afternoon. Hardly anyone had come to indulge in whiskey or beer. Gripping the chair and then the table, Old Cap was finally able to sit down.

Sam Finkel, middle-aged and looking older than his years, brought the captain's usual, a bottle of whiskey and a cigar. "Good day to you, Captain Courtland," he said as he lit the captain's cigar. "How was your ride into town?" he asked as he wiped the table with a damp cloth.

It was just enough to start a conversation; James, however, wasn't interested. He puffed on the cigar and watched the curl of smoke disappear in the air. Then he laughed, slapped the table suddenly, and said, "Bring me a glass, and bring one for my friend Old Cap."

Old Cap wiped his lips with the back of hand. He was elated that Courtland had invited him to drink with him. Sam returned quickly with the requested glasses and poured a generous portion in each. He watched Old Cap swig the brown liquid, nearly choking it down. When the glass was empty, he extended it out for more, and it was quickly filled.

"You are always good to Old Cap," he said, then poured the burning fluid down his throat. "You're not like the rest of these fools. They make fun of Old Cap. Make Old Cap eat dirt. But not you."

James filled Old Cap's glass, never once taking a drink for himself. He allowed Old Cap to drink until his head became limp and his vision blurred. Now it was time to talk. "I think you have had enough, old man," he said as he placed the bottle on the floor just out of Old Cap's reach. "You can sure put it away, can't you?"

Old Cap's head swayed for a moment. Then he placed his hand over his mouth, trying to suppress the urge to vomit. His head was spinning, and Courtland's voice seemed to ring like a bell when he spoke. He put his glass on the table and demanded another drink, but James wouldn't pour. "Come, on sonny, pour me another drink. I . . . I gotta have a drink," he said. His tongue was thick, and his voice was barely audible.

But James refused. He played on Old Cap's weakness. Old Cap, on the other hand, was not about to let that bottle out of his sight. He would beg if he had to, but James had other plans. With a wry smile, he told Old Cap, "You know, I'm glad I didn't marry that René Bainbridge. You would be surprised about things I found out about her. I'm glad I learned the truth before it was too late."

The expression on Old Cap's face was just enough to let James know that the seed had been planted. The old man had soaked in every word and, like a parrot, he would repeat what he had heard out loud. Again, his glass was filled, and the bottle placed just out of reach.

James whispered, "Yes, I am very glad I didn't marry the girl. She deceived me . . . she deceived us all. As a matter of fact, she isn't from the right side of the tracks! If you know what I mean . . . . "

Some of the words spoken in his ears escaped, but Old Cap heard bits and pieces. He heard what he thought was *not from the white side.* With his mind fogged with whiskey, he would tell several versions, each in their own way, damning the young woman to obscurity.

Old Cap belched, then looked around the saloon at all the men standing within earshot. "You mean René Bainbridge is a nigga gal?" he yelled, and then heaved as though from disgust. It was a false alarm. James, of course, sighed with relief, grateful that he was spared a spraying.

Old Cap had certainly changed the story around: It even shocked James when he heard what he'd said for all to hear. But he didn't refute what was said by the old man. He allowed the men in the saloon to absorb the ill-fated lie as Old Cap asked another question just as loud as he had sprayed René's reputation. *"You were about to marry the gal?* What a shame! What a shame!" he continued.

There were two men at the far end of the bar who heard every word. They were new to Wilmot. They appeared to be rich, well-bred business-men from the East. That, however, was not the case. Matt Wilson and Walter Cory had tried to meet with Devon Bainbridge for several months. But Devon would have nothing to do with their business venture, especially when he found their business proposal was laced with lies. They had planned to sell counterfeit stock in a fur company in New York, and take the elder Bainbridge for all he had.

But like any good businessman, Devon always investigated the prospects that were offered, no matter how great it sounded. Four days before his daughter's wedding, he held a meeting with the president of the Wilmot National Bank, who presented him with proof that the stock and promissory notes were worthless. Later, when Wilson and Cory arrived, expecting to leave the Bainbridge Estates as rich men, they were thrown off the grounds by the foreman and the groundskeepers. Their backs still ached, and the holes in their trousers were still visible.

"Did you hear that?" Matt whispered in Walter's ear. "We can use this information, maybe get a couple of bucks on the side . . . heh, heh, heh," he said with a sheepish grin.

"Yes! I heard everything. This is turning out better than I thought it would. Devon Bainbridge won't be able to talk his way out of this one," Walter added.

Matt laughed and then poured another drink. "Are you thinking what I'm thinking?"

"Yes, I most certainly am," Walter replied quickly. "If Devon Bainbridge thinks he has the best of wealth and power, he has another think coming."

"I think it's worth at least ten thousand dollars to start with, don't you?" Matt whispered.

"Then we'll go for the rest. I want to bleed him dry. Bone dry," Walter added. Then he turned to watch Old Cap and his company for a while. They would wait patiently for the younger one to leave so they could squeeze more information from Old Cap without drawing attention to themselves.

It was nearly six o'clock in the evening when Courtland made his way to the saloon door. He hadn't been able to wake Old Cap after he had finished the second bottle. He had hoped to continue the conversation, to plant more lies in his head, but Old Cap was no longer receiving. He tried to shrug off the possibility that Old Cap hadn't heard a word he had said. Maybe it was better that way. The damaging story could point right back to him. Then he turned to look back at the drunken sot, only to find him surrounded by the two men from the bar, both holding another bottle for the old man.

James looked at his watch and realized he had to get back to the fort before the colonel noticed he was missing. The evening light, the moon, and a few twinkling star shone through the night. It had suddenly become quite cool, making James raise his collar around his neck. As he rode toward the fort, he wondered who would be the first to die. He wanted to be there, at least to see it happen to René. Nevertheless, he planned to have her at *his* mercy. Then the most puzzling thing jolted him: *"Who sent the letter?"*

CHAPTER

FOUR

WORD HAD COME TO the Bainbridge household that rumors were floating around town and the people were getting very cocky. As Devon suspected, it didn't take long for them to make a mockery of his love for
René. Meanwhile, René paced her room like a caged animal. She had been
forbidden to leave the house for any reason, not unless she had an escort.
She wanted to get away, and Devon knew that she would be in more danger if she went out on her own. Everything had changed, the house, her
parents, and even her brother seemed different to her. It didn't feel like
home anymore, almost like she didn't belong. She even began to accept the
fact that she was the daughter of a slave, and Devon couldn't bring himself to talk to her about her mother.

Angry and impatient, René stormed out of her room and rushed
straight into her father's study, interrupting both her father and brother.
"René, child, I'm glad you are here. I've been wanting to talk to you all
day," he said gently.

"Have you, really?" she asked, almost coldly. "I feel like a prisoner in
my own home. I can't go anywhere or do anything without having the eyes
of your men on me."

"I know, I know. But it's for your own good," he offered with great care.

"My own good! What good is this? Our home has become a fortress.
Everyone is carrying a gun. It's almost like we're going to war. My God,
why are you doing this?" René asked, almost becoming hysterical.

Realizing for the first time that she had become disrespectful, she changed her manner and somewhat composed herself. "I'm sorry, father . . . . I feel I've lost control over everything. Someone out there is trying to hurt me, and I don't know why. What have I done to warrant this? What have I done? Oh, God, I'm so afraid."

The pain she expressed was great and so was her fear. Devon couldn't offer any explanation to soothe away the pain. He could only imagine what she was going through. How she reminded him of Sarah Josephine. Her memory had been forever on his mind since the letter had arrived. And how could he bring himself to tell Rachel of his long-term love affair with his former slave? How could he tell her that René was a product of that love and a replacement for the child he and Rachel had lost? Rachel loved Robert so very dearly, but she had a special bond with René. She was so proud of her daughter's beauty and of how well she carried herself. Rachel paid special attention to René, making sure René had everything she needed or wanted, which included making sure that René was a prime catch for the best suitors. Now Devon would have to destroy the image that his wife had created by telling her the truth. Soon there would be more to worry about, and if she wasn't able to withstand this . . . what was to come would destroy her for sure.

"There is nothing I can say to ease your pain, darling child," he replied softly. "I know it's been difficult for you to understand the way things have turned out, but—"Devon found himself abruptly cut off.

"Father, I can't stand it anymore!" René retorted hysterically. She stormed out of the study, leaving her father in a state of anguish. It tore at his soul that his own daughter wouldn't let him forget that he had lied to her.

As René rushed out the door, Rachel entered. Their voices had invaded the peaceful surroundings of her sewing chamber. She immediately called René back into the study, and René reluctantly complied. There was a mark of discomfort in her face. Her health was steadily failing, but with no concern to her own needs, she pursued the needs of her her family. They were obviously in desperate trouble.

"René, my child," she said softly, and felt her daughter pull away from her momentarily. "Something is bothering you, isn't it, dear?" Rachel appeared pale and tired, but had the strength to put the pieces together, especially since she only knew what Devon had told her, and that wasn't much at all. "It seems that it is affecting your father . . . and your brother, as well," she said gently while taking in the expressions on each of their faces. With that remark, she could see that she wasn't far from the truth. There was silence in the room as she continued to observe the trio. René avoided eye contact with her, Robert could hardly maintain his composure, and Devon had guilt written all over his face. *What are they hiding from her?* she wondered. Rachel had sensed something was brewing on René's wedding day. Especially when Devon avoided answering her questions. She recently had become even more convinced when she noticed that when she would enter the study, both her husband and son would stop talking. They seemed to be harboring some major secret. She was even more determined to find out what was ailing her daughter and would stand for nothing being left out.

"Mother, I'm sorry," René replied quickly. "I have had a lot on my mind since the wedding was canceled." René hoped that that would be a good enough excuse. She wasn't able to bring herself to explain her strange behavior of late.

As always, Rachel saw through the excuse and turned to her husband, who apparently knew more than her daughter was willing to give. The silence in the study had grown extremely unbearable. Robert, still sitting quietly in the armchair facing the fireplace, had said nothing to disturb the lines of communication between his family. He listened and watched for anything that remotely seemed to be a threat to René's composure. He knew that his mother shouldn't hear of the rumors from an unkind source. It was necessary for him to intervene and take the pressure away from René, but he would wait for his father to bid him to do so. René had to be spared any more trauma that would most undoubtedly affect their mother once she learned the truth.

Before Rachel could insist upon René justifying herself, Devon gave the signal, upon which Robert interrupted. "Mo-ther," he stammered. "Mother, René has promised to show me the new foal before the auction tomorrow. We have to determine the cost of separating the foal from its mother." He was up from the chair and pushing René out of the doorway before Rachel could dispute his retreat. Then he looked back at his father, who agreed in silence with his actions.

Rachel was thoroughly shocked by her son's rash behavior. She would definitely have something to say about that when she caught up with him later. In the meantime, she turned her attention back to Devon, who seemed to have all the answers to her questions. She knew they were hiding something from her. She didn't enjoy being the last to be informed, which had become ever so apparent these past few days. "Now that our children have left the room, I gather I will be told what is going on with René and why she is acting so strangely."

Devon inhaled, holding his breathe for what seemed like a long spell. Then he allowed the air to escape slowly. It was time to tell her . . . everything. He braced himself against the desk for a moment and then said gently, "We have much to talk about, my dear. " Now and forever, he would regret not having been honest with her for their entire marriage.

He directed Rachel to sit in the armchair, her favorite chair, where she would join him when the children had gone to bed. It seemed to be the most suitable chair in the house at the moment. He wasn't sure how she would take hearing of his past mistakes and how he had ruined René's life, but she needed to be comfortable if all else failed. He walked to the window, then turned to face his wife. She was still a very lovely woman, even though time was creeping around her eyes. In his eyes, she still looked like the young bride of twenty-two years ago.

Devon began. "Rachel, there is something I must . . . " He paused momentarily, just to regroup. The idea of telling her the truth now was too much for him. His heart ached with despair, for he knew that Rachel would never forgive him. They had been living a lie all these years, and he was to blame for it all. The news had reached town already, sooner than he had expected it to. Now it had come full circle, back to him . . . to René.

"I meant to tell you this when you were well enough to hear it, but it seems that I must tell you before . . . before you hear it from the wrong person," he continued softly. Rachel looked at him in wonder, confused. It was beyond her comprehension to know what he meant by that, but she didn't interrupt. "It started the day our children were born . . . so tiny and frail . . . passed away . . . René was born the same time . . . looked just like our baby . . . I didn't know what else to do . . . . I lost her . . . I didn't want to lose you, too."

Rachel placed her hand to her throat. She couldn't believe her husband of twenty-two years would do such a thing. She became faint, and the walls began to close in around her. At that moment, her manner changed. There was hate instead of love in her voice. She no longer wanted to be his wife. He even dared to call himself her husband. However, she gathered the strength of ten bulls, then inquired, *"Whose child have I been raising all these years?! If my daughter is dead . . . whose child?! Whose child?!"*

The coarseness of her voice shrilled throughout the house. Her heart had been weakened by the birth of her children. Now she was being told that René wasn't of her blood. "Does René know?" she asked while trying to regain her sanity.

Devon feared saying any more because she had become so dreadfully pale. He nodded only to confirm his guilt. He could lose her, if he hadn't already. He didn't want to face life without her . . . not now, not ever.

"Whose child have I been raising, Devon? she asked again, but calmly. She closed her eyes, ready to take the burden that had invaded her home twenty years ago. Imagine René was now a burden rather than a joy.

"She belongs to Sarah Josephine . . . and . . . to me," he said gently. "She was born only minutes after our children. I had to do it, Rachel. Our daughter had died. The doctor wasn't there to help you . . . and you were so weak."

"Sarah Josephine . . . yours . . . how dare you. I'm your wife, and you dared to have a slave for a lover! You touched another woman, a slave . . . who worked in my house and then out of guilt you came to me!" she continued hysterically. "How could you? How could you lie to me? How could you pass a slave's child off for being mine . . . mine?"

Rachel stormed at him, slapping him for the first time in their marriage. Never in their married life had he ever given her cause to wonder about another woman or even a child, so she thought. This wasn't what she expected to hear from her husband. Suddenly, without warning, she clutched at her breast in agony. Her face turned gray as if all the life had been drain from her body and she collapsed in Devon's arms.

At the same moment, Old Cap was talking to Ben Wright, telling him the tall tale he had heard and had been repeating for several days. Ben never cared for the Bainbridges, especially Devon, who had fired him when he had been found drunk under a tree. He had been ordered to corral the horses before dusk, but instead he had gone on a drinking spree, losing several mares and their foals. He had tried to shoot Devon for firing him that day; instead, he caused a major stampede that claimed the lives of three good young men. One of them was just fourteen years old. Lucky for him that no one in town was told of the incident, especially since Devon handled the whole matter personally. If Old Cap had caught wind of this fiasco, Ben would have been run out of town or, better yet, hung.

"So . . . the high-and-mighty Bainbridge family has a skeleton or two, heh!" Ben inquired eagerly. "I knew he would get his one day, heh, heh, heh."

"How'd ya know'd dat?" Old Cap asked. "Ain't nobody but me knows the truth 'bout dat gal . . . and . . . it'll cost you another drink, ma friend, to hear the rest," he added with a laugh.

Eager to get the goods on Bainbridge, Ben called out, "Sam . . . bring us another bottle." Then he turned to the stragglers who had wandered into the saloon. "Drinks are on me!"

He saw the two gents, Matt Wilson and Walter Cory, sitting on the other side of the saloon, trying not to draw attention to themselves. "Hey, you!" Ben called. "You, over there . . . you too good to drink with us?"

They turned away briefly, then resigned themselves to the invitation given. What better way to learn more about the Bainbridges? It didn't settle too well with their plans, but they conceded, and drank with the brutish lot. "We'll be glad to drink with you." They seemed to gain a mark of popularity when they accepted the invitation. Matt and Walter watched intently as Ben wrangled the information out of Old Cap. What they had failed to get, Ben was a bit more successful.

Old Cap was like an overflowing pitcher, spilling everything he knew about René from the every beginning. The saloon began to buzz and hum from the accusation he had hurled. Many shook they heads in disbelief, while others sat nearby, straining their ears to get the next tidbit.

Matt bought the next round of drinks, then Walter. They continued to feed the group until they became loud and angry. One or two yelled, "Let's hang 'um." Yes, they were angry, and the Bainbridge family was the enemy. "Who do they think they are?" another cried out. They continued on and on until one fired a gun in the air, breaking the momentum. They wanted blood, and Devon's or René's would do.

Matt sensed that one thing would get them started and he called it, "Are we just going to sit here and talk about it, or are we going to do something about it?" He waited a second or two and then added, "They're just sitting up there getting fat off of your sweat and you're letting them get away with it."

Like puppets, they all nodded their heads in agreement. Then Ben slammed his fist onto the table and yelled, "Let's get 'em!"

There was a rumble of footsteps, and chairs were tossed out of the way. Someone grabbed a rope from a saddle that was stashed away in the corner of the saloon, and others called out vicious recourse as they entered the street. The had death on their minds and bloodletting in their hearts.

Walter Cory was all ears. He enjoyed this part of getting over on the rich, especially if he had something to gain from it. The less he had to do, the better he liked it. He and Matt followed the crowd down the long road to the Bainbridge Estates. There the men had rallied others to follow and it soon became a mob that included the men, women, and children of Wilmot.

The grounds of the Estates were surrounded by a high, cast-iron fence with a beveled gate. The initial "B" graced the intricate design on both sides of the gate. It seemed to be a sturdy foundation, capable of keeping people out. But the first thing to penetrate the security of the Bainbridge home was gunfire, and then the taunting remarks yelled in by a brazen few.

The field hands were awakened from their sleep, and the lights to the main house were extinguished. The men quickly gathered their guns and clubs and whatever they could find to defend the Bainbridges against the intruders lurking at the gate.

Suddenly, Old Cap pushed his way forward through the crowd to get in front. As before, he was leading the mob. This time he had an ounce of truth to back his claim, and he didn't know it. Some of the people who had followed the mob had no idea what they were doing. It was just exciting to them to be a part of a lynching again. Yet, the story about René began to circulate within the crowd, causing shock waves. They felt the Bainbridges had deceived them. They wanted to take René out of her fancy surroundings and put her in her place.

The field and range hands had come to face off the mob at the gate. They were determined to protect the property of Devon Bainbridge. They stood fast and sure, never once questioning their boss's word. They stood face-to-face with many of their friends and with the fathers of their sweethearts. It was going to be tough to remain loyal.

The sheriff knew that Old Cap was up to no good. He remembered the last lynching and how he wished he had been able to stop an innocent man from hanging that day. Old Cap should have been dangling from the noose himself. That incident nearly cost him his star. Now the town was at it again, and this time a young girl's life was hanging in the fringes. Yet, the people believed Old Cap and his outrageous accounts of many mishaps while he was under the influence. When he reached the Estates, he could hear the heckling and the jeering from the crowd.

"Yah'll go home now!" he yelled as he rode up to the front of the mob. "There is no need to act like this. The people yah is try'n ta harm ain't done nothin' but good fo' the town . . . an yah knows it is true," he continued.

One rabble-rouser said in retort, "We gotta right ta be here. She ain't got no right ta be livin' in that there house, she bein' a nigga gal and all."

His words created a wave of agitation of slurs and taunts unbefitting any human being. Sheriff McDaniels knew that he couldn't contend with them unless Old Cap admitted he was lying about the girl. The old goat had lied before, and he had to make him fess up. However, the crowd began to push McDaniels into the gate. Suddenly, without warning, someone fired a shot into the crowd. Everyone scattered and ran for cover.

There was a volley of gunfire from both sides of the fence. Two men lay motionless and face down on the ground. The women who had taken part in the fiasco hid behind the trees. They whimpered when they saw the blood trailing from the fallen victims. Sheriff McDaniels tried to make a last-ditch effort to get the crowd to go home before more blood was spilled. "I am givin yah'll two minutes ta git off this land," he shouted. Then he pointed his gun toward the angry crowd. "Did yah hear? Do I have ta arrest the whole lot o yah?" he added angrily.

But Old Cap wasn't going to let up. He decided to get brave and show everyone that he was going to stand by his story no matter how much trouble it caused. As far as he was concerned, he was right about René Bainbridge. This would make him a big man, a respected man, in Wilmot. "Yah know she's a nigga gal. This town is fo' decent white folks," he continued. "Let's git her."

There was a rumble of voices coming from all directions. Suddenly, they got enough gumption to come from their hiding places to start the wave of violence again. Sheriff McDaniels couldn't get them to listen to reason. He didn't like what he heard, either, but the law was the law. They were trespassing and were about to hang an innocent woman. He tried again, but was pushed out of the way. Matt hit him from behind with the butt of his gun.

With the sheriff out of the way, the crowd rushed to the gate. Guns were being fired, clubs were connecting with heads and other body parts. Men fell left and right, some dying and others suffering from a variety of wounds. Old Cap was among the first mortally wounded. Ben Wright just stepped over him and continued to pull the crowd on.

Devon and Robert, having heard the commotion earlier, had already barricaded the doors and windows on the first floor. The servants were ordered to extinguish all the lamps and to stay low just in case they were fired upon. Robert made sure that all the men who had managed to get back to the house safely were armed with two or more rifles. Young Jonas was in charge of loading and reloading, while the others stood guard at the weakest point of the house. Suddenly, everything came to a standstill. It was too quiet outside. Jonas, just like the others guarding the door, could hear his heart pounding.

Like a loud blast, a lone voice reached in to shatter the nerves of everyone inside. "You . . . you in there. Bring out the girl. Bring out the girl, and the rest of you will live." Then the manly voice called out again, "You got to the count of five or we'll burn the house down around you."

No one moved or even made a sound to draw attention to themselves. They waited for the intruders to make the first move. Suddenly they heard footsteps on the porch, followed by breaking glass. They must have broken the large window in large hall. That was followed by a hail of gunfire, and one man lay crumpled on the floor. Again there was silence, like the wake before the storm.

"They're going to rush the house soon," Devon said in a low voice. His nerves were shattered, and he was tired. It was evidently taking its toll on his spirit. Rachel had shut him out, refusing to see him after she had come around. It was as though the life had been drained from him.

"You're right, Father," Robert responded quickly. "We have to act now or we'll lose all hope of getting out of here alive."

Reality! What a reality it was. Their home had a new face. Devon's dream of growing old and having his grandchildren around him—his son, his daughter, and his wife—would all become a part of raging flame, if he didn't act now. "Then it's time," he said sadly. He embraced Robert and said, "It's time. Get your sister and take her to the cellar. I'll meet you there in a few minutes. Hurry!"

Robert hesitated for a moment. For the first time in these few days, he realized that this was all too real and that they definitely may not survive the night. He rushed upstairs to René's room and entered without knocking. There was no time for formalities. He had to get her out without being noticed.

"Grab what things you need and come downstairs," he said as he chanced a look out of her window.

René didn't argue with him. The situation outside had reached a point of finality. The people were going to attack the house. She watched them light the torches and then burn the bushes and the beautiful sycamore tress that surrounded the house. "We're surrounded on all sides, Robert. How are we going to get out of here?" she asked finally.

"All I know is that father wants us in the cellar . . . now!" he remarked quickly, while checking the window for a possible escaped route. "Just take what you need, and hurry!"

René complied. She had no choice in the matter. Smoke was coming through the front door, and she moved a little faster when she heard the billowy sounds of the flames lighting up the sky. She snatched a dress, a nightgown, a few of her toiletries, and a small broach with a locket attached. If she needed anything else, she would just have to learn to do without it.

They were out the door within minutes and rushing down the stairs when they noticed the flames licking through the front door. Ben and his followers were seriously going to burn the house down, and they didn't care who died in the process. Some of the stragglers had wandered to the back of the house and tried to set it ablaze, but Jonas picked them off one by one from the kitchen window.

Robert threw what water he could find on the flames, but it continued to grow as if fed by kindling. "Let's get out of here!" he yelled, and ushered everyone into the cellar, where Devon waited with the others.

The evening's events had taken its toll. Devon's eyes were engraved with dark circles. His once strong, broad shoulders were now sagging from the weight he carried. He wanted one last look at his daughter. One last look and he would send her away where no one could harm her.

Shots could still be heard, and the house was now engulfed in flames above them, leaving them vulnerable to die a fiery death. Quickly, Devon embraced René and whispered, "You must leave now, my darling. I want you to leave knowing that your mother and I both love you very much. Go my child and . . . live!" Tears streamed down his cheeks. The pain of losing her wrenched at his heart. He had already lost his beloved Rachel. She had succumbed to a broken heart, dying just before they entered the cellar. She had never opened her eyes, nor would she ever know that he loved her with all his heart.

René closed her eyes, praying that the nightmare that had begun several days ago would end. But Robert brought her back to the reality of the events occurring around her. He spoke impatiently, mostly due to the flames coming through the ceiling. "It's time for us to leave, René . . . now!" He knew he was about to lose both parents and he had no control over it. He wanted to kill.

They needed a clear path to the stables. Jonas and the other field hands fired into the bushes, hitting a few who dared to venture into the open. Robert kissed his mother's cold brow, then hugged his father, who suddenly became a tower of strength. Then Devon handed him a saddlebag and pushed him out the door. René had to be pried from Rachel's side and, tearfully, she, Robert, and Lily ran straight for the stables.

The horses were already saddled and packed to leave. They were able to slip through the rear exit, which led to the woods. The last thing René saw as she and her brother escaped into the night were the flames that lit up the night's sky. Her memories of home and peace went up in those flames. She heard the crowd cheer as the house exploded. How could they do such a thing?

The three rode several, maybe ten, miles without stopping for water. Periodically they looked over their shoulders, wondering whether someone was following them. They weren't sure when they would be able to relax and slow their pace. They knew a posse would be fast on their heels, and what would happen if they were caught.

CHAPTER FIVE

FORT WAYNE WAS AWAKENED by the call to reveille. Every man jumped from his bunk and tried to be the first to visit the latrine before the morning's inspection. Private Smith was still lying in his bunk when Captain Courtland entered. Those who were within earshot heard the sergeant call, "Atten', hut!" All scrambled to their feet, all except Smith, who managed to get himself tangled up in his blanket and then winded up on the floor.

"Dad blast yah, boy, cain't yah stand on your own two feet?" demanded Wills as he walked toward him. Smith ducked when he thought he would receive a blow for his stupidity again. But Wills decided it was futile to even try to whip some sense into the boy. No matter what he did, the boy was a bungler.

"I'm sorry, sir. My foot got caught in the blanket," Smith tried to explain. "I try to right, but it don't seem ta want ta work dat way." Finally Smith managed to get to his feet.

The barrack, which he shared with nineteen other soldiers, wasn't as neat as it should have been. Their canteens weren't hanging on the hooks, and their rifles weren't stacked in the corner with bayonets fixed and ready. The men knew they would have to spend the entire day marching in the hot field if they didn't pass inspection today. It was too hot to march today. It had to be a blistering one hundred degrees or better out there. But when the men saw the condition of their quarters, they knew they were in for it. The beds were unmade, the floor hadn't been swept or mopped, and last, they were all out of uniform. Like children holding their breath, they waited for their punishment. To their surprise, Captain Courtland wasn't there to inspect their quarters at all that morning. He walked right through the column of men, who were straining to stay at attention, and headed for the bungling young Private Smith.

"Smith!" he barked. "Report to my office immediately." With that he turned on his heels and walked out. Everyone, including Wills, wondered what Courtland could possibly want with Smith. He was so incompetent, a complete idiot. But they were relieved that the inspection hadn't taken place. And no one had to tell them twice to move. They jumped into action the moment Courtland cleared the door.

Meanwhile Courtland walked toward his quarters, taking a detour by the munitions depot. He checked the cannons and powder keg, then he made sure that each barrel was dry in the darkest corner of the storeroom. Finally, he checked his holster for missing bullets and reloaded the empty casings. He was pleased with his findings, since everything was in its proper place. With that out of the way, he headed for his office, an extension of his quarters, and waited for Private Smith to arrive. He didn't even take time out for breakfast with the other officers. He knew they would notice a change in his behavior, but the least he had to account for, the better. He had an excuse that would satisfy their curiosity, but only if they inquired. "That will just have to do for now," he muttered.

Smith had finally finished dressing and preparing his bunk. He had rushed to get himself in order and hoped that he hadn't taken too much time. He didn't want any more trouble. He just shook his head remembering the mess he had made of things a few days ago. No matter how hard he tried, he found a way to wreak havoc. He ran across the quadrangle, which housed a single cannon and a forty foot-flagpole. He took time to stop and salute, even though reveille had already been sounded.

Upon reaching the captain's office, he dusted himself off and prepared himself for the worst. He puttered around for a few seconds and noticed that the sentry had left his post to help the guard open the gate. The two barely escaped being trampled by a horse and its rider. He stopped short of the colonel's office, leaping from his mount, rushing up the stairs and into the office itself without knocking.

Smith mused, "The rider must've been ridin' all night." The horse's breathing was hard and very labored. Its nostrils were flared, and sweat was pouring from its body. Instead of going into the captain's office, he went to the horse's aid. He wet the horse down with cool water from the trough and brushed away the sweat with the cloth he was carrying.

Speaking softly to the mare, he said, "Somethin' must've happed ta make the man ride yah like that." The horse responded to him with ease and began to relax. It didn't seem to matter to the horse that he was clumsy.

Suddenly Colonel Sheridan and the rider burst through the door. He wasn't happy. Whatever the rider told him must have jarred him for sure. He called to the nearest sentry, "Tell all officers to report to me immediately." He seemed frantic. He twisted his gloves and then used them to wipe his brow.

Captain Courtland was the first to report, followed by Lieutenants Birney and Gantry. They were fresh from the academy and were anxious to get more responsibility with their newly acquired rank.

"You sent for us, sir? Courtland asked, since he was the senior officer. He noted his commanding officer's state of appearance. Something was definitely wrong. The colonel never had given reason to be morose or to show sadness in front of his men. But something had happened to change all of that.

Captain, take the first battalion to the Bainbridge Estates and assess the damages. The entire estate has been burned to the ground with no sign of survivors," he said emotionally. "I want Sergeant Wills and ten of our best soldiers to go to Wilmot and check on the condition of the sheriff. The town is in a state of emergency. No one is allowed to leave the town without permission. This young man, Deputy Matt Wilson, will go with you," Sheridan added.

Matt Wilson turned to face Courtland. He was fully aware that the captain recognized him from the other day at the saloon. He played a hunch that the captain wouldn't betray himself in order to expose him to his commanding officer. After all, the captain was the true reason why the Bainbridge Estates lay in ruin. The two eyed each other for a long time before Sheridan interrupted what could have been a showdown.

"Do you two know each other?" the colonel asked. If they were aware, he was, of the strange behavior developing between the two of them.

"No sir, we haven't had the pleasure," Courtland remarked quickly. However, there was something fishy about Wilson's story. Why had he come by way of Wilmot instead of coming directly from the Bainbridge Estates? Why had it taken him so long to get to the fort? It's only a three-hour ride, but if one really wanted to, one could get there in half the time.

Then Courtland remembered the day he had spent filing Old Cap's cup and telling him René's secret. Even with Old Cap changing the story the way he did, he never imagined the town reacting like that. He thought René would be banished from Wilmot and the life she knew. But the people of Wilmot took it a step further. They resolved the matter by killing everyone. And the more he thought about it, the more he was convinced that René deserved to die. The money, the land, and all that would have been hers was destroyed in a single night.

When the first battalion arrived at the Estates, they were witness to the aftermath of the carnage from the night's rampage. They could only imagine what had taken place here and why. The bodies of the dead and wounded still lay in the same places they had fallen the night before. The soldiers immediately began to move the bodies aside, separating the living from the dead.

Courtland, Gantry, and Birney rode up to the house to see if anyone from the Bainbridge family had survived. They found, however, the charred remains of those who had fallen victim to the townspeople. There was no telling who they were. How could he be sure that René was among them?

"Captain Courtland, sir?" said Tom Butler, one of the older soldiers. "I have counted forty dead, and there are fifteen people alive . . . just barely."

Courtland looked surprised. *Could she be with the wounded?* he wondered in silence. Then he ordered the man, "Show me!"

Tom Butler led him to the spot where the wounded were being tended to. James searched each female face among them and was relieved that René wasn't there.

"Are you sure you found everyone?" James asked as he walked past one woman whose hair was the same color as René's.

Tom nodded, then said, "We looked everywhere. Those who we found wanted to be found, sir. I don't think we missed anyone. Where do you want us to set up the tents for the wounded, sir?"

Courtland looked around and decided the south gate was the best location for the makeshift hospital. It was the only area untouched by the mayhem. Then he assigned twenty men to burial detail. "Don't cover the grave until the next of kin has identified them," he ordered. "As for the bodies in the house, they must be buried immediately."

Tom Butler agreed. He divided the men into two details and sent them on their way. Courtland quickly headed back to the house to determine the excess of the damages incurred by the violence. His need for revenge took on a greater toll than he had expected. Now the welfare of those who survived were on his hands.

Lieutenants Birney and Gantry had scouted the surrounding field. They found the markings of several horses, each traveling at what seemed to be a great speed. Courtland had wandered toward the area where the stables used to stand. There he found the burned remains of several horses that hadn't escaped the blaze. There he found himself counting the the charred carcasses and realizing that four horses were missing. Since the horses would have been one of the many gifts bestowed upon him if he had married René, he knew just how many were housed there. That only meant one thing to him: Someone had survived. He trusted his instincts and knew that René would be one of them.

"She's alive! I knew it! That damned woman is alive," he mused. "I'll just have to take care of her myself," he continued as he kicked at the dirt. More and more his anger began to build. It was just like her. She had made a fool of him and the town. When it seemed he had won over the Bainbridge clan, she pulled the wool over their eyes and survived. He muttered several obscenities and then yelled, "I'll find you René and kill you myself. You're not fit to walk the earth. Cheat me, will you? I'll make you pay! I'll make you pay if it's the last thing I do."

Courtland turned abruptly only to find Lieutenant Gantry standing alone and quite shakened by what he had just heard. "Sir! Um, we found ten bodies in the basement. One of them appears to be a woman," he said carefully. He tried to pretend that he had just arrived, but the expression on his face gave him away. James smiled, then cleared his throat and made a path toward the young lieutenant. Gantry tried to retreat, but failed in his attempt. According to protocol, he was under orders and had to obey his superior no matter what the circumstances.

Tension grew between the two, enough so that it could have been cut by a knife. With Gantry being the smaller of the two, he knew that he was outweighed and outmanned by the large muscular frame of James Courtland. "You heard everything, didn't you?" James asked. His eyes changed when he asked that question. It frightened Gantry to a point where he couldn't respond. James asked again, but as he spoke, he put himself directly in front of Gantry.

James's action unnerved Gantry so much that he stepped back to avoid getting trapped. He also dropped his eyes to a downward glance to avoid contact with Courtland. "So . . . you heard everything," Courtland mused. "Well, well, well. It looks like we have a lot to discuss." With that he boldly placed his hand on Gantry's shoulder, tightening his grip, and then force the young man to walk toward the wooded area behind the Estates.

"You'll . . . never get away . . . with killing me," Gantry said while trying to fight off his assailant.

Courtland was definitely the stronger man and had no trouble overpowering Gantry as he pushed further into the woods. The struggled only lasted a moment, then Courtland applied pressure to his victim's neck and "snap," Gantry fell limp and motionless to the ground.

"I'll get away with this . . . and more," Courtland rebuffed and spat on Gantry's lifeless body. "Now to think of a reason for your untimely demise," he said sharply, and then covered the body with dried leaves and branches. He concealed it well out of the view of the main house. He knew he would have to deal with this death of one of his charges if he were to be discovered. To answer for it, now that he had plans to exact his revenge on René, was another issue. He had to put the blame on someone else, so he would be free to seek out René. With each step, he planned the details of her demise as he made his way back to the main house.

Meanwhile the fugitives had ridden all night and had continued through until noon the following day. They were tired, dusty, and worn. They prayed that no one from last night's mob noticed them as they fled. They had ridden north, concealing themselves under the low-hanging trees and staying off the main road. The didn't take time to stop for water, thinking they were only minutes away from being caught.

During the night Robert had doubled back to cover their tracks. They had to disappear without leaving a trace. He covered the horseshoes with rawhide, then cut the underbrush of several bushes to dust away their tracks. He would be gone no more than an hour at a time, nevertheless he would catch up with René and Lily without raising so much as a swirl of dust behind him.

René rode quietly and mourned the death of her parents. She knew they would never survive. She could still see their faces, and yet their images were steadily fading in and out of her thoughts like the pages being turned to close a chapter. Her mother had never said good-bye. She was so cold and so very pale when they left. René closed her eyes, trying to refocus on the road ahead, but instead she cried . . . openly cried. She tried several times to hide the tears of guilt, the shame, and the lies that had brought her to this point. She was so overcome by grief that she lost control of Strafer. She came close to falling, but Robert came to her aid. It was time for them to rest.

Robert had pushed them to ride all night and now it was taking its toll on René and Lily. Silently he led them to an enclosed area surrounded by tall rushes, with a crystal stream flowing through it. It was the only welcomed sight they had encountered since leaving home. He couldn't chance making camp, not with the possibility of them being followed.

"I'm hungry," Lily said as she dismounted. She remembered eating lunch, but that was yesterday.

"There are some biscuits in the saddlebag," Robert said quickly as he helped René down. "I'll tend to the horses."

"How would you like some hot coffee with those biscuits?" she asked.

"Just biscuits, Lily. We can't risk building a fire now. It will draw attention to us . . . something we can't afford," he explained. Even though he knew he would enjoy it, he had to do without such a luxury. He quickly removed the blankets and a rifle from the packhorse before tethering the horses to the brush.

René had already taken a spot by the water, cupping the clear liquid in her hands and feeding it to Star Fire. She had hardly spoken a word since they left last night. She needed to cry, really cry, to release all the anger she held inside. But it seemed futile to even try.

Robert decided to take it upon himself to lighten her load. He playfully tossed a blanket to her and, as expected, she recoiled. *"Stop it!"* she yelled. "I can't go on like this!" Her voice trembled as she rambled on, "I know . . . I know our parents are dead! Those people . . . burned our home and killed them both. *Killed them!"*

Robert wasn't shocked by her outburst, but he wanted his sister back. They couldn't afford for her to be wallowing in self-pity. She would be a threat to herself as long as she couldn't think straight. She didn't seem to realize that he suffered the same pain. "René !" he scolded. "René, do you think that I don't feel anything? They were my parents, too!"

René stepped back. She couldn't stop what turned out to be a barrage of horrible retorts, "Oh . . . I forgot . . . I only lost one parent last night. Isn't that a laugh? You! You can go anywhere you want, but I can't! Where can I go? North? West? No matter where you take me, someone there is bound to know. They won't let me live in peace, and you know it!"

Robert couldn't argue with her. She was right. But since he had some of his father's gumption, he was going to prove her wrong. "You're right, René ! Maybe I should just let them catch up with us and cart you away," he said sharply.

Nonetheless, René quipped, "Maybe you should. I have nothing left. Instead, why don't you just end it all? Right here, right now. Just pull the trigger."

Robert couldn't believe his ears. He couldn't take much more of her self-defeated attitude, much less the fact that she wanted him to kill her. Angry and insulted, he slapped her, causing her to fall into the water. He had never raised his hand to her, and now for the first time he had done unthinkable. "I can't believe you would ask me to do something like that," he said sharply. "If father had handed you over to that mob, they still would have burned us out. All because father dared to make you a Bainbridge. That's how much he thought of you. That is how I will always think of you," he continued, but very sternly.

René was stunned. The sting of his hand meeting her cheek made her face throb. His words also left a lasting impression in her head, ringing over and over until she realized how wrong she was. There was no doubt in her mind that Robert was determined to protect her, even if it meant protecting her from herself. She watched him as he grabbed Star Fire's reins and led him to where he had tied the other horses. Then, slowly, René stood up, half drenched from the stream, and made her way to where food and company would be. She had no desire to be alone now that she'd had some sense knocked into her.

The following morning, they were awakened by the thunder of hooves trampling the firm ground as they passed. They were extremely close to being discovered. Robert placed his hands over Lily's mouth to prevent her from screaming. Silently, he signaled for René to hide in the rushes, where he and Lily followed after retrieving their blankets and saddlebags. In the very spot where they had slept, several men rode in to survey the area. They had to be the men from town, following their trail. But these men seemed totally unaware that they were within inches of finding them. They only filled they canteens with water, talked a bit, and then adjusted the saddles before mounting again. They were there no more than ten minutes when one said, "The bounty on the girl is enough to pay for some new duds."

"Yeah! But the bounty ain't enough for me. I can think of other ways to make her pay," said the other. Then he laughed and mounted his horse, ready to join the others.

From the trio's vantage point they were able to see everything. They watched twenty or more soldiers ride past in two-by-two formation. The leader sat tall in his saddle, indicating that he was well-attuned to riding for long periods of time. He continued to stretch his horse's full potential while the others followed, maintaining the same cadence. Then another group of men rushed up, bringing up the rear. From the count, there appeared to be at least forty. Some were the very ones who had torched the Bainbridge house, killing everyone who had tried to defend it.

Robert became enraged, as he could only sit and watch the bastards ride by. He was the hunted, and they would track him until there was no stone unturned. René held her breath, praying, as she watched him point his rifle sights at the head of one of the riders. He didn't fire. As much as he wanted to, he had to consider the consequences of his actions. The slightest noise would set the whole mob on them. There wouldn't any defense with one rifle, one handgun, and two women.

Matt Wilson, the leader of the posse, decided it was in his best interest to follow the glorified captain and his small entourage. He wanted to ensure himself against any reprisals that might arise as they pursued the fugitives. Yet, as James tried to establish a lead, he was also concerned about the tasks ahead. He was satisfied with the results, until the tracks they were following had suddenly disappeared.

James knew who he was up against. He knew that Robert was as cunning as he was. Furthermore, fresh memories of the whipping he had received came to mind, as well as the face of the one who gave it. "He will be an adequate adversary," James said as he rode further down the trodden road.

Robert was remembering, as well, as he watched them ride by. He never imagined that they would follow them this far, especially when they should have been presumed dead. "Now we will have to travel by night," he whispered. If only he had pulled the trigger, maybe some of their problems would be over.

CHAPTER SIX

AN OUTPOST SAT IN the midst of the vast forest, not overly populated, but it thrived from the trade with the Indians and the French trappers. Many fur traders from the East were coming and going, either pleased with their newly acquired goods, or trying to get the best of each other. It was mid August, the season when the most trade would take on a new attitude. Supplies were in an abundance, and stocking up for the winter months ahead were the main concern of every man who planned to venture further north.

There were many tribes represented, Ojibwa, Miami, Cree, and Blackfoot—all camped in the entrance of Miller's Outpost. Some were there as permanent residents. Some offered their services as trackers or guides, while others traded their pelts for guns, dried corn, and salted meats. It was a rare occasion for a horse or mule to be up for trade. But now, they were in great demand.

The largest tribe in the territory was the Ojibwa tribe. Their population was so vast that during the winter months they would separate into subdivisions and settle in their winter camps. They were a peaceful people who shared what they had even when there wasn't enough to go around. They found trade to be an essential means of getting the supplies they needed to sustain their lands and their peace of mind. So they went out of their way to trade with the white man and other tribes. With that credibility, the Ojibwa were given the first choice of all items in trade. As always, their main interest were guns and shot, in order to hunt and to protect their land.

The time was upon them to leave Miller's Outpost, and Black Eagle still hadn't found his bride. He had such high hopes of seeing his vision come to life. He had so much to consider: his infant son, for instance. He had left the babe in the care of his mother, who continued to press him about finding a mother for the child. She never realized that he still mourned for his wife and secretly spoke her name when he was alone.

Already four moons had passed and he hadn't finished bartering over the beaver pelts and the lynx skins he was trading. He had his eye on the spotted silver-gray roan with a flowing white mane. It was a handsome animal. It would make a fine addition to the fifteen he already had bargained for. Yet the owner, Denver Brant, wasn't willing to part with it, at least not without a catch. And since there was more than one bid for the horse, he was sure to gain more than the horse was worth. Denver decided to let the best man win in a wrestling match.

The match was set. Black Eagle would wrestle Lame Fox, a Miami brave. They were tied together, hand to hand, with a leather strap. Denver fired his rifle, and the men rushed for the knife that would cut one free of the other.

"The horse is mine, Black Eagle," Lame Fox said forcefully. He yanked hard on the leather strap that bound them together, causing a sharp pain to pierce Black Eagle's shoulder. That moved Black Eagle to become more aggressive. He swayed left, then right, causing Lame Fox to falter. He wouldn't allow the man time to gain his footing while he wrapped him in a choke hold.

Black Eagle could feel Lame Fox going limp and watched as his eyes rounded upward, accepting the darkness. Once that occurred, Black Eagle loosened his hold only slightly, but not enough for Lame Fox to catch his wind. He held on until he reached the knife to cut himself free, which gave him a greater leverage. He was able to distract him with quick blows to the head and body. Like quicksilver, he finally pinned Lame Fox to the ground.

"Say it!" Black Eagle demanded. "Say it, and I will let you go." Lame Fox refused to be bullied into giving in, but he found it most impossible to shake off his opponent. "You cannot win this one, my friend," he continued while applying more weight to Lame Fox's shoulder. However, the man wouldn't admit defeat. Then he pressed Lame Fox's face to the ground. All the man could do was inhale the loose dirt, which caused him to choke and wheeze.

"I . . . yield!" Lame Fox gasped. "I yield!" Black Eagle released him and helped him to his feet. "So, you win again, my friend," he said, still choking out the last bit of dirt. He found it necessary to rub the back of his neck while inhaling the fresh air he had been denied. He never believed that Black Eagle was so strong, but after today, no one would dare argue the fact, red man or white. "Yes . . . you have bested me again. But there will be a next time."

The two embraced and showed the others that there were no hard feelings between them. And, since there were no other bids for the horse, and no one wanted to be defeated in the same manner as Lame Fox, it was given to the victor.

Denver gladly handed the reins over to Black Eagle, saying, "That was the best darn wrestl'n' match I ever done seen!"

Black Eagle handed over the furs and took the reins. Then he leaped on the roan's back in a single swoop. Ponies were scarce in his land. However, he was a natural rider, even though it was his first time on horseback. He gave the horse a slight kick and then yelped with pleasure. He rode of the grounds, straight into the wooded area and into unsuspecting travelers. Their horses reared and whinnied at the abrupt approach. One rider in particular lost control of her horse, and it sped off in the opposite direction.

"René!" Robert called out to her. "Pull back on the reins! Pull back!" he yelled.

Robert couldn't catch up with her. His horse was exhausted from the hard ride, however, Star Fire had more spit in his craw. He felt like running and for the first time he refused to respond to his mistress and her tearful screams. He moved like lightning. Black Eagle turned quickly and raced after René. She was heading for a low-hanging branch, which would have injured her greatly. Just seconds before impact, Black Eagle grabbed her from behind and pulled her out of harm's way. He held her tight and seemed unwilling to release his grip until he slowed to a complete stop.

"Let go of me!" she yelled, forcing his hands away from her waist. As she slid to the ground her hair became entangled in the fringes of his leggings. She became infuriated with him even further, twisting and flinging her arms in all directions. She was no help in the matter. Black Eagle tried to loosen the reddish-brown tendrils that caught him, but to no avail—her hair remained locked. There was nothing to do but cut her free. Before René could get a grip on what stance to take, Black Eagle pulled his knife and cut the fringes. He knew she would become unraveled if her hair had been sacrificed. However, he marveled at the long curls that fell free and brushed his hand.

"I suppose you expect me to thank you," she said mockingly. She dusted herself off and tried to bring back some dignity she had lost. Her hair lay loosely about her shoulders, and she fussed because she lost all the pins that held her locks hidden under her hat. With her identity exposed, she knew she would have to deal with him.

He stared at her without saying a word. Then he dismounted and stood within her breathing space. She wasn't sure what he planned to do with her. She imagined many things, most of them misplaced. Instead, he offered her a ride, something he was unaccustomed to doing. But he felt he had to show her that she nothing to fear from him. He gently placed his hands on her waist and lifted her to sit on his horse. She refused to look at him, yet she trembled when her joined her. He sensed her uneasiness and sat back to give her space. Just then, Robert rode up, his horse having been pushed to its limit from the run.

"Are you all right?" Robert asked while eyeing Black Eagle. He didn't hear a word she said, even the point about Black Eagle cutting her loose from his leggings. In Robert's eyes, Black Eagle was sitting a might too close to his sister, which made him reach over to retrieve her. But Black Eagle pushed his hand aside.

"Your horse is tired," he said as he pointed to Robert's mount. "Too much running . . . no time to rest," he continued. René began to fidget in her seat. She couldn't wait to be free of his grip. "And you . . . have much fire . . . like the horse you ride," he said in her ear.

René forgot herself. She started to turn around and give this big man a piece of her mind, but Robert stopped her. He had to remind her that they were in a strange land and the people would have to be dealt with differently.

When they reached the outpost, Lily was already standing by the rooming house. For days, all she had dreamed about was having a hot bath and enjoying a home-cooked meal for a change. Soon Lily stopped dreaming, for there was René riding into the outpost with an Indian on the same horse, followed by Robert, whose eyes never left them.

René sat very still, almost stiff as a board, and waited for him to stop.

To her surprise, when he did finally stop in front of the rooming house, she was unable to jump from the horse as she had planned. Her body ached from head to toe, and the stiffness that she projected so well had actually set in. She was forced to accept Black Eagle's assistance again. He helped her down and watched her slowly walk away.

His memory suddenly unfolded with pictures of her face, the bounce of her hair, and the softness of her hand. He realized she was the one he sought. His heart jumped as his vision unfolded right before his eyes. He couldn't let her disappear without knowing what was in his heart. Before she could open the door to the rooming house, he caught her by her shoulders and said softly, "It is you I see in my dreams. You will be my woman . . . my wife." The look in his eyes said he meant every word of it. He released her again and suddenly leaped on the back of the silver roan. René didn't have time to react at first; she was thoroughly stunned by his actions, but too tired to consider him seriously. It had to be the fever of the moment, yet his words echoed in her ears, and his touch—a gentle touch—sent chills down her spine. He was quite happy with her reaction and smiled before riding off. He was pleased that he had finally found the woman he wanted. Yet she felt that she would have to deal with this at another time. Now, however, she wanted a bed. She wanted sleep.

In the few hours after the trio had arrived, they were witness to several fights among the trappers over a few dollars here and a few skins there. They became even more active later on that evening, with drinking, fighting, and then drinking again. For René, it seemed like they had never left Wilmot, for the atmosphere was basically the same.

René headed for her room, after they had checked in, so to speak, to take that much-needed bath. She was glad to see that it was ready when she entered the room. She quickly undressed and stepped in. The water was welcoming to her tired young bones. She began to soak in the crude wooden tub, basking in the solitude of her room and feeling safe for the first time in weeks. She managed to smooth her hands over her aching muscles and recalled the moment when her rescuer, an Indian, had made his intentions known to her. She fretted at first that he would be so bold, but deep inside she felt excitement and wonder. Exhaustion finally took its toll on her body and soul, for she fell into a deep, uninterrupted sleep . . . where she was able to forget her pain.

She could see Black Eagle riding the silver-gray roan through a open meadow, the horse's mane gently flowing back to brush the arm of its master. They were truly magnificent together, riding under the stars. She could see herself being swept up in his strong muscular arms and then riding off to a secluded place. She envisioned that he embraced her and then kissed her breathlessly. She found herself wanting more. Then she touched the eagle feather that he had worn so proudly and had gavin it to her to seal the bond between them.

A soft knock at René's door didn't stir her from that long-awaited sleep. When she didn't respond, Lily entered as quietly as she could. She gathered René's clothing and placed it in the small cedar chest at the foot of her bed. She started to turn the covers when she noticed two feathers tied with a thin leather strip and adorned with colorful beads, gracing the pillow. She knew they hadn't been there earlier and began to survey the room. Lily noticed the open window by the bed. The curtain swayed from the warm breeze, and she wondered whether she should close it. "Footprints!" she said aloud as she chanced a look through the dusty windowpane. There was a path leading from the window to where René slept and then to the bed. Suddenly René sighed, almost out of despair, startling Lily so much that she slammed the window shut.

René awoke with a start. The water had suddenly turned cold, and tiny goose bumps had riddled her entire body. It took a while for her to focus on where she was. The room wasn't well lit, and the only thing she could see were shadows highlighted by the lamp that flickered by her bed. Then one of the shadows moved directly toward her. It was then she realized that she wasn't alone. She felt as though her heart would burst from her chest, and the scream was caught in her throat.

"I'm sorry, Miss René. I didn't mean to frighten you," Lily said softly as she clasped her hands together. She seemed more nervous than usual and very uneasy as well.

"It seems we were both scared out of our wits," René said as she stepped out of the tub. The warmth of the room calmed the chill she had received from her bathwater.

Lily wrapped René in a quilt and quickly started drying her hair. Both were happy with the company and both laughed at how silly they were acting. Then another knock came through, making both women freeze in their places. The door slowly creaked open, and a jolly little plump woman with hair graying at the temples had entered the room, holding a tray of food and some fresh linen over her arm.

She had come to appraise her new boarders, hoping to find out more about them. She had already met the young man who had paid her cash for their rooms, enough to cover more than two months. "Here you are, young lady," she said as she placed the tray on the table, then walked toward the window to let in some air. "We wondered why you didn't come for your supper," she continued as she raised the window. There was a sudden gleam in her eyes as she spied the little trinket on René's pillow. She cleared her throat and walked toward the bed, hoping to get a better look at it.

To take their attention away from what she was doing, she let it be known that many had noticed their arrival and were curious about a man traveling with two beautiful woman. "You must come and meet the friendly people of our little outpost," she continued. "It's called Miller's Outpost, you know, but it's run by Denver Brant. He's our peacekeeper as well. Oh, pardon me. I failed to introduce myself. I'm Bea Graham. And what may I call you, deary?" she said as she chanced a look in René's direction. It didn't phase her that neither one of the young ladies had offered to tell their life story to her. "No matter . . . I'll find out for myself. I'm good at things like that. Besides, it seems you are all planning to stay for a while."

René and Lily were puzzled by Mrs. Graham's remarks. She would prove to be meddlesome if she wasn't appeased . . . and quickly. Any excuse would do to keep this woman from becoming a pest. "As you can see, Mrs. Graham, I'm not quite up to visiting anyone just yet. Maybe, maybe tomorrow . . . yes, maybe tomorrow we can all join you for breakfast or tea," René answered in a genteel manner. "I'm quite sure that you will be able to convey my regards to your guests. Thank you, Mrs. Graham, for bringing my supper . . . you are most kind."

"Well . . . then I will leave you to finish your supper," Bea stated as she placed the little trinket back on the pillow. It was obviously a gift of great importance, from a chief or the son of one. It was customary for the intended bride to receive a token of power and great strength from her intended groom. She wondered who was the lucky so-and-so. From the looks of things, René must have made a great impression on someone. *Lucky man*, she thought to herself. *Better yet, lucky woman.* "Maybe you will feel like joining me for tea later?" she inquired as she stopped short opening the door.

"Maybe," René responded. "It's been a long day, Mrs. Graham. I think I'll call it a night."

"Well, then . . . good evening," Bea said, and smiled as Lily opened the door for her and let her out. But she couldn't help thinking about the little treasure that lay on the young woman's pillow.

"The nerve of that woman," Lily whispered. "Did you see how she looked you over?" Lily finished braiding René's hair and finally tied a small ribbon to the end to keep it in place.

"I most certainly did. I also noticed that she was quite occupied with something on my bed," René stated as she neared the bed. "Ooooh! This is very lovely," she continued as she admired it. "Where did it come from?"

Lily shrugged and then glanced at the window. She remembered that she had closed it when she'd entered, and that the footprints were leading straight to the tub where René slept. *Better not say anything to frighten René,* she thought to herself. *The room is safe enough for now.*

René was still concerned about the untimely visit of Mrs. Graham. She totally forgot about the feather and beads and carefully voiced her opinion. "If we are going to be here for a while, as Mrs. Graham stated so well, we'd better get used to unwanted company and to answering questions without giving ourselves away. I don't know about you, but I don't know how much more I can stand being on the run."

Lily agreed with a silent nod and continued to tidy up the room. There wasn't much for her to say since she was just there to be of assistance to René. Who was she to question where they went or how long they would stay there? Long before they had arrived, she had pined over Robert and his closeness. She hoped that one day he would just say her name without sounding like her employer. However, she knew her station in life wouldn't permit him to consider her in his future.

While Lily mused over her none-too-exciting future with Robert, René ate what she could of the mutton stew and then placed the napkin over it. It was a very hearty meal, but too much to suit her taste. "Can you imagine that this is the only dish on the menu for breakfast, lunch, and dinner?" René asked. She held her stomach, hoping its contents would stay down.

When her question was met with silence, René dared broach another subject. "Have you told my brother how you feel about him?"

Lily remain silent for a moment. She had forgotten that René had noticed the way she had been looking at her brother. Her insight into family matter was all too uncanny. "No, I haven't, Miss René," she said, almost embarrassed to look at her.

"Just call me 'René,' Lily. If you don't mind. I'd rather have you for a friend. From now on I will do everything for myself. As for you, if you care for my brother like I think you do, you should let him know. He needs someone like you," René continued softly.

As Lily left René's room, she blew out the flame that flickered in the oil lamp and then quickly slipped out as quietly as she could. She had received René's blessing to pursue Robert in matters of the heart. If she only had the courage to confront him with this matter. *But that can never be,* she thought to herself.

Lily was in the hall for no more than a second when she ran into Robert himself. Her heart pounded as he came near her. She couldn't bring herself to tell him how she admired his strength. That was a private thing to her. Being around him for all those weeks, sharing the same sleeping space and sometimes the same horse, had brought her awareness even closer to him. She could never amount to the kind of woman he would want. She could never tell him, yet . . . she hoped. She hoped.

"Uh, René is safely tucked away in bed," she said as she tried to ease her way by him. The very idea of René knowing what was in her heart made her feel small. She apologized for her impertinence and again started to walk toward her room.

Robert stopped her and closed the distance between them. He was grateful for her support and especially for her company. She had never once complained about their living conditions and had never asked why they'd had to leave Wilmot. She was a wonderful woman, desirable and beautiful in his eyes. For the first time he admitted what he had been feeling for a long time. He brought her close and kissed her forehead, then slowly without hesitation, kissed her full on the lips.

René heard and witnessed enough of what transpired between Robert and Lily. It made her heart glad to see that the two had finally found in each other what she already knew. Slowly, she closed the door, so as not to be noticed. "Soon . . . very soon, those two will be married," she said as she scooted of to bed.

René slept comfortably throughout most of the night until she heard the sound of thunder pounding around her ears. The walls seemed to be caving in around her. She felt the hands of doom were at her throat. The feeling was so overwhelming that she woke up to find her own hands bracing tightly about her throat. In the darkness that surrounded her, she surmised that it was nothing but a bad dream. She tried to convince herself that she was safe, and that no one from Wilmot could possibly think to travel this way. Furthermore, it must have been the hottest night ever, which may have contributed to her continued restlessness. She lost most of her night's sleep tossing and turning. In her sleep, she was running for her life . . . still.

The following morning René realized that she didn't hadn't had a nightmare. There were many soldiers milling around the outpost. Many had tied their horses in front of the rooming house, the trading post, and the small corral that housed a few horses and mules. Some of the men were shouting orders, keeping the trappers who came to the trading post at bay. They shoved many of the trappers out of their paths, causing great commotion and unrest. The whole outpost was thrown out of kilter. Business had stopped. No one was permitted to come or go without being questioned.

"What is goin' on here?" Denver demanded.

None of the soldiers bothered to answer him. However, one soldier managed to point toward the trading depot, where a tall and very well-built man was standing. He was like a stallion among the mules. He walked with determination, and commanded respect from all. He had just finished making inquiries inside and was seeking out the peacekeeper. The commotion drew his attention away only briefly, and to Denver's dismay, the tall one allowed his men the liberties of disrupting the lives of the occupants.

Courtland felt that the law in theses parts wasn't well-organized. Yet, there wasn't really any need, since no crimes were committed. If any wrongdoing were to come about, the settlers would handle it. Sometimes the matter never reached them since the trappers rarely reported any misdeeds in their travels. But he needed information and decided to get it any way possible.

"You there!" Courtland stated abruptly. "Are you the law here?" He marched toward him, making sure every step counted. Denver nodded and waited for the man make to stake his claim. "I'm searching for two fugitives, a man and a woman," he stressed as he checked out the rooming house and the teepees in the area.

Denver listened carefully, making sure he didn't tip his hat to a possible enemy. There were many fugitives here in the outpost. Many were standing within a hair's breath of him and the captain. "Who yah lookin' fo'?" he finally asked.

"It's no matter to you," Courtland snapped. "But there could be a sizable reward for their capture."

"Reward, heh! Nope, ah ain't seen nobody but these old goats," Denver answered, while pointing to the men surrounding them.

Courtland looked around just as Denver had directed him to do. He was surrounded from all points by the shabbiest-looking bunch he had ever seen. No one cracked a smile. No one dared give him a clue, much less take him under their confidence. Courtland became angered by Denver's brevity. He knew the man wasn't telling the truth. He was too cool and too quick with his answers.

"I followed a very skimpy trail to this outpost. I know I'm not wrong. I know they are here. They must be here," he snapped again.

"Nope. Ah knows it fo' a fact. Are yah sure 'bout the trail? Sometimes them Injuns play games, mark'n' things here an' there," Denver said jokingly. "An' besides, we ain't got no place ta lock 'em up, even if yah do finds 'em."

At that, the captain fumed, "I know they are here! If you will just turn them over to me, I will make sure that no charges are brought against you and the people of this outpost."

Denver laughed, almost to a point of hysterics. "Charges! Heh, heh, heh. Yah has no place here. We's protected by the French militia. Yah cain't take one man o' woman from here."

Seeing that he would get no assistance from the peacekeeper, Courtland decided to look for himself. He attempted to cross the walkway leading to the rooming house, when his path was diverted. A tall, half-naked man riding a silver-gray roan was careening toward him at full gallop, yelling, "Eayah . . . ey . . . eayah!"

Courtland fell into a mud puddle trying to keep from being trampled. Angry that he had been humiliated by a heathen, he pulled his gun. He wanted to put an end to the rider's pleasure . . . quickly. But he found his arm locked from behind by an unknown assailant. The gun was forced from his hand and put back into his holster.

"That'll be a major mistake if'n yah shoot that Injun. Yah'll have the whole mess o' dem down on our necks!" he said sharply.

Courtland looked back into the face of Simon Ashe, a trapper and friend of the peacekeeper. He had lived in the mountains for more than thirty years and knew the Indians well. His crusty voice and unshaven face repelled James. Without responding to the warning he had received, he jerked his arm free, glared at the man and then headed for the rooming house again, while cursing under his breath.

Simon just shrugged and walked back to his furs. He figured the man was too much trouble for him to be concerned with. If the people in the rooming house were the ones he was looking for, bullets were sure to fly. He was better off minding his own business.

Courtland reached the rooming house without a hitch. He knew it would be necessary to take a room for the night, at least to have a warm bed and some hot food. He even thought about freshening up his mud-caked uniform. But from the looks of the place, it was more in need of repair than he was. The floor on the front porch creaked as he walked. The windows were dirty and covered with spiderwebs. He hesitated, thinking that he was better off camping out again.

He was about to enter the establishment when one of his soldiers rushed up with news of the two fugitives. "Sir, Captain Courtland . . . there is a man on the other side of the compound who says he saw the people we are looking for," he stated quickly. "He said they were heading west along the southern tip of the big lake, but that was a week ago," he continued as he pointed in the direction where the man was located.

Courtland wasn't happy with that bit of news. "You mean I've been following a bum trail all this time?" he yelled. "They could be anywhere. Is that all you could come up with, soldier?" he asked as he brushed the mud from his trousers.

"That's all, sir. No one wants to talk to us. They think we are going to stir up trouble between them and the Indians, sir," the boy answered. Courtland noticed how the trappers had followed him from place to place. Some were angry that their way of life had been interrupted. Others followed just out of curiosity. "Do you see what I mean, sir? They don't want us here!"

He would be blind not to notice what was happening around him. He was thoroughly outnumbered in this small outpost. He realized that a quick exit would suit these people rather than trying to shoot it out with them. Courtland decided to relent; a retreat would give him time to regroup his forces. He called out, "Men, apparently the people we are looking for aren't in this outpost. Mount up!" Courtland ordered the bugler to sound retreat, and the entire horde left the trappers in a huge dust cloud.

Denver opened the depot for a night's drinking in celebration of their victory as darkness finally set in around the inhabitants. Miller's Outpost had begun to settle down after their near brush with the Americans. They hadn't faced the likes of such men since they had made the wilderness their home. Even the French militia wouldn't treat them in that manner. In as much as they didn't want to think about it, each man knew that the captain would return, but they didn't bargain on it being so soon.

Courtland slipped back into the outpost by the rear entrance, angry that he had been rousted out by what he called no-accounts. This time he was going to check out the areas he had missed earlier. He passed two Indian maids, who were preparing their evening meal. They watched him as he quietly walked through the gate and passed the men who were busy drinking and talking about the day's events. His stiff, yet quiet movements were undetected by the next group of men sitting by a fire in front of their old cabin.

Simon Ashe, the man who had stopped the captain from making a fatal mistake, was one of them. He spoke of the three new arrivals and wondered if they were the ones the captain was looking for. The description of one of the women was very similar to the one staying next door. "Aye, she's a lovely one, yah know. *Ah* could do a lot wid dat, she tak'n care o my home an' all," Simon claimed.

His friends were quick to agree. "Yeah, but howd yah think she'd fare in da winter months?" one asked.

"I think she is too skinny . . . no meat. I like a woman I can hold on to," he said, laughing.

James listened to the conversation in depth. He knew he was right. René and her brother had made it there. Those unsuspecting tongues would never know that they had helped him to seal René's fate. He swore he wouldn't allow her to slip through his fingers again.

Covered by the darkness of the two structures, James casually made his way to the rooming house. All the lights were out, with an exception to the one flickering in the kitchen. He entered through the east window, taking care not to disturb anything in his way, and headed for the single rooms located in the rear of the house. The floor creaked under the pressure of his weigh. He would stop, wait, and then proceed again, looking around periodically, hoping to catch the right someone unaware.

Then Mrs. Graham walked in carrying two lamps. She was humming a tune she had learned from one of the French trappers. She checked the dining table for any dishes left behind before she blew out the extra lamp she carried. She took the other lamp so the path to her room was well lit. Suddenly she felt the need to gasp for air. She felt a large hand cover her face. James knew from her reaction that she would scream, therefore he continued to muffle any sound that would betray him and he eased the lamp from her hand before she could drop it. In her struggle, Mrs. Graham could feel the hot breath of her attacker, which frightened her even more.

In a low voice, James said, through gritted teeth, "What room is she in? René Bainbridge . . . what room? He pushed her against the wall, keeping her face away from his.

Bea shook her head. She didn't know the woman he had mentioned, at least not by that name. There were three arrivals since yesterday, and she had yet to get their names. As James tightened his grip around her neck, she panicked. She decided that her life meant more that the life of a stranger. She finally pointed to the last door in the hallway, the one facing them, hoping that would appease her attacker. James thanked her and then gave her the butt end of his gun against her head and let her slump to the floor.

James eased his way down the corridor toward the last room in the hallway as he was directed. He placed his ear to each door in the surrounding area to make sure that he hadn't disturbed anyone. The hallway had become pitch black, forcing him to feel his way to the end. When he finally reached René's room, he opened the door and quickly entered, slowly closing the door behind him. He was grateful that no one else was up and about, blocking him from his quest.

He could hear her stirring under her sheets as he walked toward her. A light breeze brushed his face and stopped momentarily to gather his wits. He noticed that the window was wide opened. That made it simpler for getting her out without being seen. Then his eyes caught René. The light of the moon was shining on her face. She shifted her position on the bed and turned away from him. Through the light filtering through the curtains, he was able to see each curve and swell of her body. He drew in a breath, holding the vision of her in his mind. It would be justice served if he took what was once almost rightfully his.

He closed in, nearing the bed where she laid, and stood hovering over her, watching, waiting for the right moment. He wanted her to be awake when he punished her. Without so much as a thought of being heard, he seized her by the throat and forcefully threw her covers aside. René's eyes were wild with fright. She couldn't see the face of the one who was attacking her. However, her body turned to stone when she recognized James's voice. "Now, I have you, my lovely. Don't scream, don't!" he demanded. "Scream and I'll break your beautiful little neck."

He placed his cheek along side of her neck and then brutally kissed her—full, long, and hard. His weight seemed to crush her ribs as though they were about to break. Then he released her, saying, "You though you could escape me, didn't you? Didn't you?"

René pleaded with him to stop, but he refused to hear her. He pinned her to the bed with one hand and fondled her breasts with the other. Even in the darkness of her room, James could see the fear in René's eyes. He rallied in her despair, enjoying every minute.

Each time she struggled free to cover her breasts, he would bite her hands. Then to punish her further, he would take the same pleasure on her breasts. The pain sent shock waves through her spine. He was a brute, and there were no ears to hear the torture he issued. Casually, he raised her nightgown, bringing it well above her hips. James groaned with pleasure as he let his hand wander over her belly and then to her Venus mons. That's when sheer panic set in for René. Her heart pounded in her ears, almost deafening her. She was certain of one thing: rape. He was going to rape her, and there was nothing she could say to stop him. She suddenly became wild and struggled again to free herself from his grip. And in his frenzy to maintain control, he tore her nightgown to shreds. He was a man on a mission of pure hate.

Tired of the fight, René absolved to the inevitable. He felt he had succeeded in his plan to totally humiliate her. "I've been waiting patiently for this for a long time, my . . . "

There was silence. René heard nothing but silence after such a frightening ordeal. The man had treated her so brutally . . . without honor. He had shamed her by attacking her body and now his body was very heavy and limp. Something or someone had interrupted him from completing his torment. She tried to push him off, but he was all dead weight. She prayed that Robert had come to rescue her, but she couldn't see or hear him. However, she knew she wasn't alone with this brute. Without any regard, James was thrown aside like damaged goods. He landed on the flood with a loud thud . . . knocked cold from a blow to the back of the head.

Even though she was shakened by the traumatic experience, René sat up, clinging to what was left of her dignity. She couldn't believe that James would act so callous, so thoughtless . . . so hateful in one breath. She felt a chill rack her entire body and tried to cover herself again. Then a familiar set of warm arms surrounded her and lifted her from the bed. She was quickly wrapped up in a blanket and swept away with great celerity through her opened bedroom window, deep into the shadows of the night.

It all happened so fast, that she didn't have time to react or cry out. Yet, the man who carried her managed to run in a quick pace without faltering on the uneven ground. She heard horses approaching from her right and flinched when one came near her. She was then hoisted on the back of a horse and was instantly joined by its rider. His movements were swift, but he took great care with the precious cargo in his arms.

CHAPTER
SEVEN

THE SMALL PARTY HAD covered many miles during that evening, putting enough distance between them and the outpost. They had traveled at least forty miles along the shore of what is now called Lake Erie. The water was crystal clear and reflected the deep blue color of the sky. The lake stretched out for miles and miles into the horizon. The trees surrounding the lake were twenty, maybe thirty feet tall and draped like a curtain over the edge, creating a graceful dance as they slowly reached the ground. The gentleness of the quiet breeze that brushed against the riders' bodies let them know that the season was changing. The sun finally reached through the trees to warm them. The smell of the forest was very powerful. The scent of evergreen, pine, and maple seemed to shroud over them as they trekked northward.

Further down the shore, they came upon a clearing behind several large bushes. This would be René's temporary shelter until they were ready to depart again. All night long they had traveled in silence. But now, they were talking and laughing without a care.

René and her captor were the last to arrive at the camp. She never had a choice of the position she would be in as she rode draped over his horse to this little hideaway. She heard a language that she never heard spoken before . . . beautifully spoken as it rolled off of their tongues. Yet, she wondered what they were saying and where they were taking her.

Someone brushed by her, moving the blanket that covered her head.

The light was very bright, but slowly everything came into view. She saw a young man kneel down on one knee to start up a fire. There were horses roaming to and fro, and untethered. She saw bundles wrapped with deerskin placed under an evergreen tree. It was clear she wasn't near the outpost any longer. Nothing was familiar in the slightest.

Suddenly the same arms that had put her on the horse were now bringing her down to the ground to stand before him. He removed the blanket that covered her head. For the first time since her ordeal with James, she was able to see the face of the one who had saved her from certain death. She was glad, but she was also very frightened.

What did he have in store for me? she wondered. She saw the same look in his eyes, the same when they had first encountered each other. The memory of his touch and the words he had spoken in her ear were forever branded in her mind. She didn't really expect him to take her away, not like that. Apparently, he lived by his word. But how could he do this to her —take her away —away from the only family she had left?

René couldn't bring herself to look at him, to even speak to him. As far as she was concerned, she was no better off than she had been before. "How am I going to get back?" she asked as she tightened the blanket about her shoulders. "Why did you bring me here?"

Black Eagle didn't answer her. He felt that his reasons were self explanatory. Her life was in jeopardy, and he had removed her from the danger that threatened her. Besides, he had claimed her as his own in public and he felt he had the right to take her for his own. Now she was his to do with as he pleased.

René felt as though she had been passed from one hand to the other. No longer was she able to consider her life in the company of her brother or with Lily. They would be free to do as they wished, after all, she wasn't going to be a burden to them ever again. That's when the gleam of the crystal lake caught her eye. It was the most inviting sight she had ever beheld.

With the blanket securely wrapped about her, she walked toward the lake's shoreline. She was sorely in need of water to wet the dryness that had formed around her mouth and to soothe away the ache in her ribs that was more profound as she walked. Black Eagle followed, keeping a close watch over his treasure.

The water was welcoming, but was colder than she had expected. She cupped her hands and dipped them into the water, splashing some on her face and hair. The blanket was in her way, water dripping and then soaking through. Yet, she bore the chill. Black Eagle was eager to enjoy the coolness of the lake as well. He quickly removed his leggings and shirt, leaving only his loincloth to cover his manliness. René blushed, trying not to notice the expanse of his shoulders and the muscular lone of his body. He was beautiful, more beautiful than she ever dared to imagine. His eyes were dark, but the reflection from the lake made them glisten like the stars in the heavens . . . and they were fixed on her. She wasn't able to hide from his glances, nor could the blanket act as a shield.

They were alone on the shore together, out of the watchful eyes of his traveling companion. He was taller than she recalled, like the trees over the lake, and he overwhelmed her with his nearness. She couldn't retreat or run even if she'd wanted to.

Black Eagle reached for her, tugging at the blanket. But René held it as tight as she could. All she had left of her nightgown were the pieces around her neck and shoulders. James had done a thorough job in leaving her totally vulnerable. Black Eagle sensed her fears and said, "I will not hurt you. The water will refresh you." he tugged at the blanket again, practically prying her fingers away from the edges. What he revealed took his breath away. She was standing before him virtually naked.

René snatched the blanket out of his hands to cover herself again, but his hands were faster than hers. He quickly tossed the blanket over his shoulder and into the water. Infuriated, René leaped into the water after it, more so to protect herself from his advances.

The water was so cold that she screamed. Her teeth nearly shattered as she clamped them together. René realized as she neared the water's edge that he had her right where he wanted her. He wanted her to become familiar with her surroundings and with the ways of his people. Or else, she would become a hardship. Yet, in his eyes, she was worthy of that hardship.

She was forever on his mind, especially since the moment he had touched her. He envisioned her waiting for him to arrive home from the hunt, of her caring for his infant son as though he were her very own, and of course of the day when she would present him with another child shared in their love. His heart was glad . . . glad that she was here with him.

Slowly Black Eagle entered the water to join his young prize. She retreated trying to avoid him. He, however, advanced quickly, taking her in his arms and holding her tight. It seemed strange to her that his touch didn't offend her, even though her mind said it was wrong. She felt the wild beat of his heart as his hands moved over her back and down her sides. With every move he made toward her, she became more receptive. He had her full attention and it bothered her that she hadn't tried to stop him . . . not until now.

"What do . . . you . . . think you're doing?" she stammered as she pushed his hands away. "You can't! We can't." She looked into his eyes again and saw that he had left himself open to all that she could muster.

"You are mine!" he said forcefully. He wasn't in a mind for relenting so easily when there was something he wanted. "You will be my wife . . . soon."

"Your wife! You can't possibly think that I—" René snapped, but was cut off.

"You are here with me. I am the one who saved you!" he retorted. "You cannot change what has taken place. I have seen you in my mind and I know you are the one I seek," he continued as he pulled her closer.

But René pushed against him, trying to free herself. She didn't understand why he wanted her. Her behavior irritated him to a point where he left her standing in the water by herself while he swam into the deeper section of of the lake. He hoped that she would follow him, and she wondered if this was his way of courting her.

However, René was just being stubborn and refused to move. She refused to play into his game of cat and mouse. At least that's what she thought it was. "How dare he," she said. "He can't possibly believe that I would . . . "

René suddenly felt something rough rub against her leg. Then she felt a stinging pain in the same spot. She cried out when she saw a snake slithering away from her, taking refuge in the reeds. Some blood oozed from the wound, and that made it all the worse. She had never been bitten by a snake, much less seen one in her life; that alone made her panic.

Black Eagle was at least twenty feet away from her when he noticed that she was in distress. Quickly, he swam to her aid, covering the distance faster than he had earlier. He could tell just by looking at her face that she had been injured, even though René tried to repress the fear that swiftly overcame her.

He lifted her from the water and took her to a shaded spot under a large evergreen tree. There was no time to get a blanket to cover her, and there was no time for René to be modest. He quickly examined the wound. There were two tiny puncture marks on the inner portion of her left thigh. Without hesitation, Black Eagle brought out his knife and cut a line deep enough between the two wounds. Then he proceeded to suck out the poison.

His mouth was cold, like ice on her skin. And each time he drew out the poison, she cried, for the pain was too great. René trembled from within and suddenly became very weak. She also dropped her guard and leaned against him for security. This was the third time she had come close to death and he had been there to save her.

She needed to be taken care of now, and he had to leave her for a spell to get another blanket, since the one she had was still quite wet. It was important to keep her warm until the crisis had passed. "I must get something to keep you warm," he said, trying to ease her fears. I must go back to the camp. I will return soon."

René acknowledged him by shaking her head. Never in her wildest dreams had she ever encountered a man of his caliber. However, there she remained, very still and motionless. Where was she to go? She could get far on one leg. Besides, it was possible there was still some poison in her system. So, she waited for him to return, and she prayed that she wasn't going to die. She tried not to close her eyes, for fear she wouldn't awaken, but fatigue had already set in. She slept all day and into the night.

Earlier that same day, Robert had entered René's room and found it virtually destroyed. James Courtland was still stretched out on the floor near her bed. From the looks of the room, there had been a major struggle. And . . . René wasn't among the matter that was spread around the room. He found pieces of her nightgown on the floor and on the bed. Her broach was still on the table where she had left it. All he could do was pray that she had been able to get away. He wondered if she had called for help. *Why didn't he hear her cries?*

James was beginning to stir. His vision was blurred, and he had a hard time focusing on the form hovering over him. Before he could ask what had happened to him, Robert had cuffed him under the chin, pressing him against the wall, demanding, "Where is my sister, you son of a bitch?"

James looked around the room. He remembered entering her room without any trouble at all. He remembered grabbing her and torturing her. He even remembered ripping her nightgown and trying to have his pleasure. However, he couldn't remember anything after that. All he knew was that someone, somehow, had gotten the best of him before he could finish. For all he knew, Robert had knocked him out.

"I don't know where your sister is," he said, smirking. "Anyway, you and your sister—or is she?—well, you are both under arrest," he laughed.

"Under arrest! For what? For someone's lies? Your lies, perhaps?" Robert issued. "I know you are the one who started the rumors going around town. And now you stand here claiming that we are under arrest. That's funny, very funny!" he continued.

"Funny indeed," said Mrs. Graham, who had just entered the room brandishing an old broom. The door had been left ajar, and she had heard everything that transpired. She was sure James was the culprit who had hit her last night. "So you're the one!" she bellowed. "It was you sneaking around here last night . . . the one who hit me and messed up my best room. Look at this mess!" Her head still ached, but it didn't stop her from wielding the broom at his head. But James ignored her. He was still under the close scrutiny of his nemesis and he was proving to be a pain.

"So, René is missing. Well, you know what that means, don't you?"

"No. I know what this means," Robert snapped as he smashed James's head against the wall. "If you know where she is, you had better tell me. Or, I'll let the lady of the house tear you to shreds."

The man had no scruples when it came to the Bainbridges. His only excuse for existence was revenge, sad though it may be. However, he felt he was justified under the circumstances. It would suit him well if he had succeeded in dishonoring René and her family. But the satisfaction of accomplishing his task had been thwarted. He was now at the mercy of Robert and the broom-wielding witch, which made him even more impossible to deal with.

"Now, I'll ask you again," Robert bellowed. "If I don't hear the answer I want to hear, I'll hand you over to Mrs. Graham and let her beat the hell out of you."

Mrs. Graham stepped forward, eager to accept the honor. She would be more than glad to accommodate James with a beating. And he was well aware of his status at this time. James had nowhere to run, and there was no possible means of escaping, now that a mob had formed outside of the room and window. He was definitely trapped, just like he had trapped René.

A few trappers entered the room to make sure that his escape was blocked. With that sign of power, Robert continued to push for answers.

The room became deathly quiet. Each waited as though his life depended on what the other had to say. James stared at each man, moving sharply from face to face. Yet, no one flinched or wavered from his glare. He had no authority here, and the threat to his life had broadened.

"Well, where is René ?" Robert demanded again. Again, in his frustration, he pushed James against the wall, the force causing him to hit his head.

"I don't know where your damned sister is. I don't know any more than you do," James retorted quickly. "How could I know? You found me . . . I was just coming to when you found me!"

There was some truth in the matter, but Robert wouldn't accept it. "I don't believe you. You and that mob of yours have been tracking us since we left our home. You and your stupid greed and jealousy caused the death of my parents and the burning of my home. So, shall we get to the truth, or is that something you are truly unfamiliar with?" Robert demanded again.

James was a sick individual to track René out of revenge or greed. But he was able to put one over on Robert. "Innocent people don't run when the law is on their side. You and I both know that there is more to this than you are willing to say. Shall I enlighten your benefactors with what I know, or will you?" James snapped harshly. It was his way of gaining the upper hand or at least trying to buy some time until his men came after him. James had control again. He was sharp and clever and knew how to turn many situations around to suit his needs. It was René's fortune not to have married him.

"You're good," Robert replied with a smile. "Real good about trying to change the subject. But it won't work—not now or ever again." That's when Robert placed the point of the barrel of his revolver at James's forehead. With his finger on the trigger, he pressed the gun against his brow. "You are a hair's breath away from dying, my friend. This is your last chance to do something good for those you have caused so much pain and suffering," he continued. The gleam in his eyes made it clear that he had nothing to lose by killing him. The look on the spectators' faces led him to believe that he could die at any one of their hands if Robert was so inclined. He was definitely at the mercy of his captor, which was the same fate he had planned for René. It had come full circle . . . right back to him.

"Okay . . . okay! I'll tell you! I really don't know what happened to her. I was planning to take her away myself, but someone knocked me out! *It's true! I'm telling you the truth!*" he babbled. He could hear his heart beating in his ears.

Robert didn't want to believe him, but he had no choice in the matter. The man had to be telling the truth. His sister was missing without so much as a clue to where she might be. There was nothing for him to grab hold of. He had failed his father's last request by failing to protect her from harm. When all seemed lost, Lily suddenly entered the room. She was the only thing Robert had left of his past. She was the only link that gave him solace when realization of his loss finally hit home.

René and her companion had been traveling steadily northward and maintaining a steady pace with the lake to their east and the forest to their west. Periodically during the ride, she would awaken, thinking that the land they were traveling was home ground. However, later on, she would remember that she was no longer in her native Ohio.

Black Eagle wanted to maintain as much distance between him and those who would search for his prize. It was necessary to travel by both day and night, which meant Robert would give up looking for her sooner or later. Yet, his pace was slowed by René, since she hadn't fully recovered from the snakebite.

He was forced to set up camp about 160 miles into their trek. He was supposed to rendezvous with his brother near the great fish line, but he had to make adjustments. René required a lot of care, even though she slept most of the way. Her wound needed to be checked from time to time. She also needed water and rest.

There was supposed to be a great celebration when the brothers joined in the return trip home. He had planned so much, and nothing was working at all. So reluctantly he ordered his braves to set up camp again and make sure that a signal fire was set for his brother, who traveled by canoe, to see from afar.

Even though the air was misty and cool, the small fire crackled and sparked from the fat dripping from the meat cooking over the spit. The sleeping area had been tidied up, and they were canvassing the area for more firewood and kindling.

René was finally beginning to show that she was with the living. She stirred and shifted her weight from one side to the other. She hadn't done that for several days. She could smell food cooking, and her belly ached to be filled. Slowly she opened her eyes, seeing the men make the camp ready for their night's stay.

Black Eagle had joined her by the fire after he had tended to the horses. He knew she was awake, although her movements were a bit sluggish. He was glad to see that the color had come back in her cheeks again. For a while, he thought he might lose her. But she was strong—a fighter. She had survived death's grip.

"You hungry?" he asked, and then handed her a small chunk of meat from the spit. It was hot and greasy, but a welcome to the empty well in her belly. René devoured it, then looked at him for more. But he wouldn't allow it.

"You eat too fast," he warned as he put his finger to her lips. "Rest; you will have more later," he cajoled.

It didn't appear to be in her best interest to argue with the man. He was very persuasive in his manner and forced her to rely on him for everything. As she lay down, his words continued to echo in her ears. She tried to understand what he wanted from her. She had never been in the company of a man who demanded so little, but gave so much.

She sensed compassion from him, and yet she dared to ask him, "What are you planning to do with me?"

He wasn't shocked by her query, he just laughed and then said calmly, "You will know in time. But . . . for now, you must get well."

Without fear she closed her eyes again, feeling somewhat at odds with what he meant by "You will know in time." He hadn't answered her question, nor had he said anything about taking her back. She was his prisoner, and he would decide what she was worth in his own time.

The following morning the group uprooted their camp and headed steadily northward. There were times René would inquire where they were going or how much longer, but the only answer she would receive was "home." They traveled sometimes through the night making up lost time and periodically stopping to water the horses and to rest. With the weather seemingly to be on their side, they were able to get to their appointed rendezvous without further delays.

CHAPTER EIGHT

BLACK EAGLE AND HIS party finally reached their destination. This time when they set up camp, they set several fires and built a few lean-tos. It appeared they were going to be there for quite a spell. Everyone went about their work with such ease that it reminded René of home, where she was able to take part. But here, she was limited to one place, where Black Eagle had deposited her.

When he finally settled down and all seemed to become quiet with him, René decided to approach him again with the question of home. "Are you planning to take me back to my brother?" she asked with a little excitement.

Black Eagle didn't answer. He continued to feed the fire with small pieces of wood. But René pushed him for an answer again. "Please, can you tell me . . . are we going back?"

"No!" he snapped. "We are not going back. I have taken you for my woman! Your brother could not protect you! I protected you! You are mine!" he said, and stormed away from her, only to look back and wonder if he was doing what was best.

Shocked and bewildered by his reaction, René stayed quietly by the fire. She stared into space, neither connecting with his glances nor with those of the others who followed him. Her only outlet from the lack of not knowing was the pain she experienced. She never expected to be abducted by the man who had protected her from certain death. She lay back on her makeshift bedroll and happened to catch a glimpse of the sky creeping through the trees. "I'll never see Robert again," she said, with tears flowing. There was no turning back now. James would surely find her if she left Black Eagle's protection. She had no other choice but to follow him wherever he chose to go.

Out on the lake, far off, at least a mile away, several small figures could be seen rowing in the direction of Black Eagle's band. As they approached the shore they signaled by waving their paddles over their heads. They had seen the smoke from the campfires. René watched with great curiosity as one tall, similarly built Indian approached Black Eagle. They embraced and then held each other at arm's length. She could only figure that he was Black Eagle's friend. But they were too far away for her to make any judgments. Eventually, the distance between her and themselves was closed. As they drew nearer, the similarity between the two men was more than astonishing. They were obviously twins. The brother's hair was cut shorter than Black Eagle's, but the face, the build, the walk, and the manner were all similar.

"I must be going crazy," she said as they approached. It was ironic, indeed. Robert was believed to be her twin all these years, only to find that they were only half-brother and half-sister. Now she was in the company of true twin brothers, one just as handsome as the other.

"So, brother, you have found the woman who has haunted your dreams," Black Eagle's twin, Running Bear, said as his eyes wandered over every angle he could see of René.

Black Eagle nearly blushed and smiled, knowing that her face had been one thing stirring him on. Then he answered, "Yes . . . yes, I have found her." He was proud not to be going home empty-handed. She wasn't just a dream, she was real!

"Good woman . . . yes! She does not talk much! I like that in my women," Running Bear reflected.

René was stunned by his interpretation of what women should be like. Yet, she decided it would be harmless to ask, "You have more than one wife?"

Running Bear nodded and then quickly remarked, as though trying to prove his worth, "Yes, sometimes they are a handful. But I am strong. It is good to have more than one woman."

René noted that Black Eagle's brother certainly had only a talent for bragging. His ego appeared to be inflated well beyond his means. She was glad that it wasn't he who had taken her away from the outpost. It wasn't her desire to become one of his many wives. Then again, she wasn't ready for the adventure ahead.

Black Eagle sat next to her again; this time, he planned to stay as close as possible. He knew that tonight would prove to be a chore, especially if she refused his advances. He had to bring her to his bed soon or lose her to another, possibly to his brother. He had to tell her of the customs of his people, and he needed to do that immediately. His brother was an adversary when it came to women. He refused to let René fall into his clutches, like Two Moons had. If he did, he would lose his love and his honor among his people. The cost was too great.

That night, Black Eagle wasted no time in taking René to his secret place. He had taken great pains to prepare it, making it as special as he could. He had made sure they had the comforts of a soft bearskin robe to lie upon and a small fire to warm them. He had chosen a beautiful spot near the lake where they would have a magnificent view of the sun at dawn.

The moon was full that night, bright and dancing on the lake . . . inviting enough to bring two people together. A single night owl was perched on an evergreen branch. Its eyes glistened like twin beacons, blinking on and off. It was to be witness to the joining of two souls—or to a refusal.

Nothing escaped Black Eagle's glances as he laid René on the soft bearskin, where he immediately joined her. She wasn't sure what he expected from her, but they were separated from the main camp—alone. She was in the wilderness, a place that he was accustomed to. It didn't matter that he wanted her. It only mattered that he had taken her away from the people she knew and loved. René watched him with speculation, never offering so much as a sweet gesture or gentle smile for his perusal. She became stiff and rigid when he caressed her cheek, but wasn't unaware of what the touch meant. His breath was warm and sweet with fresh peppermint. It sent a pleasant reminder of her mother's favorite tea.

Everything was getting away from her when he gently pressed his lips to her shoulder and a soft moan broke through. She couldn't tell whether it was she who made that sound or if it was Black Eagle, caught up in a moment of passion. She had to stop him, to squelch his desire. Oh, he was making her heart dance with his gentle way with her. But this was too much. "What do you want from me?" she asked as his hands smoothed over her shoulders and arms.

"It is you I want," he answered slowly. "It is you I crave. Now and always."

René wasn't surprised by his declaration. All she knew of passion was what her mother had tried to tell her just before her canceled wedding. Now this magnificent man was making a claim to her. She had to block his advances, if only to question his motives. But Black Eagle wouldn't be put off so easily. Again he tried to quiet her words with gentle kisses and soft caresses. But René pushed him back, trying to keep her virtue in check. His hands were too much for her. She finally had enough and yelled, "Stop! Don't touch me!"

Puzzled by her reaction, Black Eagle released her. He couldn't understand why she would refuse him. He had been good to her. He had taken care of her, even protected her, and now she was holding him at bay.

René ' pushed away from him again, almost stumbling into the brush. Her heart nearly burst from her chest. She couldn't imagine consenting to his advances. She was no longer under the protection of her brother, and she was sure Black Eagle would continue his pursuit without hesitation. The look in his eyes made that very clear. He had every intention of getting what he wanted.

"I've never been with a man before!" René said angrily. But she changed her tone as he drew her closer to him.

"If you have not been with a man before, why was he—"

"You mean why was that man, uh, in my . . . bed?" she finished for him. "He would have killed me if it hadn't been for you. I am very grateful to you for that," she continued slowly. "But that doesn't mean that he and I . . . well, it never happened."

Black Eagle sat up, somewhat angry at being put off, and yet, he seemed to understand her fears. Maybe he was moving too fast. But he had a lot to consider. One thing for sure, he didn't want to lose her—at least not before he could prove to her that he was worth having in her life. Even though she wanted to keep the peace between them, she was afraid to give in without a fight.

"I've been raised to believe that before I give myself to a man of my choosing, I must marry him. You see, that man, James Courtland, and I were supposed to be married, but something went wrong." The unusual look on Black Eagle's face indicated that he really didn't care, but she told him anyway. "There are so many things that you wouldn't understand, and it would take too long to tell you," she continued as she tried to bring some sense into what she was actually trying to say.

But Black Eagle didn't understand. His head was full of her scent. He wanted her to return the gentleness that he had bestowed upon her so willingly. His blood was hot, and he was quickly becoming discouraged with her and her refusal. On any other occasion he would have won the woman's heart and he would have had his way with her. But here was a woman who had managed to keep away. He wasn't accustomed to being led by a woman. He was supposed to be the stronger of the two, and he wanted her to know his strength as a lover and as a *husband*.

René tried again to convince him, hoping that he wouldn't pursue her any further. But it didn't help in the slightest. "Then . . . you refuse to be my wife?" he asked. The bitterness in his tone gave away his disappointment. He moved away abruptly, taking all the warmth in his body with him. "Then you are faced with another choice," he continued. The manner in which he spoke made her wary of what his next statement would be. Then he said, "You can either become my wife, or you will be forced to take another as a husband. It is the custom of my people that a man take the woman he wants to live in his home, to bear his children. They have agreed to be one, of one body."

René listened to the full scope of what Black Eagle said. Each time he spoke, he sent a strong message. Then he faced her again and said, "It is also custom among my people that if a woman refuses a man who desires her, she will live in his house as a slave, with no honor."

René sat up and looked him straight in the eye. She wanted to see if he was trying to force her hand, but all she saw was concern in the depths of his dark eyes. He was telling the truth. There was so much at stake that she didn't know what to believe anymore. She tried to replay his exact words in her mind, and each time she recalled the words "wife" or "slave."

Black Eagle then lowered himself onto one elbow. It was enough to give him a better view of her face. He enjoyed being with her, looking at her . . . touching her. He stroked a loose wisp of hair from her shoulders, exposing their slim line. He wanted to touch them again, but he waited. It would do more harm than good to push her further away because of his desire.

Everything she had been taught about life would have to be thrown out of the books or rewritten. She was with a very unusual man. His heart was genuinely good. He wanted her to have the best he could offer, and from what she saw, he was rich beyond compare. If she had to pick a man for his worth, she would have to say that he was a far better catch than the ones she'd dealt with in the past.

René gazed into the eyes of the man before her. She saw desire, hope, and pain. She would have to overcome the deep-seated fear that assaulted her nerves as she recalled the frightening moments before he had taken her away. If being with Black Eagle would soothe that fear, she would gladly give up any chance of going home again. Then she remembered: *"There was no home to go back to."*

René took a leap of faith, allowing the newness of the moment to finally sink in. Impulsively, she reached up to caress his brow, and Black Eagle quickly and happily returned the gesture. Then he let his lips glide a path over hers. They found their mark, for he kissed her with all of his hidden passion and she answered with her own. The signals were all in place, and Black Eagle closed the distance between them. While looking into René's eyes, he removed her blanket, the only barrier she had, and tossed it into the wind. Their bodies melded together under the full scale of the moon. They couldn't stop the tremors of passion or the unbridled need for each other. René had unleashed all her inhibitions and allowed him to enter. There was pain, but only for a moment, and then her body became one with his. He was her first, and he called out his pleasure for being her first. They were transfixed, one to the other. Never to be separated by another.

The following morning the camp was quickly dispersed, and the party separated into two groups. Black Eagle and his party traveled by land, while Running Bear's traveled by by water. Each kept pace with the other, but maintained good speed. René was glad to be on the move again. The farther away she got from James, the safer she felt. She began to reconcile herself to the fact that she may never see her brother Robert again, but was glad that he wouldn't be alone. He had Lily in his life now, and she had Black Eagle.

She watched the land change around her as she ventured deeper into uncharted lands. There was so much to see, yet she hardly remembered watching the low-flying bald eagle or the red fox that scurried away as they approached. Her mind wandered back to the days when she was forced to leave home, Wilmot, and sometimes to the night when Black Eagle had saved her. If she could only forget. But the emptiness and the pain were forever etched in her thoughts. She had no idea where she was going, and she wasn't sure how she would handle living in the wilderness.

She could only imagine what she would have to face. She missed being able to take a hot bath with her favorite scented oils. She missed the silver hairbrush that her father had given her on her sixteenth birthday. She no longer had the luxury of sleeping late, something else she would grow accustomed to. They may have seemed trivial to Black Eagle, but they were her memories. Somewhere, they would be lost in the depths of the new land she would soon call home.

"You have much on your mind, woman," Black Eagle said softly in her ear. He had interrupted her thoughts several times before, and she hadn't responded. "You have said little since we left the camp," he continued.

This time she reacted without thinking. "Yes! I do have a lot on my mind. My family, for one thing. I want to be with them. But I know . . . I know you won't take me back, will you?"

Her abruptness didn't change his manner in the slightest. He continued to speak with her patiently, knowing that she was becoming nervous and edgy. "Woman, I cannot take you back. Not now or ever. You will learn to accept that soon," he said slowly.

She didn't want to accept it at all, so she tried again to appeal to his sympathy. "I know you protected me when there was no one else there to help, but you never gave me a chance to say good-bye to my brother. I know he is worried about me," René said gently.

Black Eagle soon became weary hearing her go on and on about the same things. He had to make her understand that the journey they were taking together was for keeps. He couldn't return her to her brother and still keep his position in the ranks of chief among his people. The vision had been fulfilled when she had fallen into his path that day, and now he must follow his destiny. He must make his vision come to pass. "He will worry, and he will learn to live without you. He has someone to care for," Black Eagle said as he recalled the other woman who had arrived in the outpost with René and her brother.

For the first time his words rang in her ears, sealing any hope of returning. He was right about one thing: Robert wasn't going to be alone. But she had to find a way to get word back to her brother, at least so that he would know she was alive. With Black Eagle so close all the time, she wouldn't be able to escape him.

"Thank you for being honest with me," she said sadly. "At least one of us will have what we want. And, by the way, my name is not 'woman,' it's René " she added with an angry tone.

Black Eagle didn't like the way she sounded. She appeared cold and withdrawn, very much unlike the woman he had made love to the night before. He knew he had to realize that she wasn't acquainted with his ways nor of the ways of his clan. He had to be patient with her and help her to adjust to every transition that would eventually arise. Then softly, he repeated her name, Re-nea . . . Re-nea."

They traveled like that for several days, sharing only glances, Black Eagle's horse, and the bearskin robe at night. But she never brought up the issue with him again, and she kept communication to a minimum. It was her way of keeping peace within herself.

Ten days went by, and the group continued its slow trek northeast by the curve of the lakeshore. Today would be the last day Black Eagle and Running Bear would be traveling together. Running Bear was due to return to the village with dried meats from the hunt and most of the supplies that would carry them through the winter months.

As Running Bear paddled away, he looked back to see his brother preparing the fire. He noticed that the woman sat quietly by, watching Black Eagle intently, and a streak of jealousy ran through him. "She is a beauty," he remarked sullenly. He wished it had been he who had found her. She would have made a nice addition to his home.

It would take less than a week to travel the distance across the lake and an additional few days by land to reach the main camp. But it would take Black Eagle and his party at least a month by land, as they planned to hunt and to tap maple trees on their way. It was Black Eagle's plan to make sure he was well ladened with gifts for his people, since he planned to return with a bride, which was a gift for himself.

CHAPTER
NINE

THE JOURNEY BY LAND caused Black Eagle and his party to miss the harvest ceremony. They could hear the ceremonial drums being played, even though they were a few miles away from the village.

In the village, men and women danced around the huge bonfire, while others sang songs of thanks to the sun and the rain for a good harvest. There was more food than the eye could behold, as each household had contributed their share to the celebration.

Running Bear had reached the village by canoe a week before . He told the story of how his brother had rescued a young fiery-haired woman from certain death. He had repeated the story from one household to the next, and each time he told it, the story grew.

News had reached all points of the village, especially the home of Black Eagle and Running Bear's parents. He had made that his last stop before heading for his own home. But before that, he wanted to take part in the night's festivities, where he danced with the young warriors and played his flute with the elders.

Gray Wolf and his wife, White Feather, were sitting by the cook fire and watching the festivities. They had rabbit roasting on a spit and wild rice simmering in the black cast-iron kettle they had traded beaver pelts and deer skins for last winter. Gray Wolf had seen more than fifty winters, and his wife, still lovely and aging gracefully, was a few months younger. Both had put a lot of their energy and time into raising their sons, hoping that they would become strong leaders. Only one of them, however, would become chief, taking Gray Wolf's position. He was greatly admired by his people, and it would be hard to fill his shoes. Only time would tell.

Finally Running Bear left the celebration to join his parents. He was greeted warmly by his mother, "It is good to have you home again, my son."

Gray Wolf gestured openly, taking his son by the arms firmly and smiling with pride. His wrinkled lips curled as his grin broadened. "Yes, my son, it is good to have you home," he said deeply. He missed his sons and tried not to show favoritism. But he noted the seed of envy in Running Bear was growing steadily, even though he appeared to have everything he wanted. Then he stated, "I hear there is news of your brother returning soon. Is that true?"

Running Bear's manner changed. The jealousy he felt had been rekindled. There were many instances where competition with his brother was interpreted as war, to see who was better.

White Feather invited her son to eat. She handed him a bowl filled with chunks of rabbit, cornmeal, bread, and rice. Gray Wolf waited patiently for his next serving, for he had consumed a good portion before his son arrived. They both licked their bowls clean and gave a healthy belch to show they had enjoyed the meal. Running Bear wiped his mouth with his sleeve and smiled at his mother as she took his bowl. She was pleased to have at least one of her sons home.

Knowing that his mother wouldn't ask, Running Bear decided to tell her about the young woman who would be accompanying Black Eagle. He described her as a gentle woman and explained that Black Eagle was very protective of her.

"I believe Black Eagle has taken the woman for his wife," he continued. He wasn't sure, but he thought he saw signs of disapproval in his mother's eyes. "And I am sure she is willing." His father still showed no expression. "She means trouble for us all. She will bring the whites to our land. We may need new blood in our clan, but hers may cause us great harm," he added finally.

Without so much as a word to acknowledge what he had heard, Gray Wolf donned his heavy bearskin robe and his bonnet of eagle feathers, then walked to the open portal of his home. He had taken each word spoken by Running Bear under consideration. Yet, he also heard the underlying tone that marked jealousy. "We will not speak of this again until your brother returns," Gray Wolf said quickly.

"But father, they are at least a few days' away. By the time they get here, the woman may be with child. Black Eagle's feeling for her are very strong. He will not give her up without a fight," he pressed.

"You mean, he will not allow you to have the woman. You have always been a thorn in your brother's side. You would deny him the woman he wants for your own pleasures. Have you forgotten how you cheated him out of marrying Two Moons?" Gray Wolf stressed sourly. "When your brother returns, we—your brother and I—will decide what to do. But until then, *you,* my son, will speak no more on the matter. *Eni-penkissemo ki-siss.*" ("The sun is setting.")

The trio departed for the harvest ceremony, which was coming into full cadence. The drums and flutes were played all night long. Gray Wolf and Running Bear danced around the bonfire with the other men. They would dance until dawn. The holy man sang songs of blessing for the coming winter, for fresh meat to be plentiful, for peace to reign supreme over their lands, and for each newly wedded couple to be fruitful.

Meanwhile, many miles away, Black Eagle and René came to another place with a small brook running through it. It didn't take long for Black Eagle to notice the disappointed looks on his men's faces. They were missing the event of the year, the harvest celebration. Now it was up to him to get them in better spirits for the long journey ahead. He was sure the Great Spirits would be pleased if they were honored here as well as at home.

He ordered Tall Elk to dig a pit for the bonfire and then to collect firewood, selecting the best birch and maple he could find. Little Beaver prepared the fresh meat for roasting, while Black Eagle constructed a drum from a hollowed-out tree trunk. While they were making final preparations for the night's festivities, René sat quietly on the side, watching with great interest as they completed each detail. This celebration seemed to be very important to them.

Black Eagle stopped working on his drum suddenly and turned abruptly. He heard the sound of snapping twigs from a short distance away. He and Tall Elk elected to investigate, but before leaving, he gestured to René to stay put. The two disappeared into the woods without making a sound.

How dare you tell me what to do! she said to herself. In her own fury, she practically leaped to her feet and started to follow Black Eagle. She ducked behind the trees that fell into her path and suddenly realized that she had lost her bearings. The trees were all beginning to look alike, and she wasn't sure which one was the last she had passed. There wasn't a track or a trace of the man she intended to follow. Now she wished she had obeyed. What she didn't know was that Black Eagle had had her in his sights from the time she left the camp. Suddenly, she heard something, at least four, maybe five separate voices coming from the opening just ahead of her. That made her quicken her steps from a slow walk to a run.

When René reached the small camp, she heard a small child whimpering and another child playing with a doll. René hesitated for a moment, but soon pushed on hoping to find help. Fear gripped every fiber of her being. This could be a trap. These people may turn her over to James Courtland. Then again, she could convince these people to help her find her brother. After battling with these thoughts, she wondered, *How could they be a threat to me with children around?*

René closed her eyes for a second to try to drum up enough courage to go talk with these people. Someone had to help her or she would be lost in this wilderness forever and lost to her brother. René slowly left the cover of the tree that had protected her from their sight. The first to see her was a little girl named Rachel. Startled and then excited that she finally had someone to play with, Rachel exclaimed, "Momma! Poppa! there is a pretty lady with long, curly hair!"

She was a pretty little thing, of about five years of age, with shiny dark hair covered with a lacy hand-sewn bonnet. She smiled at René and gave her a delightful curtsy. My name is Rachel, and my dolly's name is Mary, like my mother's."

René still hadn't said a word. She was somewhat taken by the little one's friendliness. Rachel took René by the hand and led her to the other side of the wagon, still talking about her doll and her new baby brother. Rachel's parents must have thought their daughter was still playing make-believe, because they certainly weren't expecting her to actually bring a young woman into their camp.

"Momma! Poppa! Look who has come to play with me!" Rachel exclaimed. She was anxious to have a playmate and wasn't willing to wait for her brother to get older.

Rachel's parents were stunned seeing René standing next to their child. She knew she was oddly dressed, and to have appeared out of nowhere made them panic. "Rachel! Come here, child," Jacob said as he reached for his daughter's free hand. He yanked the child away, scaring her half out of her wits. The poor child whimpered, thinking she was being punished.

In that same instant, René tried to ease their fears by saying, "I'm sorry if I frightened you, sir. I have no weapons, as you can see." René turned around with both hands extended outward, allowing them a chance to see for themselves. Then she exclaimed, "I need your help! Please!"

She paused momentarily and looked into their fearful faces. They didn't notice that she was just as frightened of them as they were of her. For all she knew, they would be the ones to tell James of her whereabouts. She would be taking a great chance exposing her identity to them.

"Help?" Mary echoed. "How can we help you? We are poor people trying to find a better life away from the madness in the South. With talk of war stirring up everywhere and the people killing those poor slaves . . . well, we just couldn't take it anymore."

A lot had happened in the few weeks since René and Robert had left home. She knew that relations between the North and South were strained. There were times when she detached herself from such issues, trying to remain impartial. And yet, her father had ways of bringing her attention to the needs of others. His respect for human life weighed more than the desires of those who want to dominate others, and this became more apparent when she found out that her father had aided many runaway slaves as they reached Wilmot. He had risked everything, his home and his family.

"You say there is talk of war? The last I heard, they were still discussing the rights of each state to govern itself. Have things stopped? Have they really stopped negotiating?" she asked, sensing some relief that she wasn't caught in the cross fire any longer.

"I'm not sure. But it appears that the talking will eventually turn to war. Neither side is listening to what the other wants. The South wants a separate government from the Union, and the Union wants the South to accept their laws. It will be brother against brother if they don't settle their differences soon," Jacob said painfully.

/René listened carefully, knowing that her situation was no different from that of the runaway slaves, who wanted freedom above all else. She was forced to run for her life. But was she alive? If only she hadn't read the letter that day. Maybe her life would have been better after all. The day she was forced to leave home suddenly flashed before her eyes as did the dreadful way James had treated her when he found her. She could hardly envision anything being different. Not with James or with the people of Wilmot.

"As you can see, we are powerless to help you or anyone else. We had to leave our home in Virginia so that we could live in peace," Jacob stated quickly. "Now, young lady, you must go. Leave us!" he snapped. Even though he felt sorry that he couldn't help her, he had to consider his own family. Their safety came first. Besides, someone could be lurking in the bushes just waiting to pounce on them.

René was the stranger, and her appearance didn't make it any better. She could only wonder what they thought about her. And they wondered where she could have come from. Yet, they decided that it was too dangerous for them to get involved. They would have to forget that they ever saw her. But how?

René broke the silence again, hoping to at least convince them that she wasn't a threat to them. If she could only impress upon them the importance of leaving a word or two for her brother, it would set her mind at ease. And even if they didn't go to the outpost, she would know that someone apart from the man who had saved her

"Sir!" René exclaimed. "All I am asking is that you remember my face . . . my face, please! Just remember me! I'm not asking you to take me back. *He* won't allow it. But one day, you will meet my brother . . . my twin brother. You will know him when you see him," she said as she looked into the woods. "Please tell him that I am well . . . that I haven't been harmed in any way. He will know that I have said this to you."

She could hear the man's wife saying, "The poor thing. Jacob, we must do our Christian duty. What harm can it be to tell her brother—if we see him? What harm, Jacob?"

Jacob grumbled a few words under his breath. It wasn't something he wanted to do, knowing the way things were in this strange land. He may never see the girl's brother. Then again, he may not see another soul until spring. The girl might die between now and then.

René had reached the other side of the wagon, when Mary rushed to her side and grabbed her hand. "God be with you," Mary said sweetly and then added, "you never told us your name."

René's smile was almost painful, but she spoke with pride. "My name is René Alexandra Bainbridge. I am the daughter of Devon, Rachel . . . and Sarah Josephine."

Then she quickly headed back into the woods, hoping that she would find her way back to the campsite. As though a blanket had been pulled over her head, René was now facing the darkness of the wooded area alone. She had difficulty maneuvering as it settled in around her. Each step took her farther away from the camp. There were no signs of light to guide her in. The trees and bushes seemed to mesh into a woven canopy.

Suddenly, René had the feeling she was being followed, and again she wished she had listened to Black Eagle. Then she heard footsteps on the hardened surface behind her. Whoever or whatever it was, was closing in on her fast. She had to feel her way around in the darkness. The speed of the footsteps increased, and so did her heartbeat. If she ran, she probably would run into a tree. If she didn't, she would fall victim to whomever or whatever was lurking in the shadows. Panic rose in her throat as a hand grabbed her from behind. Another hand covered her mouth. For all she knew, she was about to die. But a familiar voice squelched that thought immediately.

Black Eagle had followed her from the time she left the settlers' camp, letting her feel his presence, but not letting her see him. He felt it necessary to teach her that she must listen to him even if she didn't want to.

"*Wegoonen wenji?*" Black Eagle asked calmly. Then he translated, "Why did you leave?" He ran his fingers through her hair and then placed his hands on her shoulders.

"I don't know . . . I really don't know why I left the camp," she stammered. "I can't stay put when something might . . . "

René walked away from him, around the tree, putting it between them. She was still shaking inside. Even though she was grateful that it was Black Eagle who had found her, she still felt out of sorts with him. His voice changed in a way that let her know that she had made a major mistake.

Black Eagle wasn't about to allow her to keep the distance between them an ongoing thing. Even as he closed in on her, his first instinct was to yell at her, but instead he flipped her over his knee and paddled her rump. The shock of his action made her fly from his grasp. She ran aimlessly through the woods in tears and angry that he would be so bold. It would suit her if he just let her go.

René thought she had put enough distance between Black Eagle and herself and she slowed to a walk. But she soon collided with him again. This time, he wouldn't let her go.

Realizing that she couldn't get free of Black Eagle, she stopped fighting. She knew he was persistent and he was too strong. So, as it would be, the two of them wound up on the leaf-covered ground, one feeling defeated and the other feeling a chance of hope.

Black Eagle stopped momentarily to absorb the radiance of his prized possession, then gently said, "I want you for my wife, Re-nea. I will make a good husband. I will provide for you and give you all you will ever need."

Black Eagle's proposal was met with silence. For a long while, René just looked into the darkness, trying to put things into perspective. Then, she answered slowly, allowing his proposal to sink in. She wanted to keep some kind of assurance that he would keep his word. "If . . . if I say yes . . . what guarantees do I have that you will do all these things for me? I mean . . . you haven't even asked my brother for my hand. And . . . since you haven't shown him the respect that he deserves, I am sure that you should consider his wishes above all other things," she said with conviction.

There was no argument. Black Eagle knew she was right. If she were the daughter of a chief, he would have paid a bride price for her. However, her brother had been denied that right. It meant going back to the outpost, and he still had to return to his people. Suddenly, he blurted out, "I agree to do as you ask, but I cannot go until the snow melts and the planting season is over. Will that be to your liking?"

"Are you sure you can't go back any sooner?" René asked quickly, hoping that he could be reasoned with. But he shook his head no, leaving her to answer his proposal, such as it was. His eyes remained fixed on her, intent on a response. There was nothing to keep her from acknowledging him. Her lips quivered as she answered. "I will be your wife, Black Eagle, but only if you keep your word. You must keep your word!" she said nervously.

Black Eagle accepted her conditions. She had consented much too quickly, but he didn't care. He had what he wanted. But he would, for her sake, keep a close watch on her. "I promise to speak to your brother," he stated without hesitation. "I live by my word."

René didn't relish being kept against her will. If there was a way for her to escape, she would find it. In the meantime, she would allow him to think that she was happy with her new situation. She would marry him and hope that nothing would come from it. Yet and still, Black Eagle was elated. The woman he wanted most had given him a great gift by consenting to be his wife. *She will love being my wife,* he thought to himself. Then, without much effort, he removed his breechcloth and leggings and pulled closer the woman he adored .

There was no turning back from that point. His blood was hot with passion, and she was at her wit's end. If only she could open her heart to him, to return the love that he gave so freely. She wouldn't be able to keep up with the pretense for much longer. Black Eagle was in love with her. For the first time in his life, he was vulnerable, but only to her and her charms. He loved the touch of her soft skin, the aroma of her hair, and the gentle way her mouth curved when she managed to smile.

Every muscle in René s body began to tingle as Black Eagle worked his magic. He was able to make her body respond so well that she nearly cried out for him to stop. So ashamed by her own behavior, her own need, she tried to hide her face from view. She never knew that the joys of being with a man would make her want more. Nor did she expect to become so demanding. She wasn't the same woman who had made love to him several nights before. Aglow with passion, René allowed herself to release what was hidden deep within her and she called his name, "Black Eagle."

He was hungry for her, so much so that his heart quickened as he continued his amorous gaze. In his arms he held the woman he had dreamed of. She had honored him with her presence and would honor him later with a child from their union. René had his heart. Never had he been so happy, so content.

A thump of a single drum reached the ears of the two in the woods. Black Eagle's men had started the ceremony without him, and he was glad that they had. It had blessed the union that he and René had shared. "We must join the others," he said quickly, anxious to share the news with his friends. Then he offered, "The harvest ceremony has begun, and a blessing must be given to those who are fruitful." He rose swiftly and then turned to give René a hand. He lifted her to her feet in one swift motion and pulled her close to him. He regretted not having more time with her.

René hadn't responded as quickly as he would have liked. She was still somewhat taken by her actions. She wondered if he would always be like this, loving and caring. Would he see her with the same intensity in a few months, even years, or was this a passing phase? She began to worry. There were many thing she hadn't considered that might go wrong; a child, for instance. She could become pregnant. How would she manage with the birth of a child in the wilderness? How would she care for it? "I'm frightened, Black Eagle," she said softly under her breath. "I don't know if I can . . . "

Black Eagle eased his arm around her waist and placed a finger to her lips to quiet her. She seemed more relaxed with his closeness and didn't pull away as she had before. He was glad that she had accepted her new life, even though she was afraid of what it had to offer. "My heart is full of you. You are mine. You are my wife and will one day be the mother of many new sons . . . and the mother of my son," he said gently in her ear, not realizing that he had said more than he intended.

However, René had heard every word. "You have a son already?" she asked. The world stopped spinning, and she came back to her old self.

It was too late to take back what he had already stated. If he wanted her to be with him freely without reservation, he had to tell her everything. "Yes, I have a son. He is still very small . . . only born a few moons ago," he explained slowly.

"That means . . . you are already married," René snapped. "You were about to make me one of your many wives?"

Black Eagle became flustered all of a sudden. He was so caught up in having René in his life that he had forgotten to tell her about the child and the child's mother. Realizing that he, too, had made a major error in judgment, he decided to tell her all and keep to the tradition of protecting the spirits of the dead. "You will be my only wife, but you are not my first. The woman who bore my son . . . died. She was not a strong woman like you. My son and I are alone," he said while putting on his leggings. "He needs a mother like I need a wife. I want you to love us both. But if you cannot love us both, then at least love me. I need you."

René wasn't sure if she should be angry or satisfied with his explanation. Yet, everything he told her was the truth. His honesty was impeccable. She couldn't doubt the man who had saved her life and vowed to care for her. She would wait and see for herself. In the meantime, the drum was calling them to dance. Black Eagle handed her a small bundle. René unwrapped it and found a beautifully beaded deerskin dress. She quickly donned the dress and ran her fingers through her hair to set free the snarls and to loosen the leaves. The moon finally broke through the trees, just in time to shine on her features, making Black Eagle catch his breath. She was a vision to behold. He had to close his eyes to keep from wanting her again. She was about to braid her hair when Black Eagle gently moved her hands aside and braided it for her. He sang a lilting tune in her ear and then kissed her neck. René accepted the caress and turned to face him. "Am I your wife now?" she asked softly.

It appeared she had accepted her plight. Few if any who tried to escape from their captors were only to be faced with the wilds of nature. They would either come back or vanish into its depths. The forest was thick with underbrush and densely populated with bear, moose, elk, and fox; it would be more than a trial for anyone to undergo.

That thought alone frightened René. She remembered the stories James had told her when he came to call, about women being carried away by only God knows what. She'd shudder to think that she could fall into the same predicament. She didn't have a horse, and she most certainly didn't know her way back to the outpost.

"By our laws, you have taken me for you husband. It is I who should be proud," he added. Secretly, he was rejoicing. He had finally chosen the right woman, someone who his brother had no claim to and someone who would love only him.

Black Eagle's words had brought her back to reality. She had to stop thinking of escape so that he wouldn't suspect that she wanted to leave. But in the few weeks they had been together, she found herself wanting to be with him every second of each day. She had to keep her mind on her family, Robert and Lily. They were all she had left of her family. Now, Black Eagle was standing before her, wanting to give her the world if he could. "I will try to be a good wife, Black Eagle . . . I will try," she said softly.

They held to each other as they walked back to the campsite, each feeling satisfied that they had gained something from the other. Black Eagle stopped short of entering the camp and said, "I will dance the marriage dance for you tonight. When I call to you, my bride, you must come and wrap your robe around my shoulders . . . like so." He demonstrated each movement like the wind would carry them both away. "Then, I will take you in my arms to show that you have my heart and that I have yours."

"Is this how you take a wife? No vows, no reverend to say 'I now pronounce you man and wife'? It's silly. I don't think I can do that," she answered.

Again, Black Eagle had to use patience to explain the ways of his people and their traditions. She had to understand that what he asked wasn't really unlike the ceremonies given by the white man. "When two people are joined in this manner, they are considered of one body. A man and a woman must show that they will share the domain that the man has provided. Our holy man will bless the union and pray for us to be fruitful," Black Eagle continued. "It is our way! My people will now be your people. You will learn the ways of the clan, and they will take you to their hearts, just as I have," he added while placing an assuring hand on her shoulder.

His eyes never wandered from hers. She was caught up in his world, almost picturing to the last detail of what life would be like with him. In a way it seemed more intriguing than frightening. René suddenly felt queasy for a moment, but it passed just as quickly as it came. He was the most handsome man she had ever encountered. She was glad that he wanted her in an honorable way. "Well . . . I will do as you ask," she said hesitantly. "But you will have to learn some of my ways as well. Fair is fair."

In partial agreement, they performed the marriage dance in front of Black Eagle's traveling companions. There was much excitement and merriment in that one gesture of acceptance. Tall Elk fired his rifle in his leader's honor. Little Beaver danced and played the drum. As Black Eagle had stated, they accepted her with open arms and greeted her as a new member of the clan . . . and as Black Eagle's wife. As Running Bear had foretold, Black Eagle would bring home his new bride.

CHAPTER

TEN

BLACK EAGLE AND HIS party finally arrived home by midday one month later. They were greeted by everyone, especially the curious, who wanted to see that woman who had sparked Black Eagle's attention. They touched René's hair and tugged on her clothing to make sure she was real. Some smiled and welcomed her, while others stared in disbelief. There was only one familiar face in the mass of faces, and it belonged to the exact copy of Black Eagle's. She could tell the way he stared her down that her presence would cause difficulty between the two brothers. There wasn't any kindness to be found in that face.

Gray Wolf and White Feather watched as their son approached from the southern point of the village. They were impatiently awaiting his arrival, especially since Running Bear had brought them news of Black Eagle's new interest. They walked part of the way to meet him, wanting to close the distance between them before the clan surrounded them.

As soon as he spotted his parents, Black Eagle leaped from his horse and rushed to greet his father and mother. The union was warm and sweet. They were pleased at receiving such public attention from their son. However, their eyes went from their son to the woman in his possession.

"My son . . . it is good to have you home after such a long journey. You have traveled far and must be hungry," Gray Wolf said aloud, so all of his people could hear.

"It is good to be home and among my people again," Black Eagle stated, just as clearly. He wanted to talk privately with his father, but the people willed him to stay.

Then Gray Wolf said, "So, I see you have brought back a slave to help your mother. That is good. She is getting on in years and needs someone to do the heavy work." His eyes sparkled with delight as he spied the treasure that his son had stolen. *He will never be bored at night,* he thought to himself.

All ears turned to Black Eagle, waiting to to hear his response. He hadn't told his father who the woman was. The people were so quiet that the dog barking in the northern section of the village could be heard. They wanted to hear from his own lips what she meant to him.

"Kuwa pema na aw akkwe?" ("Do you see that woman?") Black Eagle asked while turning to look at each person who stood nearby. *"Nesa keʔa aw akkwe,"* ("I love that woman!") he announced loud and clear. He knew that once he proclaimed his love for her, no one would dare challenge that. "I have taken her for my wife and I have witnesses to the fact."

First there was silence, then a low hum of voices among the masses. Even Gray Wolf appeared surprised that Black Eagle would declare such a union in public, when he had not given his blessing. "But my son, she is not one of us. She is an outsider. And she can only bring trouble to our land," he stated with a critical note. "It would be better for us all if she were a slave. She could be sold to another tribe."

But Black Eagle wasn't about to let his father win when he knew that his father was only repeating the shallow words of his brother. He could lose the woman he loved to his father's fears and to his brother's treachery if he didn't act now.

From the midst of the crowd came a gentle voice. White Feather, his mother, had come forth to speak. She couldn't bear having her favorite son spend the rest of his life alone. "Gray Wolf! If you deny your son the woman he wants, he may leave with her, never to return again. He will not give her up," she said with conviction. She was saddened by her son's choice. He had taken an outsider for his wife.

René remained on the horse, sensing that the conversation taking place was about her. She wondered what had happened when the old man pointed in her direction and all eyes fell on her and then turned to talk among themselves. She noticed how freely Black Eagle used her, planting in their heads a message that she was here to stay. Now and then he would gaze at her and smile, knowing that he would be taking her home very soon.

"She is not a slave and never will be. She is my wife!" he announced with pride. "I will have no one treat her in any other way!" With his last statement, he rushed to her side and then gently brought her down from the horse. His eyes sparkled as he smiled into hers, and slowly he led her to the place where his parents stood. They appeared bewildered or at least a little frustrated that they couldn't convince him to pick another for his bride. No other woman would do at this point. Black Eagle presented René to his parents, face-to-face.

René was unaccustomed to the ways of the Ojibwa. When she was introduced to her father-in-law, she inadvertently extended her hand. And when he didn't understand the gesture she made, he frowned upon her with ridicule. René quickly withdrew her hand and backed away. From the look of things she was going to have in-law problems.

But White Feather took René's hand and gave her a broad handshake. She must accept this woman, no matter how she hated René for taking her son. In her heart she felt betrayed, but she would let them all believe that she had accepted her.

So when White Feather had acknowledged René, it created a wave of acceptance from all who could reach her. René shook many hands, shared smiles with those who couldn't reach her, and held several crying babies. She was amazed at how quickly they accepted her, but there was something gnawing at her very nerves.

Black Eagle saw through that gaze as clearly as if he had read her mind. He smiled at her, gently trying to ease her fears of what was soon to come. He was going to stand by her until the day came when she could and would stand on her own in this land. He had made a promise.

Later that day, Black Eagle and Running Bear sat in council with their father. He was still intent on putting René into the hands of another tribe, preferably their enemy, the Sauks. Black Eagle argued with them until nightfall, only to have his words fall on deaf ears. He later stormed out of his father's home, only to find René sitting by a fire in the middle of the village . . . alone. Without a word, Black Eagle snatched her up and took her to his horse. He wasn't about to let his family destroy what he had tried to build for himself.

The two rode until Black Eagle finally felt he had put enough distance between them and the village. He had picked the most spectacular place in the wilderness to stop and rest. The most magnificent waterfall that René had ever seen splashed the large rocks below it and sprayed a beautiful rainbow across the early evening sky. It was so inviting, beckoning René to enter into another realm. Black Eagle let her down and watched her remove her moccasins and leggings. She sampled the water and laughed as it trickled down her neck. René quickly removed the rest of her clothing and rushed into the pool of cool, delicious water. She laughed again as the water tickled her spine.

It was the most refreshing moment she had had since her arrival into the village. The water cascaded over her skin like a satin sheet. She captured Black Eagle's attention. She no longer felt threatened in his company , which he attributed to his continued attentiveness. He was willingly caught up in her passion. Her manner had changed. She no longer appeared cold or standoffish. She was in want of him.

Black Eagle quickly leaped from his horse and joined her in the cool water. He reached out to her, and she flew into his arms. She felt his torment and knew that it all involved her. She kissed him, first gently caressing his lips with hers. She allowed her breath to escape before kissing him again . . . full and without fear. She held him as tight as he was holding her. The moment she allowed him into her world, all the anger he once felt turned to passion. He couldn't imagine being with anyone else. She was his life, his soul, and his very existence. René had succeeded at tugging at his heart . . . making it hers.

"Love me," he said in a low drawl. "Keep me inside of you and let my seeds grow in your body." It was the one thing his family couldn't spoil. Even if the white man did come, they would never know her. They could never connect with where she came from. He was determined to have her. His heart pounded wild and furiously when she let him in. René let him take her to paradise, and the pool became the warmest sanctuary in the forest.

They were so in tune with each other that they didn't know they had company. Running Bear had followed them and had witnessed their joining. His jealousy clouded his reasoning. He had planned to make René a part of his life. He couldn't allow his brother to have something better than he had. *She would enjoy being a slave in my house,* he thought. Then he recalled how he had stolen Two Moons and Dancing Wind away from his brother, always trying to outdo Black Eagle in every way. "Now Black Eagle has a woman devoted only to him! She should be mine!" he said aloud, shattering the confines of the trees above. He disturbed the passion between his brother and his brother's wife. It was enough to let Black

Eagle know that his brother needed some attention. The rivalry between them must end.

It didn't take long to find him. He sat boldly in the open, hoping to be recognized. Not only had he deliberately disturbed their love play, he had come to offer something that would have made anyone sick to their stomachs. She is good in love play, isn't she? Maybe we can trade? Two Moons for the woman," he said with a wry grin. "Now I see why you sided with Father. You wanted Re-nea for yourself," Black Eagle yelled.

"Yes, I sided with Father. I told him what I wanted him to know so that he and Mother would convince you to give her up. You know I am the better man for her. Let me have a chance with her. She will never know the difference, I promise you," he answered, thinking that he could outwit his brother.

"That will never happen! She is and will always be my wife. Stay away from her. Stay away or I will . . . kill you," Black Eagle stated forcefully. He pulled his knife from its holder and shifted it from one hand to the other.

It seemed Running Bear had pushed his brother much too far and once too often. He never imagined that his brother's feelings for the woman were so strong, as they must have been for Two Moons once upon a time. However, he had damaged that before it got started. Then there was another matter concerning him: He had no wish to die, especially over a woman. There wasn't any honor in that.

"You already have two wives. I think you have more than you need," Black Eagle added. "Now, go home to your wives and make them happy. Or are you so busy trying to keep me miserable that you cannot satisfy them? Are they too much for you, brother?"

Black Eagle's words stung. Running Bear had always been envious of his brother. The two women he had taken as wives were, in fact,in line to become Black Eagle's at one time. But in his absence, Running Bear had taken them for himself, leaving his brother to find another. First it was Two Moons, a beautiful maiden with long black hair. She was chosen to be Black Eagle's bride by none other than White Feather. Many pelts were given as a bride price for her hand, but Running Bear pretended to be Black Eagle and took the woman as his own. Then he took Dancing Wind under the same trickery, although she wasn't the one he actually sought. His treachery knew no bounds when it came to his brother.

The woman Black Eagle finally married without any interference from

Running Bear had suffered under the hands of the tribe with whom they they traded. She was swapped for rice and the privilege of hunting on the lands belonging to the Ojibwa clan. She was frail, yet very beautiful. So full of life was she, but she died under mysterious circumstances. She left Black Eagle with a son to care for and an empty bed to lie in.

"You are much stronger . . . since I saw you last," Running Bear stated as he backed away from a potential fight. "If she means that much to you, keep her! I will treat her like a sister. I will not betray you, my brother," he offered, hoping that would calm him. He hadn't seen this side of Black Eagle before. "It is good . . . good to have you home again."

However, Black Eagle knew his brother. But he would be considered a fool for not accepting his brother's apology as offered. He knew all too well that Running Bear wouldn't give up so easily when there was something he wanted. "Yes, Running Bear, I am stronger. I have a home, a son, and now I have a wife. It is more than good, dear brother," he said slowly, so not to miss his brother's reaction. "Yes, it is good. I could not have asked for more. She is all I have ever wanted. What is more, she has not been touched by anyone but me. She is truly mine. She is carrying my child, as well," Black Eagle stated finally with great pleasure.

And Running Bear knew that his brother really wanted him to know how it felt to have something taken away before you've have a chance to enjoy it. It was a bitter pill to swallow. In disbelief, he said, "That cannot be. But, then, she must have bewitched you. You must be bewitched, dear brother, to have fallen so shamelessly into her trap. She must be lying about the child. It is impossible!"

"If there was a trap to be set, it was I who planted the snare, Running Bear. She just fell in and I caught her. It wasn't the other way around. And if I appear to be bewitched, it is because I am in love for the first time in my life and I want her more than I have ever wanted anything. If you cannot understand that and allow me to have the greatest gift of all —a companion—then you are not my brother. You have not acted like my brother since we were children."

"But this cannot be true!" Running Bear stated again.

"Oh, do you think I would lie about that? She has not seen her woman's time in all the time we have shared together. She carries *my* child," Black Eagle pressed.

"Then I have wronged you, Black Eagle. I will leave you and your bride to yourselves," he said sheepishly. "I will not trouble you again."

The woman had succeeded in bewitching his brother. Now she dares to carry his child. He would have to think of a way to destroy the closeness that was sure to develop between them. He wanted the woman, and that was all that mattered to him at the time. He slowly backed away from his brother and then slipped into the shadows of the night, vowing to get her for himself.

After the confrontation with his brother, Black Eagle wanted to take René as far away as possible. Maybe it had been a mistake bringing her to his village. His people weren't ready to accept her. Even his mother had seemed distant at their meeting. And yet, he knew running away with her wouldn't solve anything. He was still very devoted to his people and he had to convince them, even his father, that René was worthy of being a part of the clan. Besides, he was subchief to this clan, a title given to him by birth. He had privileges, some of which he hadn't taken advantage of. It was only fitting that he should be able to pick the woman who would share his bed and raise his children. It would be necessary to make them understand that he must live out his vision and that she was a major part of what would keep him strong. By then, Black Eagle had walked back to the place where he left René. His little hideaway had been discovered and was no longer a fitting place to bring her for their private moments. With Running Bear roaming around, spying on them, it would be difficult for him to be free to be with his wife.

Later that same evening, Black Eagle and René arrived home to a dark and cold cabin. There was no fire. The place hadn't been tidied up. Several blankets and a few furs had been tossed carelessly over a makeshift bed. But René could see that that someone had made an attempt to clean up the cabin, for the fresh scent of evergreen was everywhere. The person must have left in a hurry, because the cabin entrance was opened when they arrived.

Black Eagle quickly sparked a small flame in the pit, which grew into a friendly crackling fire. It immediately began to warm and light the cabin. René drew nearer and put her hands up the flames to warm her cold fingers. She then took a good look at the cabin for the first time since their arrival. The walls were covered with deerskin, which prevented the weather from coming through. There were large rocks surrounding the pit, from which she warmed herself, and a hole in the roof where the smoke filtered through. Her new home appeared to be very comfortable and quite spacious.

René noticed the large pots near the pit and quickly inspected their contents. One was filled with fresh water and the others were filled with cornmeal, rice, and dried meats. From the looks of things, someone wanted to make sure that Black Eagle's home was well-stocked. A few other odds and ends were noted, such as the small pouches filled with spices near the pots and the kindling piled neatly behind them.

Judging by the thoroughness of the supplies given to the newlyweds, Black Eagle knew that his mother had paid them a visit bearing gifts, even though she didn't care for René. She wanted her son to have the best. It was her way of welcoming him home without intruding. "My mother, White Feather, has been here," he said quickly as he touched each item, acknowledging the importance of her effort. "She must have done this while we were away," he continued as he pulled a piece of dried deer meat from the pot.

René recognized the same and said, "I must thank her. She is a very kind woman to do this." But René felt a little uneasy about speaking to her new mother-in-law. Somehow she sensed that White Feather was putting on an act for the sake of her son. But for now, she would play along with hopes of gaining her friendship. The only way to keep peace in Black Eagle's family was to win over his parents. She would try very hard to make them feel welcome whenever they came to call. It was important to Black Eagle. Therefore it was important to René. She busied herself straightening up the bed and putting Black Eagle's weapons where he could find them. The only thing she had of her own was the blanket, which she neatly folded and placed by a cradle board. René stood up holding the cradle board and turned to Black Eagle. He had watched every move she'd made during her few minutes of being there. It was evident that she was going to inquire about the child, a child he hadn't seen in months.

Before she could pose a question, Black Eagle said gently, "You want to know about my son. He is not far from here. Soon he will join us. But for now, you must rest. You must come . . . .now," he ordered as he led her to the spot where they would share their nights together. Reluctantly René followed. There were many questions to ask, and he seemed to be avoiding her. Maybe she was mistaken, yet she complied to his wishes. They curled up on the makeshift bed, keeping each other warm through the night.

It was the shortest night René had ever spent. When she awoke the following morning, she found Black Eagle had already risen and was gone without so much as a word as to when he would return. But White Feather was there. She had come to show her new daughter-in-law how to care for her husband. It was her duty to show her daughter-in-law what was expected of her, especially now that she was the wife of a subchief. René had to learn how to prepare the meats for drying and how to tan the hides and to sew them. It was going to be the hardest task White Feather had ever undertaken. "There must be some other way to get through this without losing my son," White Feather stated without caring whether René heard her.

René also knew that it wasn't going to be easy dealing with someone who only appeared to like her when Black Eagle was around. It was within those few seconds after she had awakened that she knew her work was cut out for her. The woman had spoken loud enough to let the dead know her feelings. So there they were at odds with each other before the day had actually began.

Black Eagle had gone hunting with the others and hoped that his mother would make things easy on René while he was away. One of the warriors, Tall Elk, happened to be out during the night and had found the track of a large herd of deer heading north away from the village. And since this was the time to fill the cache with meat for the winter, he was sure that things would be in order upon his return. So when René awoke, the only thing she had to look forward to was the glaring eyes of her mother-in-law.

White Feather was wearing a simple dress with soft leggings and mocassins. She was dressed for work and had plans to get her lazy daughter-in-law moving. She tossed René a simple deerskin skirt and top that she no longer had any use for. Then she rustled up some corn cakes and rabbit for René's breakfast and watched René consume each morsel until her bowl was empty. Finally, without wasting time on any formalities, she said in a huff, "It is time for you to get to work, girl. I have chores for you to do." She was determined not to like René, but softened her tone when she saw the tiny bulge of René's belly that had been hidden under her blanket.

René was embarrassed to be under such scrutiny. "I'll be ready in a moment," she said as she stepped into the skirt. She tidied the bed and quickly put on the leather top. It felt scratchy and rough as if it hadn't been tanned very well. It made René itch in parts she couldn't reach. Her discomfort was noticed but ignored by White Feather, who rushed René out the door.

"Now we go to work!" White Feather snapped.

"But this top makes me itch. Let me change into my own clothes," René said. She felt the urge to rip off the top and scratch all over.

No! No time! We must go now! The work must be done by the time our men come home from the hunt," White Feather said and forced René to follow her into the woods.

As they approached the enclosure, White Feather placed a wooden object on René's shoulders and led her to where they gathered dry kindling and firewood for the night's fire. They walked several yards away from the village when White Feather started piling wood on René's carrier. She continued to pile it on until René went down on one knee. Her load had become so heavy that she was unable to walk without feeling the pressure on her back and stomach.

White Feather knew it was too heavy. She had never been forced to carry such a heavy load, even in her youth. However, she wouldn't allow René to gather her strength or footage, and kept piling more wood on top of the weight that was already there. "You are a lazy girl!" she accused. "You cannot be a good wife to my son! You must learn that a woman's work is hard. And if you wish to stay among my people, you will not complain . . . you will do as you are told," she snapped.

But René heard only one statement and quickly admonished her. "I am not lazy! I will always do my share of work. But this . . . this is ridiculous," she yelled as she removed the heavy burden. "I will carry enough to satisfy my husband's home.I will make two trips," René snapped as she walked away with an armful of wood. She walked away, leaving White Feather to steam in her own anger.

René knew she had jeopardized any positive relationship that could have been kindled. René had to tell Black Eagle of this incident before it was blown out of proportion. In the meantime, she made the two trips and delivered the wood as she had promised. She didn't stand around to receive any thanks, because she knew there wouldn't be any.

While René made her way home, another person followed. He had witnessed the small altercation between White Feather and the young bride of Black Eagle. He also saw the abrupt change in the younger one's behavior and decided to follow for a pace. He tracked her to the area where she had left a reasonably sized pile of wood behind. She appeared weak and tired after she placed the wood onto the burden, the makeshift carrier. When she leaned against the tree for support and held her stomach, he knew something had gone wrong with her. Before he had reached her side, she was vomiting violently. She was no longer concerned about the itchy top or the silly old woman who had mistreated her. She had another problem to deal with.

With each spell, she became even paler and more light-headed. She finally fainted, falling back into his arms. He was unable to help her or take her back to his son's cabin. So he waited to see if there would be any change in her condition before deciding to go back for help. He checked her breathing, placing a small feather under her nose. It hardly moved. Then he raised her head and looked inside her mouth to check for blockage of any kind. All seemed clear as far as he could see. So he continued to cradle her head and wait for assistance, which he hoped would come soon.

An hour had passed when René finally began to stir. Some color had come back to her cheeks, and she opened her eyes slowly to accept the light. She couldn't imagine what had happened to her or why. She was surprised to see that Gray Wolf was holding her head on his lap and was singing a prayer. She was about to jump up when he stopped her and forced her to relax and to lie back against his shoulder. "I will not hurt you, my daughter," he said in a gentle manner that lulled her back to sleep . . . trusting him, for she had no strength to move. He continued to sing, until he heard light footsteps approaching them from the east.

"*Pesa n eya n,*" ("Stay quiet") he said gently, trying not to disturb her. "She became ill, and her soul is fighting from within," he added.

"She was fine this morning, Father. What happened to her?" Black Eagle asked without seeming forceful. He was still bitter over the way his father and Running Bear had tried to force René out of his life. He wondered how long he was supposed to suffer and live alone, since they were so convinced that René was a bad choice.

"I believe she is the only one who can tell you. Besides, I think you have reason to be proud of her. It seems . . . she stood up to your mother. Do not think ill of the girl. She had a right to stop your mother from being so bossy. I think it is good that she can handle herself," he said with a smile. "But, my son, she has a long journey ahead. It takes time to build trust. She must be strong."

Black Eagle agreed. René had to be strong to live in this land. The only other thing facing her besides his mother's wrath was the winter, which is never gentle. Then he lifted René with ease and carried her back to his cabin. In route toward his home, Black Eagle chanced to ask his father if he had changed his mind about his new bride. "Does this mean I can keep my wife?" he asked. "I should have the right to have the woman I want, since I have been denied of the right by my brother so often. Or is it my destiny to be alone, because you will it?"

"No, my son. I do not want you to spend your days alone. You have a right to happiness. But it would have been better if you had selected a girl from amongst your own kind. This one has little to offer. She is frail and may not make it to the summer months. Beware of your heart," Gray Wolf stressed with great concern for both of them.

"She is strong. She will see many summers and winters with me. I will see to that," Black Eagle pressed.

"Only time will tell, my son. Time will tell," Gray Wolf answered. "If you want her, you must do right by her . . . and by your son, One Shoe."

Black Eagle had heard these words before, only they were spoken by René. There was a lot of wisdom in this young woman. As if it had been only moments before, he had memorized each word, hoping that something would will her back to life, bring her back to him. However, she hadn't moved, not once, since he'd found the two of them.

Immediately upon entering the cabin, Black Eagle laid her down and quickly applied a cool wet cloth to her brow. He did this several times until René pushed it and his hand aside. It was still daylight, and the sun hurt her eyes. She turned away from the light and from him. The room was spinning, and all she could do was close her eyes and bury her head under the covers. Black Eagle felt helpless. He didn't know what to do to help her, so there he stayed with her through the day and through the night. She slept without stirring, while he kept a vigil and watched over her, praying.

The following morning his mother paid René a visit, but Black Eagle sent her away with no excuses. He didn't even ask her for help in tending to his young wife. White Feather left, feeling somewhat put out, but said she would return on the morrow.

Later, about midday, René sat up feeling a little fatigued but somewhat rested. She was hungry and she wanted to wash up. She hadn't had a chance to do that while with her pushy mother-in-law was around. And with it still being daylight, René expected her to show up again, demanding that she complete her chores. She still had a pile of wood to bring back to the cabin.

Suddenly Black Eagle's voice broke through her thoughts. "Re-nea, you are well!" he said while bringing her close to him. He held her as though she had almost disappeared. "I was worried about you! You slept through the night. You were as white as the snow in winter and sometimes very cold," he continued.

"What do you mean, I slept through the night? I just took a nap, that's all," she said softly. However, the look on Black Eagle's face told her that she had frightened him. He wouldn't have acted so overly concerned had it just been a nap. "I guess I took on more than I could handle," she said, flushing. She was still feeling a little weak. "I'm glad you found me."

"But I didn't find you until later. My father found you and stayed with you until I arrived. You could have died and I never would have known where to look for you," he admonished. He wanted her to understand the importance of what his father had done for her. It wasn't something to be treated lightly.

"You say that your father found me? I don't remember him being there, I really don't," she said calmly. Then she sat back quietly, suddenly remembering the gentle voice, a voice that didn't belong to Black Eagle. She looked up at her husband and said, "I do remember someone telling me not to move. But I didn't see his face."

That's why Black Eagle was acting so strangely. His father had made a gesture of acceptance, and both she and Black Eagle had to come to terms with it in the way it was given. Gray Wolf was wise and very much aware of his son's desire to have someone special. He knew René was just what his son needed.

René's back began to burn and itch again and she quickly she removed the deerskin top from her body. There were tiny red bumps on her shoulders and in the center of her back. Her perfect skin had been marked by the tiny quills that had been laced into the seams. Black Eagle quickly snatched the top from her hands and demanded, "Where did you get this?" He examined it and pulled the quills from the seams. "It is not fit for any human to wear," he snapped.

René leaned back, trying to keep her head from spinning. "Your mother . . . gave it to me. She said I had to wear it to do my chores. I tried to do as she wanted, but we . . . argued. She piled too many pieces of wood on that thing . . . that harness. It was too heavy. I couldn't walk," she answered quickly. "And then . . . she said I was . . . I was lazy. She doesn't like me. I know it. Maybe I should leave," she said finally.

"No!" Black Eagle yelled. "If you leave, I will follow. I do not think my mother would like that very much," he added with a little mockery. "But, you still have not told me what happened to you."

René pulled the blanket away and exposed her abdomen. Right away his eyes caught the tiny bulge that he had run his hands over nearly every night. "I think I am carrying your child," she said softly. "I have suspected it for several days now."

"How can you be sure of this?" he asked while squeezing the deerskin top in his hands. He should have been pleased with the news, but he wasn't ready to share her yet. He had told his brother that she carried his child only to keep him away from her. He never dreamed it could be true.

"Well . . . I have been keeping a calendar ever since you took me away from the outpost," she said in a quiet manner. She knew what the next question would be, so she answered it quickly. "My calendar . . . is on something that you carry with you everyday. I used . . . I used your spear." She walked toward it and picked it up to show him her handiwork. "I placed a notch for every day I was away from my brother. I stopped . . . when you brought me here."

Black Eagle walked toward her and removed the spear from her hands. He saw the markings, which counted more than three score, and wondered what purpose they served to account for her condition. She waited for him to say something, to explode or even ask why. But nothing passed through his lips, except a sigh . . . one of disbelief.

"I'm sorry. I didn't think it was important at first, especially to tell you about it. I didn't know how I would feel toward you. What I am trying to say is . . . I love you. I hope you believe me. Do you . . . believe me, Black Eagle?" she asked, almost pleading with him. However, his silence was more than just overwhelming, he just didn't seem to have anything to say to her. His pride had been damaged.

For the first time in the many weeks they had shared together, Black Eagle seemed very distant and betrayed. "No!" he yelled. "I cannot believe you. You lied to me. You do not wish to be my wife. That is why you kept a calendar," he snapped as he tossed the spear against the wall. He paced the floor and stopped short to look at her and then he stormed toward the door. "I must leave you for a while. I must think about what you have done," he said as he left her standing in the middle of the cabin.

He wasn't completely out of the door when she asked, "Where are you going?" She couldn't understand why he was upset with her. She always had kept track of her monthly flow and now for some strange reason the calendar made him feel rejected. "Why are you so upset with me?"

"I have much to think about," he said as he turned to her. "And so do you."

It was the first time Black Gale had ever indicated that he didn't trust her. She, on the other hand, couldn't blame him. He had been honest with her from the start. There were no surprises, not even about the way she would be received by his family and by his people. She suddenly felt frightened and she was sure he wasn't going to return, at least not right away. He was the only one she could turn to and she had let him down, like a rock being dropped over the edge of a cliff.

All she felt when he departed was the cold breeze that attacked her shoulders. The coldness and the emptiness was all she had between her and the man she had insulted with her small secret. She couldn't move from the spot where she was sitting, the only place where she could gather what strength she could. Yet, she watched the door, hoping that he would come back . . . soon.

Minutes turned into hours and night slowly turned into day and Black Eagle still hadn't returned. So, rather than sit and do nothing, René decided to take a chance and get out of bed. She needed to relieve herself and freshen up. She dressed quickly, taking the barest of necessities with her. Then she made her way to the small stream that led to the large lake that happened to be several miles away.

She found several tall bushes to hide behind while she relieved herself. She was grateful for the cover. Then she found a nice spot near the water where she place her blanket and lay upon it to rest. She listened to the water splash up against the rocks, and the gentle rhythm seemed to say Black Eagle's name over and over again. The emptiness in her heart attacked again as she pondered over the last words Black Eagle had spoken before leaving, and a tear escaped the corner of her eye. However, she quickly pushed her emotions aside. She needed to bathe and soothe away the aching pain in her heart. Maybe there, she could learn how to deal with her problems.

The water was icy cold, but René didn't care. She went about her routine, washed her hair then her face, and finally dried herself as quickly as possible. She allowed the water to soothe away the pain of the small bruises that were affecting her back and shoulders. A chilling breeze wisped by her, making it necessary for her to put on her dress before drying off. Finally she wrapped herself in the blanket and continued to run her fingers through her hair.

Time had lapsed, maybe an hour or two. René didn't realize that she had been gone that long and without an escort. It wasn't long before she heard branches snapping and leaves rustling in her direction. Someone was coming . . . fast-paced and unyielding. She held her breath, waiting for a familiar voice to call out, but no one spoke. Instead, a hand had come from behind and lifted her to her feet. She couldn't bring herself to scream for help. She just closed her eyes and said, "If you are going to kill me, do it quickly!" René's heart beat wildly in her chest . . . afraid, but ready to die. She would rather die than live without Black Eagle. She had come to love him . . . dearly.

"Then . . . you have not learned anything. And you have put yourself and my child in jeopardy," the familiar voice stated softly in her ear.

René's eyes flew open, and to her surprise she was being held in Black Eagle's strong arm. Overcome, she turned away from him to hide her emotions. He had come after her, even though she had caused him great pain. The thought of being without him frightened her just as much as it must have frightened him. And she had to rely on him to survive in this wilderness. She wanted to live. How she would accomplish that was apparently up to him. He was in total control. Although she had told him of her love, something she hadn't shown—not yet, for him—she felt a sense of loss. He, too, felt a great loss when he found her gone that morning. He wondered if she had run away. He would blame himself if anything happened to her.

René hesitated for a moment, praying for the strength she needed in order to speak. It was important for her to pick each word carefully, and when she spoke, she spoke from the heart. "I wasn't sure how I felt about you . . . until you told your parents and all the people of your village that you loved me. You made me feel special and wonderful at the same time. You have treated me with such care . . . I feel like I am one . . . with you. I never thought I could feel this way. But you gave me something to look forward to. I look forward to being with you every day. And . . . I am very glad to have you in my life," she continued softly. She smiled and then drew in a breath as she placed her hands together. She was certain that she would burst, thinking about how her feeling had changed during their long journey. "I never thought that I would fall in love with you, but I did. I do love you, Black Eagle. I do."

Black Eagle had waited for what appeared to be an eternity for this moment. Her words were like music to his ears. When he had made love to her, he'd thought that she had only allowed him to have his way since she was his captive. But maybe he had expected too much from her. She had been snatched away from her family without her consent. Therefore, he should have expected René to be distant or to even retreat from his advances. And what did she have that was her own? He had her body, but he didn't have her heart. When he had left her alone last night, and slept under the stars, he'd wondered if she could ever return the love he had entrusted to her. They would have to build on the strength in their love and hope that it would continue to grow.

"Let's go home," he said softly. He was frantic to be with her again. No more restless nights and no more loneliness to creep into his world. René was there to fill the void that had been tearing him apart day after day and night after night.

When they arrived home late that morning they were greeted by Tall Elk and his wife, Morning Star, both bearing gifts for the newlyweds. Morning Star was a beauty who stood tall and sleek next to her husband. Her manner was gentle as well as graceful. Tall Elk beamed with pride as he gazed upon her. They had only been married for eight months according to their calendar, but from René's point of view, it appeared that they had just fallen in love. There was a spark between them, something only people in love share.

The foursome sat down to a hearty breakfast of corn cakes and broiled fish, something Morning Star had been preparing while the lovebirds were away. She was most handy in homemaking skills, which had been attempting to learn herself before she was forced to leave Wilmont. René watched her hostess avidly, asking periodically if she needed help. But Morning Star just shook her head and directed René to sit by her husband. The food was quickly served, and everything tasted wonderful. René relished every morsel and cleaned her bowl. She wanted more, but thought that her new friend would think she was a pig for eating so much. Yet, each bowl was filled again, and everyone ate until they were satisfied.

"Have you had your fill?" Morning Star asked René, hoping that she was pleased. She was so graceful in her ways, that René thought she was a princess. She shared a gentle smile as René admitted that she was full. Then she took her bowl and placed it in the pile with the rest.

Moved by the young woman's capacity for kindness, René smiled in return. It was the first time she had ever felt truly welcomed since her arrival. Then Black Eagle and Tall Elk excused themselves and took a brief walk around the village. They checked on the elders and made sure there was meat at their fires. Some complained of the cold, and others were in need of blankets.

It didn't take long for René and Morning Star to become good friends. Morning Star had promised to teach René to cook and tan hides, and René had promised to braid Morning Star's hair and to teach her to speak the white man's language. It was a small thing compared to what she received, but it was worth the bargain.

As the day went on, René learned from Morning Star that she, too, was new to the village. When she arrived nearly eight months ago, no one had welcomed her as they had for René. No one had taken time to show her how to build her cabin either. She had learned mostly by watching the other women when they went about their duties, and she did everything, including her share of the work, by herself.

René noticed a change in Morning Star's behavior, most of which was attributed to her pregnancy. Unlike René, she had yet to tell her husband that bit of news. He had been away so long, traveling with his closet friend. It was obvious to René that the young woman had been left out of a lot of things. And now that René was no longer the center of attention, she, too, would have to fend for herself while Black Eagle was away. The picture she envisioned wasn't a very happy one, but she had no alternative to accepting it.

CHAPTER ELEVEN

FOUR MONTHS HAD PASSED and now the snow was knee-deep. The air was very cold and crisp, and the wind would swirl the loose flakes and create a deep mound on and around each cabin. The only thing that could be seen was the smoke coming from the top of each mound. Like tiny mountains, they sustained the lives of those who dwelled within.

René had kept close to home as Black Eagle had suggested. She was far into her fifth month and showing signs of approaching motherhood. Since it was her first, she wasn't sure how she could handle delivering a child without the proper supervision from a doctor, especially out here in the wilderness. But, then, René remembered, there were many children born to the women here. Sometimes the knowledge that they were born healthy seemed to help, but then she would start worrying again. Her plight was to have a healthy child,too, but not alone. If only she had the medicine necessary with Black Eagle out in God-knows-where.

Meanwhile, Black Eagle and Tall Elk, along with a small band of warriors, had gone hunting again to fill the cache with as much meat as they could find. Everyone, including René, had cut back on their rations. Sometimes she shared what she had with one or two of the elders who would come to visit with her. Then there were days when she would just serve them the last of whatever was cooking in her pot. It wasn't easy keeping her stomach satisfied.

Today, however, was one of the days that René' planned to enjoy a decent meal. She had prepared rabbit stock, which was simmering in the pot, and had just dropped in some wild carrots, onions, and a handful of wild rice for a light soup. Her appetite had changed so much that many of the foods she prepared didn't agree with her. She had resorted to eating raw vegetables and sometimes a few eggs if she could get them. But, today, she had to eat something.

The wind whistled through the ceiling vent and rattled the roof. Sometimes it felt as though the cabin would blow apart. René, however, continued to stir the soup mixture as she questioned the stability of her home. "I could sure use a carpenter right now," she said as she reached for a bowl. She could see her home in a different light, with brick walls and plaster instead of stick, stones, and skins.

A gust of wind shook the cabin, and snow managed to come through the vent opening and put out the fire. It also ruined her meal. René tried to start up the flame again, but the wood was too cold and wet to ignite. "This can't be happening," she said angrily. "I can't stay here without any heat." Her voice fell silent when she realized that she was only talking to herself. The weather was really getting under her skin. And since she wasn't able to get around the way she used to, the condition of the house made it all the worse.

Just then the door flap opened, startling her out of her wits. A wet, snow-covered man had entered, leaving snow scattered on the floor and wall. At first, René thought it was Black Eagle home from the hunt. But he didn't extend his usual greetings. He remained silent as he removed his heavy robes. As he did that, he checked out the cabin. He didn't make a sound, nothing that would identify him. But he watched her as she reached for the knife that was close to the pit.

"No need to reach for that," he said briskly. "I have come to see my friend, Black Eagle. Where is the big man, anyway?" he asked finally.

René made no attempt to speak to him. He was a white man, a threat to her very existence. She felt sure that he would know who she was the moment she uttered a word. It had been so long since she had spoken her own tongue, save a few moments when she spoke to Morning Star, who was trying to learn. And yet, she had to keep her identity secret, especially with a man she didn't even know, not that she didn't want to go home.

"*Nessa kkussin eskwa nte m,*" ("The door is opened") she said while pointing to the flap behind him. She prayed that she had pronounced each word correctly. She wanted him to leave, but found it difficult to form the words that might convince him that he was not welcomed in her home.

"Damn it! This woman does not understand me! But maybe . . . I . . . have . . . not . . . learned . . . your . . . tongue. Maybe . . . you . . . someone . . . can tell me . . . when . . . your . . . man . . . is . . . coming back," he continued to press.

"Kwa eya n ma meppi!" ("Go away from here!") she ordered. She wasn't in a mood to deal with a lusty man or his unwarranted behavior. If she revealed her identity, she would be running out of options of how to get rid of him. Also, the fact that he was blocking the door, the only exit to the cabin, gave her something else to worry about. Then there was the rifle he was carrying, which never left his hand.

Ethan came forward to tend to the fire and René expected the worst when he approached. Since René wasn't expecting him to make himself comfortable, she grabbed for the knife by the pit. But he was too fast for her. He snatched to knife and tossed it completely out of her reach. Then he grabbed René's wrist and forced her to face him. His breath was foul, and his beard was unkempt. His clothing was wet, and to top it off, his body odor made her ill.

René felt a wave come over her as her stomach released its confines. That was the first sign of freedom she had experienced since his untimely arrival. There was an unwanted visitor in her home, someone invading her territory. If anything, she wanted him to leave immediately. René', weakened by the turmoil happening in her midsection, crawled toward the door, hoping that someone, anyone, was nearby and could hear that she was in distress. However, everyone was snug in their homes, waiting for their husbands and fathers to return just as she had to.

Showing some concern for the woman, Ethan asked, "Are you all right?" But he was met with silence and an evil stare. Then he spied the bulge that was hidden from his view earlier. "Ah, ha . . . I see you are going to have a child, little missy. You are, aren't you?" With that, he wiped off his sleeve, which René had sorely christened. He realized he was getting nowhere when his questions were met with silence again. He considered the woman to be too frightened to communicate with him and she made no effort to make him feel welcome. "Well . . . maybe I had better go," he said as he gathered up his belongings. "But it sure is cold out there," he continued, hoping that he could get some sympathy. But she gave no signs at all that she would allow him to stay.

René pointed to the door, directing him to leave. There was nothing he could do to change her mind. She very well understood a lot more than he gave her credit for. If he had stayed in the cabin without Black Eagle in attendance, her status in the clan would definitely change. She would become a marked woman, and Black Eagle wouldn't be able to protect her from that.

Realizing that he wasn't going to get anywhere with her, Ethan left the cabin in a huff, angry that he had been thrown out and furious that he hadn't been received warmly by his friend's woman. he had no sooner picked up the remains of his gear when Running Bear confronted him. He was very aware of where Ethan had come from. With a sly look on his face, he proceeded to question Ethan, implying some kind of wrongdoing.

"You have entered my brother's house without his permission. Did *you* touch his wife?" he asked, while loosening the sheath that covered his knife.

Ethan was flabbergasted. He was looking into the face of Running Bear, his friend's brother. This one had always made him feel uncomfortable when he'd come to visit. Ethan always found himself looking over his shoulder every now and then, making sure an arrow wasn't aimed at his back. He always considered Running Bear a tricky bastard. He had no heart and was definitely, without a doubt, the opposite of his brother.

"Yeah, I was there. But . . . the witch . . . ah . . . threw me out," he remarked quickly. Then he realized that he had missed an important note. "Did you say . . . his wife?" he asked nervously. "Oh, my God . . . ha-ha! I didn't know that Black Eagle had taken another wife." He tried to chuckle. Now he understood why the woman had reacted so violently toward him. She had to think he was crazy for entering her home the way he did, unannounced and unwelcome.

"Yes, she is Black Eagle's wife!" he snapped. His eyes jetted from the cabin back to Ethan and then he said, "If you touched her, I must know it . . . now! I saw you leave my brother's cabin, and that, my friend . . . will put you with the woman in question. Now, tell me what I want to hear."

It was as though he wanted to find something wrong to say about the young woman, which confused the old man. She had made it very difficult for him to stay, and he had made a beeline to get out of there before she took his head off. However, Ethan decided to tell him everything and made no bones about it. "I wasn't there long enough to warm my butt, much less try anything with that wildcat. She is a mean one, you know. She pointed to the door and shouted something. I didn't understand her. I didn't mean to upset her. You know . . . she tried to kill me! Really, she did."

Running Bear listened to the man babble on, until he heard the last statement loud and clear. "She tried to kill you? How?" he inquired. It seemed he had misjudged René once too often.

Then Ethan continued his story, elaborating on the moment René had grabbed for the knife. From his declaration, he had spent a few minutes of hell in that cabin. "Yeah, the woman tried to kill me. She pulled that knife on me. I guess you could say that I am a lucky old bastard, especially since she didn't have the strength to fight me. She is going to have a child . . . you know?"

Running Bear was stunned with this bit of news. He had hoped that Black Eagle was lying that day when he'd warned him off. He had been watching René for months, hoping to sneak into the cabin, pretend to be Black Eagle, and have his way with her. But Black Eagle had planted his seed securely in her womb before venturing off on the hunt. The child she carried should be his, not his brother's.

"Yeah, the woman is having a baby. I wanted to stay, but she wouldn't have it. And you say that she is Black Eagle's wife? She's a mean one, she is," he said laughingly. "Black Eagle has bitten off more than he can chew."

Running Bear had been defeated in his attempt to get the woman away from his brother, but he had to put an end to this problem . . . soon. It was necessary to get Ethan out of the camp as soon as possible. With the way the old man was talking, René would be looked upon with great respect rather than as a wife who had betrayed her husband. It was necessary to make sure that there was no one around to corroborate her story until he had told his version of it. He knew he could count on his mother to act as witness to whatever he planned, since she didn't care for the girl at all.

"It is best that you leave our camp before Black Eagle returns tonight," Running Bear stated quickly. "I know that she will tell him of your visit . . . and when she does, *I* will be there to tell your side."

Ethan was a little skeptical at first, but agreed. It would do him no good to stay when there might be trouble brewing, and he might be the cause of it. "Uh . . . good. I don't want Black Eagle to think me an enemy. I didn't mean to disrespect his home in any way. You know that we have done business . . . trade together," he said softly and gathered up his property. He was no fool in the matter where Running Bear was concerned. There was something up his sleeve, and the person who should be wary should be Black Eagle. "Maybe you would like to trade with me?" he asked, thinking that he could at least get a good meal out of the deal.

But Running Bear didn't respond. He had other things on his mind, and Ethan was in his way. Neither man knew that Morning Star had heard every word. Anything that involved her friend, whether it was good or bad, she made her business to know. As far as she was concerned, both Running Bear and Ethan were her enemies because they dared to harm her friend. She especially hated Running Bear because he had tried to steal into her bed, but Tall Elk had come home before he was due and nearly killed the man. She knew that he would use the same tactics to make trouble for her friend.

Morning Star had planned to pay René a visit when she had finished her chores. Since the weather had changed so drastically, she'd found it difficult to get around in the snow. Today, however, she would make every effort to get to her friend regardless of the depths she had to traverse. She stumbled several times due to her haste, and pain struck her with the swiftness of a blade. In a panic she called for her friend, praying that she would be there to receive her.

"Re-nea!" she yelled as she watched the snow turn red at her feet. Re-nea!" Morning Star cried out again, and fear washed through her when she found she couldn't move. This was her first child, and seeing her own blood in the snow made her panic even more. before she could say another word, René was at her side. She wasted no time getting Morning Star to the birthing room, which had been built by both women several months ago. Both had promised to be there for the other without question.

"You will be fine, Morning Star," René said softly as she helped her friend into the birthing room.

The room was ice cold and had never been used. But Morning Star didn't feel any of it. The waves of pain began to come closer together, and all either woman could do was wait until it was time for Morning Star to bear down. To keep the cold from setting in, René opted to start up the fire. At least they and the new babe wouldn't freeze to death.

"We can't have your baby greeted by the cold," René stated gently, trying to ease the tension that was building. At least with that she received a friendly smile from someone who was grateful for her just being there.

"I would like some of that heat . . . now. But . . . the pain . . . is getting worse. I don't think I can stand . . . much more of this," she cried. It was getting to be more difficult for her to speak as the pain continued on its path. She had brought nothing with her except the herbs that the medicine man had given to her last month. Other than that, she was on her own.

The fire was going nicely, and the room was getting warmer by the minute. It was relaxing to watch the flames crackle and spark within the pit. It also helped to subdue the onslaught of pain that had waged war on the young woman's body. Now peaceful, she slept, awaiting to the moment when the pain would start up again.

René took this time to run back to her cabin for the cradle board, blanket, and maybe a little food to tide them over. When she entered, she walked in on White Feather rummaging through her belongings and destroying her home. The woman stopped momentarily when she realized that she had been discovered. They stared each other down, each hoping the threat of discovery would make the other one yield. However, neither would waver from her stance. And yet, René's anger was a bit more apparent since it was *her* home being trashed. In less than one hour she had had two unwanted visitors invading her home. She wanted to yell at the woman, but the cries of her friend brought her back to her senses.

René grabbed the items she had come for and headed for the door. She decided to state her case one last time, in hopes that her mother-in-law could be reasoned with. "I don't know what you want, and frankly . . . I don't care. But if you are planning to do me any harm by destroying *your son's* home, remember: You will have done the harm to your grandchild as well," she said sternly. "Do what you will. What can I do to stop you? You *are* my husband's mother. I will be with my friend. At least I know the people I can turn to. It most certainly isn't you."

White Feather said nothing to rebuke her daughter-in-law's accusations. She knew what she had done was wrong and that René was right about her silly behavior. From the time the young woman had arrived, she had never offered her a word of kindness. Even the people noticed the contempt she had for the young woman. And here she was, challenging her and making her see what she had become, a bitter old woman. She watched René leave, not even bothering to look back at her. It appeared René had had enough of her and wanted nothing more to do with the old woman. René just walked back to the birthing cabin and remained there, at her friend's side, just as she had promised.

By the time René returned, Morning Star was soaking wet from perspiration. She would sleep periodically and then awaken to the pain. When the strongest wave of contractions came, René helped her to bear down. The baby's head was now quite visible, and René moved quickly to place the blankets and the hot water within reach. Without warning, Morning

Star grabbed René's hand and held her as tightly as she could.

"I think this is it, Morning Star! The baby's head has come through now and, oh, God . . . the shoulders and arms are free!" René said with excitement. It was the first time René had ever witnessed the birth of a baby. She had watched the horses foal their young, but never had she participated in the birth of a human child. In her hands lay one of the most beautiful creations of love between two people. The baby was free of his protective covering, and the mother was elated.

The baby had big brown eyes and short, thick, straight hair. His arms moved freely as he tried to reach for the one who would claim him. René placed her hand carefully and securely behind the baby's head to give him support. Then the little one stretched and wiggled, trying to move his little legs. "You have a son, Morning Star! You have a beautiful baby boy!" René exclaimed as she cut the cord and then quickly cleaned the baby with the water she had heated earlier.

Morning Star was too excited to relax. She was ready to burst. She wanted to hold her son. "Is he all right?" she asked while holding out her hands to receive him. She was most anxious to hold the child who had kept her awake at night and forced her to eat when she thought she was full. She greeted the darling babe with open arms and suckled him right away. She held his tiny hands and then kissed his chubby red cheeks. She expressed her love just as the women of René's world would have done and more.

"Yes, yes, he is just fine . . . just fine!" René responded with excitement. However, she soon was overwhelmed by what she had just witnessed and found herself speechless and frightened, too. In a few months she would be going through the same thing. It hadn't dawned on her until now that she was truly on her own. She wondered whether she would be able to have her child under the same conditions. There were no doctors to speak of, and it seemed that the women of this village looked upon birth as an everyday occurrence. She rubbed her tummy, hoping that her little one would be just as strong and just as beautiful as the one she had just watched come into the world.

René and Morning Star stayed in the birthing hut until dark. The snow had started up again and covered their tracks. No one but White Feather knew where the two young women had gone and she wasn't about to tell anyone, especially the one coming toward her. She noticed Running Bear making his rounds throughout the village, sometimes stopping to ask questions or to take a token from those who offered. His path led straight to Black Eagle's cabin, which he entered without being acknowledged. Within minutes he was out again with an angry streak across his face. The person he sought was nowhere to be found. It was then that White Feather realized that her first-born of the twins was trying to outdo his brother again. Even in Black Eagle's absence, he was trying to steal the only thing that would bring him home. She had never seen this side of him before, or rather had refused to notice the rivalry between the two. It was he who had poisoned her thoughts about the young woman, never giving her a chance to even like her. And with such a lovely bride, taken away from the people she knew, who had only reached out for a friendly hand, had been treated poorly by her husband's relations. She could only see René pushing her aside and taking her son away from her.

It was time for her to act like René's mother, a duty she had forsaken all these months. There were times when she had wanted to truly welcome René into her heart, but her pride had stood in the way. After all, Running Bear did see to it that René appeared to be a bad influence on Black Eagle, keeping him to herself. *So much time lost because of pride,* White Feather said to herself. *So much wrong has been done to that poor child.*

She walked toward the birthing hut, something she should have helped to build with a grandchild on the way. She was truly ashamed of her behavior, destroying her son's home and expressing hatred toward René'. As she approached the hut, she could hear René's praises of the newborn child and of his mother, and thought she had many other good qualities . . . qualities that only Black Eagle was able to see. And now she was finally witness to what her son had already known. White Feather decided to protect René in the only way she could, by blocking Running Bear's attempts to get to her. His inability to take care of his own home bothered her greatly, but she had been seeing him with a mother's eye at the time . . . a son who could do no wrong. If she had to, she would lie to protect René's status with the people. She would offer René her friendship, with hopes that René would forgive how she had treated her in the past.

Running Bear closed the distance between his mother and himself quickly. He was intent on getting what he wanted and hoped that his mother would help him. White Feather heard the tiny babe wail, knowing full well that her son would also hear the child as he approached. He could tell that something had captured his mother's attention, and he quickly called to her, "Mother! Mother! Have you seen Black Eagle's woman?"

White Feather wasn't shocked by his question, but she was disgusted with him. She had grown tired of this meddlesome side to her son and decided not to play into his hands. She stared at him, saying nothing to help him on his quest. *"Nekkwe ttuswissin. A ni ss pwa nekkwe ttuwiyan?"* ("Answer me. Why don't you answer me?") he demanded. But White Feather said nothing. She stood stoically still and dared him to move around her.

René and Morning Star became aware of who was standing outside the hut. Neither made a sound to bring attention to their presence, and prayed that the babe wouldn't give them away. White Feather was the only person standing between them and the man who seemed determined to wreck his brother's home.

Suddenly Running Bear realized that he was not going to get any answers from his mother. He quickly turned and left her standing there alone. No one, not even his mother, wanted him to have any part of Black Eagle's woman. It seemed they were all trying to protect her. Again, a wave of jealousy struck him. Why should his brother have the woman and not he?

White Feather watched her son disappear into the storm that had soon begun to strengthen. Then she entered the hut and said softly, "It is safe for you to leave now. He has gone home."

The two women breathed sighs of relief and were glad they didn't have to stave him off. With their husbands being away, it made it more difficult for them to relax knowing that Running Bear was lurking about. It was clear to them both that they couldn't stay here without someone to watch over them.

"But he will return!" René said frantically. It wasn't something she wanted to endure during the next few months of her pregnancy. She should be allowed to have a peaceful and restful time while her husband was away.

"Yes, he will return, but you will not be alone. I will stay with you until Black Eagle and my husband return. You will not face him alone," Morning Star said as she wrapped her son in the blanket René had given her.

"And I will be there, too," White Feather said as she made sure the way was clear for them to leave. She helped René to her feet and then assisted Morning Star. The women and newborn left the hut huddled closely together, trying to keep warm.

René led the way and, upon entering her cabin, found food cooking in the pot. She turned to look at White Feather, who smiled, knowing that she had finally done right by her son . . . by accepting the woman he loved. René didn't know what to expect next. The woman was full of surprises. One moment, it appeared she hated René, and now, she wasn't sure. But the aroma from the food simmering in the pot sent hunger pangs through René's stomach. She stopped thinking about what had happened between them before; she wanted to fill her belly. Maybe . . . this time . . . she could enjoy a meal with any interruptions.

They quickly made up a new bed and tucked Morning Star and the baby away in it. White Feather checked on the food and began to serve generous portions. It was deer stew. There were lots of carrots, potatoes, and a few wild onions swirling around in the savory mixture. René ate a healthy bowl and leaned back to allow the food to find its mark. White Feather was glad that her cooking was appreciated. She was happy to be with her daughter-in-law, and was beginning to see her in a new light. She was sure that her son, Black Eagle, would be proud to see them together like this.

"Would you like more stew, Re-nea?" she asked. Her manner had changed so much that even White Feather herself felt the difference.

René smiled. It had been a long spell since she spent time with anyone. It felt like home, and she sensed tears forming in her eyes. "Everything is wonderful! But I can't eat another bite," she responded quickly, hoping not to offend her. "But thank you . . . White Feather. This was the first meal I have been able to enjoy," she continued slowly.

"Then it is good that you have had something. The children you carry must be fed, too," White Feather remarked. There was a pleading look in her eyes. She wanted to touch her unborn grandchildren and make amends for all she had done in the past. René answered her with a smile and allowed the old woman to caress her belly. She sang a lullaby and then smiled as she felt her child move from within. It was the first real sign that it was alive in its protective wall. "Black Eagle will be so proud that you are so fat. You will have your children when the snow melts. You will find it hard to get around soon, but stay close to home," White Eagle said with care while she gazed into the fire. She was suddenly aware that René had locked in on what she had said only moments before. "Yes, my daughter . . . you are going to have two babies," White Feather said with a smile.

How could she know after only being with her for a few minutes? Excitement welled up in René quickly as she thought about the prospects of having twins. Then her fears broadened once again. Twins? One child was a lot to think about, but twins . . . how?

"When the time comes, you will have me with you," White Feather offered.

"And I will be there, too, my friend," Morning Star echoed.

Overwhelmed by the generosity of her friend and her mother-in-law, René broke into tears. She had been frightened because she'd thought she would have to face the birth of her child alone. "I don't know what to say," René said softly and sniffed the last tear back.

"You do not have to say anything. I understand how you feel. I will understand if you do not want me to be here with you when your time comes, but I would be proud, anyway. I . . . hope in time . . . you will trust me, daughter," White Feather added with a smile, and took René's hand to seal the trust.

The trio spent a very quiet evening together, laughing and telling funny stories. The wind outside picked up and whipped the outer wall of the cabin, causing it to shake. The flames crackled and sparked as a new piece of dry wood was placed into the pit. René cleared away the dishes, Morning Star nursed her son, and White Feather repaired the cradle board that her first-born grandson had used. She was home.

For the first time in two months, René was able to close her eyes without fear. There were many times when she would hear the sounds of someone prowling around the cabin or the sound of someone lurking nearby, but only when she was alone. There were so many things that kept René awake at night that she barely had time to do any of her chores during the day from lack of sleep.

Just as it seemed she was going to get that much-deserved rest, the door flap was pulled open and quickly closed from within. This time the tall figure shook the snow from his robes at the door and then placed his weapons by the door. He looked around the cabin and saw three women sleeping soundly instead of one. He canvassed the room, looking for the one who was close to his heart. She was in the bed that they had shared months ago and was more beautiful than ever. Her hair caught the glow from the flames and made his heart lurch as he gazed upon her.

Slowly, he tiptoed to her bedside and let his hand find hers. She was soft and warm to the touch. He couldn't resist lifting one of her braids and placing it to his nose to inhale the gentle fragrance. The scent of wildflowers and leather made his mind reel. He had missed her tender touch and her sweet smile. She had been the light in his dark and lonely nights on the trail.

René turned from one side to the other, trying to find a comfortable spot. She was finding it difficult to sleep without her husband supporting her back. She sighed. Even in her sleep she missed him. He tightened his grip ever so lightly, making her eyes flutter and then open. She frowned at the face that had robbed her of her most-needed rest, and then something in that face said, *"Black Eagle has come home at last."* Two months he had been away from her.

"I am home . . . my love," he said in a heavy voice. He kissed her with great ardor and passion. She could feel the intensity of his longing, and he was aware of hers as well. She knew this was her husband. No one could make her feel the way he did. Quickly, he climbed into bed with her and covered them both with the heavy bearskin robe. His hands explored every inch of her, from the swell of her breasts to her belly and beyond.

Their moment together was long and beautiful. "I love you, Re-nea," he said deeply. "It has been too long . . . to long without you," he said in her ear. His breath became heavy and strong and took René to the heights of pleasure with him. She, too, felt secure in his arms again. If only the night could last forever, but the reality of the dawn would make it difficult for her to let him go.

Suddenly, Tall Elk came in search of his wife. He didn't have the same reunion as Black Eagle had had. He was worried about her. When he had left Morning Star, he'd promised to return before the baby was born. He knew Morning Star wouldn't ask for help from the midwives in the village. He knew that she would undertake the task of giving birth on her own if she had to. She was the only thing on his mind. Again, his voice quaked as he called to his trusted friend.

"Black Eagle! Black Eagle! My wife . . . she is missing!" he said frantically.

Black Eagle put on his clothing while under the cover of the bearskin. He had forgotten about his friend. He was so caught up in being with his own wife that the sleeping Morning Star hadn't been considered. Quickly, Black Eagle opened the flap and invited his friend to enter. Worry was etched across Tall Elk's face, more frightened about losing his true love than ever.

"Black Eagle . . . Morning Star is missing. I must find her before it's too late." There was great panic in his voice. He cursed himself for leaving her.

He shouldn't have left knowing that the child was due soon. But it had been necessary to fill the meat cache before the winter really set in. He was honor bound to the tribe to fulfill his obligations. But when he'd returned home, he'd expected to find Morning Star waiting for him, at least that is what he'd pictured in his mind. When he'd arrived home, all he'd found was a cold and abandoned cabin. There were no signs to indicate that she'dhad any problems or had left him for another.

Tall Elk's expression was that of a bereaved man. His heart had been sorely wounded, and to make matters worse, he had shown his friend his weakness. "My Morning Star is missing," he said again. "She is so heavy with child . . . that she could be anywhere out there in the snow. You must help me search for . . . " his voice trailed off, for in perfect view was his wife, and in her arms lay his infant son. Both were sleeping soundly near the warm fire.

A sigh of relief escaped his lips as he looked in wonder at the sight of them. The fear he had once felt had weakened him, but he vowed never to leave Morning Star like that again. Black Eagle knew what was going through his friend's mind, for he, too, had had the same feelings toward René. The need to cherish and protect the ones he loved most was very powerful indeed.

"I should have come to your cabin last night after I saw her, but I wanted to be with my wife," Black Eagle responded apologetically. "She is safe and well . . . and so is your son."

"I have a son?" he asked. But he didn't wait to hear the details. He could only hear the gentle cry of his newborn son being held by his beloved. He rushed to her side, carefully placing a kiss upon Morning Star's cheek. He was thoroughly relieved to find his family . . . safe and among friends. "It is good . . . good to be with my family again and my friends," he said as he lay down with Morning Star.

Everything seemed right with the two brave men. They had the devotion and trust of their wives, good homes, strong spirits, and the drive to maintain the life of the tribe. It was a good life for the both of them.

"Yes . . . it is good that you are home, my son," White Feather interrupted for the first time, allowing him time to notice that she was listening in. "Your gentle wife has had many hardships to befall her since you left. She will not complain, so I will do it for her."

Black Eagle was puzzled by her genuine concern for René when it hadn't there before. Still, he gave her his full attention. For some reason she appeared to be overprotective of René', like a mother watching over her young. Then he realized there must be some credence to what she said, since the three women were together. There had to be a reason other than the birth of Tall Elk's son.

"What has happened here that it has put you in such a state? You never really cared what happened to Re-nea before, so why bother now, Mother?" he inquired.

White Feather knew that she had to face him with this issue eventually. She wanted to make amends for her ill doings. "Please believe me, Black Eagle . . . I only want what is best for your bride. She is my daughter now. I want that more than anything," she said softly. "Last night, a man claiming to be your friend entered your home. Re-nea told him to leave, but he would not. She tried to defend herself with a knife, but he wrestled it away from her," she continued. "When he found she was with child and would have nothing to do with him, he left."

Black Eagle walked toward his sleeping wife and gazed upon her with endearment. "I should not have left her," he said in a voice that nearly shattered the dreams of those sleeping around him. A sudden guilt washed through him as he listened further.

"My son, you must be ever watchful of . . . " her voice trailed off again. It was difficult for her. Undoubtedly, she knew there would a rift in the family unit if she said more, but it was necessary. "You must be ever so watchful of your brother. He has eyes for your gentle wife, too. He wants to be you, Black Eagle."

"Did he touch her?" Black Eagle asked. He wanted to kill, but that would serve no purpose when he could lose everything in a single act of violence.

"No, he did not have a chance to. I stood in his path," she stated. "She is a good woman, Black Eagle. I pray that you will both forgive me for my actions. I want us to be a family again."

Black Eagle heard her, but his mind was elsewhere. The threat was again upon them. He had to make it known to his own brother that René was his and his alone. He thought he had made that clear several months ago, but apparently the point wasn't strong enough. He remembered the day he was about to announce his interest in Two Moons. He'd had no idea that Running Bear had bedded her, not until it was too late. He was also suspected of being the cause of the early delivery of Black Eagle's son. And then he wondered if he was the fault of his wife's untimely death. Again,

Black Eagle had been away from home and his wife was found lying face down, motionless, on the floor. He refused to live through that again.

"I will settle this. Running Bear will learn not to invade my home again. As for the man who claims to be my friend . . . I will find him," he said sternly. Again he gazed upon René'. He had her face memorized, from the smallest dimple on her cheek to the slim curve of her neck. She was connected to him in body and in mind.

"Then you understand that you must protect her. Protect her and your unborn children," White Feather said as she walked to the door. "I have come to like her. She is a good woman and she is loyal to you." She left Black Eagle to think on all he had and all he could lose if he made the wrong choices.

The day had begun with much excitement. White Feather went home to tell Gray Wolf about Black Eagle's return and where she had stayed for the night. She knew he would want to know every detail from beginning to the end. Each step she took through the snow was arduous and difficult. She stopped momentarily to catch her breath and then begin again. She had so much on her mind that she didn't notice Running Bear approaching her from the right.

"So, you spent the night in Black Eagle's cabin. Do you have news of my dear sister-in-law? Where is she?" he inquired most insidiously. "Maybe . . . she will will welcome my company . . . don't you think?" All of a sudden he noticed the cold stare that his mother presented him. Apparently her opinion of him had changed greatly overnight. It appeared that the young woman had bewitched his mother and had taken her loving spirit, and he was taking a chance asking her about the girl at all.

"Yes, I was there all night, but that was to make sure that you didn't harm her," she snapped. "She is a good woman and she loves your brother very much, but you can't stand that . . . can you?" she said, smirking. "She will not come to you willingly. She knows who you are and she knows what you are capable of."

Running Bear's eyes gleamed with excitement. His mother had provided him with an outlet, or so he thought. The unsuspecting bride wouldn't know him from his brother. That alone would allow him to get his hands on her. "We will see what she knows. But first . . . I will take you home. It is cold, and the weather will affect you, Mother."

White Feather didn't like the manner in which he addressed her and she didn't want his help. Yet, she accepted it. She allowed him to walk her home and deposit her at her door. She then watched him as he headed for his unknown fate.

It didn't take long for Running Bear to get to his brother's cabin. He felt secure that he could get away with this farce and that his mother would support him in his efforts. He planned every moment that he would spend with his lovely sister-in-law down to the last. Then he would surprise her by exposing his identity after he had had his way with her. What could she say? She could never deny that it wasn't he who had fathered her child.

He looked in all directions, making sure that no one was monitoring his movements. Then he slipped into the cabin unnoticed. René felt a slight breeze and covered her shoulders. She appeared to be alone, just as his mother had said. He took great care not to awaken her as he removed his robes and placed them on the floor near the door. He walked toward her, proceeding slowly and deliberately, making sure each step counted. He hovered over her breathing in the gentle fragrance that made his heart flutter with excitement.

René had the feeling of being slowly devoured. She was awakened by this towering figure who reached down and placed his hand over her mouth. The intensity of his grip made it hard for her breathe. She knew this wasn't Black Eagle, because of the glare in his eyes and smirk on his face. This wasn't the face of the man who had made love to her so warmly before. Running Bear took his time and slowly leaned over to press his lips to her ear and asked, "It this the way you greet your husband after a long journey? I have been looking forward to being with you for months, and you act as though I am a stranger."

He released his hold over her mouth and waited for her sweet voice to reel him in. He was sure that he had pulled it off, but she gasped, *"You are not Black Eagle. You are nothing like him. I know the difference. I know my husband. There is much about him that you will never be! Never!"*

Shocked at first that she would be so bold, he then softened his embrace and said, "Ahhh! But I am that . . . and more. I will have you, and there is no one here to stop me!" He spoke with assurance and was quite pleased that he had gotten this far.

She struggled to free herself, but realized that he was too strong for her. *"You can't do this! I'm your brother's wife! Have you no shame?"* she yelled as she continued to wriggle away from his grasp.

Out of the corner of his eye Running Bear saw a shadow moving quickly toward him. He then turned to see his brother standing over him holding a spear within inches of his heart. He couldn't offer an explanation or any excuse for the behavior that his brother had just witnessed.

"No! My brother has no shame, Re-nea! He has no honor when it comes to my wife . . . or my home," Black Eagle said angrily. He was greatly bothered by his brother's betrayal. "You were warned to stay away from my wife and you chose to ignore me! Why?"

"I want her, Black Eagle. You and I can trade . . . I will give you Two Moons for the woman. Two Moons will please you. You wanted her once! Remember?" Running Bear added with desperation, and held on to René as though she belonged to him.

"I will not trade with you. I will have no other woman in my life. Re-nea is my wife! Now . . . get away from her, or die!" Black Eagle ordered. There was no way in hell he would let Running Bear have her. Too many years of his selfishness had gone on without anyone trying to stop him . . . always excusing him or allowing him to have his way. He had cheated many out of their just dues and no one had stopped him. Now, when he finally had found something that his brother had never touched to call his own, here he came to destroy any amount of happiness he had ever felt.

Tall Elk heard the disturbance and made his presence known in support of his friend. To his surprise, Running Bear had worn out his welcome even before he had dared to enter his brother's home. He was outnumbered with two men, both stronger than he even on their own terms. He had stepped into the eagle's nest and tried to make off with its precious and most prized possession. He had no other recourse but to release René'.

Then Black Eagle nailed his brother's fate with a final insult, saying, "As for Two Moons . . . she was mine for a while, but you took her like you have taken everything else. She is yours until you die. Go to her . . . and to your other wife. If you touch my wife again, I will kill you!" With that he threw Running Bear's robes at him, slapping him in the face with the force. The intense stare that followed the blow was enough to let him know that he was close to walking with the dead.

Meanwhile Two Moons and Dancing Wind had just finished preparing the evening meal. They were waiting patiently for their husband to return home and join them. It had been a good day for Two Moons, and she planned to spend the evening alone with Running Bear. There was news she wanted to share with him tonight. Dancing Wind was a little upset at having to sleep in the extra cabin for the night. She, too, had plans, but being the younger of the two wives, she had to do as she was told.

"I hope he comes home soon," Dancing Wind said as she fretted with her braids. "I am hungry and I want to eat." She had become very irritable and anxious with his untimely arrivals and started sneaking her food. Dancing Wind, who at a young age was snatched from her people by the Sauks and was later traded for several deerskins and a cast-iron pot, nonetheless, had wound up in Running Bear's house, second to Two Moons.

"Be patient," Two Moons said calmly. "He will be home soon, I assure you." Being the older of the two, she seemed more relaxed with his temperament and torrential flares of anger whenever things didn't go well outside of their home. She, on the other hand, was a lovely young woman, but had gained weight over these past few months. While her husband was away, her only solace was eating, and when he married Dancing Wind, her habit had increased.

"He's always late. He never seems interested in coming home anymore. Do you think he has found someone else to warm his bed?" she asked childishly.

"Well . . . if he has, we will have to make some changes around here. Now stop worrying and let me finish my sewing, you lazy girl," Two Moons scolded.

Just then the door flew open, snow and wind, accompanied by a tall, familiar figure of a man. He was angry and tired from the walk. The door was still flapping in the wind, and Dancing Wing rushed over to close it. She saw the anger on his brow and decided not to press the issue of the door. Two Moons saw the same look, dropped her sewing, and began to prepare his meal right away. Then Dancing Wind took a chance and ushered him to his favorite spot by the fire and placed his feet on her lap. She wrapped them with a blanket and rubbed them until her hands felt hot. He didn't respond to the gentle treatment she had administered. He was stiff and uncaring and only watched the coals spark as they burned.

Two Moons handed Running Bear a bowl of stew, made of deer meat and rice. He made no attempt to eat it, and that caused great concern for both women. Something was very wrong with him. When his behavior didn't change, Two Moons decided to take the matter in her own hands and sent Dancing Wind to the other cabin for the night so that she could be alone with him. Besides, it was her turn to enjoy the nightly pleasures. She hurried and prepared the bed and then called to him, "Running Bear, come to bed and let me warm you. It has been a long time since we have enjoyed each other's company."

Yet her words fell upon deaf ears. Running Bear hadn't moved, nor did it seem that he planned to. His eyes were glued to the fire, and his mind was totally fixed, but not on her. He ignored all her pleas to come to bed. Finally, Two Moons made her way to his side, thinking that she needed to use drastic measures to get him to respond to her. She massaged his shoulders and pressed her body against him, only to face his icy stare. She thought that a gentle maneuver would snap him out of his trance. However, instead of desire, she saw the look of disgust in his eyes. His lips curled up like a wolf snarling at its prey, frightening her. She tried to retreat as he lunged at her, but her weight worked against her. He pinned her to the floor with her arms above her head. She could neither move nor shake him off.

"Running Bear! Running Bear! What are you doing?" You are hurting me!" she cried. There was nothing that she could say or do to penetrate his madness. He wasn't the same man who had pursued her and stolen her away from Black Eagle. What had she done to deserve this?

Her cries did nothing to deter him. He attacked her, driven solely by his anger. He wanted to hurt anyone who caused him trouble . . . anyone, when, in fact, it was he who had created the problem from the start. Now his wife lay huddled in a ball, fighting off the pain from his assault. Slowly he moved away from Two Moons, finally taking note of what he had done. But he didn't care. It was her fault that he had raped her. He had done so with such force that she lay bleeding. She cried out again in pain, unable to understand why he had treated her so horribly.

"*Leave me!*" he demanded. "I don't want *you* anymore. You have given me nothing . . . *nothing!* You . . . you are the reason why I cannot get the woman I want. I should have let Black Eagle have you a long time ago. Look at you! You are fat, and your beauty is gone. You have nothing I want . . . . *nothing!*"

There was no remorse in his voice or in his face as he watched her try to get to her feet. She lost her footing several times, trying to do as her husband had commanded her to do. In her weakened state, she fell to her knees, breathing hard and feeling faint due to the loss of blood. And yet, she gained enough of her composure to say, "You believe . . . that I have

. . . given you nothing. I would . . . have given you . . . a child. I am fat because I carried your child in my body. But he is gone. He is dead! And you killed him!" Then she collapsed into a void of darkness.

For the first time in his life, Running Bear was unable to move. Her words had opened a new wound. He could have been a father and he had destroyed that without so much as a care. He had deceived so many for so long that he didn't know he had the greatest of all gifts, the gifts of love and devotion, right under his own roof. He had forgotten that he had pursued her when her heart had belonged to Black Eagle. Now that he had Two Moons, he wanted to trade her off for a woman who had stolen his brother's heart.

He finally realized that his brother had spoken the truth all along. He didn't deserve to have the wealth that he had stolen so freely. He had so much, but didn't appreciate what he had. His heart softened, a trait he always considered a weakness in a man, and he lifted his wife's limp body from the floor. He gently carried her to the bed they shared and, with care, placed her in it. He brushed her hair aside, which had fallen out of place, and took a good look at what he had.

"My brother was right . . . and so were you, Two Moons. I have no shame. I have done many wrong deeds to get what I want . . . including taking you," he said apologetically. "I should not have taken my anger out on you. You have always been a good wife to me."

Running Bear called out an alarm and prayed that he had acted in time. The door flap came open again. This time it was White Feather who entered. She knew what he had done the moment she saw Two Moons' crumpled body on the bed. Something had told her to stay nearby, especially when she had seen how angry he was when he left Black Eagle's home. The look of disappointment was etched across her face as he ushered him out of the cabin. She said nothing to calm him and she quickly closed the flap . . . closing him out.

CHAPTER
TWELVE

THE WINTER MONTHS WENT by very slowly, and spring was approaching in its solemn way. The snow hadn't quite started to melt, but the birds could be heard chirping and singing in the trees above. A hazy mist covered the land like a blanket as the warm air approached from the south. All the signs of spring were in the air, and the harvests of the long winter were about to come forth.

René, now, was very heavy with the child she carried. She was having a great deal of difficulty sleeping at night for the past few weeks and found it necessary to prop herself up with many bearskins and pelts to give her back some support. Throughout the entire ordeal, she never complained. She had learned the way of the Ojibwa and found strength in knowing that she wasn't alone. With Black Eagle staying so close at hand and her mother-in-law spending more time with her, she had little to be worried about.

And yet, there were times when she would pace the floor of the cabin, sometimes becoming emotional or fretful. The pressure of the baby made it impossible to stay in one spot for long periods of time. With her constantly moving about, Black Eagle had no other recourse but to stay awake and keep her company. She was becoming a handful of late, and he found himself doing things he never thought a man of his stature would be caught doing. He, on the other hand, helped out with the cooking, which was usually the final meal of the day. René always found herself chewing more than swallowing. The rice was sometimes over or undercooked. The cornbread usually wound up burned, and sometimes he would attempt to make rabbit stew. He would either add too much water or not enough rabbit.

That morning Black Eagle quickly turned on his side to face her and cleared his throat. That was his way of letting her know that he was awake, but she always waited for him to speak. He had maintained the same vigil every day since he'd returned, taking in everything about her. He had missed being with her and wanted more than just to hold her at night. So many times he had to hold himself at bay, knowing all too well that she wouldn't be able to give him what he wanted. He could only swallow his need for her and learn to accept the change in their relationship.

"Ah . . . you are awake and ready to face the day with me," he said softly.

René smiled, glad that he had greeted her. She had been up and moving for many hours, tidying their home and repairing the cradle board White Feather had given them. Finally satisfied that she had accomplished her task, she headed for the cook fire. She decided to make some hot cornmeal mush with honey. The pots were already filled with the food which Black Eagle tried to pass off as edible. In as much as she wanted to allow him to help, she had to take over where the cooking was concerned. She even dreaded having to toss out what he had worked so hard to prepare for her. But, she only had a few pots to work with and it was necessary to clean the pots before breakfast.

"I'm starved," she said gently, then looked at the pots she had to clean, took a deep breath, and started to gather everything she needed.

As though Black Eagle was reading her mind, he rose quickly from their bed, donned his leggings, and then took the pots that she had started to lift outside. She didn't ask where he was going; she was just glad that he wasn't hurt by her gesture. He couldn't blame her for not wanting to eat his cooking, even though he had grown accustomed to it, always eating on the run. He was meant to be chief, not a cook.

"I will prepare all the meals today," she said with a smile as he walked out. She had to have something in her stomach or she thought she might get sick from trying to eat his strange concoctions.

He was hungry, too, and missed the special way she prepared his meals. "Will you be all right handling these heavy pots?" he asked, realizing that they were a bit heavy for her to be toting around. Even when they were empty, they were a lot to deal with.

She heard the concern in his voice and added, "I think so . . . just as long as you are here."

He was trying so hard to keep her from overdoing, that he never considered her palate. He had discovered that there were some foods that her taste buds demanded and he wasn't able to prepare them. However, every dish she prepared was simple and very tasty. She had learned a lot in these past few months with the aid of White Feather and Morning Star. Even René thought it peculiar that she could learn housekeeping in the wilderness. Her parents would have been surprised at how well she had adjusted to this way of life.

Black Eagle took the food to the southernmost part of the village, where the stream emptied into the big lake. The ice bed in the lake had begun to melt, and large chunks were floating and crashing into each other. There were several dogs tugging on a piece of raccoon nearby. It appeared they hadn't received their share in a long time, so he dumped the food in front of the dogs and watched as they devoured every morsel. With their stomachs full, they ran off to find a warm place to sleep. Black Eagle quickly washed out each pot undisturbed by either man or beast. He didn't relish having to explain why he was doing menial work. But he was ready for anyone who dared to make a joke of it.

He return to his wife as quickly as he could with all pots scrubbed and rinsed thoroughly. He made sure that he had one filled with water and the other filled with clean snow. Meanwhile, René had already placed more wood on the cook fire and had placed all the ingredients where she could reach them. With all he had brought back, she was able to prepare their morning repast without a hitch. René had just served Black Eagle a healthy portion of mush when a sharp pain assailed her. She held her ground, trying not to waiver or make a fuss. She put a little mush in her own bowl and was caught by another wave that made her tremble.

"With the warm season coming, I must make more space in the cabin," he said gently as he surveyed the walls. "We will need more room now that we have a child on the way."

René nodded, gripping her side as the pain became intense. She wanted to cry out, but held her breath until it subsided. Black Eagle noticed how she had tightened up when she had handed him the bowl. He was well aware of her silent agony. Her time had come and she needed help. Without a word, he put his bowl aside and reached over to draw her close to him. He could feel her muscles tighten and then release, where she would catch her breath and hold it. She would exhale as the pain subsided and tighten up again, not having time to prepare for the next wave.

0 "Your time has come, Re-nea," he said eagerly, and gently kissed her brow. In a swift motion he lifted her and placed her on the bed. Another wave assaulted her and all she could do was grab his arms and hold until it passed again. It brought tears to her eyes, something she had tried to hide from him. Her weakness was showing, but Black Eagle had already seen that side of her. There was no reason to shield her face from him now.

"I didn't know having a baby was . . . like this," she almost cried. "I'm frightened. I don't think I can do this!" Even though there was no choice in the matter, she knew she couldn't stop what was happening . . . the babies were coming. She was afraid to attempt this venture without help.

"I know," Black Eagle said softly, wanting to take her pain. "You cannot do this on your own. I must get help," he said as he reluctantly released her hands. He was out the door before she had experienced another pain. He made his way to his mother's cabin and ran into Little Beaver, who wanted to tell of his exploits on the hunt. But Black Eagle, who had no time to dally with words, rushed by him, not giving him a chance to act out his story. He pouted and hung his head in defeat. It wasn't like Black Eagle to be so rude.

White Feather had just come from her cabin and had inhaled the fresh morning air. She had planned to make her way to her sons' cabins, but she wasn't sure which one to visit first. It appeared, though, that the decision had already been made for her, because she saw Black Eagle approaching with great haste. She grabbed her medicine pouch and several herbs and met him halfway. When she reached him, her only words to him were, "Get Morning Star. I will need her hands." Black Eagle's eyes moistened, only slightly. He was grateful that she knew without him having to say it. They were separated, one heading for René and the other reaching for another hand to help.

René experienced severe pain after Black Eagle departed. There seemed to be no end to it and she wanted to scream at the top of her lungs. Many things had crossed her mind while she suffered alone; dying in childbirth or losing the babies frightened her most of all. There were no doctors, at least not the kind of doctors she was used to. Yet, she had risked everything to have her children in the wilderness.

Suddenly the door to her realm opened and some of her fears began to disappear. Tears of relief finally escaped the confines of her eyes as White

Feather touched her cheek and greeted her. "So, my daughter . . . your children are ready to be born. Relax . . . child. Do not fight the pain," she said soothingly as she gently stroked René's brow. It was as though she had given René a tender kiss . . . it calmed her almost immediately.

Then White Feather proceeded to prepare an herbal mixture in one of the bowls, then poured in hot water and let it steep. She moved quickly, since she knew that René was in full labor. "What is that?" René asked.

"It is an old medicine. It will make your pain easier to handle," she answered quickly. "You must drink it. It will make you relax, and your little ones will come without much strain," she continued.

René was struck again by White Feather's words. She wondered if her mother-in-law only wished for her to have twins. How could she predict something that only God would know? And yet, White Feather was very confident. Even René had started to believe it was possible when she heard her say it months ago. "You keep saying 'children' . . . how do you know this?" René asked.

White Feather's voice suddenly became very soft. "I just know, my child . . . I just know," she offered as she made sure that René drank the mixture. Patiently she waited for her to feel the euphoric effect of the brew.

It wasn't long before René was yawning and talking about the joys of motherhood. Now it was safe to move her to the birthing cabin without fear of her doubling over. Morning Star had caught them as they were about to exit. Together they escorted René to the cabin without much delay. Black Eagle had already been there. A fire had been cast, and the warmth was there to welcome them with open arms. There were several blankets and a small basket with leather batting inside. They would use this to cradle the baby when it left the protection of the mother's womb.

Seeing that they had all they needed, they closed the door behind them and waited for René's labor to come to full affect. They waited for an hour, then two had passed, but René was in her own dreamlike world. Upon the third hour René's pain hit like a fabric being torn to shreds. Her mind reeled as one pain ended and another one began.

Outside of the cabin, Black Eagle paced the snow-covered ground until it had melted away. It was as though he was waiting for the birth of his first and only child and yet, it was his first . . . with René. He hoped that her time would be an easy one, knowing that their ways may be strange and sometimes frightening to her. His musing was suddenly interrupted by the sound of a wee babe crying. He was so excited that he nearly tripped over his own feet. Then another tiny voice matched the first, both echoing in rich chorus to his awaiting ears. He couldn't move for a moment. Then reality struck when he heard his mother call out to him, "Black Eagle! Black Eagle . . . come quickly! Come quickly!"

Like a nervous bridegroom, he entered the small, well-lit room. In his excitement, he wasn't sure where to look first. Finally he focused on the two little bundles resting in his mother's arms and then to his wife. René was so totally exhausted from the ordeal that she barely noticed his presence. He knelt by her side, taking both hands into his and placed a kiss on each. He thanked her for blessing him with two wonderful children. There were no words to describe the feelings he had for her. All he could see was the face of the woman he cherished the most in the world. Even as she drifted off to sleep, he was overwhelmed with her never-fading beauty . . . how he loved her. No other could take her place in his heart, and the gifts she had bestowed upon him was one of great honor, great honor indeed.

The village was quiet again. Another day was coming to an end. The only sound that could be heard was that of the barking dogs in the southern section of the camp. Yet, their barking was insistent and regular. All the braves, including the chief and his council, left the shelter of their homes with weapons in hand to check on the ruckus. Three men on horseback approached them with a beautiful black horse and two pack mules in tow. They continued in an undaunted pace toward the band of men and silently watched as their entrance was closed up behind them. Gray Wolf held up his hand, causing the three to come to a halt. They obeyed without hesitation. Neither rider moved from their horses, waiting instead for the old man to give them a sign. Any sudden movement or gesture on their part would be more than likely considered a threat. So they waited calmly.

Black Eagle and Running Bear joined their father in the center of the camp, while the others held their ground and waited for the signal to attack. However, Gray Wolf signaled to the lead rider to come forward. The rider complied, keeping his hands in full view as he dismounted. Then he walked slowly toward the trio, being ever mindful that he was in their land and he wasn't welcome. As the stranger neared, Black Eagle managed to gaze into his green eyes and thought how similar his eyes were to his wife's. The stranger removed his hat and allowed them to get the full view of his face. Black Eagle's own expression gave way to recognition: He was looking into the face of his brother-in-law. Both men stared at each other, knowing that there was a lot to be said between them.

Gray Wolf interrupted the reunion and said casually, "You are a brave man to come into my village at night. It must be very important for you to risk your life in this manner. " He also noticed the reaction between his son and the young man before him.

Robert couldn't believe that the search for his sister would bring him to the very one who had saved her life almost a year ago. The same arrogant man who had announced that he would have René as his woman was now standing only a few inches away from him. Carefully Robert spoke, saying, "My friends and I are not brave men . . . but we are tired men. We come in peace and hope that you will allow us sanctuary here for the night." He deliberately made no mention of why he was really there.

"Sanctuary? Why do you need sanctuary?" Gray Wolf asked as he examined the possibility of it. "You seem able, and your companions seem able, to endure the wild as we know it."

In the course of his travels, Robert had learned that if he asked for protection of the village when he entered it, he wouldn't be refused. He had stayed in several villages while searching for his sister and was accepted with open arms after he presented no threat to them. But somehow, this was different.

"We only ask that you allow us one night. We are hunters and we have traveled far. It would be good to sit near a warm fire with friends," Robert answered, hoping that would satisfy the old one.

Gray Wolf was confused since the reaction in both men still went unanswered. Something was definitely amiss, and neither his son nor the young man offered any explanation for their behavior. "I must sit in council," Gray Wolf offered as he turned to Black Eagle and gestured that he follow.

Robert nodded in agreement to show that he would accept whatever they decided, even though it would prove beneficial if he could get the old man's permission to stay a bit longer. Maybe he could win him over, just long enough to get information about his sister. Since the encounter several months ago with the Quaker family, who had been quite adamant about seeing René, finding her had become an obsession. And now he was in the company of the man who was openly wanton of her, making it known to all that he would have her.

Black Eagle followed his father, looking briefly over his shoulder at Robert, who openly stared at him with distrust. Black Eagle found himself in a real dilemma, one of uncertainty at the possibility of losing his wife and his newborn children. He knew that René would never forgive him if he allowed her brother to leave without her knowledge. Then again, she would probably leave with him. He recalled the night they wed, what she had asked for, and his promise to make things right between them.

He was suddenly compelled to honor René's request and dared not to leave anything out. "Father . . . I know this man. He is my Re-nea's brother," he said slowly. "He has come in search of Re-nea. He is not aware that it is I who took her . . . but I did so only to protect her from another."

Gray Wolf wasn't pleased with this bit of news. The thought of someone tracking that young woman to his village made him feel very uneasy. He knew more could and would eventually follow. In any case, he would have to take great care before allowing these strangers to stay. His son had brought these people down on them, but he prayed that his son's loyalty to the clan was stronger than his desire for a mere woman. And yet, his son was happy and had been for many months. She had brought him back to life and Gray Wolf couldn't deny that it was for the better. Then again, he couldn't help thinking about Re-nea and her brother and what was to come.

"Black Eagle . . . you have been a good leader, a good warrior, and a good son. Yet you did not consider your people when you brought that young woman here. I must say, you acted foolishly. You let your heart speak, and you acted without thinking. That young man who you say is her brother has much courage to have come so far and to have come among us to find someone he cares for," Gray Wolf stated carefully. "You must tell him the truth! You must put an end to this . . . and think of your people."

The subchiefs were in total agreement with Gray Wolf. They all stood about, nodding their heads and offering their points of view. They, too, were concerned about the possible threat coming from the south. They had heard so many stories from their Sioux brothers, telling how the white man was pushing them farther west and farther north, away from the Ohio Valley and Wisconsin woodlands, no longer able to hunt the deer and bear of their vast lands. The sacred burial grounds were being looted for the yellow dust and laid waste of the land of plenty. There was no pride in the violation of the land . . . or of its people.

"I am loyal to my people, but Re-nea is also my wife. I vowed to protect her, just as I have done for my people. *Do not* ask me to give her up!" Black Eagle stated vehemently. He felt the sting of anger boiling in his veins.

Tall Elk and Running Bear voiced their concerns to the council, but in truth they supported Black Eagle's claim on the woman. To Gray Wolf's surprise, Running Bear had actually convinced the others of the need to know more about the white man and his ways. They knew that they could easily defeat the white man should he ever decide to attack them on their land. The white man lacked the knowledge of the wilderness and couldn't survive for long under these conditions.

Soon Gray Wolf saw the logic in their words. "It is good to learn more about the white man before he becomes your enemy," he stated. "Then I shall let the young man and his friends stay. But, my son," he said as he turned to face Black Eagle, "you will be his host and see to his needs. You must also tell him that his sister is here. I will say no more on the matter."

Black Eagle had to resign himself to the inevitable. His father and the council had made it impossible for him to back out of it. The truth had to be told, tonight. And yet, he was somewhat grateful for the chance to honor the pledge he had made to René months before. She must have known that her brother would come for her.

The small group walked back to where Robert stood waiting patiently, hoping that his request would be honored. He was sure that Black Eagle had the answers to the many questions resulting from his sister's disappearance. He had traveled too far and for too long to be turned away without being given a chance to inquire. He needed to talk to Black Eagle. He needed to find René. And since Black Eagle's eyes betrayed him, he was sure that he had come to the right place.

Gray Wolf approached the young man with ease and said, "You do not honor your host . . . I must know what to call you."

Robert cleared his throat; he hadn't spoken in so long that his voice cracked from the cold. "My name . . . is Robert Bainbridge. I am the brother of René Bainbridge . . . my only surviving relative," he said as he directed his attention toward Black Eagle. The tone in his voice projected a sincere plea for help. "And they are Denver and Jacques, my friends," he said while pointing to his companions.

"Well, well . . . Ro'bert Bainbridge', you are welcome to stay for as long as you need. There is an empty cabin near where my son Black Eagle lives with his wife. He will show you the way," Gray Wolf stated clearly. He had purposely put Black Eagle on the spot to make it easier for him to do his duty.

Robert acknowledged the invitation with a firm handshake. It had been a long time since he had encountered a man as fair and just as his own father. Again, the memories of his loss flooded his consciousness. He wanted so much to find his sister that he had left the only other person who cared for him.

"Come . . . I will show you where you can rest yourselves," Black Eagle stated sullenly. He led them to the cabin, which just happened to be right next door to his home. The trio followed in silence, hoping that the shelter offered would contain them all. Denver and Jacques finally dismounted and nearly stumbled when they reached the ground. Their legs had become stiff from the cold and their breeches weRe-near ready to crack from the sudden movement.

Black Eagle entered the cabin first and lit the fire in the pit. Robert and his companions rushed to the flames to warm themselves, nearly falling over one another. This was the first real shelter they had been able to settle into since René's disappearance. Robert slowly walked around the cabin, patting himself on the shoulders to get warm. He was pleased with his surroundings and considered the generosity of both of his hosts. He came to an abrupt stop near Black Eagle, who had just sparked up the flames again with another log.

"Warm yourselves . . . the night is still very cold here," Black Eagle stated quickly. It was his way of breaking the silence that had hovered over them since they'd left the others. When Robert didn't respond, Black Eagle rose to his feet and made his way to the door.

In as much as he didn't want any contact with this man, Robert placed himself between the door and Black Eagle, who had all the answers to the many questions that had haunted him for months. "Don't go yet, my friend," he said sternly. "We have much to talk about. I think you know what I mean, don't you?"

Sensing the change in the tone in his brother-in-law's voice, Black Eagle decided to put the man's worries to rest. "I was not planning to leave. I wish to speak to you . . . my brother. Please . . . sit . . . and warm yourself," he insisted as he gestured toward the fire. Each man realized they had nothing to fear from the other standing before him. He complied with Black Eagle's wishes and welcomed the warmth that was offered. Robert, aside from the other, was very set on the reason he had visited every village between the outpost and their present camp.

Denver cleared his throat, giving a friendly warning that Robert should take great care not to act foolishly. He had been against coming to this village from the beginning, knowing that these people didn't trust strangers, especially whites. He had even tried to convince Robert that René could be almost anywhere, maybe even dead. Then again, they might very well find the girl here among the Ojibwa. Then what would they do with her? They wouldn't be able to get two feet out of this village without someone sounding an alarm. There was no doubt in his mind that if she were here, she would be keeping the big man's house. She would be a fine catch for any man, including him.

Fear made Denver speak up, "Son . . . before you say something that we all may regret, remember where you are," he added in a fatherly manner. He had many close calls and had escaped by the skin of his teeth. He realized that the only way he could keep his scalp was to maintain calm between the boy and his host.

"*Oui, mon ami!* Now I must sleep," Jacques added and then pulled the bearskin over his head. He was snoring almost immediately.

Robert took everything in stride. He was determined to make his point known to Black Eagle no matter what the older gent said. The months of searching for his sister had soured him. He was angry. He was angry at the one who had taken her. He was even more angry with himself for not keeping her out of James Courtland's hands. He was doomed by his own failure, forcing him to look for René if need be till he died.

"I remember you. You are the one who saved my sister's life back at the outpost," Robert said sternly. He cleared his throat and then rubbed his hands together. "You know, René is the only living relative I have left. I promised to protect her . . . and I failed. And what's worse, she was taken away from the outpost and no one heard a thing. You know, I don't remember seeing you around after that, either?"

Black Eagle nodded at first. He recalled all too well the circumstances around their first meeting. That day was branded in his memory and in his heart. "You remember well," he stated. "I too remember that day. It was the day I saw sunshine," Black Eagle offered.

"Then you remember saying that René was yours. *Don't deny it!* I remember every word you said as though it were yesterday!" Robert snapped. He wanted more than Black Eagle was willing to give at the moment, but he pushed on.

Black Eagle nodded again, very calmly and reassuring. "You speak the truth. Your sister, Re-nea, is here. She is safe," Black Eagle continued. "She is my wife."

"*You what?*" Robert yelled. You can't expect me to believe that you . . . that you and my sister . . . " he gasped. "Oh my God." Robert couldn't contain his anger any longer. He lunged at Black Eagle, who quickly moved aside, avoiding any violent contact with him and watched Robert crash into the wall. He was shakened after that fiasco and didn't move when he inquired, "Then you are the reason she disappeared. You . . . it was you who took her that night . . . *damn you!*"

"Yes . . . I did take her. I admit . . . I wanted her from the first moment I saw her . . . touched her. But if I had not, she would be dead. Both of us . . . you and I would be in mourning," he said as he gestured to Robert and then to himself. "The man I found in her room, was there to harm her. I wanted her to live."

Robert was infuriated by his statement. How dare Black Eagle assume that he should be a part of her life. "You presume much. Besides, I know she didn't want any part of you," he shouted angrily. Then he picked up a burning log from the pit and aimed it at Black Eagle's head. And still, Black Eagle sat calmly, never wavering, causing his brother-in-law to feel foolish and less than civilized. Frustrated, he tossed the log back into the flames, and sparks flew in all directions.

"You are angry with the wrong man, my brother. I have done your sister no harm. I care deeply for her. She is my reason for living," Black Eagle said forcefully for the first time. Then he tossed another log into the fire, pulled out his pipe and tobacco pouch, and offered Robert a smoke.

Robert refused it, just as he refused to allow this farce to continue. "I am angry with the wrong man? I don't think so. I have every reason to be angry with *you*. You stole René away. Do you expect me to believe that you had her best interest in mind when you did that?" Robert demanded.

There seemed to be no end to the mocking tone of the man to whom he had shown respect. In any other case he would have tossed the man out on his ear, but he was Re-nea's brother. He must try to make him understand that taking her saved her life. "Yes . . . my brother . . . I feared for her life. She was being attacked that night. He had been spying on her," Black Eagle offered slowly.

Robert was definitely on his own on this one, because he found James in her room the following morning complaining about being hit from behind. "James . . . yes, then, it was true. But I didn't believe him. Then, that must have been you. You did a lot of damage. So, where's my sister?"

Black Eagle stood up and with a small gesture bade Robert to follow.

"Come!" Black Eagle commanded. "I made a promise as you say . . . I vowed to protect and care for her. I have done that. Re-nea wanted you to know that she was well. You will see that for yourself."

Robert wasn't sure if he should trust the like of this man, but he had no choice. The Quaker family was his only lead and he would never forget how they described her. Every detail, from her hair to her eyes and the way she was dressed, brought all kinds of thoughts to his mind. Then James Courtland's face flashed before him and the deep-seated hatred began to well up again.

Black Eagle, still conversing, was telling him of their journey north and of the Quaker family when Robert finally clued in again. The only words he managed to hear rang in his ears. "She honored me in many ways." Now Robert clung to every word. He was confused by Black Eagle's last statement and wanted him to clarify himself. It implied more than he was willing to believe. Before he could ask what he meant by it, they were both standing in front of Black Eagle's home. He opened the door for Robert and bid him to enter.

The cabin was warm and lit only by firelight. Robert saw René sleeping with her back to the door. From the angle it appeared that she hadn't changed in the slightest. Her hair was neat and well kept. Her skin was still as radiant as when he last saw her. Robert closed the distance between them and gently called her name. "René, René, I've come to take you home," he said with excitement growing in his voice.

René's eyes opened in a flash, as though she had been struck by lightening. She couldn't believe it: Robert, her brother, had finally found her. She turned to face him, hoping that this wasn't someone playing a mean trick on her. But the man kneeling by her side, dark green eyes dripping with tears, and sandy brown hair, now long and wavy, was truly Robert himself.

"Am I dreaming? Is it really you?" she asked as she touched his face. He had a full beard, which hadn't been shaved in months. There was no mistake, though—it was he, and she cried with joy for the second time that day. They hugged each other, both exploding into tears.

"You are alive . . . I felt it. Oh God, how I've missed you!" he said as he embraced her again, practically squeezing the air from her lungs.

In René's excitement, she exposed the two babes who were at her side. Their bright eyes sparkled from the light of the fire. They were alert and actively moving their little arms and legs from under the cover. Robert's eyes widened, first in shock, then in dismay, and last in anger. He hadn't been told about them. His attitude changed most abruptly. He looked away from René to Black Eagle, who was standing by the door.

"Tell me that the babies aren't yours, René. Tell me!" Robert insisted vehemently. "How could you do this?" he asked as he strained to maintain some control. His tone had changed so much that there was a mark of insinuation directed toward both René and Black Eagle.

"It seems you've answered your own questions, Robert. I won't tell you what you want to hear. They are mine. They were born just hours ago," she responded gently. Then she lay back down on her bed and cradled the little ones in the crooks of her arms. "Would you have me deny my own children? I can't do that. Are you ashamed of me . . . of them? Well . . . I am proud," René said firmly as she lifted her son and kissed his forehead.

Robert exploded with accusations that were directed toward Black Eagle. His anger had reached its peak. If only he could undo the damage that his foolish sister and her lover had done. "So . . . that is why you kept calling me your brother. I should kill you for what you have done," he yelled.

"And what has he done, Robert, except to marry me? He has given me a home and he provides for my every need.I haven't had a hungry day, nor have I suffered in the cold. I haven't said this too often, but I love him . . . dearly," she continued without hesitation and then gazed at Black Eagle with admiration.

Robert didn't know what to think about the conditions she was living in. This wasn't what his father had meant by taking care of her. How could she stoop so low and allow Black Eagle to even touch her? She should have killed herself rather than allow him to make love to her.

"I know what you are thinking, Robert. You are thinking that Black Eagle is a savage and that I am no longer fit to be a part of the civilized world. What white man would want to be with me? Am I right, Robert?" she asked while showing concern for his feelings. "Think . . . think about our home . . . .our parents, Robert. Those people wanted to kill me. They wanted blood. All that was due to the secrets surrounding my birth. So . . . what white man would want a woman of mixed blood? Answer that one, Robert," she continued calmly. She knew all too well that should she ever return home, her life would be miserable. She would undoubtedly suffer from ridicule and the hatred of those who would eventually learn of her past. That wasn't the life she wanted to live.

Robert's eyes narrowed toward Black Eagle, but he heard every word René had said. She never failed to bring him back to reality. She had accepted her fate and she refused to consider any other option that wouldn't include her new family. She had learned to survive and to deal with her new way of life. She had also made a place for herself and even though it was small, she was the richer for it.

For the first time in months Robert was grateful for the selfish act of the man before him. Not only had he saved her from certain death, he had given her a reason to live on. She had done well by Black Eagle. He could only imagine the happiness that warmed their home. It wasn't long before Robert started fumbling with his words. He had already spoken in haste and had made threats of which under normal circumstances would have been considered a challenge.

Black Eagle finally opened the door for peace between them, speaking for the first time since they entered the cabin. His voice was strong and firm, which allowed him to command the attention of his tongued-tied brother-in-law. "You act as though I have dishonored your family by taking Re-nea as my wife," he stated quickly. "It is you who have dishonored my wife and my home. Speak no more of what should have been. She is here! She is safe!" he stated coldly. "You will take this time to think of what will be good for you . . . and your sister. If you take her back, she will not be treated as the good woman she is. I know nothing of her past and I will not let you bring her past back to haunt her."

"But I came . . . " Robert tried to explain himself, but his mouth failed to produce any logic behind his undertone.

"You came to take her back. I will not give her up!" Black Eagle stormed. He had taken every insult Robert had hurled and out of concern for René, he allowed him to press his views. And yet Black Eagle was guilty of wanting René so much that he would have taken her away that night even if she hadn't been in danger. In many ways, Robert had a right to be angry.

Suddenly, Black Eagle's manner softened after spying the reaction on René's face. She hadn't seen this side of the man she had called her husband and was truly frightened that her brother was going to sent away. "It is not my wish to keep you and Re-nea apart. Her heart is good. I am learning more about her as each day goes by," he offered slowly.

Robert didn't understand how a man like Black Eagle could be so caring and so gentle with René. From all the stories he had been told, he expected to find his sister in a mindless and ravaged condition. Instead, she was beautiful, healthy, and totally aglow with love. He never saw such happiness in René while she was courting James Courtland. She had a look that he hoped would never disappear.

René began to yawn, and the fatigue of the day's event were showing in her eyes. She could barely stay awake, while her brother and husband continued to iron out their differences. "Come," Black Eagle said softly, noticing that she was quite tired, "I will walk you back to your cabin. Re-nea must rest now."

Reluctantly Robert agreed, then kissed René on the cheek and bid her good night. He was sure he had worn out his welcome and was quickly ushered out of the door before he could utter another word. There were no signs to indicate whether he would be permitted another visit with his sister, for he had said too much; some of which he wanted to take back if he could.

The night's sky was like black velvet sprinkled with tiny diamonds. The air was still quite brisk, even though spring had finally come. It had been an exciting day, one of joy and one of fear. Neither one had expected the other to listen, and neither had considered the affect it would have on René. In a way, it seemed as though Robert had delivered René into Black Eagle's hands to fulfill the vision. Black Eagle strongly believed that she belonged to him, and now, with the new additions to his family, he felt complete. Robert, however, still felt he had failed to complete his father's request.

When they reached the door of his cabin, Robert inadvertently put his hand on Black Eagle's shoulder to prevent him from leaving. He wasn't sure, but he took a chance and extended his hand in an act of friendship. "I don't really know how to . . . it is hard for me to admit when I am wrong. But . . . I want to thank you for keeping my sister safe. Where I failed, you succeeded. She seems very happy here. I have to admit, she wasn't happy at all before," he said apologetically. "I've been a damned fool thinking that I was the only one who knew what was best for her. I know that she is in good hands with you."

With that, Black Eagle took his hand, remembering how René wanted them to accept one another. There was so much to consider now that they had two little ones to care for. "It is good . . . you and I have said what needed to be said," Black Eagle offered. "Re-nea has much to be proud of. She will be pleased that we do this."

CHAPTER

THIRTEEN

THERE WERE MANY BLESSINGS bestowed upon the Ojibwa during the long winter months. They had survived the harshness, while the food and wood had remained plentiful. Babies were born healthy and strong, some were already trying to crawl or walk. There was a sense of contentment throughout the village.

Gray Wolf was pleased with his decision to allow young Robert and his friends to stay a little longer. So much was learned in the short time the small group had dwelled among them. Gray Wolf's clan hadn't learned much from the missionaries, who would come twice a year. But the missionaries wouldn't explain why the white man wanted their land and was taking away their brothers' main source of food and trade.

The weary trio spent most of their time in council, being grilled daily with questions, and sometimes accusations were hurled by disbelievers. There were many days when it seemed they would lose their lives, but Gray Wolf would remind the council again Robert and his friends were under the protection of the village.

Denver proved to be more useful than the others. He had been trapping in those woods for many, many years. He had learned to survive on his own at an early age. He couldn't recall exactly how old he was at the time, but he knew that he was no older than the boys playing with their bows and arrows in the field. All he could remember was that he was born near or around the time it was planting season.

Denver spent most of his free time with Gray Wolf, talking about their past adventures and smoking their pipes. There were surprised to find that they shared many common bonds them and took great care in acknowledging their differences. "Yep, Old timer . . . I mean Gray Wolf, those youngins have gotta learn respect. They's gonna lead a hard life if'n we—that is you and me—don't show 'um," Denver said sheepishly.

"Yes . . . I agree. They act before they think, but sometimes they see things that we elders do not," Gray Wolf added, taking a puff from his pipe. He was, without a doubt, a very striking man with bold features adding depth to his character. He held himself with esteem and pride. His strength in decision making and leadership had proven to be of great influence to his sons and to his people. He enabled him to know that his new-found friend would shed light on the answers he sought.

"How true! I am still tryin' to teach that young whipper a thing or two. Robert is more headstrong than any of your warriors. I worry about him, like I would my own son, if'n I had one," Denver continued. He hadn't spoken openly about Robert to anyone before. He hadn't even confided in Jacques, who had been his traveling companion for many years.

Gray Wolf noted the sincerity in Denver's heart and considered him a good man. He, too, felt a kinship with Robert; the young man obviously had a great sense of loyalty for his family and a strong desire to protect his loved ones at any cost. "You have chosen your friends well. My daughter-in-law has learned much living among us. At first, I was sure she would bring sorrow to my people. I see now that she has brought us were new friends. It is good. She has made a place . . . . "

The two were interrupted by the sight of a woman who rushed into the village crying and screaming. Her clothing was practically torn to shreds. Blood dripped from her arm, and mud and dried leaves were clumped in her hair. Her eyes were wide with fear, and she was barely able to speak. She only pointed toward the field as she collapsed, falling to the ground like a wounded deer.

Both men rose to their feet and quickly rushed through the crowd to get a better look. Fear seemed to beset the onlookers. No one wanted to go near the bleeding woman. She wasn't one of the clan. She was an outsider, probably a Sauk, someone who had breached the security of their peaceful village.

Gray Wolf called out an alarm and ordered those within the sound of his voice to arm themselves. "It appears this woman is a runaway. Look . . .

those men yonder. Her wounds are fresh. She must belong to one of them," he added while surveying the open field for more. Even from that distance, Gray Wolf's sharp eyes picked up the blunt edge of steel that glistened in the sun and shoulders laden with many bows and arrows. "They have come to kill. We must arm ourselves."

Black Eagle and Robert pushed through the crowd after spotting the small group. The two had already surmised that a raiding party was definitely afoot, looking for food and women . The women and children silently gathered their belongings and headed for the caves hidden in the northern section of the village. Only a few opted to stay behind. Since Robert and his friends were guests in this territory, it would be wrong to assume that they would take part in this foray. However, Robert offered without forethought, "My gun is yours. I will help you in any way I can."

"So is mine," Denver added. he hadn't had as much excitement since he left the outpost with Robert several months ago.

Jacques, on the other hand, was a little shaken by the prospect of being clubbed to death. He had no desire to have his brains garnishing the club or his scalp on the breastplate of the likes of them. Therefore he made no offer to assist.

Gray Wolf hoped that the other two would stay out of the fight like their friend Jacques. But he accepted Robert and Denver's aid reluctantly, hoping that this wouldn't turn into a full-fledged battle. He was greatly impressed by Robert, who had shown he was ready to sacrifice his life for that of his sister. And yet, there were the other two: One openly followed Robert's lead, and the other cowered, unwilling to help those who had sheltered them. His death would be shadowed by fear.

The cabin that housed the tribe's rice and grain over the long winter may not have seemed like much, but it was their main source of survival. There was much planning and very little time to prepare for the ensuing battle ahead of them. "Clean her up and fix her wounds. She has much to tell us!" he ordered. "You . . . my friends, this is not your fight. You have nothing to gain from it. But I am grateful that you offered to help."

Robert acknowledged his host and said, "I do have something to gain, Gray Wolf. My sister's life as well as the lives of her children . . . my family." Then Gray Wolf nodded, understanding the logic behind Robert's actions. Then he gestured for the woman to be taken to a shelter.

The closet cabin belonged to Black Eagle. Without any warning to the occupants within, the door opened and the woman was rushed inside with hands and legs bound. She was roughly placed on a mound near the fire. René had just finished nursing her daughter when the village women intruded. There wasn't much she could do to stop them as they went about destroying her home. The women used the water that she had planned to use to wash her children. They knocked over the pot of stew into the flames, causing the cabin to fill with smoke. There was so much confusion with everyone coming and going that the babies became frightened and fretful.

That was the last straw for René . She couldn't take this invasion of her privacy any longer and yelled, "Stop! All of you . . . get out! Look what you've done! You've destroyed my home!"

Everyone stopped and finally took in what they had done. The tiny clothes, which René spent many hours, even days, sewing by hand, were torn to shreds. The cradle board belonging to Black Eagle's first born lay crushed and scattered on the floor. And the worst occurred when one woman stood within inches of stepping on René's son. René rushed over to him and snatched him up as quickly as she could without frightening him. She managed to compose herself long enough to pick up her daughter as well.

"Gray Wolf told us to clean her up and fix her wounds," one woman snapped angrily. The smirking look on her face expressed power. She dared René to say another word.

Another added with just as much venom, "She is Sauk. She is an enemy to our people. *They* have come to take our food . . . to kill our womankind."

"You know nothing of the dangers that cloud us from day to day. Your man protects you from such things. He thinks you are too good to suffer. You, an outsider, like she is. But not an enemy. Or are you *our* enemy?" asked the first.

René clutched her children to her bosom. She didn't know they were in danger of being attacked. She hadn't felt this way since the people of Wilmot had invaded her world. It was more than she could bear. These women knew nothing about her and from what she observed in those fleeting moments, they wouldn't care. Their own needs were controlling their every thought. Who was she to judge or condemn them?

"You are right! I know nothing of what you go through from day to day. It is also true that you know nothing of mine . . . like what it is to suffer. I know that kind of pain. I have dealt with it for a far greater time than you will ever know. The only joy I have ever known since I lost my parents was Black Eagle and now . . . my children," René stated without reservation. But even though she regarded them with respect, they laughed at her. Some mocked her words, creating a wave of laughter and jeering. Sensing that there was nothing she could do to convince them that she wasn't the enemy, René rebuffed, "You have said nothing but cruel things to me! You've destroyed my home and you nearly killed my son! So, before you do any more damage . . . leave! I will care for the woman!"

"Ahhh, you speak with great strength, but you cannot send us away. You will learn in time. You . . . who will never be a part of the clan," the woman said bluntly. The she proceeded to dress the woman's wounds and ignored René and her whimpering children.

Black Eagle heard the woman's words of cruelty and entered his home to find his wife standing by the door protectively holding their children. "Which one of you speaks with such boldness to my wife?" he asked sternly as he looked at the damage caused by their thoughtlessness. "It appears you all feel that my wife is not important. I heard much talk before I entered. You have been told to leave . . . so leave!" Black Eagle stormed.

His voice seemed to shatter their bones. They had dared to pose themselves as a threat to his wife and to his children. They even tried to make light of her status as wife of a subchief. He then cast a gaze upon those who dared to stay, making them lower their eyes to the floor. They treaded out the door in single file, without uttering another word. The bold one was the last to leave. She spat on the wounded woman's face and then tossed René medicine bag into the flames. It wasn't hers to destroy, but she did it as a final effort, to create another problem for René. Finally she stormed out of the cabin, practically tearing the deerskin from the door.

"Who was that woman?" René asked carefully. "She has a mean streak that would frighten a mad dog!"

Black Eagle couldn't agree more. "Her name is not important now. She has the mark of the evil spirit," he answered quickly while packing up some of their belongings. His mind was elsewhere, worrying over the hostility lurking outside of their village. He could lose his family in a single swoop if he didn't act quickly enough.

René, however, who was still shaken by the entire ordeal, was glad that the situation hadn't turned ugly. "It must be sad to live like that," she thought, not realizing that she had spoken aloud.

Again Black Eagle agreed, only in silence. Then René noticed that he had placed food in a sack and had gathered their blankets and more of their belongings. It dawned on her that the danger the women had spoken of was, in fact, true. She placed both children in the protective surroundings of the bearskin wraps, which weRe-neatly piled together and ready to be used. With a little hesitation she then turned her attention to the blood-spattered body of the woman who watched their every move.

René wiped the blood away from her wounds, only to find that her injuries were superficial and appeared to be self-inflicted. She was only pretending to be hurt, so that she could infiltrate the Ojibwa village occupying their attention. She had succeeded in maintaining her farce until her wounds were dressed. She was likely a plant or a spy, sent there to find the weaknesses.

Black Eagle then broke her train of thought, bringing her attention to his words alone. "The woman is not important. But you and my children are. I must take you to a safe place. Come!" he cajoled. "Leave the woman! She will be dealt with later!"

Then, with a swift chop of his club, Black Eagle made a new opening in the wall opposite the door. He checked the area and then secured the door. This left the woman, bound and gagged, with no way to warn the enemy.

Black Eagle led his little family to a large cave on the outskirts of the eastern most part of the village. The journey there was trying and exhausting, yet they continued on their way. René never asked where she was going; she only knew that it was important to Black Eagle for them to get there.

There they joined White Feather, who held a small child; Morning Star and her son, Two Moons, and Dancing Wind were there as well. They were all quickly ushered inside. The cave was dark and smelled of the last inhabitant, which happened to be a female bear and her cubs. René was completely repulsed upon entering and tried to walk out, but Black Eagle insisted firmly that she and the others stay. There was no other place for her to go, and the safety of her children should be more important than the smell of their temporary shelter.

"Black Eagle, how long must we stay here?" she asked with great concern. He had stopped Dancing Wind from starting up a fire and quickly made sure that they had enough brush to cover the entrance.He placed his children on the bearskin robe and then stroked their little hands before kissing their tiny foreheads. He appeared to be saying a final farewell.

Then he turned to René, kissed her with the fullest passion, and held her close.

"You must stay here until I come for you," he responded finally. He inhaled the fragrance of her hair. He wanted to take in as much of her as he could, for strength. Finally, he turned to his mother, who held a beautiful, chubby little baby. The babe's eyes flashed with excitement when Black Eagle reached out to take him. His small arms wrapped tightly around Black Eagle's neck, and a little chuckle escaped his lips.

René watched the union between the two and caught what sounded like *"my son"* come from Black Eagle's lips. Before she could asked him, Black Eagle eagerly presented the babe to her for safekeeping. "Re-nea . . . this is my first born, One Shoe. He is now our first born," he added. He watched how lovingly she had cared for the children she bore him and wanted the same care for One Shoe. He waited with some hesitation, knowing that this wasn't the best way to introduce the two to each other.

He could only imagine how hard it was for René to take care of two children, each having the same demands on her time and each having different eating and sleeping patterns. Now Black Eagle was presenting her with another young child to care for. A child he shared with another woman. The same child he had told her about months ago, and never brought home. But when René looked into the child's big brown eyes, she couldn't refuse him. She smiled at Black Eagle and gently took the babe from his arms, holding him close to her heart and then allowing him to suckle at her breast. She knew Black Eagle wanted to have his son home. One Shoe now has a mother of his own.

Black Eagle kissed her again, "You have made me proud many times, my love," he said while taking in the sight. "Now you have opened your heart to another . . . my son, who is now your son. You have made him your own. My heart is glad. Now my family is truly complete," he continued with reverence toward her. Then he turned to his mother and his sisters-in-law and said, "Do not leave the cave for any reason. The enemy will be watching."

As unpleasant as it was, René complied. She was finally in the company of her in-laws, one of whom whimpered like a child whenever she didn't get her way, and the other, who seemed quite reserved and well-mannered. She sat quietly by the large rock formation and began to eat the little morsels she had hidden in her pouch, while the other paced the floor, wanting very much to see what was going on outside.

"Sit down, Dancing Wind!" White Feather ordered. "I grow tired watching you pace the floor like a bear cat

"But I want to see! Running Bear never lets me see him at battle. I want to watch," she babbled.

"You are so childish," Two Moons offered. "You will never be happy until something goes wrong!"

"That is not true!" she stormed aloud, frightening the children. "Quiet them down. Do you want the Sauks to find us?" she demanded, turning her anger on René and Morning Star.

"If you hadn't startled them, they wouldn't be crying," René stated firmly. But White Feather placed her hand on René s shoulder to quiet her. She had had enough of Dancing Wind constantly creating a problem without thinking of the welfare of others. "If you do not sit quietly, I will have you bound and gagged until our men come for us," she snarled.

Fearing that she would spend the next few hours in the condition White Feather had described, Dancing Wind sat down abruptly. Each woman had given her an evil stare. They were all testy and quite put out. If anything, Dancing Wind would bring the enemy upon them.

René was thoroughly mystified by the wayward woman and her silly behavior. She had little respect for anyone and created an unhealthy atmosphere by her presence. Everyone grew angry listening to the young woman banter on about things she didn't understand. And White Feather wondered what her son ever saw in her in the first place.

The Sauks, a warlike people, believed in taking from others to sustain themselves and many times they had to show their strength in battle. The Ojibwa, however peaceful they appeared to be, were most treacherous whenever they were attacked or forced into battle. A victorious win in battle over the Ojibwa would be considered the greatest coup ever for the Sauks. They would acquire the rich and fertile land, the bounty of fine hunting in any direction they chose, and there would always be plenty of food throughout and after the winter season.

The drums sounded like thunder. It continued for at least an hour. Soon the songs of the dead were sung. Each brave prayed to the Great Spirit for strength and endurance, each knowing they would soon meet their death in battle. Many of the young warriors danced around the large fire and then smoke the ritual pipe. One by one, each warrior received a blessing from the tribal priests, who painted their faces and bodies for war.

After receiving his blessing, Black Eagle—joined by Robert, Tall Elk, and Running Bear—took their places at the eastern point of the village. They were armed with bows, arrows, clubs, spears and a few single-fire rifles. From their vantage point they could see far into the valley and the large meadow beyond, which surely housed their enemy. The cave where the women and children were hidden was just out of sight, but Black Eagle could see the landing, which led to the mouth of the cave.

Everything appeared to be secure from the east to the north and to the west of the village. Now, they had to wait . . . wait for the Sauks to make their move.

CHAPTER
FOURTEEN

THE SAUKS MOVED IN on the Ojibwa with stealth. They used the trees and the low-hanging brush to conceal themselves. Their leader, Chief Pa Te' Nea, wanted more than the rice fields—he had come for the women, as well. His people were dying, mostly from starvation and poor health, due to the lack of proper shelter during the long winter. There were many braves without wives, and their population was doomed to nonexistence. They had heard of the vast tribe of the Ojibwa, and Pa Te' Nea promised his braves that each would come away with a bride or two.

He counted his blessings after seeing the beauty of the land the Ojibwa cared for. "Look . . . they will be easy prey to our arrows. Let them fly with the wind and hit every man in the village," he said, knowing that taking the land or even the women of the village would be costly.

His braves were willing to fight as long as they could. They had the taste of blood on their lips, and their palms were sweating, eager to feel the warmth of the flesh of their victims squirming and begging for their lives. Pa Te' Nea was sure that he would fulfill his greatest quest: He would defeat his long time adversary and make them all slaves.

Pa Te' Nea closed in for the kill. He could see Gray Wolf sitting at a fire in the center of the village. He saw a few children playing with a barking dog and several women tanning deerskin on a rack. Everything was quiet for the most part. He didn't suspect that he was entering a trap. So he waited until darkness was about to set in. The drums were still beating and the chanting shaman could be heard from all sides, getting louder and louder as the Sauks approached. Then all went silent. It was as though he heard his own heart stop beating. He wiped the sweat from his brow and leaned closer to the ground to get a better look. From what he could see, Gray Wolf wouldn't know what hit him if he fired now. Then Pa Te' Nea raised his arm and let it fall. The signal—as though thunder had rumbled—for a hundred or more men converged upon the village. Each Sauk brandishing a club in one hand and a knife or spear in the other rushed into the village.

It would be written that the door had been left opened and the serpent was allowed to enter. His fangs bared, and venom spewed in all directions. Arrows were flying everywhere, some connecting and others lodging in the outer walls of the cabins. A Sauk brave sounded a war whoop, which was followed by others. They charged the village, vowing to take many lives and many scalps.

The women and children who were once in sight had suddenly vanished. Gray Wolf and his warriors stood their ground, waiting for the enemy to come completely into the center. Once he drew them in, he in turn sounded an alarm, and the Ojibwa came in from all sides, firing arrows, chopping and stabbing at their enemy. In their hearts they were protecting their homes and their people. But, in their minds, they were facing death without fear. The tables had been turned, and the Sauks were astonished.

Many men had fallen on both sides. Blood soaked the moist earth, draining the life's force from the bodies that lay crumpled on the ground. The Ojibwa never wanted to have blood on their hands. They only wanted to live peacefully on the land they had tilled for centuries. Now the blood of their enemy mingled with the blood of their people, tainting the land.

The battle was still raging, until the last of the Sauks, Pa Te' Nea, stood alone. He slowly turned to look upon his brave and fallen warriors. He saw the youngest, who was only fifteen summers old, lay gasping for his last breath, before dying. He saw the bravest of the brave struck down, as though struck by lightning. Never had he suffered such loss, such humiliation. Surrounded by the Ojibwa, who brandished the clubs in the air, he waited for the death blow, which in his terms would be a death of honor.

But, Gray Wolf was a man of peace. It was his nature to allow the beaten man to depart and to account for his losses in peace. But that wouldn't be the case with Pa Te' Nea. His honor had been destroyed. He had planned Gray Wolf's demise, and it proved fatal to only to him and his warriors. He couldn't return to his people a broken man, a man defeated by rice growers and tillers of the soil. He was a warrior, a strong man with many followers. Now, many of his followers lay dead. All except the warrior band who were awaiting his next signal.

"I have not been defeated yet. I will spill your blood and that of your sons . . . and their sons," he said bravely. "You think you have won this battle? *Well . . . I will win the war! Ha ha ha haaaa!*"

Pa Te' Nea was sure that Gray Wolf would signal for his braves to kill him on the spot. His arrogance continued even after defeat. Yet, he was totally surrounded on all sides, with no way out, unless Gray Wolf gave way, and he did. He grew tired of the bloodletting. It was time to bring the killing to an end. But before Gray Wolf could respond to his vehement statement, Pa Te' Nea roused a loud war whoop that shattered the nerves of every man and woman in the village, then he fled, leaving the dead and the wounded behind

Black Eagle and Running Bear were still holding the eastern point of defense. They heard the war cry and knew that something was afoot. It had been too quiet for too long. Darkness was all around them. The moon was shrouded by the clouds, and there was no light to see what was coming their way. At one point it seemed as though the moving shadows were caused by the wind, but the sound of the shrieking eagle pierced the air. The only bird to hunt by night was the owl, and the call of the eagle touched the ear of every man at the point.

"They come," Black Eagle whispered. "They send the call of the giant bird. A bird that will only hunt by day."

"How can you be sure?" Robert asked without thinking. Yet, before he could say another word, he found Tall Elk's hand over his mouth.

"They hear everything. They know we are here. But they do not know we hear them," Black Eagle whispered.

Their bodies were still covered with war paint made of blackened ash and bear fat. Even their eyes seemed to disappear into the darkness. And with that cover, they readied themselves for the grueling battle. Again, the eagle call came, but this time it came from their left flank.

Fear and excitement gripped Robert's stomach when he heard it. The realization that Black Eagle's logic never seemed to fail began to bother him. How could a man of such simple means know so much and have so much wisdom? Death, fighting—for what? A few sheds filled with grain? Then he licked his thumb and lightly touched the siting on his rifle. As suddenly as a breeze touched their brows, the Sauks attacked. They fell back and then attacked again. They continued the battle through the night, and then it came to an abrupt end.

In the cave just over the hill, René and the others waited patiently in the dark for a familiar face to came for them. Dancing Wind became restless again and started pacing the dirt floor. Everyone had something to do, except her. "I cannot stand this anymore! This place is dirty and smelly. I want to go home!," she whined. "I want to sleep in my own bed, not on this," she admonished as she kicked at the dirt on the floor, creating a swirl of dust. No one spoke. No one wanted to reveal that they wanted the same things.

René covered her newborn son's face with her tunic. She was relieved when the dust finally settled and Dancing Wind took her antics to the other side of the cave. Then René gently placed her son on the bearskin robe, next to his sister, who was still sleeping. She covered them with a tiny blanket and watched them sleep. Then she turned to White Feather, who cared for One Shoe. The little one had slept through the night without as much as a whimper. She could say the same for Dancing Wind, who again started pacing the floor.

A glimmer of light peeked through the opening where the branches couldn't reach. Daylight. They hadn't heard any war cries or gunshots for the most part during the night. They wondered whether the danger had passed, or if it was still in full scale. Then Dancing Wind started up again, fussing with her blanket and complaining of hunger.

If only René could make a small fire and warm the cave a little. But to do that would endanger them all. Instead, René settled for the light coming through the opening. It gave her a chance to see the tiny faces of her children. She played with them, making them smile. At three months, they were very alert and were changing every day. René was afraid to miss a moment of time with them.

Suddenly, dancing Wind blurted, "I am going home! I cannot stay here another minute."

"We all want to go home. But, Black Eagle told us to stay here. We will wait for him to come for us," René said sternly. She felt just as uncomfortable as Dancing Wind, but what good would it serve to complain about it?

"Re-nea is right! We must wait for our men to come for us. Have some food. You will feel better after you have eaten something," White Feather offered. She was sure Dancing Wind would be more agreeable when she had a full stomach.

Even Two Moons was having difficulty convincing her to stay put. Her jealousy over the attention afforded Two Moons, now that she carried Running Bear's child, made Dancing Wind feel left out. She was no longer allowed to sleep in the main house. In their home, she had to do whatever Two Moons ordered her to do. Her life wasn't her own.

Again, she heard Two Moons say, "Dancing Wind, you must stay. Our husband will not be happy if anything happens to you."

"Our husband . . . you mean your husband! He cares nothing for me. I have not warmed his bed in months. You have had him all to yourself, ever since that night. He cares for you. He cares nothing for me!" she retorted.

"That is not true! He has treated you well. You want for nothing. You have clothes and food. You have everything a wife should want," Two Moons continued. For the first time since that horrible day, she was protecting Running Bear's honor.

Dancing Wind smiled ruefully. There was nothing anyone could say to convince her that Running Bear wanted her for anything other than a slave. She closed her mind to reason and sensibility. She pouted and made a place for herself on the far side of the cave. She fussed and fidgeted with her blanket again. A frustrated sigh passed through her lips as she tried to rest her eyes. It was apparent to all of them that Dancing Wind was scared and that she would be a great hardship until their men returned to take them home again. Maybe they would come soon, since daylight was peeking through.

Later that morning, nature was calling and Dancing Wind was not able to keep her composure. Quietly, without waking the others, she moved toward the opening. With great haste she made her way out of the cave, never once checking to see if the area was safe. She walked out on the ledge and headed for the cover of bushes that happened to be fifteen feet away from the opening of the cave. She took time to stretch and then she relieved herself where the bushes were at their thickest. She was totally unaware of the probing eyes of the men hidden in the bushes below the ledge. She took her time, inhaling the fresh morning air that surrounded her. The grass was damp with the morning mist and felt cool against her ankles. She felt free and happy and even more relaxed than she felt before. She pondered over the cruel words she had spoken earlier and wondered whether Two Moons and the others would forgive her. She wanted to make amends. After taking in another deep breath, she headed back toward the opening of the cave.

The probing eyes belonged to the Sauks, who happened to choose this route as another vantage point to attack the Ojibwas. Instead, they came across Dancing Wind, who suspected nothing as she slowly walked back toward the cave. The lead warrior and his small band silently approached her from behind. Just as she reached the opening of the cave, she was grabbed and thrown in. Her abrupt entry had awakened everyone from a painful sleep. White Feather and Morning Star were about to scold her when they noticed the tall figure blocking the only way out. From the strange regalia he wore, he most certainly wasn't Ojibwa.

"How many women here?" he asked as a few of his men rushed in and probed the cave. He proceeded to walk the length of the cave and then a torch was placed firmly in his hand as though he summoned it. He adjusted his eyes to the light and finally focused them on René and her tiny babes. She kept them close to her, hoping that he wouldn't take them. He brought the torch closer so he could get a better look. White Feather panicked after she saw the concerned look on René's face. She put herself between him and her daughter-in-law. But, his cruelty knew no bounds. He just threw her aside so that he could gaze upon the treasure that was once blocked by the feeble old woman. *"Um, I want this one. She will keep me warm during the travel home. But, first, I must part her from those sucklings,"* he said as he examined the rest of the cave. Then he walked around her, touching her face, then her hair. *"Yes, this one is mine. Pa Te Nea can choose from the others."*

"What is he saying, White Feather?" René whispered in her ear. "I don't understand. What does he want?"

White Feather knew all too well what he wanted and she wasn't sure how much to tell René without getting her upset. But, she was sure the children would die if she didn't act. She simply took the babes from René's arms and held them close to her body. "The babes are my grandchildren. Please . . . do not harm them!" she begged.

He laughed at White Feather and swung his club only inches away from her head, saying things only she understood. White Feather cast her eyes downward as if in prayer and he stopped short of cracking her skull. He laughed again and was quickly joined in by the others, who had been rummaging through their belongings.

"You!" he said forcefully toward René. *"Come! Come with me!"* When she didn't move, he grabbed her by the arm, practically dislocating her shoulder in the process. Then he rushed her out of the cave and tied her hands tightly to the bushes with a piece of leather stripping. He reentered the cave and returned dragging Dancing Wind and Morning Star behind him. With a jerk of his head, he signaled his men to enter the cave again.

Suddenly White Feather screamed. They had taken the children from her. She cried aloud again, such a bloodcurdling cry that René felt a gripping pain in her heart. She tried to loosen ther bonds, tearing at the leather with her teeth. René stopped suddenly, with tears streaming down her cheeks. She heard the cries of her babies silenced almost as immediately as they had started. She knew what they had done. She knew that they had killed her children. And poor White Feather, feeling she had failed her son, begged to die. The men in the cave laughed at her and left her in the cave alone, so they thought, with two tiny bodies of her grandchildren.

Dancing Wind's head finally cleared, and she was now aware of the situation she had put her family in. She could never console René for her loss. And yet, Morning Star was was somewhat composed. She had hidden the two older infants, One Shoe and Tiny Sparrow, under a larger bearskin robe near where Two Moons had slept. She was sure that Two Moons had taken them when she slipped out of sight.

"I will mourn with you, Re-nea. I feel your pain," Morning Star said gently. "You have lost two children, but you still have one to care for," she continued. "Our sons, One Shoe and Tiny Sparrow, are safe. They live!"

Yet her gentle offering was met with silent anguish. René had gone into shock. Her mind was focusing on the image of her children when she last saw them moments ago: Their bright eyes flashing with excitement when she touched them and spoke to them, even their chubby little hands reaching for her, clouded her vision. Now they were gone, murdered without mercy. René cried aloud, "Oh, God, how could they do this? How? My God, they were just little babies . . . babies!"

Morning Star had to maintain the composure of a strong woman, even if she happened to be frightened of the outcome of their new ordeal. Her gentle mystique and quiet ways always led René to believe that she was raised with care and tenderness. She would learn a great lesson of strength from this woman. "Be still and listen. Do what they tell you to do and you will live," she said sternly. Then her voice went silent, but her ire remained high. She was ready to protect the ones who had survived, even if it meant giving her life. She hoped that she could convince René to do the same thing. But how could she tell René not to think of her little ones? They were her first, and she held them with great pride. This was also the month the children would have received their names, and now all was forsaken. The enemy had touched their innocent lives without pity to their helplessness.

On the battlefront, Black Eagle had swung his club into the body of his enemy. He had grown tired, but refused to allow the fatigue to set in. He stopped momentarily, sometimes casting a gaze upon the hill where his family was housed. Many times during that morning, he wanted to check on them, but the Sauks had attacked in waves, coming at them from different directions each time. In all the activity, he hadn't considered the possibility of the Sauks getting through them, to the cave or even into the village. His gut feeling said that they were only being distracted while the Sauks pilfered their way through.

Suddenly a sharp pain in his shoulder brought Black Eagle back to the battle at hand. He found himself facing another Sauk bearing clubs and knives. Again, Black Eagle was the victor, taking down the leader with a crushing blow to the head. The other Sauks who witnessed his tyranny cowered and ran into the forest, leaving the bodies of their kin behind. Never had they encountered such brave and fierce fighting men. They had expected to find a people who would fall under their blades without a fight. The Ojibwa pushed them back without giving them a chance to gather their wits as they ran with their tails between their legs.

Black Eagle had proven his bravery more than the rest, facing each Sauk hand to hand without faltering. He hadn't taken any scalps and he refused to consider that distraction when he put all his energy into the fight. He took no pleasure in the killing, and yet, he had to regard the lives of his family. Even after the last Sauk ran away, he felt something wasn't right . . . that something had gone wrong elsewhere.

CHAPTER FIFTEEN

WHILE RENÉ AND THE others were being ushered away by the Sauks, the battle had calmed on the eastern point. Robert had just exhausted the ammunition from the rifles. Black Eagle and his warriors wiped the blood from their hands. Many lay dead, while other were gravely wounded. The men were tired and feeling the pain from the strenuous blows they'd had to inflict upon the enemy.

Running Bear had taken several scalps. He waved his new trophies and sang a song of triumph. The ferocity of his attack made the Sauks take notice. It seemed they had walked into the pit of hell and the only reprieve was to die or to retreat. They chose the latter and fell back, working their way down the hill and into the open meadow.

Robert was appalled by the acts he had witnessed. Yet, he realized that this was Black Eagle's way of life. Now it would be René's. He followed Black Eagle step for step down the hill in full pursuit. His arm felt heavy and totally useless. Never in his wildest dreams had he ever taken part in such a bloodbath. He had his share of saloon brawls and had fought off several men at one time, but this was the first time he had ever killed.

"They run. They run like scared rabbits," Black Eagle said while stopping to check for stragglers. He knew that the Sauks would try to take as many lives as they could before fleeing to their homeland.

"Aren't you going to follow them . . . maybe to their camp?" Robert asked. He was sure that Black Eagle would hunt them down and kill each and every one of them.

"No! They run with the mark of cowards. They have nothing . . . "
Black Eagle's voice suddenly trailed away. His eyes were set on the opening of the cave where his family had been safely hidden away. The bushes
that had covered the opening were no longer in place.

There was something different, something usual in the way Black Eagle
was acting. Something was apparently wrong, but Robert couldn't think
beyond the bloodletting that had taken place a moment before. He wondered what had taken Black Eagle's attention away from their conversation so quickly. Suddenly Robert noticed a small gleam of light coming
from a cave just above the ledge. There was no movement, at least nothing that should have drawn his attention to it. The look on his face was
one of worry, which made Robert's heart jump like a stricken horse. Before
he could ask, Black Eagle had rushed off in the direction of the cave.

As Black Eagle had dreaded, the light had displayed more than both
men had expected to find. Black Eagle's worse fears had come to pass.
White Feather and his twin babes, who hadn't been named, were lying face
down in a different part of the cave. The smell of death seized his very
nerve. Robert watched as Black Eagle gently picked up his children's limp
and lifeless bodies. His heart had been ripped out and torn to shreds.
Robert felt the pain that wrenched at Black Eagle's soul, and felt a closeness he had never expected. His sister had married a good and sensitive
man. She had chosen well. But, René was nowhere in sight.

"Is there anything I can do?" Robert asked while surveying the rest of
the cave. He probed each part, hoping that René had escaped the fate that
had claimed her children. Then he quickly went to White Feather's aid and
found her breathing, but ever so slightly. He removed the dirt from her
face and gently placed a rolled blanket beneath her head.

Even though her breathing was shallow and somewhat painful, White
Feather wanted to speak. She pushed Robert's hands away and reached for
her son who cradled his children in his arms. She ached with the pain of
telling him what she knew would make his anger flare, saying softly, "The
Sauks . . . the Sauks . . . they came and took your Re-nea. They had no mercy
. . . no mercy for the little ones. They took the women out one by one, Re-
nea, Morning Star, and Dancing Wind. I do not know what happened to
Two Moons The little ones . . . the little ones . . . my poor . . . ," she moaned.

"Mother, say no more," Black Eagle said as he wrapped his children's
bodies in their blanket. "Save your strength. We will find them," he continued soothingly in her ear. "The Sauks will pay with their lives for ask-

ing the lives of my son and daughter. They will pay dearly."

There was rage in Black Eagle's voice, yet he appeared calm. It drew a sign of concern from Robert as he began to feel his blood boil with anger. He questioned every move Black Eagle made. He even followed him from place to place, wanting to be sure that René was making the right choice in staying. Was he a savage or a man just like himself, one who loved without question? Was he René's protector or would he leave her to her fate?

Just as suddenly as she disappeared, Two Moons came into full view holding two small bundles in the bearskin robe that Morning Star had passed to her. She had hidden herself in a small, dark crevice that was set deep within the cave. Although the place was well-concealed, she couldn't keep them in that damp hole much longer. Besides, One Shoe and Tiny Sparrow were getting hungry, and it was necessary to bring them back to the main cave. At least there she would be able to feed them until help arrived.

Relieved to see Black Eagle and another friendly face, she finally sat next to White Feather and stroked her brow. "What your mother says is true, Black Eagle. The Sauks would have killed your oldest son and Tall Elk's son had they found them. I saw what they did. I heard White Feather beg for their lives, but they laughed at her," Two Moons continued with tears flowing. She had confirmed White Feather's account of what had taken place only hours ago.

The only thing that Black Eagle could concentrate on at the moment was the sight of his son. He was alive, hungry, and very fretful. His heart was strengthened knowing that his son was alive and that he would eventually find René. "One Shoe lives!" It was the first spark of happiness in Black Eagle's voice since he had entered the cave. "My son lives! Now . . . I must find my wife!" He had a look of determination on his face, which let Robert know that he was planning to go after her. He hadn't been defeated . . . not yet.

"What ever you are planning to do, Black Eagle, I must be there. René is my sister. She's the only family I have left, except for . . . you." Robert said it, he had embraced Black Eagle by the arms. "Now, let me help you with our family."

Fifteen miles away, where the trees were so plentiful and thick that hardly any sunlight came through, the Sauks had set up a small temporary camp. They made no attempts to start a fire or to pull out their blankets for the night. They only sat facing the four winds, watching and waiting for their fellow warrior to return. There was no honor in the defeat they had suffered. They had nothing to show for their losses but three women captives. Their bellies were empty, and what food they had, had to last for the journey home. They waited, sometimes silently. Their egos would create friction and a great amount of discord between them.

The only solace that the women had was the knowledge that their men would come for them. René had suffered the most. Her arms were light and empty without her tiny babies to care for. She could only wonder if they had been found. She wondered if Black Eagle would blame her for their deaths.

"It is all my fault," Dancing Wind said apologetically.

"It doesn't matter now. They would have found us, anyway," Morning Star added quietly.

"But I'm hungry and I'm tired. I do not want to die! I want to go home," Dancing Wing continued. She hadn't even considered that they all shared the same fate as she.

"We are hungry, too. You have to wait and see what these devils have planned to do with us first. Do not make trouble, Dancing Wind. They will kill us . . . or even worse, they might rape us. They have never shown mercy to our women before," Morning Star added quickly. She was the oldest of the three, and her knowledge of the people would serve them well, but only if the other two would listen.

She touched René's shoulder, hoping to get a response from her, but René's eyes were focused on one of her captors. She wanted him to feel the pain she was feeling. For the first time in her life, René wanted revenge. If she had Black Eagle's strength, she would surely kill him without giving it a thought.

It was as if her thoughts were being read when she noticed the one she was staring at was the one who had ordered her children killed. He had turned to face her. She had no idea that her stares were being interpreted at all. She didn't hear Morning Star's warning. She only saw the man who had created the emptiness in her heart. He was the one, the biggest one of the all. He had to be at least four or five inches taller than Black Eagle. His muscular build was about the same, though. The sides of his head were shaven, leaving a thick line of jet black hair from the front to the back. He wore two gray and white eagle feathers pinned to a single braid. His arms and hands were still covered with blood, and he still wore war paint, a red stripe and a yellow circle etched to the contours of his face. His broad features were fierce and very vicious. He rose to his feet slowly. He never once dropped his glance from her, nor she from his. Before she knew that he was in motion, he was standing in front of her. Then Morning Star's warning came ringing in her ears.

"Re-nea! Re-nea, look at me! Look at me! You must not stare at him like that. He will kill you! He will kill us all!" she implored.

But it was too late. He grabbed René's arm, twisting her shoulder. The pain from that alone had awakened her innermost fears. Then he pushed her up against the tree and pressed himself against her. With one hand on her throat, he held her securely against the tree. It was rough on her tender skin, but that was the least of her concerns. He snatched his knife with his other hand and cut open the front of her tunic. The tiny beads that made her tunic colorful, were popping off in all directions. René just closed her eyes and waited for him to plunge the blade in her middle.

But he wanted her to have a taste of real terror. He wanted her to know that he had the power of life and death over her. He kept his face within inches of hers. She could smell the dried blood . . . the strong scent of death that hovered over him. She felt the urge to heave, but held her breath instead. Every time she tried to turn her head away from him to gasp for air, his hand would tighten at her throat. To further intimidate her, he pressed his bare chest against hers. His weight created such pressure on her breasts that they began to leak.

"Your eyes are green! You are not Ojibwa! You must be a slave!" he said as he tightened his hold on her. "You do not understand me, do you? Soon . . . soon you will understand. You pushed me to take you like this. So . . . you will suffer. I will make you forget the father of those sucklings. Besides, he will not want you after I have had you," he laughed repeatedly in her face. "You will like that. I make all my women happy. I will make you happy," he prattled on while he continued to maintain his grip on her throat. He smiled as small warm droplets trickled down his abdomen,which he knew would bother her greatly.

"Ahhh! That is good. Now . . . you truly belong to me," he continued and then placed his lips to her nipples. Her breast were hard and ached painfully from the missed feedings.

Morning Star couldn't help her. She only translated his words for René to understand. Her words were his words, and there was no doubt that René's virtue was in danger. His actions didn't need translating as far as René was concerned. He wanted her to feel his strength and domination over her. How could he not have power over her? Her hands were bound from behind.

But René found renewed strength. She challenged his right to put his hands on her by saying, "Don't touch me! Keep your hands off of me, you foul . . . . ! I will never give in to you! Never!" Her manner was forceful, and she managed to stop him momentarily. It was all she could do to keep her sanity. Even as she spoke, her eyes revealed hatred and contempt for him. Yet, his manly ego would prove to be her undoing.

He was about to backhand her when the other warriors warned that Pa Te' Nea was approaching the camp. Everyone hurried to their places to greet their chief, each having a story to tell about their near-death experiences and to show that they hadn't left the Ojibwa encampment empty-handed.

"Ah! Welcome, Pa Te' Nea," each said as he reached the campsite. He was glad to see familiar faces, even though they had been defeated in the battle. They came together for a brief moment to sit in council and to smoke the ritual pipe. They would either plan the journey home or attack the Ojibwa again. Excitement grew when he signaled his approval of the captives. He knew at least one would prove to be valuable.

"You are in good fortune, today. Your life is spared for the moment," the warrior said, sneering. He squeezed René's neck tightly, making her gasp for air. He planned to punish her as well as have his pleasure.

After he released her, René sat down quickly trying to hide her disheveled appearance behind Morning Star. Her throat ached, and she could barely catch her breath. Dancing Wind was in tears, seemingly more so than René. She never expected to witness such treatment of women. But then again, it could have been her on the receiving end. Then the trio huddled together for protection and from the prying eyes of their captors.

"Are you all right, Re-nea?" Morning Star asked. She felt René trembling against her body. But the look René expressed earlier was still plastered on her face.

"No! No, I am not all right!" she snapped. "How else could I be?" she asked bitterly. " I will see him die for the death of my children. I will see him die, whether by my hand or Black Eagle's. To harm innocent children for greed is no excuse. I will suffer no more," René spat. Her words were like the venom from the serpent.

Morning Star wasn't ready to die. She wanted to spend the rest of her days with Tall Elk and raising healthy children. She also liked René, mostly because of her compassion and sense of fairness. But, at the moment, René wasn't being fair, not when it came to their lives. How could she calm the storm that was raging in her friend? How could she help her cope with her loss and still manage to live?

Almost immediately the words were forming on her tongue, and she spoke sternly, "Re-nea! Re-nea, you must stop this before we are all killed. If you force his hand . . . he will certainly harm you. He does not care about you or me or Dancing Wind. He will have his way with you, and you will not be able to stop him."

"I can't help the way I feel. He killed my babies. They were only three months' old . . . three short months. They didn't have a chance to live. What harm could they have done to him by living? Then . . . he killed White Feather. You heard her scream. You heard it, didn't you?" René looked into Morning Star's eyes and waited for her to acknowledge all she had said. "And now, this monster wants to take us to God knows where," René whimpered until she fell into full tears. The tears were long in coming. She buried her head into her friend's shoulder and let go of all the anger and pain that was ripping at her very soul.

"That is so, my friend. That is so," Morning Star answered, feeling the sting of her pain. "But you must go on living. You still have Black Eagle . . . and One Shoe," she continued soothingly.

René heard her words, but the guilt surrounding the loss of her babes made it difficult for her to put it into prospective. She blamed herself and felt that Black Eagle would never forgive her. Morning Star and Dancing Wind began to sing a gentle song to ease René's troubled heart. The melody was soft, like the one Gray Wolf had sung to her months ago. Between tears and a grieving heart, René was finally sleeping soundly, with her head cradled on Morning Star's shoulder. For a while there was peace, a quiet that not even a galestorm could disturb. There, under the tree, the trio slept side by side, accepting the outcome of the new day that was yet to come.

Black Eagle sat in council with Gray Wolf to determine the outcome of the kidnapped women. Many were willing to follow after the small band who had escaped their wrath. A large group sat outside, waiting to hear the decision. While others continued to prepare the dead for burial. Denver and Jacques helped with the wounded; some wounds could be repaired, while other were more deadly. Injuries inflicted by the knife or the club were more common. The dying prayed for death, and the dead no longer suffered. This was the vision Gray Wolf saw while sitting in council with his subchiefs.

Many souls have been taken to the Sun. I do not want any more bloodshed. Our people must move on with their lives, just as you must move on with yours, my son. Our once rich and fertile land has been tainted with the blood of our enemy. I am sure . . . they will not return to our land. But, I know the chief, Pa Te' Nea, acts only on revenge, when it suits him," Gray Wolf said with patience. He knew his son. He knew Black Eagle would take it upon himself to get their womenfolk back at any cost.

But Running Bear interrupted. "Father, Black Eagle is not the only one to lose his woman. Dancing Wind and Morning Star are missing as well."

"I know, my son. I also know they may die before they reach the Sauks' village or they may already be dead as we speak," he said with a sense of finality.

"We must not sacrifice our lands for only a few women," one said without regard.

"But it is our womenfolk who bear our children and keep our lodges. They deserve our protection," Tall Elk blurted. Morning Star was his second wife. She was his pride, his excuse for living from day to day.

But Black Eagle knew in his heart that René was still very much alive. She was worth all his efforts to find her and bring her home. He could see her face and he could hear her voice. He couldn't imagine life without her, nor was he planning to. He would defy his father even if he had been ordered to stay.

"Re-nea is not dead! I will not rest until Re-nea and the others are home again. Re-nea has earned that right. She is Ojibwa, just as if she were born of my mother's womb," he answered sternly.

"Nor shall I, Father!" Running Bear added.

"Then . . . my sons, you and Tall Elk must seek the vision of the Holy man. If his vision is what you seek, then I will order a coup," Gray Wolf implored. "But first, seek the truth. What you may find may change how you feel."

"To be the seeker of a dream, especially one that could determine the life or death of one's loved ones, is to be a seeker of destiny. You must cleanse yourselves with the herbs and the oils of the earth. You must first purify your mind Black Eagle . . . you Running Bear and you Tall Elk. You must purify your hearts," the shaman said as he led them into the sweat lodge.

Once inside, the trio shut the world out of their minds. Without saying a word, the shaman handed Black Eagle the pipe of dreams and directed him to smoke. He tossed water on the hot coals and created a heavy mist that filled the room. Almost immediately, Black Eagle began to feel light-headed. He inhaled the vapors from the steam and allowed the herbs to take him to his quest. He became one with the sky and with the earth. His soul was no longer his own, but was part of the universe.

Robert watched the trio attentively, but was totally bewildered with what he saw. Black Eagle appeared to be in a trance. He neither moved nor flinched when the shaman threw his spear just above his head. Then the shaman chanted, and it became louder and louder as the steam began to build up. It was so thick that Robert found it difficult to breathe. Yet, he refused to leave as long as Black Eagle remained.

In Black Eagle's mind's eye, he could see himself walking down a steep slope to the Sauk village. He passed many trees, and a gentle creek with cool water. He could feel the small rocks and pebbles beneath his feet. There was a mist that covered him as he approached a lone teepee, which was a few feet ahead. He saw himself go through the opening, where he came in contact with a large warrior. The two began to struggle, to get control over a knife that appeared from nowhere.

Black Eagle's breath became more shallow. Sweat poured from his brow and forehead. His facial expressions changed with his vision. He saw more bloodshed, but the men he saw were wearing uniforms like the one worn by the one who had come to the outpost. Then he saw his love, Re-nea. He reached out for her only to see her running for her life from the very man he had taken her from months before. What he saw made Black Eagle get to his feet. He was completely awake . . . completely aware of what he had to do. Then the shaman made him drink a bitter potion to clear his head and allow him to focus on what he had seen.

It seemed they had shared a similar experience. They all had faced the Sauks in combat, but that was where their vision parted. Running Bear saw the death of Dancing Wind. She had sacrificed herself by taking the arrows that were meant for Re-nea. It convinced him that both Dancing Wind's and René's time was short, shorter than Gray Wolf had predicted.

All three were taken to the lake, where they were stripped of all their wrappings and were bathed in the cold and still icy water. Then they were to spend the night in prayer, with no contact from their loved ones. Black Eagle sat with his legs folded and began to sing his prayers in full voice.

Running Bear began to sing his soon after, but his voice was barely audible. However, Tall Elk remained quite solemn, singing his praises with his head lowered.

Throughout the night until dawn, Robert watched his brother-in-law, waiting for the moment when they would rescue his sister. The morning veil had lifted, and the sun had reached out to warm those who greeted it. Even though Robert hadn't taken part in the ritual, he felt that he had renewed strength and could undertake any task put before him.

Gray Wolf and his council were waiting in the shaman's cabin to hear the results of his sons' and Tall Elk's visions. He knew before his sons' arrival that they were going to the enemy's camp. He also knew the only one of them would return with his wife. The shaman's prophecy was coming true and had started the moment Black Eagle entered the village with his bride. Even though she was the model daughter-in-law, she posed a threat to his people. Now he might lose his sons in the process of rescuing her.

"Before they come, I must say . . . the prophecy of the attack on our village was well-known before my sons were born. It was said that a woman . . . not of our people . . . would be a part of the destruction of our lands," he said.

Tall Elk was the first to arrive and he overheard Gray Wolf's statements. It troubled him that Black Eagle's father was so apt to believe that a mere woman would bring so much change. He quickly interrupted. "Gray Wolf, Re-nea did not harm our lands. But, a woman was the cause. Remember the woman who entered our village bleeding and claiming to have been assaulted by the Sauks? She was the cause . . . not Re-nea. My woman, Morning Star, was taken along with Re-nea and Dancing Wind. Do you blame them, too? Do you blame them for the loss of our brothers who fought so bravely to protect our storehouses of meat and grain.?"

"He speaks the truth, Gray Wolf. Black Eagle's woman did not cause this, nor did the other women. We must show the Sauks that we will not allow them to attack us so freely and then take our women without a fight," one blurted out.

There were many voices expressing their agreement. They all believed that Black Eagle and Running Bear should go after the Sauks. Many were willing to follow the brave sons of the chief, which filled Gray Wolf's heart with pride. His people were truly his people. That was all Robert had to hear, for he leaped to his feet and rushed off to tell Black Eagle what he had learned. Now it was time to plan the strategies of attack.

René and the others were roused from their sleep early that morning. Their hands were freed only to be put to work gathering wood and preparing the morning meal. The food was for the men. Even though the women had prepared it, they received nothing.

The fire had been stamped out and the bundles were given to the women to carry. They followed their captors on foot, in single file, for what seemed to be ten miles. René knew she was traveling southwest. She had passed through this portion of land once before, but that was on her journey to her new home. She planned to leave Black Eagle a trail to follow, leaving the beads from her tunic to fall in various places. She knew that the trail would guide her back to the Ojibwa village, back to Black Eagle and her brother.

Dancing Wind, as always, tired easily. She wasn't used to carrying such weight and trudging on for so many miles. René and Morning Star handled their bundles as they would have handled the weight of their children on their backs. They neither complained nor fretted about the journey. After last night, René learned not to provoke any trouble from her captors. The time would come when she would exact her revenge.

"I plan to escape, Morning Star," René whispered. "I want to know if you—"

"Yes, I want to. But this may not be the time. They are expecting us to run," Morning Star interrupted. "We must be careful not to bring attention to ourselves."

Dancing Wind began to worry. René and Morning Star were talking among themselves and didn't include her. "What are you two planning? Do not leave me behind!" Dancing Wind begged. She was very weary of the journey and sobbed aloud when they just looked in her direction. Her sobs brought unwanted attention their way.

"Shush! Keep your voice down!" René said sternly. "We don't want them to know what we are planning to do."

Without warning René was grabbed from behind by the tall one. She hadn't yet learned his name, but at this point, she was more interested in getting his hands off of her. He seemed to know when she had something on her mind and would stop at nothing to thwart her efforts. He turned her around to face him, so that he could instill more fear in her. But his glare went unnoticed.

"No talking! Say nothing to each other or I will kill you all here . . . and now!" he yelled. "Woman! You do not fear me, do you?"

René knew he was speaking to her. His face still in hers, shaking her as he made his demands known. "I don't understand what you are trying to say!" She looked at Morning Star, hoping that she could at least help at the moment.

His threats were interrupted by Pa Te' Nea, who grew tired of hearing of Osa-a's exploits. It was widely know throughout the tribe that Osa-a wanted to be chief, but he lacked the support of the young braves who wanted to see Pa Te' Nea dead. They all seemed to fear their chief rather than revere him. They thought that his spirit would haunt them if they tried to kill him or overthrow him. They wanted him to die with honor as in battle, not by their hands. Yet, the man had power. He seemed to overcome the odds when things were at their worst. Osa-a believed that, as did the others who followed him.

"You waste time with idle threats, Osa-a. You give the woman cause to hate you. If you want her to come to you, you must show some kindness. She is only a woman. She cannot think for herself. I should know . . . I have had many women warm my bed. They are all the same," he said with a wry grin on his face.

Osa-a wasn't sure whether to listen to his chief or to maintain his grip on René's arm. He enjoyed tormenting her and watching her squirm. It gave him pleasure when he humiliated her in front of his companions. It also gave him a sense of worth to have a woman cower from him, especially since the Ojibwa made them flee for their lives.

"Yes, but this one is a fighter. She will be hard to break," he answered.

"Be careful, Osa-a. She will be the death of you," Pa Te' Nea added.

"Yes! And what a way to die," Osa-a admitted. He was still holding René's arm tightly, with no regard to whether he was causing her pain.

He roughly shoved her aside only to plant a threat in her ear. There was no doubt he was a cruel man. His size overwhelmed her and made her wish that Dancing Wind had kept to the confines of the cave. The very thought of this man taking liberties with her made her skin crawl. She would rather die than allow this man to touch her. He used everything he could to intimidate her and to keep her in fear.

"You will soon come to me for pain as well as pleasure. I will not let you go! Never!" he snapped as he pushed her along.

Even though he had her in his sites, René planned her escape. She knew it wouldn't be long before he would take her to his lodge. She had to make a way back to Black Eagle and One Shoe. She could only hope that Black

Eagle would understand why she couldn't stop them from killing her babies. Throughout her musing over her husband, René had deposited a good amount of beads on the ground where she was standing. Osa-a neither looked at what she was doing, nor had he any reason to suspect that she would leave such a colorful trail behind.

The Sauks and their captives continued to walk. The women were weary of the travel, but tried not to let on. Dancing Wind had learned not to whine as she had done earlier. Her back ached, and she had blisters on the balls of her feet. René and Morning Star were ready to lie down, but refused to appear the least bit out of sorts. René never realized until now that the journey with Black eagle was far less a strain than this one.

The women noticed that the leader, Pa Te' Nea, was upset. He was looking for something that must have been hidden under the broken bushes that he fiercely tossed aside. He searched for what appeared to be an hour, but came up empty-handed. "The canoes . . . they are gone! We must plan another way back to our village," he stormed. He kicked at a mole that had poked its head out of its little hole. Then he flung his arms in all directions, hoping his hands would come in contact with someone's face. His warriors knew his temperament and beat a path away from him until he cooled off. Finally, he ordered them to get a fire going. They were many miles away from the Ojibwa settlement, and there was no way for their enemy to catch up with them now.

So, they set up a temporary camp near the lake. There was a coolness that seemed to envelope them. Since there were no blankets, they dared to pitch a fire to warm themselves. They never once considered the women and their needs. While the men prepared their food, the women huddled together hoping that one might be generous and give them something to sustain them for the night. But their vigil was all in vain.

René took this time to survey the area and sighted a small island about a mile or so into the lake. She knew that she could swim the distance if she had the strength. Some food would definitely help, but her captors weren't into sharing. She leaned back and stretched her arms out to remove the strain in her muscles. A slight yawn escaped her lips and a drowsy mist filled her eyes. She made it seem as though she was ready for sleep.

Even though darkness had engulfed them, Morning Star and Dancing Wind could see what had captured René's attention. They knew what she was planning to do and waited for her to signal them when the time was right. Morning Star had learned to swim as a child, but wasn't strong. She could make the journey, but only if she had help. However, Dancing Wind had never had the chance to learn. She was never taught something that may one day take her to freedom. That alone would prove to be a task for the other two to endure.

As René pretended to rest quietly next to Morning Star, she whispered as she directed her attention to the island, "Can you see that tiny island? I think it's about a mile or so out there. We can swim there when they have settled down for the night."

"I see it," Morning Star said with hesitation. "It is so far away. I am not a good swimmer. I can do it, but I do not think I can without help."

"It's our only hope. They won't think to look for us there . . . I am sure of it," René continued softly.

Worried that she would be left behind, Dancing Wind whined, "But what about me? I cannot swim at all. You cannot leave without me. I want to go home."

"Quiet! Do you want them to hear you?" Morning Star scolded. "We all go or not at all."

After the mess Dancing Wind had gotten the trio into, she would be the one to keep them from escaping. René had to think of another way home; that was all she could do to keep from breaking down. And so they waited, waited for the last man to put his head down and fall into a deep sleep. It seemed to take forever, but soon they were all snoring after consuming such a hearty meal.

The only sound that could be heard was the crack and spark from the fire. Each, in her own way, observed the movements of the sleeping men until they were sure that it was safe to depart. The women slowly crawled away from the center of the camp, where they had been placed for safekeeping. Thank God Osa-a had forgotten to tie them up before he had turned in for the night. As they reached the man-made barrier, a small branch snapped under René's knee. She held her breath and prayed that the sound wouldn't awaken the warrior who was resting in her path. He only turned over and continued the slumber that was momentarily interrupted.

Without a sound, the trio continued to crawl out of the camp. They kept themselves low and well-hidden in the underbrush. They crawled then turned into a run when they had surmised that they had put a good distance between them and their captors. They could see the water glistening through the darkness, and that gave them a sense of peace. They were closer to freedom . . . to home!

René reached the water first and quickly removed her leggings and moccasins. Morning Star and Dancing Wind did the same. Each treaded deeply into the water until it had reached their necks. René came upon a log that was drifting by. God had answered her prayers. It was just what she needed to keep Dancing Wind afloat. She and Morning Star then used the support of the log and swam toward the island.

"Dancing Wind," René whispered softly, "lean up against this log and hold on. Morning Star and I will help you stay afloat." She place Dancing Wind's hands on the log and continued to show her what to do. "You must move your legs so that the log will move," she continued while periodically looking over her shoulder.

"I will do as you say, but . . . I am very frightened," she answered quickly.

"I am, too, Dancing Wind. But we must move now or they will find us," Morning Star interrupted. She had just looked over her shoulder and had seen a man's figure under the tree. He had to be at least fifty paces or less away from the shore and was closing in on them fast. "Someone comes, Re-nea! Someone comes! Push . . . hard!" Morning Star exclaimed. She felt the wall of terror closing in around her

She wasn't alone; fear swept through the trio as the figure entered the water and swam toward them. They had a good start, so the distance between them and their unknown pursuer was too great for him to catch up. Their attention was taken away from their destination, where they found themselves floating away from the path to the island. The undercurrent had caught them and had swept them deeper into the lake.

Even though René was frightened, she wanted to maintain a calm outlook. There was certainly nothing simple about the new danger they were all facing. Yet, it was better than having to deal with the prospects of being raped or killed by the Sauks. "Don't give up! Swim . . . swim for that island. We are three on a log. He is one. He has no support. Now . . . swim!" she implored.

At that moment it seemed Dancing Wind had come alive. She began to move her legs like flippers and helped to get the log moving in the direction of the island. It took nearly an hour to get to that rocky mass that would be their temporary hideaway. René glanced around several times trying to locate the one who followed, but saw no one. She sighed with relief and thanked her maker for giving her the strength not to retreat.

When they reached the tiny shoreline, they found a dugout canoe washed up on the beach. It must have belonged to the Sauks, because they seemed to be looking for something earlier. Apparently this was what the leader was looking for when they arrived. The canoe was laden with two paddles, a blanket, and a knife—everything they needed to survive. But they had put all their energy into swimming to this point and were extremely tired. As much as they wanted to get underway they wouldn't make it in their present condition.

René took one last look, peering over the large rocks back toward the main shore, and then checked the water for any movement. A sigh of relief escaped her lips as she noted the area was free and clear of any danger. "He isn't on the shore or in the water," she offered slowly. "He may have been carried away by the current. If he did, they will be looking for him come morning. We must leave before that. At least we will get a head start."

"But . . . we cannot be sure that he did not make it back to the shore," Morning Star stated quickly.

"I know. We will just have to take our chances that he didn't. And besides, if he had made it back, don't you think those brutes would be on the shore with torches in hand and ready to swim this way? Now . . . we need to get some rest before we get on our way."

"I will keep watch," Dancing Wind offered. She seemed very eager to help now that she was on her way home.

"Good! We will rest for only a short while. We cannot afford to be caught now that we have dared to escape. They will surely be angry on the morrow when they find us gone. If they catch us, they will kill us!" Morning Star quickly put in. She felt that would convince Dancing Wind to stay on her toes.

René agreed, pointing out the advantages of traveling by night. "What they can't see, they can't track. We must use the darkness as our blanket," she added, thinking of how Robert led them away from the Estates during the night without being seen. "Yes . . . we will travel only at night and will rest during the day in the rushes along the shoreline. It will be hard on us. There may be times when you will want to give up . . . but don't!" René demanded. She wanted to get back to the place where she felt like she belonged: home.

Dancing Wind and Morning Star knew that René was right about the dangers they were facing. They had come this far together; it would be fitting that they returned home together as well. Then René and Morning Star slipped into a semirestful sleep. For the first time in the three days since their capture, sleep came somewhat easier to them.

CHAPTER

SIXTEEN

THE DAWN WAS THE most magnificent sight ever to behold. The sun just reached out and put a golden glow on the shimmering lake. Even the shoreline of the tiny island was touched by its warmth. The flowers opened their petals to receive the gift of life, and the small woodland creatures scampered into their burrows after a night of hunting and playing. Even the sparrows took time to bask in the sunlight and sing a merry tune in thanks. The air was sweet, as though it had been scented with jasmine and hyacinth. These were the many things that had awakened René from her much-needed slumber.

René felt the warm rays of the sun and embraced them. Then she realized that they had slept too long. "Oh, my God! It's morning! We should have left hours ago!" she exclaimed.

Dancing Wind had fallen asleep, and now they were trapped on the island until dark. Then René heard a commotion on the mainland. Apparently the Sauks were very aware that their prisoners had escaped. The trio could hear them as the leader yelled at his braves for their stupidity. His voice seemed close, even though a body of water separated them. Nervously, René took a chance to peek over the large rock mass again. She saw Osa-a running toward a body that lay face down near the shore. From his size alone, René could tell that he was one of the younger braves. Whoever he was, he tried to follow them and didn't make it to the small island where they were resting. The same undercurrent that had caught René and her friends must have pulled him under. She watched as they lifted his body from the water and took him to dry ground. They took such care to check to see if he was still breathing. But the leader, Pa Te', Nea just shook his head. The young boy was dead.

The Sauks were angry now, especially Osa-a. His prize was nowhere in sight. It was as if the earth had just swallowed her up. A moccasin floated toward the shoreline, right in his direction. It was René's, and he yelled at the top of his lungs in fury. Never in his life had he possessed a woman as lovely as she. It was the ultimate insult to his character that she was able to slip from his fingers. Then his mind reeled. He remembered that the women's bonds weren't replaced when they arrived at the camp. He refused to let Pa Te' Nea know that he had failed to tie them up the night before. He would never hear the end of it.

Osa-a had followed the women's trail all the way to the shore. He checked the bushes and then followed the shoreline both north and south. René could see the frustration and anger building in him. Moving from the island at this point would put them all in jeopardy. René eased back down the rock to where Morning Star was waiting to help her. Once down, she looked back, grateful for its size. The large rock served to protect them from the probing eyes of the ones who were searching for them.

"They are everywhere, Morning Star. We can't leave until nightfall. If we leave now, they will surely catch us," René said as she tried to repair her tunic. It was impossible to fix with the threads fraying, but she tried anyway.

Morning Star could see where René's concerns were aimed. There were no words to soothe away the damage that had already been done. She knew that her friend had great pride, but was a very gentle woman as well. She saw a new side to her friend every day. Now that they had taken this step together, it was more and more apparent that she had become a true sister in every sense of the word. She was Ojibwa.

"How long will they look for us?" Morning Star asked. She was hoping that René had the answers, but she realized later that the only one who could answer that question was her captor.

"They will look . . . I guess . . . until they get tired. We can't leave now. They are sure to see us if we try. Even we can't stay in the water forever. We must have food and water. We can't last like this for much longer," René continued.

"We should have been on our way a long time ago. I wish . . . I wish

Dancing Wind would . . . oh, I wish," Morning Star said as she fumbled with her words. She was angry and hungry. There always seemed to be an obstacle in the way at every turn, and Dancing Wind was an obstacle for sure.

René understood more than Morning Star knew. She tried hard not to hate the woman who had caused their capture. It was difficult for René not to snap at her whenever the woman began to whine or complain. "I know how you feel, Morning Star. But it's too late. We are here and we are safe for the moment. That is all that matters right now," she said as she looked at Dancing Wind. "Dancing Wind will have to face her own weaknesses. But for now, her problems are our problems. We can't leave her behind. She isn't strong enough to protect herself alone, but with us, she . . . we have a chance to get home," René finally stated. It was her way of convincing herself that Dancing Wind was worth the risk. However, she also made sense. There was no doubt that the young woman, although scared and hungry, had a level head. Even if they died in the process of trying to get home, it was her strength that made it possible to take a chance.

Morning Star's belly made hungry noises, but she refused to let it weaken her desire to get home. René went back to sleep so that she could ignore her hunger pangs. Dancing Wind was already taking advantage of the extra rest. It was her way of avoiding the angry looks from her companions, especially after she overheard them talking.

Nightfall came very slowly for the trio. They had awakened hours before the sun went down, and they could still hear the voices of the men on the shore. They hadn't given up on their search for the women. One of the braves found a canoe and was bringing it back to shore where the men were located. René watched as Osa-a entered the canoe. At first it seemed that he was heading toward the island. Instead, he pointed the craft in a southern direction, away from them.

René practically jumped from her perch and landed on her feet. Her heart was beating wildly. "They have a canoe! I think they are going to get the others. We must leave!" she said as the bile began to rise in her throat.

"We will wait. He is sure to see us if we leave now. Wait till he passes that bend over there," Morning Star said while pointing. Her nerves were on edge as she watched him round the bend. As he disappeared from sight, she said, "Wake Dancing Wind!"

The women rushed to the canoe and set off into the semidarkness. They headed east first, keeping the island as cover. They managed to maintain good balance and speed for several hours before they sighted a campfire, which acted as a beacon bringing them to shore. Their arms ached from paddling the canoe without stopping. The fire was set in a secluded area, where the trees arched over it like a canopy against the night's sky. The closer they came to the shore, the more inviting the fire became. Each could smell the fresh deer meat and corn cakes cooking over the flames. But no movement could be detected by the fire.

What they didn't know was that the campsite was a trap and that they were about to be snared. As if tied by a baited hook, Dancing Wind leaped from the canoe and ran into the center of the camp. She quickly devoured the simmering meats and corn cakes. She had filled her mouth to capacity when she realized that René and Morning Star hadn't joined her yet. They were still in the canoe waiting for the first sign of danger.

"It does not feel right. Someone is here, but they hide from us, Re-nea. I can feel it," Morning Star whispered.

"I know. I can feel it, too, and Dancing Wind has made our presence known. I fear it is too late for us to make another escape," René added as she surveyed the area.

It was Osa-a's plan to bring the women back at all costs. They were only moments away from being captured themselves. Black Eagle and his party were very close, so close that Osa-a felt his hair rise from his scalp.

René felt uneasy about landing in this spot. It seemed all too convenient. The silence bothered her. The fire with no one around it was inviting, but that dreaded knot of fear in the pit of her stomach was ever so apparent. Since René was in front of the canoe, it was only practical that she be the one to bring Dancing Wind back. Reluctantly, she slipped from the canoe, taking great care not to create much noise. She walked slowly to the center of the camp where Dancing Wind was located. She, too, realized that she had endangered them once again. Out of the corner of her eye, René saw a shadow closing in on them. She grabbed Dancing Wind and turned to run, but a familiar hand had seized her. She had been thrust to the ground with extreme force. Dancing Wind panicked and started to run toward the canoe, and René quickly got to her feet and tried to follow. René fell to her knees after losing her footing, just as an arrow whizzed over her, hitting Dancing Wind in the back.

When René finally got the dirt out of her eyes, she took in the full view of the man she had come to hate. Osa-a grinned. He was happy to have outwitted such a rebellious young woman. She challenged his very fiber and forced him to come back to the land of the Ojibwa. She was someone to reckon with, someone who commanded his full attention.

"Do not move . . . little fox. You thought you could outsmart me!" he said as he fingered the small whip at his waist. It had at least four or five thin talons, each of which was knotted at the ends. He let it dangle over her head as he walked around her to show his power.

In the next instant, which she would never forget as long as she lived, he snatched her up from the ground and carted her off, away from the camp and away from Morning Star. He passed through many trees and found a place that he felt offered him the privacy he needed with his prize. He threw her to the ground like a rag doll, and René screamed from the force and pain. Her back ached, and her right arm was bruised to the wrist. He completely destroyed her tunic, tearing it to shreds. He used it to bound and gag her so that her screams would go unheard.

He quickly hung her by her bonds from a large branch that was draped overhead. She was totally at his mercy. He smiled as he cut away her skirt and exposed the parts he had been denied when she ran away. He was pleased with his catch and had no interest in sharing his bounty with anyone. He inhaled her fragrance, teasing his nostrils and making her uncomfortable. He walked around her to take in the view from every angle. With his whip, he stroked her breasts and abdomen. He marveled at the way she reacted to him. He knew she hated him, and that fed his mistreatment of her.

"You will enjoy this night of pain . . . and of pleasure. I will show you what kind of man I am," he said brutishly. Osa-a knew she didn't understand him, but she would understand his manner.

He took one of her breasts between his teeth and pulled on the nipple until it snapped back. The jolt angered René, and she instinctively kicked. Her foot connected with his groin, and he fell to the ground in pain. He wasn't sure which part to grab first, his ears or his groin. While he lay on the ground moaning, René struggled to free herself, but her bonds were too tight. She heard him grabble for control over his breathing. He moaned again in agony and then staggered over to the tree for more support

When he felt secure, he again approached his lady fair. This time he tied her feet together. He used the root of the tree as an anchor to keep her from moving. Then he picked up his whip again and slowly extended his arm. He attacked her buttocks, her legs, and her breasts over and over again. If she could have screamed, it would have awakened the dead. Tears streamed down her face. Her body was racked with pain from the intensity of his blows. She fainted into a void, a place he couldn't reach.

After he had taken his anger to such a ruthless extent, he wondered whether he had killed the fair beauty. He slowly removed the gag from her mouth to see if she was still breathing. Osa-a then cut her limp body from the tree. His breathing was still quite hard and ragged. He could hardly catch his breath after inflicting such fury on the girl. Finally, he removed the leather strappings from around her legs and gently touched her face and hands. He let his fingers roam where she wouldn't let him before. He took her tender breasts into his mouth and gently sucked on them one by one. His body quaked with delight as René's breasts yielded their sweet nectar. He wanted her to respond to his touch, but she neither moved nor spoke. He had tormented this beauty, only to regret it.

Hours must have passed, because daylight was illuminating the entire field. Osa-a had awakened to find himself wrapped around the woman he had abused the night before. His lips were still holding one breast and his hand kneading the other. René's eyes were opened, but the light was gone from them. She didn't say a word. What could she say? Who would listen? And there were no signs that she enjoyed his touch, which angered Osa-a even more.

"You are my woman!" Osa-a exclaimed, forcing her to look at him. He took her into his arms and held her tight. Then he pried her legs apart with his. His weight was more than she could take, but he pressed on. René couldn't breath at all, and he in his own way wasn't concerned with her discomfort. He was more concerned with his own pleasure. He wrestled with his loincloth and snatched it off. She could feel his manhood on her thighs. Her eyes widened as he entered her canal with such force that she screamed in despair.

"No! No! You brute!" she spat. "Noooo! I would rather die," she screamed. She never imagined having another man inside her. "Black Eagle HELP ME!"

"You . . . will . . . please me. I . . . will please you," he panted.

He took her nipples between his teeth and held them tight. He pulled and squeezed on them as much as her flesh would permit. He wanted her to affirm that his lovemaking was great, but she said nothing to gratify him. He tightened his lips and bit into her nipples again. The sensation made René arch her back. She couldn't tell which pain was worse, and when her head began to spin with indecision, Osa-a's body became limp. He had spent all his energy, but refused to release her.

In another section of the wood, Morning Star was enduring the same treatment. Her cries were the echo of René's. It seemed they were both tormented by the same thought. They knew that the life they shared with their husbands would be forever changed. Everyone would know that they had been raped. They might become with children. And worse than that, their husbands wouldn't want them or the child. These thoughts and others were passing through their minds, and a cry of despair escaped from their lips. That pain was the greatest of all.

Since Black Eagle's party was only a few miles away, it was necessary to put as much distance between them as possible. Osa-a and Pa Te' Nea rushed the women into separate canoes. René and Morning Star weren't extended the courtesy of being allowed to dress themselves.

"You will not go far without your clothing," Osa-a said with pleasure. He rubbed his hands over René's shoulders where a few scars from the whip had developed. She flinched at his touch and gave him a glare of dissatisfaction. "You will learn that what I say is law. You will learn, my little fox. And when you bear my children, they, too, will know," he continued.

René hoped that he would choke to death on his own words. She had learned some of his words and was beginning to understand them. Yet, her learning his language wasn't attributed to the type of schooling she was used to. He had killed her children with no regard for their lives. Now he expected her to have his sickening brats.

They set off again for the Sauks' homeland stopping only to fish and hunt. They traveled day and night until they finally came upon a small secluded village near the lake itself. There was a lovely little stream that passed through the center of the village. There were women, old and young, repairing the hides on their teepees. Some were preparing their evening meals, while others were feeding their young. Apparently, they had all the comforts necessary to maintain and dwell on this land. But they were use to taking what they wanted from other tribes. They would never spend time tilling the rich soil beneath them.

The women dropped everything to greet their chief and warriors. It had been nearly three weeks since they had been with their husbands and sons, the few who had them. Now they were home. Tired, hungry, and anxious to tell the stories of their exploits. But the women were more interested in their naked captives. One pointed at René and laughed. The others talked among themselves, waiting to see which brave would claim her.

Osa-a was greeted by a young woman who appeared to be the same age as René. She used her hands to speak in sign while she told him about his mother. He thanked her and swiftly ran toward the teepee directly ahead. The teepee was covered with wolf and deer hides and there was a small fire burning in front, with a small portion of deer meat cooking on a stick. On the side of the teepee were two poles, both of which had been pounded into the earth. They appeared to be a makeshift hitching post for horses. But the only animals in the camp were dogs. Some were tied to their poles, others ran free.

Osa-a returned shortly thereafter and escorted her to a teepee located just opposite the one he had entered. From the outside the shelter appeared small, but once inside, René saw an amazing amount of space. It wasn't as roomy as her home, but it was adequate. It also appeared that he held as much pride in his weaponry as Black Eagle. He kept his quiver of arrows and his bow near the entrance. His spear and tomahawk were always at his side.

Without saying a word he put a robe around René's shoulders. It was the first sign of kindness that he had shown since the trip to his village. René, however, still felt the humiliation of having been raped and the rage of having her children murdered. She in no way planned to soften in her manner toward him. She felt lost to Black Eagle. She had no way of knowing that he was coming for her. All she could do was pray for deliverance or death.

"My mother will come to help you care for your wounds. She is good with herbs and plants. She will make your scars go away," he said gently in the language she had spent many days trying to learn.

And still, René was unmoved by his thoughtful attention. She wouldn't have needed his mother's help if he had kept his hands to himself. Of all the places in the world, she had to wind up with another version of James Courtland. They were of different worlds, yet the way they treated women was uncannily similar.

It wasn't easy for René to relax around him, with his behavior being so inconsistent and erratic. One minute he was cruel and aggressive, in the next he was calm and giving. She didn't know what to expect from one moment to the next. He made a complete pest of himself and talked to her as though she had been a part of his life. He made advances, which made René cringe and shy away. He offered her food, which she refused. Then he gave her his oversized tunic to wear, but found it carefully folded on the mat. He presented her with many beads and charms, things he thought she would like, but René pushed them all away.

Osa-a's temper began to flare up. He paced the floor, periodically taking time to stop to look at her. Her manner was unchanged, and her contempt for him was more than apparent. And he didn't like it. She wasn't pleased with him or with her new surroundings. Since there was a slight language barrier, he knew he would be unable to convince her that he wanted her. Although he had no plans of making her his wife, he considered the prospects of what might come later. Right now, he was more interested in possessing the lovely creature who sat only inches away from him.

Like a lovesick boy, Osa-a tried another ploy, hoping to get René to drop her guard. He stroked her hair gently and loosened the thick braid that held her curls together. But René was true to her commitment to Black Eagle. She would never allow it to be said that she was overtaken by his charms. As far as she was concerned, the man was sorely lacking in everything but brutality. With Dancing Wind's death on her mind, it was another means for her to want this man out of her life.

"You are a hard woman to please," he said in frustration. "You will learn in time to accept what has happened. No one will come for you. On one would dare take you away from me. I will soon be chief and leader of my people. I am a great man . . . a great hunter. You will see this," he admonished.

It appeared he was spellbound by his own sense of being. There was no place in his world for a woman. He proclaimed himself to be greater than his chief. He had no concept of what it really meant to be a thoughtful human being. He killed helpless children and old women, then he expected René to feel admiration for it. Without a doubt, he was sickening and she could find no words to further express her dislike for the man.

"You think I am an animal? I am so displeasing to you? Then maybe you would rather sleep outside . . . with the real animals! They will keep you company. Until I hear from from your own lips that you will come to me, they will be your company!" he stormed.

René was somewhat in the dark about what he was trying to say to her. She recognized only a few words he had spoken. Yet, from the force of the way he spoke, René didn't react. At least not until he yanked her up from the floor and dragged her outside. Once there, he tied her to one of the poles. He waited for her to beg . . . to plead with him, but René refused to give him the satisfaction. If he wanted to be master of someone, it wouldn't be her. When he realized that she wouldn't commit to him, he stormed into his teepee.

Within minutes after Osa-a's unfriendly departure, she was surrounded by yapping puppies and several grown female dogs. One growled, showing all of her sharp teeth, and another licked her hand. At first René thought they were about to tear her to shreds, but they put their heads on her lap and went to sleep.

Osa-a thought that she had learned her lesson and would act more compliant toward him after spending several hours outside. He felt she had enough time to change her mind and would beg to be released from her bonds. She would take anything he had to offer, so he thought. With confidence he walked outside to release her from the pole, but when he arrived he found René resting quietly, totally oblivious to his presence. He thought he might find her shivering from the cold of the night, but instead, the dogs served as a blanket against the night air.

Pa Te' Nea laughed, saying, "She is a smart woman. The dogs treat her better than you do."

Pa Te' Nea had just left Morning Star. It was apparent to all that his woman was just as unyielding as Osa-a's. The condition of his face was evident of the fact. He had received deep scars on his neck and face, where she in turn had been beaten for her misdeeds until she collapsed.

"I have a wildcat and you have a demon. We should have let them escape," Pa Te' Nea said as he wiped his face. The open sores burned as the sweat dripped from his forehead.

Osa-a wasn't pleased with that prospect. He wanted an obedient woman, one who would rush to do his every bidding. "I will tame her," he bragged. "She is strong, but I am stronger." He wanted to believe his own words as he threw his head back in an abrupt manner. He finally untied René very hastily. The less he had to deal with Pa Te' Nea and his remarks, the better. Then he pushed René into the teepee. He had had enough of her antics as well. She would suffer greatly as long as she fought him. Once he had her alone, he said lightly as he brushed by her, "You have had a taste of what can happen to you if you do not obey me."

Again René sat quietly. She couldn't speak his language and wasn't making any effort to try. She had been forced to do unthinkable things. She had witnessed death from both of her worlds and had even endured his fury. Her strength and fortitude were the only things that were keeping her sane. She managed to focus her attention on her husband, her brother, and the life she had learned to love with all of its simplicities. She missed making Black Eagle's morning breakfast and she missed talking to him about his adventures.

Osa-a interrupted her musings and pointed to a place where she could lay her head. René waited for him to leave, but he made himself comfortable on the floor next to her. He appeared to be quite content with the present state of things, but she wanted privacy and rest. To sleep alone, unscathed, was all she desired.

There was a pile of plush bearskins on the floor; apparently it was his sleeping place. There wasn't another place made up like it, and it looked like they were going to have to share the accommodations. He smiled as though he had won the first battle, but René snatched one of the skins and made a bed for herself on the far side of the teepee. She would have to deal with the lumps and bumps that hadn't been smoothed out. She would rather face the bear that had once owned the robe she had wrapped herself in than be pushed into sleeping another night with him.

René turned her back to him, a sure signal that she wanted to be alone. She waited patiently, hoping that the hint was well-taken. It seemed an hour, maybe two hours, had passed when she finally closed her eyes. Although painful, it was the first bit of rest she'd had since the nightmare had begun.

The following morning Osa-a had gone into council with his chief. It was his duty to prepare for a retaliatory attack on the village, just in case the Ojibwa planned a coup. They were under the impression that the women were quite valuable and were of great importance to them. They would bargain, trade for horses and guns. They had no defenses when the guns were fired upon them. They were forced to run. They left without the food cache and the many skins that were known to be in the settlement. So prepare they must.

René finally had awakened the stares of an old woman with straight silver-gray hair and a tiny, wrinkly face. She appeared to be about fifty or sixty years old, from what René surmised. Yet, she was a strong old woman, who quickly helped René to her feet. Without asking she started pulling on the robe that René had securely wrapped around her. And René was forced to grapple for the cover, trying to keep everything she owned under cover. The woman was persistent. She made René sit down and quickly opened the top portion of the robe to expose the damage. The bruises had blackened, and there were bite marks on René's breasts. The old woman shook her head and mumbled something that René understood.

"Do you speak Ojibwa? Are you one of the clan?" René asked, hoping not to betray herself.

The old woman nodded. It had been a long time since she had spoken the language of her people. She thought that she would never see the day when she would be able to talk to or touch a member of her tribe. Although René wasn't a member, she spoke the language as though she were born to it. It was pleasing to her ears . . . the sound of home . . . the land of peaceful people, where rice fields were plenty and the game was overflowing.

"ekwane? oteson wa po wya n. a ni ss ka -esiwe pesiyan?" she said quietly. ("Cover yourself with the blanket, my child. What has happened to you?") she asked as she examined René's wounds.

In her own way she already knew that the poor child had been brutally raped by her son. She had hoped that he wouldn't treat a woman with such cruelty and disrespect. It gave her no comfort to know that her own son was no better than the men who had stolen her away from her home. She remembered that day all too well. She saw herself nearly nearly thirty years ago, taking care of her little brother, while her parents traded with the white trappers in the area. The man who had stolen her away and later taken her for his wife was the leader until his untimely death. he wasn't a cruel man, but he never believed in trading for something unless he could take everything he wanted without giving anything. It seemed all the women in the village belonged to other tribes, Sioux, Miami, Cree, and Fox; all stolen one way or another.

"What are you called?" René asked carefully. "Can I trust you, or are you here to get information for your son?" She eyed the old woman with caution. The slightest twitch would indicate that that old woman was a plant, a means of getting René to expose herself and maybe her plans to escape.

"I was called Wondering Flower many, many years ago. But after I was taken from my family, I was called Jaewa. I have not said my true name in many years. You are from my home. I have always wanted to see my homeland and my people again before I die," she continued calmly.

How ironic that this woman had also been whisked away from her family without a trace. She could be Gray Wolf's long-lost relative or even . . "Yes, I am from your homeland, but I am not Ojibwa . . . at least not by birth. I am"—René hesitated for a moment, then continued as the old woman placed her wrinkled hand in hers—"I am the wife of Black Eagle. He is the son of Gray Wolf, chief of the Ojibwa clan." She hoped that at least one of the names might be familiar to the old woman, but she seemed to be at a loss.

"My son has taken the wife of one who will one day be chief. That is not good. That is not good at all," she responded quickly, and then glanced over her shoulder. "Then your husband will surely come for you. Does my son know of this?" she asked suddenly.

"No! I cannot speak his language. It is so different from Ojibwa," René offered. She was skeptical to offer any more information than she already had. She had to be sure that the old woman wasn't spying on her.

The woman didn't run. She stayed in the teepee and dressed René's wounds, taking great care not to cause her any more pain. Then she gave René an herbal tea that was bitter. René frowned as the woman pushed her into finishing the last of it. She told René that the tea would help her sleep and would soothe away the pain of the bruises on her body. She then promised to look in on Morning Star as soon as she was permitted by the chief.

René didn't hear Jaewa leave the teepee. She was floating into a sea of bliss and no longer felt the pain of her wounds. She was so relaxed, her mind wandered to the last time she had spent with her father. She remembered his eyes and how they had brightened up when she would come near. It all seemed so real. She saw her mother, Rachel, and in the shadows stood another woman, her face hidden by the shade of a tree. The harder she tried to see, the farther away the woman became. She never felt more alone. Suddenly, she felt as though Black Eagle had abandoned her. her brother had probably given her up for lost again. And the people she had learned to love would probably be glad that she was no longer there.

René slept the entire day away and continued through the night. She had no contact with Osa-a at all. His mother had seen to that. She was convinced that he would do the young woman more harm if he found out about her husband. The less he knew, the better it would be for René.

Osa-a entered the teepee in a huff. He was excited and seemed eager to share his news. But when he saw that his mother hadn't left, his shoulders drooped and his head dropped like a scolded child. She could see that he was disappointed with her presence. Yet, she wasn't concerned about his ego or his wants.

"You have news, my son?" she asked and pretended to be interested.

Not wanting to show his ill will, he answered quickly, "Yes, I have news, but I must tell the woman!"

"It is strange, my son, that woman has been with you for five days and you do not know her name," she said coolly. "How is that, Osa-a?"

He wasn't sure how to answer Jaewa. Yet he wondered why the woman wasn't awake. She was sleeping when he came home earlier. "What is wrong with her? She cannot sleep forever," he said as he touched René, hoping she would look in his direction.

"She has a fever. Her wounds are festering. She needs rest, not more torment. How could you do such a thing to her?" Jaewa asked, nearly raising her voice.

"It does not concern you, Mother. She must learn that I am to be obeyed. She refused me! I punished her!" he lamented.

Jaewa knew that he wouldn't be fooled by her mettling much longer. She had to convince him to treat this woman with some kindness. At least allow her to get better. She would have to make him understand without telling him everything, especially since she learned of his treachery. Since the day he was born, there would always trouble where he was concerned. He was never a good child. He stole from the other boys and, when caught in the act, he would run away. He always wanted to get his way. He never shared, not his food, or his teepee when others were in need. He was like his father in that respect.

"Osa-a, she will die if you continue to treat her in that manner. Look at her!

"Do you think she can stand another beating?" she asked finally.

He was forced to look, but was unsympathetic to his mother's pleas. He wanted power over René. He wanted her to submit to him. If he could prove to his people, through her, that he was all powerful, they might want him as their chief. It was his dream to one day be the most important man in the village. He was strong. He was a great warrior. He provided food for the people when he desired to do so.

"She is too strong to die! I will have her when I am ready. I am ready now! Wake her! Wake her and leave! She has had enough rest!" he demanded.

Frightened of what her son was capable of doing, she did as she was ordered. It saddened her to think that she had given birth to such a monster. His heart was as black as a starless sky . . . devoid of any feeling. He felt no sympathy, no warmth, and no love. She turned to the sleeping woman, and gave her a gentle shake. She watched René stir from one side to the other. Her fever hadn't broken, and a yellowish-white film oozed from one of the open sores on her shoulder, to which Jaewa quickly applied a poultice. Then, giving her motherly touch a final impact, she covered René with another blanket.

"As you can see, my son, she is no good to you as long as she is like this. She cannot run. She is too weak to do anything that might spoil your plans for her. Let me . . . let me help her, Osa-a," she implored. "Allow her to get well, then you can talk to her."

It didn't matter. The woman had spurned him and she had insulted him by running away. It was more than he was willing to put up with. No woman, not even the women in his village, had treated him with such contempt. She was the only thing in his sight that he hadn't fully possessed. "Ha! I do not care if she is ill. She will not fight me as long as she is like that," he said angrily.

Jaewa was at her wit's end and powerless to protect René from his wrath. "I see I have a son whose heart is evil. You are a cruel man," Jaewa admonished. She had hoped she could prevent this act of force. Her son seemed compelled to violate a defenseless woman, and she prayed that someone would have the decency to stop him.

Jaewa left her son's home in the same manners he had entered. Each step she took made her sick. She looked back hoping Osa-a would change his mind. He was definitely his father's son. Jaewa remembered the nightmare of the night that Osa-a was conceived. Chills ran down her spine as she recalled the laughter of the village women as she begged to be saved. That vision was forever etched in her memory.

"Osa-a must be stopped! That poor girl . . . " she said as she made an about-face and returned to her son's home.

She had only taken a few steps when she heard something or someone stirring in the shadows. The sound of a branch snapping in two and seeing shadows move toward her made her heart lurch. But she passed that off as her imagination. She called to her son, but he only ordered her to go away. She pleaded with him to allow the young woman time to heal, but her pleas fell on deaf ears. She could hear the young woman beg him to leave her alone, and her pleas were also ignored. Jaewa regretted not having been more helpful to the girl.

"Osa-a! Osa-a!" she cried out. "You must not! She will die!" she yelled into his teepee. It didn't matter that he would be angry with her, as long as his anger wasn't directed toward that poor child. It saddened her to know that her son didn't feel the same way.

Osa-a grew tired of his mother's crazed behavior and rushed out in a complete rage. No one in their right mind would be standing on the other side of the door when it opened, but Jaewa was. It was her way of getting her son to come to his senses. He felt that he was being deprived of his only chance of proving his manliness. He wanted Jaewa to go home, to leave him to his pleasure. However, Jaewa was unwilling to budge and she stood her ground with him.

"Mother! You are crazy to be out here! Go home now!" he ordered. "She deserves everything I give her. She thinks she is too good for me, but I know better. She will live to please me!" he finished.

CHAPTER
SEVENTEEN

OSA-A'S VOICE CARRIED HIS message loud and clear to the ears of those lurking in the shadows. One in particular understood very well what he was planning. His eyes narrowed as he observed the man who was only a few feet away. He brandished a club in his right hand and a rifle in his left. He slipped closer to his prey, making sure the light of the fire didn't expose his presence. He signaled the others to surround the camp from the left, while his group advanced from the right. Each step they took was as silent as the night was young. No one seemed to be aware of their presence, except for the old woman arguing with her son. She seemed to draw all of her son's attention away from his quest and to center his aggression on her.

Black Eagle slipped behind the teepee from which the bold one had come. He used his knife to cut a rear entrance and surveyed the small area. He entered, only to find René completely naked and huddled in a ball. There was no doubt she had suffered at the Sauk warrior's hands. Black Eagle quietly eased next to her and gently touched her, hoping that would spark some memory in her. She reacted only in terror. It hurt him tremendously to see her like this, but he had to cover her mouth to muffle her screams. He then whispered her name in her ear, over and over until she calmed down. Her eyes were wide and full of anguish and shame. She had hoped for so long that he would come, she even prayed. It was hard to imagine that she was actually touching her husband's face.

As though in a daze, she closed her eyes and then forced them open again. But the vision of Black Eagle was clear and solid. "Oh! Black Eagle! Is . . . is it really you?" René gasped. She could barely hold her head upright, as she was still feeling light-headed and drowsy.

Black Eagle had just taken in the full view of his wife's condition. Anger ignited shear hatred, and it burned his heart. He couldn't believe a man would terrorize a woman to the brink of submission. The man who did this must die. He held René close, wanting to wipe away her pain and suffering in a single instant. "Yes, I have come for you, my love," he said tenderly. He could barely keep his mind on the task ahead of him. René was alive, but was she . . . would she . . . ever be the same woman . . . loving and in love with him? Then he whispered in her ear, "I will take you away from here . . . now!"

Black Eagle could hear the pain in his own voice. The last thing he needed was to show any weakness, especially since they were still in the enemy camp. He quickly wrapped a blanket around her and started to lift her from the floor when Osa-a entered. He was startled for a moment, but pulled his knife ready for battle. He tossed it from hand to hand and grinned with delight.

"So . . . you have come to take my woman! She is mine!" he yelled.

"What makes you think she is yours?" Black Eagle asked sarcastically.

"Ha! And will you want her after I have had her in my bed? Will you want her?" Osa-a asked sneeringly. It was his plan to make his opponent crumble.

But Osa-a's tactics weren't working. At least, Black Eagle didn't let him know that he had injured his heart. He felt the pain, thinking that he had come too late to protect her and now their love was tainted by another. Calmly, he placed René on the floor, but urged her to move out of danger's way, since he had to fight to keep her.

He never let his eyes wander from his adversary, not even to find René once she moved out of his sight. As expected, Osa-a lunged at him and the fight began. They kicked over a pot and then fell onto the pelts piled behind them. Osa-a. Black Eagle pinned Osa-a to the floor and tussled over the knife he was wielding. Blinded by his own sweat, Osa-a swung furiously in all directions, hoping to connect with flesh, but missed every time. Osa-a lost his footing and tripped over his own pelts. His head collided with one of the clay pots and shattered it to pieces.

That sound brought Jaewa back into the teepee. She saw what she wanted to see. Osa-a thought that she was there to support him, but because of his impudence and gall with her moments before, she moved to the aid of the woman. He called to her, but she totally ignored him, leaving him to face the man he had robbed of a wife and family. His hostage was slipping safely away from him, and his mother helped the enemy. He became even more enraged with everyone in his sight.

"If I cannot have her, she will die!" he snapped as he rushed over to stop his mother and René from departing.

But Black Eagle tripped him again, Osa-ato drop the knife. Black Eagle then gained the upper hand and ordered the woman to leave. It was better for them not to remain behind, for a killing was about to commence. "Now we will see who lives and who dies. You will never live to harm my wife again. That, I promise you," Black Eagle stated.

Osa-a nervously scrambled for another weapon and found one by the pelts. This time he planned to plunge his knife into Black Eagle's ribs. He held it firmly in the palm of his hand. Again, sweat poured from his forehead, stinging his eyes and blurring his vision. Then he noticed that the other door to his home was blocked by another warrior, who entered as the women left. He was there to make sure the fight was a fair one. Osa-a never counted on that. He hoped that the people outside heard his calls, but no one cared. No one was listening, for he had cried wolf once too often.

Now both men were brandishing a knife. Each had strength on his side. And each had something to gain if they won. They collided like two charging rams. The impact made both men inhale in a rush. Osa-a tried to push his knife into any open space he could find, but Black Eagle held the knife at bay. And he, in turn, wrestled the man to the floor. Both had the same thought on their minds . . . the woman. One was willing to bring down heaven on earth to protect his love, while the other just wanted to possess her.

"You are a clumsy man. You cannot fight me falling over your own feet. You seem more willing to terrorize women and to kill defenseless children," Black Eagle remarked. He was sure that the man before him had either killed his children or ordered their deaths.

"Ah . . . so you have come for revenge! I will have your scalp on my spear. I will . . . ." Osa-a's speech was cut short.

Black Eagle had attacked. They were struggling hand to hand, each trying to thrust his knife into the other. Osa-a felt his arm tremble from the strain and panicked. That's when Black Eagle put all of his weight into the battle, causing the other to retreat and break away. Osa-a found himself on the other side of the teepee, cowering from the overpowering strength of his opponent. He had never met the likes of a man like this before.

"I will leave when you die," Black Eagle said as his eyes narrowed on him. He could feel the hate and rage build up in his body. It gave him the strength and speed of three men. With a loud war whoop, Black Eagle attacked again, slashing Osa-a across the abdomen. Osa-a went crazy when he saw his own blood oozing from the wound. He had been slashed before, but never so deeply. That's when Black Eagle struck again; this time, he caught Osa-a completely off guard. Black Eagle had him pinned to the floor with his arms securely behind him. "Now . . . you die!" he snapped as he slit Osa-a's throat.

Black Eagle could hear the air and blood gurgling from the opening. He watched as the man tried to wiggle free, but he held him fast until he stopped moving. No mercy for the man who offered none to his children. It was fitting that he die at his hands. The man's death had given him a finality to his pain, in a sense. He never blinked an eye when he took Osa-a's scalp from his head. The he turned the man's bloody body over and presented him with the scalp he deserved . . . his own.

René had no idea where Jaewa was leading her. All she could do was follow her lead. She turned just in time to see Black Eagle as he came out of the teepee. He was weary from the battle. Now that he had to finish what he had set out to do, Black Eagle sounded another war whoop, one that launched the attack on the Sauks. They would remember the night as long as they lived . . . the night of hell. teepees were set afire. Men with weapons were cut down in a single blow as they exited their homes. Women and children scurried into the wood for shelter, running for their lives. The old men weren't considered a threat, so they were spared. As for the young warriors, those who didn't run were massacred.

The only Sauk they hadn't encountered was Pa Te' Nea. He had taken Morning Star into the woods when he overheard the fight in Osa-a's teepee. He was well out of range, or so he thought. But Tall Elk and Running Bear were right on his trail and had pushed him into a corner. Apparently, he wasn't as knowledgeable about his homeland as he should have been and he cursed when he found there was no way out except the way they came in. When he realized his error, it was too late.

Morning Star broke free of Pa Te' Nea when she saw her husband approach. Like a little bird, she flew to Tall Elk's side with glee. He looked into her eyes, and tiny sparks seemed to be dancing even as she smiled. She was truly his. Yet, the main reason why they were there in the first place was standing several yards away, unarmed and scared. Then Running Bear arrived seconds later. He was troubled. Dancing Wind was nowhere to be found. He wanted her to come home. Two Moons needed her, and so did he.

"I cannot find Dancing Wind," he said. "I looked in each teepee, but she . . . I cannot find her!"

The gleam that lit Morning Star's face had gone. She suddenly became sullen and dark. It was the hardest story she had ever had to tell in her life. To tell it was to relive it. It pained her to delve into the scene and describe how and why Dancing Wind had died. "It was him! He ordered his warriors to shoot at Re-nea. But Dancing Wind . . . put herself between them," Morning Star said softly. From what she remembered, both Dancing Wind and René were running back toward the canoe. She saw René fall to the ground, and then Dancing Wind. "She took the arrows that were meant for Re-nea. She died because . . . "

"She is dead? How long? How long ago?" Running Bear demanded.

"I do not know. I only know that after we escaped, they found us. Like someone had left them a trail to follow. I know none of us did," she continued slowly. "She was so hungry and tired. We all were . . . but when we saw the campfire, we knew it was a trap. But Dancing Wind didn't hear us. She ran into the trap. Re-nea tried to get her out, but . . . we were surrounded. That is when she died, Running Bear. He ordered it. He did it!" she said as she pointed her damning finger at Pa Te' Nea. Then she buried her face in Tall Elk's chest.

Pa Te' Nea couldn't deny her words. There was nowhere for him to go, with his village destroyed. He knew his life was over from the words of a mere woman. He didn't want to die like an animal . . . not like he'd had Dancing Wind killed as she'd tried to run away. But Running Bear didn't want to hear any more. He raised his bow. The arrow was aimed straight for Pa Te' Nea's heart. He would cut him down as his wife had been. She'd had nowhere to run, either. In the instant he thought of her, he released the arrow. Pa Te' Nea fell to the ground, grabbing at his chest, squirming until he died.

The trio finally headed back to the main camp to catch up with Black Eagle and the rest of their tribesmen. When they arrived, the mayhem had subsided. There were bodies everywhere. The women of the village were chanting the songs of the dead. The children cried for their fathers. If there was a lesson to be learned, the ones who lost finally realized that they had met the grim reaper in the night. They had touched a people who chose peace over war, but when forced to, they fought with their heart and their souls. The Ojibwa were leaving survivors behind. They didn't want captives or scalps.

Robert wasn't allowed to enter the camp, but he knew what the outcome would be. There was no doubt in his mind that Black Eagle would bring his sister back safely. However, something had changed between them as he watched them approach the canoes. They seemed to be worlds apart, even though Black Eagle carried her all the way.

Then Tall Elk and Morning Star arrived, followed by Running Bear. They left the land of the Sauks, taking three women back with them. Jaewa was invited to come, after she disclosed her true identity. She knew what had transpired between her son and Black Eagle and was glad that her son wouldn't be able to harm anyone else. She wanted to close the door to her past as quickly as possible. Never again would she feel like an outsider. Never again would she have to beg for the things she needed.

Robert followed the entourage and maintained a steady pace behind Black Eagle and his sister. He noticed a change in the direction in which they were traveling, wondering why they going out of their way. Then he realized that Morning Star and René were taking them to the last place they had seen Dancing Wind alive. It took them three nights and two days of traveling without rest. On the day they touched shore, it was raining quite heavily. At times, they had to bail out the canoe to keep from sinking, and because the leader refused to stop until they reached their destination.

Upon their arrival, they found the camp fully intact, just as the women had disclosed. The Sauks had left some of their canoes behind under the bushes, more than likely to be used on a future raid. They also left the hole where the place set their campfire . . . all the stones were still in place. There was some food scattered in several areas around the site, as though they were trying to entice the animals to enter.

René and Morning Star headed for the place where Dancing Wind last stood, before being cut down by a Sauk arrow. In an opening, only fourteen feet or so from the shore, lay the body of Dancing Wind, with an arrow still sticking in her back. The memory of the incident had struck both women with guilt and shame. It made them wonder how they were allowed to survive after all the punishment they had to endure, where Dancing Wind was spared. There were times when René sensed that death was only a breath away, and Morning Star begged to put an end to all the hell she had to bear.

Running Bear knelt beside his wife's rain-soaked body. His head dropped as if he were trying to conceal his anguish. Both René and Morning Star joined him in his sorrow and cried the tears he refused to release. It was final. Today would be the last time they would say her name aloud. René was so overcome, she collapsed, still feeling very weak from the trauma and abuse in those few days before their rescue.

Jaewa insisted, "She needs to be dry and out of the rain. You must build a shelter for her or you may lose her, too."

"How can she be ill?" Black Eagle inquired. His heart was sorely wounded by Osa-a and his last testimony of passion with René.

Jaewa understood his behavior more than Black Eagle did. A man's ego is only as strong as his belief. He felt René had betrayed him. "Do you expect her to complain? She will not. She is trying to be brave . . . for you!" Jaewa explained as she wrapped another blanket around René.

"For me? How?" Black Eagle said, almost sarcastically. "Your son said that he had René in his bed. That she was his! No man makes a claim like that . . . unless, he has done such. That means, he . . . has put his seeds in her," Black Eagle admonished. Osa-a had struck a nerve before he died. It was apparent to everyone that he wasn't pleased with his perfect wife any longer. She was tarnished. He wondered if she had gone to him willingly.

"And you believed him," Jaewa put in. "You are a fool . . . and so is any man here who believes that. I have no grandchildren . . . none! My son has not been able to give me grandchildren, and there have been many wives. If he could not seed them . . . he could not seed your wife! Do not act foolishly with her. You will lose her," Jaewa warned as she continued to care for René.

But Black Eagle's heart had been wounded far more savagely than his brother's. At least Running Bear's wife had been spared rape. But Tall Elk was taking the matter much better than Black Eagle in every respect. When Morning Star fell to her knees in grief, Tall Elk was right by her side, giving her the support she needed.

"If you do not want her, it would be kinder if you told her how you feel. She is a good woman," Jaewa stated calmly. The rain forced her to look away from him momentarily, then she added, " She has strong feelings for you. I believe she would rather die than shame you."

It was the last word she dared say, since she was that stranger. Black

Eagle was unmoved by her words or her gestures. But René was still his wife, and he had to care for her whether he wanted to or not. Jaewa followed him to the place where he would deposit René for the rest of the night. In all her years of captivity, Jaewa had never encountered a man with such pride. She wished they had met under other circumstances. She felt the Spirits had planned her future. She was destined to be there, and they had given her another chance to be with her people again.

The rain stopped suddenly, but the woods were too wet to start a fire. Robert and the other warriors rigged a makeshift shelter to protect the women. Then they set out to find food. Running Bear, aided by his brother, prepared Dancing Wind for burial. Jaewa and Tall Elk assisted the women and then secured the canoes.

The following day, René awoke to find herself alone and covered from head to toe in a dry blanket. She no longer felt feverish, and the color had come back to her face. She could hear her brother issuing orders about drying the rifles and keeping the ammunition away from the water. Anxious to see him, she started out of the shelter, only to realize that she had no clothes to speak of. She wrapped the blanket around her and tied it with the leather strips that were still dangling from her wrists. Then she placed the bearskin robe over her shoulders and primped her hair into place. When she felt sure of her appearance, she crawled out of the shelter and headed for the familiar voice.

"Robert! Robert!" she called. She could still feel her knees trembling, but she refused to let them stop her.

Robert tuned to greet her the moment her heard her call. "René . . . Oh René !" he said as she leaned his rifle against the log. "You are a sight. Look at you!" he said as he hugged her tightly. "I just knew you were going to be okay." then he turned to where Black Eagle was standing and said, "Look! Look who's up and about!"

Black Eagle was nowhere to be seen. At first he was puzzled about his brother-in-law's behavior at the mention of René's name: Black Eagle would walk away or set himself apart from him and the others. Robert gently helped René sit down so as not to sap her strength. He offered her a piece of rabbit met, but she refused it. She was in need of her husband's attention, and he was unwilling to comply.

"Where is Black Eagle?" René asked as she looked around the campsite. She was saddened that he wasn't there when she opened her eyes. "He isn't hurt . . . is he?" she asked as she probed her brother's face.

"On . . . uh . . . I saw him a moment ago. Maybe he had to see about his brother. You know . . . uh . . . Running Bear? If you want, I will bring him back," Robert stammered. He couldn't tell her what he really suspected. To tell her that Black Eagle no longer wanted her.

"I must see him. I must! He must think the worst!" she exclaimed. "You know I would never . . ." She cried and then tried to compose herself. "It seems I will never be able to wash away the terrible things that have been done. He will never forgive me . . . will he?"

Robert could never hide anything from her. She knew when he was trying to protect her and when he was hiding something from her. To look into the depths of her dark green eyes and tell her that everything would be all right was one thing he couldn't do. "I think . . . Black Eagle needs time to heal. He has been hurt just as much as you have. With the deaths of your children and then your being taken away . . . I think that is a lot for one man to handle," Robert said.

But it didn't work. René knew all too well what was bothering him. "And he blames me for all of it. He does! Is that why he left you behind to deal with me?" René asked painfully. "I need to heal, too! I need! I need!" she exclaimed.

She stood and paced the moist soil. When she moved, she forgot to catch the bearskin robe about her shoulders. Robert gasped when he saw the scars from the beatings she had received. All he could do was grab her and hold her her close, again feeling that he had failed to protect her from harm.

René was so shaken by Black Eagle's lack of attention that she considered going back to the outpost with her brother. But the laws of the Ojibwa had to be respected. She would have to seek permission from the chief and the shaman in order to be set free of any vows that she and Black Eagle had shared. That meant she would have to wait until they arrived home and Black Eagle was in charge of that.

René walked back to the shelter only to find Morning Star and Tall Elk making love to each other inside. They were trying to bring back the feelings that they had shared so willingly before. A bitter feeling washed through René as she realized that Black Eagle no longer felt the same way toward her. The events that had taken place these past few days no longer ruled her friends' lives like it had for her. The two lives inside were one again.

With nowhere to put her head down to rest, René took a walk along the lakeshore. The water was so blue, it was as though the sky just reached in to take a drink of it. She marveled at the way each cloud appeared to be shaped like lovers floating in air. How she wished to be one of them. So far her life wasn't the picture of perfection, and her dreams of having a loving husband were far out of her reach. Maybe she should go back to the outpost with Robert.

René walked for so long, she didn't realize that the camp was no longer visible. She found an open space under a perfect evergreen and spread the fallen branches to make a small bed. She placed the bearskin over the branches and quickly sat down. After a few minutes of gazing into the open lake, she rested her head upon her knees. Time passed quickly while she slept. She didn't even see the sun disappear. There were no stars to light up the sky, and no moon to reflect upon the waters. As far as she was concerned, she had lost everything all over again through no fault of her own.

If there was a way to measure the weight of her heart, the scale would break. So much pain for one person to bear. So much guilt that even her husband was ashamed to be with her. She couldn't bring herself to go back to the camp, knowing that Black Eagle's feeling had changed.

René had been away from the camp for several hours before she was awakened by voices calling her name in the dark. She didn't think she would be missed; after all, she was damaged goods. But then again, why should they bother to find her. She had no one to turn to. She was better off lost. Her brother would be hurt for a while, but he would get over it soon enough. He had Lily to go home to. Black Eagle would be rid of her . . . of the shame and embarrassment she had caused him. He would be free . . . free to marry one of his own kind.

René heard them coming closer, begging her to answer, the other demanding. She said nothing to draw them in her direction. It was her way of setting them all free. She pinned herself against the low-hanging evergreen and held her breath as someone approached . . . in anger. She recognized his strong gait, but wouldn't reveal herself to him or to the others. René watched as Black Eagle stopped just a few feet away from her and surveyed the area with his torch. She continued to watch in silence as he turned toward her, but the tree blocked his view and he swiftly walked out of sight. She waited a minute or two and then moved silently around to the other side of the tree only to find him standing behind her. Her heart nearly stopped beating when he grabbed her by the arm. She saw fury in his eyes . . . fury and disgust.

"You're hurting me!" René cried. "Just let me go! You're hurting . . . me!" She struggled with him in vain and stopped when she saw no relief from it.

But he disregarded her complaint. He only wanted to insure his power by keeping her where he could see her. "I have found her. She is safe!" he yelled. "Go back to the camp! I will stay with her!"

Robert and Jaewa were relieved to hear that she hadn't met with any danger, but they were hesitant when they heard the tone in Black Eagle's voice. They had all feared the worst when she hadn't returned to the shelter. It seemed René was under a great strain and needed more than brotherly affection; she needed to talk to Black Eagle. But his manner had soured toward her. Jaewa warned him earlier of the effects his behavior might have on René and she was right.

"You shouldn't have bothered to look for me. I am of no importance to you anymore!" René snapped. She hit him as hard as she could, but only managed to hurt herself in the process.

Black Eagle quickly grabbed both of her wrists and held them behind her back, pinning her close to him and preventing her from striking him again. In his anger, his only thought was to discipline René, to put her in her place to remind her of what a wife was supposed to be. "And you do not need to shame me anymore," he said forcefully. "Your brother told me you wanted to see me. Well! I am here. You want to talk? Talk!" Black Eagle snapped.

His manner was severe. His voice was like ice. René heard him loud and clear. There was no love in his heart for her. She finally loosened his hold on her and turned away from him. The longer she stayed in his company, the more she felt like a used-up rag. He had even added new bruises to the old ones, but they all felt the same . . . they all hurt.

"You act as though I brought all this about. You must really hate me to act like this," she said as she rubbed her arms. "Perhaps you would have preferred to find me dead instead of Dancing Wind. And, judging by the way you are looking at me, you even believe that I am to blame for the death of our children . . . and of your poor mother," she added as she choked into tears.

"My mother lives . . . Re-nea," he offered coolly. "My mother lives."

"I . . . am very pleased that she survived that horrible day." A sign of happiness was etched on her face, but it changed again to the grim, solemn state she had been in earlier. "I cannot change what has happened, although, I truly wish I could, Black Eagle. I had no power against the evil that attacked our home or the evil that attacked me. I had no power over him . . . like I have none over you," she said as she walked toward the opening in the trees. She could feel a sob well up in her throat again.

René turned to look at him again, but his eyes were cold and uncaring. She could feel his anger penetrating the ebony darkness that surrounded them. She reached out for him, hoping he would just take her in his arms and hold her, but he ignored her. "I love you, Black Eagle. You were my only reason for living. I prayed for you to come after me . . . to save me," she implored. She tried to convince him of her sincerity. Too many days and nights were between them where doubt would certainly build a wall that couldn't be torn down. "Do you believe that I love you, Black Eagle?"

Black Eagle still refused to answer. He felt betrayed by her. He was sure that she had allowed a stranger to touch her, to make love to her. The vision of their small and helpless children lying dead and his mother's broken-hearted cries haunted him. The dream that he had prevented her death or her being carried away by a white man and not the man he had killed, rankled at his very being. He loved her, but at what price? He loved her, but his heart and his mind were at war with each other. He had been foolish to bring her to his village, and now he was the fool for having trusted her.

"You cannot love me . . . or anyone else," he snapped. "No! I do not believe you!"

His words stung like a whip. Confused, she asked, "Do you think I wanted this to happen? That monster . . . raped me and he beat me. I didn't give him my body, he took me by force. ..by force!" René screamed. "How could I stop him. We all tried to escape, but he . . . they . . . tracked us . . . my God . . . he . . . "

"He is dead! And the truth about his mating with you died with him. You and that woman . . . expect me to believe that her son was not able to father any children. I have never met a man who could not," he interrupted angrily. "I am not stupid, woman! If a man can rape a woman, he can father a child!"

"Wait! Are you saying that he was incapable of siring children?" she asked, almost relieved.

But again, Black Eagle's hostility came forward. "That is of no importance to you. You have betrayed me. You allowed another man to make love to you. And for that, I will never forgive you," he said squarely, noting the shock in her eyes. He slapped her with his words, just as sorely as if he had used his hand. There was no reasoning with him now. There was no change in his manner or his tone. Black Eagle had cut the bonds of their relationship to shreds.

"How can you say that to me? It isn't true. It just isn't true!" she cried.

To further add to her pain, he slapped her with one blow that was worse than the last. "I do not want you anymore. I should not have brought you to my village . . . to my home. It was wrong," he answered.

René stood within inches of him and felt his hatred and contempt for her. She had nothing to gain by arguing with him. And yet, she had hoped that his wounds would heal as she hoped that hers would. "Then . . . I will set you free from your vows. I will . . . not stand in the way of your happiness," she said. Her shoulders had lost their strength. "I will go away . . . back to the outpost with Robert as soon as possible. I won't cause you any more shame."

"Shame . . . this shame that I will always endure is because of you. You willingly gave yourself to him. While I mourned for our children, you were making love to our enemy," Black Eagle admonished.

"You honestly believe that?" she asked. Shocked and dismayed, she wasn't sure where to turn. Why he would believe such a thing was far beyond her grasp. And she received no response from him, nothing but a shove, with him forcing her to the ground.

Black Eagle frightened her with his action, so much so that she thought he might force himself upon her. He was close to doing just that as he pinned her down to the ground. All of Black Eagle's inhibitions were working against both of them. To think that she had been treated in the same manner by the man he had killed made her tighten and prepare for a punishment. He finally saw the fear in her dark green eyes and the tears flooding to the surface and streaming down her her pain-stricken face. She was powerless against him. She couldn't have stopped him even if she had wanted to. She was reliving the hell all over again and there was nothing she could do.

Black Eagle snatched himself away from her and leaned up against the tree. His heart was pounding wildly from all the hate and anger he had kept within. He quickly slammed his fist against the tree and knocked large pieces of bark to the ground where he had left her. René still lay on the ground holding herself, tears flowing to a brink of blinding her. In her mind, that was Black Eagle's way of cutting her out of his life. She no longer doubted that she didn't matter. She had nothing to hold on to, but death. Where could she go now that she had lost everything? What more could he say to break her heart that he hadn't already said? Finally, she managed to get to her feet after stumbling over the blanket she had wrapped around her. The only place of solace that she could escape to was just ahead, glistening like an onyx pool, ready to swallow her up. She bolted straight for it, wanting only to end the torment. She had lost her children and she now knew she had truly lost him.

René was in the water before he had turned to see if he had injured her. He found himself standing under the evergreen alone. And a few yards away, he saw René in the water. The water splashed upward with each step she took. She fell several times, the blanket hindering her from running the way she wanted to. The water was too shallow for her to swim, so she treaded through as much of it as she could before it reached her waistline. Black Eagle realized he had driven her to this point. She could be dragged under by the current if she continued. He had to stop her. The only light he had to guide him came from the campfire, and that wasn't enough to keep her in his sight. He found one of the canoes that was used in the search for her and leaped in and paddled with all his strength in the direction of the splashing sounds and prayed all the while that he would make it to her in time.

René wasn't handling the water very well at all. She pushed herself as far as she could go. With her strength finally drained, she no longer had the will to stay afloat. She took one last look at the camp and said her final good-byes. It was useless to keep pretending that Black Eagle would eventually come to his senses. His actions toward her were proof enough. It was useless for her to go back to the outpost when she would face the ridicule of her birth. And since Robert and Black Eagle were so close, maybe they would be able to help each other go on with their lives

Black Eagle was a few yards away and he called out to her, hoping that she would turn back. She was shocked to hear him out there, then again, maybe he wanted to make sure she completed what she had set out to do. He called her again, and this time there was a change in the way he said her name. He sounded almost sincere, but René continued on her quest, pushing herself farther into the lake.

When Black Eagle saw that she really intended to harm herself, he panicked. Calling her would only push her farther into the depths that would consume her. he had to act quickly. He dove into the blackened depths and swam to her side. He slipped his arm around her waist before she had a chance to flee. René tried to loosen his hold on her, but Black Eagle was the victor in that contest. He held her securely to his body and swam back to the canoe. Then he helped her climb in and he quickly entered himself. Hurt by his behavior and now his intrusion, René kept her back to him all the way back to shore.

Once they touched land again, René bolted from the canoe as quickly as she could. She wanted to put as much distance between them as possible. However, Black Eagle was right on her heals. He snatched her up into her arms and headed for the little spot where he found her. Within a breath's time they were standing on the bearskin, staring into each others eyes. She trembled from the cold breeze that just surrounded their wet bodies. He seemed unscathed by it. But he had changed. If he had been a moment too late, he would be mourning *her* death just as deeply as he was mourning the death of his children. He loved her like he could love no other. To deny it would be a lie.

"Re-nea! Re-nea!" he said gently. He had never apologized for anything in his life. He had never loved a woman so completely that jealousy and hatred clouded his mind. It was so hard for him to express his pain without showing anger, but he tried for both their sakes. René, on the other hand, was withdrawn and confused by his sudden change. Pain wasn't new to her, and she had suffered greatly from it all. She wanted the stabbing pain to be relieved, but she wasn't ready to hear what he had to say.

"I want us to have what we had before," Black Eagle said softly. "I . . . need you, Re-nea," he added. He could feel his heart pounding, or was it hers? He missed her so much that his body ached.

René held her breath when his arms tightened about her. She was so close to him that she felt his breath on her neck. She took a chance and looked into his eyes. They had never lied to her before. She wanted to believe he wanted her, but the sting of his words was still there.

Black Eagle gently placed her on the bearskin robe and tenderly stroked her chin and then her shoulder. He placed a kiss on her forehead and let it trail down the bridge of her nose to the gentle swell of her lips. He kissed her with the full intensity of his passion. At first, she was reluctant to allow him that privilege, but she accepted his kiss and kissed him back with as much furor. The tension that had once separated them had slowly begun to disappear.

René and Black Eagle finally learned to communicate with each other again. René was able. for the first time, to tell what had taken place the day her children died. She needed to be open with him. She needed him to listen when she described the horrible things Jaewa's son had committed against her. He in turn told her how he had found their children, and he listened to her heart-wrenched cry when he described their burial.

"And . . . One Shoe . . . you've said nothing about him. Is he okay?"

René's words seemed to echo in his ears. She missed a child who wasn't even born of her body. Black Eagle never realized that she had developed an attachment in such a short period of time. Then again, she was a wonderful mother. He had seen that on the day the twins were born and the many days after. He remembered the smile on her face when she knew she had given him a son and a daughter. He was touched by her capacity to give.

"He is getting fat," he answered. "He is happy, but I know he misses you," he added sheepishly.

"He has probably forgotten me by now. One day with him wasn't enough to build a mother-son relationship," she said softly. "I can't wait to see him."

"Soon. You will see him soon enough," he said while he carefully examined her wounds. He wondered why he had been angry with her. Then he realized almost too late that it wasn't her fault that the Sauks had taken her and the others as hostages.

"We are two or three days away from the village. But first we have to travel by land to get to the other camp. We should get there by nightfall in two days," he offered. "We will travel at your pace, so as not to tire you. It will not be long for us to get home since the horses are at the other camp. Now . . . sleep, my love," he continued softly as he caressed her abdomen.

She had taken so much abuse in these past few days that Black Eagle kept his arms around her all through the night. He hoped beyond all hope that she would forgive him. He had acted foolishly and he even pondered for a time on his own emotions. Suddenly a little moisture filled the corners of his eyes. He quickly wiped it away and sighed. Yet, these were the tears of joy, sadness, relief, and anger all about to explode from a man in love.

They spent the entire evening wrapped up in each others arms. René slipped into a restful sleep, and Black Eagle finally overcame his guilt for not having protected her from the dangers of his world. He in turn slept very well until the wee hours of the morning.

A gentle mist formed over the lake and hovered like a cloud. The weather had grown warmer than expected after the deluge that had poured on them for three straight days. The ground was dry, and the heavy scent of pine and flora was everywhere. Black Eagle had awakened to find his arms empty. René was missing again. He almost started to panic, but all that subsided when he heard her humming a little melody while she bathed. The light of the mist created a haze over the water, which only allowed partial visibility. He could see her . . . a silhouette of her through the cloudlike mass. It surrounded her like a curtain. It was lovely to see . . . she was lovely.

Black Eagle found himself hurrying toward her, silently and with even steps. He reached for her as though she was a part of heaven itself and touched the softness that was hidden from view. A soft moan escaped his lips as his hand caressed the one he desired. He couldn't stop the feeling of need that was enveloping him, and René felt the quickening of his need build as his hands wandered.

"I cannot wait for your monthly flow to pass. I am not willing to wait," he moaned in her ear breathlessly, and joined her in the massive pool. "Whatever comes, I will accept it."

"Are you sure you want to take such a chance?" René asked. That nagging threat that Jaewa's son could have fathered a child through her made her quake inside. But Jaewa could be right, after all. Her son may very well have been impotent.

Black Eagle's pleas rested solely on René shoulders, something she wanted very much not to think about. The underlying fear of her attacker continued to haunt her. If she could only push it out of her mind . . . push the nightmare aside and begin anew. She needed to take Black Eagle's strong hand and allow him to penetrate that wall she had built to protect herself. Yet, as she weighed all the things that could go wrong, Black Eagle continued to yearn openly for her. Her needs as a woman suddenly began to outweigh her fears. Black Eagle embraced her and kissed her with the full intensity of his love. He said nothing to sway her in any way. It had to be her decision and hers alone.

"I want you . . . Black Eagle . . . with all my heart," she said slowly. She had no time to be timid . . . not now . . . not with him.

No other words needed to be spoken. Black Eagle heard her and removed the bonds that had separated them one by one. Their passion couldn't be compared, for they loved each other freely, openly. As they slipped farther into the water, hidden by the mist, they became one again. The were happy in the melding that had first brought them together, and now it was healing their wounds. As the mist lifted, it unveiled the two lovers as they drew each other nearer . . . accepting . . . yielding.

The following morning René and Black Eagle were all abloom and very happy as they joined the others in the camp. Everyone, including Running Bear, was relieved that they had mended their differences and were lovers again. They knew it was a matter of time before Black Eagle's stubborn streak would break. As in all relationships, there were many obstacles to overcome, some painful. They would have to find strength to move on with their lives and to keep the past behind them.

The party finally set off for the other campsite the bright noonday's sun had cooled. The men handled Dancing Wind's body with care and carried her for the twenty-five-mile stretch. The women carried some of the supplies, stopping sometimes to rest and periodically looking over their shoulders. By nightfall, two days later as Black Eagle had promised, they had reached the main campsite. Home was just a breath away.

CHAPTER EIGHTEEN

THE THREE DAYS PASSED so quickly that the weary travelers hadn't taken time to rest when they arrived home. Robert had taken time to set up a temporary camp outside of the village in order to make his journey back to the outpost easier. He knew he couldn't stand the long good-byes and it bothered him knowing that he had to leave. He had been away from Lily for far too long. She may have given up on his ever returning. He worried that she grew tired of waiting for him, mostly because his ties to René were stronger than they were to her.

He and René spent a lot of time talking. It was difficult for René more so than Robert to come to terms with his plans to leave. She assumed the next time they would come together, they would both be too old to travel. She studied every detail of his face. She memorized his smile from the sparkle in his eyes to the curve of his mouth when he laughed. Already . . . she began to miss him.

"Would you believe it . . . it's almost been a year. It is about July or so. Yes, you were about to marry you-know-who," Robert said slowly. It would have been a major mistake if she had married the fool.

René remembered the event, but she wasn't quite sure what month it was. She stopped worrying about the time eons ago. Yet, she was never so relieved no to have that monster around to mess up her life again. "Yes, Robert . . . I remember," she said as she handed him a pile of furs.

"It wasn't easy trying to find you dear sister . . . traveling from village to village. I couldn't believe my luck when that Quaker family you ran into

. . . remember them and their little girl? Well, they told me they saw you. René. ..I still can't believe it sometimes," he said as he packed away his supplies and wrapped the furs into a single bundle. "At first when I got here, I made a fool of myself, making stupid claims about Black Eagle and his intentions. But . . . I am glad you are here. I couldn't have done what he has done for you. I probably would have messed things up trying to take you away," he continued while looking in her eyes. "He is a strong man . . . better than the best. I like him," he said without hesitation.

René smiled, knowing Black Eagle felt the same way toward Robert. She found it hard to accept his leaving, although she knew it was inevitable. "I don't want you to leave, but I know you must. Lily is waiting for you, isn't she? she asked, trying to change the subject.

"Yeah! I sure hope so. She has been very patient with me, but I'm not . . . I mean, I can't imagine . . . not having her," Robert answered, somewhat emotionally. He truly loved Lily and had almost said it himself. René knew how it felt to love someone so much that she became speechless. The only way to comfort him was to set him on his way . . . back to Lily. Then she slowly touched his face so she could keep him in her memory.

Later that afternoon, Denver and Jacques came to the small camp. Their time with the Ojibwa had been prosperous in many ways. They had traded together and had been through a small war together. And the Ojibwa were, above all, triumphant in their cause. "Ho, hooo, youngin! It is mighty good ta see yah!" Denver exclaimed as he approached them. "I see yah found the little missy."

Both René and Robert stopped talking and waited for Denver and his friend Jacques to join them. "Greetings to you both," Robert stated quickly, and extended his hand. The two men clasped each other's hand firmly and smiled.

"Well, well, little missy . . . you gave us a scare," he said as he placed his hand on René's shoulder. She was a vision of pure loveliness, and his heart pounded at though it would burst when he touched her. "Is she . . . uh . . . are you comin' with us?" he asked, hoping that she would answer.

However, Robert spoke for her, saying, "No. It is better that she stay here. She will be safe here." He didn't like leaving her behind any more than she wanted him to go, but they each had to do what was best for the both of them. Besides, there was no other solution with James Courtland plotting to kill her.

Denver didn't approve of a white woman or even a woman who looked white living among the Indian folks. He liked them, but wouldn't share a bed with them. For the most part, his mind was set on convincing Robert to take her back. Now that her children were dead, there was nothing to keep her here. He could handle her, if she would have him. She was a mighty fine catch at that.

Denver quickly raised his voice, nearly shattering René's eardrums, "Holy horse feathers! Are yah crazy? I don't want ta get into yah'lls family business, but . . ."

"That's right . . . it is family business, and you have nothing to say about it. It would be wrong and dangerous to take her back and you know it!" Robert yelled. "She wouldn't be happy there, anyway. She would be treated as an outsider or even worse." He knew that as long as James Courtland was alive, René would be hunted. It made sense to keep her out of his reach. Besides, there was no doubt Black Eagle would came after her if she did manage to leave with him.

"Yah fool! Yah stupid fool! Do yah think she is safer in the hands of the likes of him?" Denver asked. He was showing a side of himself that Robert never expected to see from a friend.

"Why is it so important to you? Black Eagle has claimed René as his wife and she accepts him as none other than her husband. If I didn't know any better, I would think you wanted my sister for yourself," Robert stated with certainty.

And he was right. The man wanted René and presented his case very poorly. It was a clumsy attempt to persuade Robert into bringing her back. Denver even tried to convince himself that René would settle for him over the handsome young buck who had swept her off her feet.

"I do . . . I mean . . . yes, I admit it. I want her! She would be better off with a white man. Why shouldn't it be me? I know about her past. I know she has a black mama. She looks white and can pass just like she did before," he stated. "Yah see, a white man would make her respectable. She would be accepted as long as I was her man."

Robert couldn't believe what he was hearing. It took a lot of nerve for Denver to present himself as a suitor or possible husband for his sister. "That won't work for me, Denver, and I'll tell you why. First of all, you don't love René. You'll eventually treat her cruelly, because she will never come to you willingly. Second, you will never let her live without the knowledge that you saved her from her past. Third, she will never again be accepted by her old friends, and that would upset your plans for wanting to be a part of a world she no longer desires. And finally, it just won't work!" Robert stressed fiercely. Then he eyed his friend and wondered whether it was a mistake to have allowed him to come along. He remembered how Denver had warned him about his attitude when they first came to this village in search of René. There was so much at stake then. But now the people trusted him. They accepted him as Black Eagle's brother-in-law and friend. He would never do anything to jeopardize that.

"You speak well for someone so young," an older voice interrupted. "You have much wisdom. One day you will be a man of importance."

Both men turned to see who had slipped up on them. It was Gray Wolf who drew their attention. In their battle of words, they hadn't realized that René had left them and made her way to Black Eagle and his father, who stood only a few feet away from the argument.

Gray Wolf had come to see how his daughter-in-law had fared since she hadn't returned to the village with the others. He wondered why Black Eagle entered the village alone and unattended by his wife. It was his decision to see for himself that the woman Black Eagle loved was in fact well and willing to stay after suffering at the hands of the Sauks. Black Eagle and Running Bear carried Dancing Wind's body to the center of the village, where they paid their last respects to her before burial rites were given. Morning Star and Tall Elk retrieved their son and had taken him home. However, René was the only one who hadn't truly come home.

"So, old friend, you wish to take my daughter-in-law away. I think you will find that to be a difficult task. As you can see, Black Eagle will not give her up as he has told me many times," the old chief accounted.

Robert had already noted the strong connection between them, even before they arrived home. The strain that had separated them before no longer existed. They had started anew, which let Denver know that he didn't have a prayer. The old man was right. René never made any inclination that she was dissatisfied with her present way of life or with her husband. "I guess I saw more in her friendly smile than it was truly meant to be," Denver said shamefully. "I am truly sorry. I should never have compromised your sister in any way. But . . . she sure is a pretty young philly," Denver finally admonished.

"I can understand how one's judgment can be clouded by a pretty face. And yes, she is pretty . . . pretty as the day I stopped treating her like a tomboy. My, our father took so much pride in her. He called her his precious jewel. God, I miss him and my mother. René is all the family I have left, so you can see I will do anything to safeguard her happiness," Robert promised.

Growing up with René and having her as a friend as well as a sister was one of his previous memories. Something he would carry with him for a long time to come. Their father would be proud knowing that his children hadn't cowered under the threat of death and the prospects of a new way of life. Devon's legacy would live on in them.

The relationship between René and her brother was strong and solid. Gray Wolf was pleased to have them both as part of his family . . . part of the clan. Then he passed the pipe, first to Robert, who had finally learned that this gesture was a sign of peace. He puffed slowly, to build the intensity of the smoke and then exhaled. When Robert had his fill, he passed the pipe to Denver, who was still feeling somewhat put out. But his disappointment was short lived, so he celebrated with the rest.

Later that evening, the drums made the forest come alive. A large bonfire had been cast in the center of the village. The men wore their finest plumage and the women, their best dresses. They danced the Grass Dance. It was the most exciting spectacle René and Robert had ever seen. The women danced in a side step motion to the beat of the drums. The warriors danced in the center circle with their weapons in hand. The older men played their flutes and rattles to the rhythm of the drums.

Now that René was officially a part of the tribe, she was expected to participate in the rituals. White Feather and Morning Star guided her through the dance steps and motions. She learned the movements quickly and took her rightful place in the outer circle with the women. She never expected them to accept her after her ordeal, but they greeted her with open arms. They danced for hours, until the circle finally dwindled down to the younger dancers. Black Eagle and René were among the few to remain in their circle, and Gray Wolf was pleased. The spirits of the departed were being honored well.

It was dawn. The sun crept over the trees and beamed its rays in all directions. The bonfire, no longer flaming in its glory, was now down to a few smoldering cinders. The dancers had all headed home to rest up for the new day. The only activity that could be seen happened with the young boys practicing with their bows and arrows. Two dogs barked repeatedly until someone threw them a bone. A tiny babe cried in the distance and was quickly suckled. It was so quiet that no one heard the trio leave early that morning.

Although tired from the night's parlay, Robert made the decision to leave before René was due to awaken. He knew it would be difficult to go, and the longer he stayed, the worse it had become. Black Eagle and he agreed upon how he would leave. His presence alone made it difficult for Black Eagle to be the supporting factor for René. She relied too much on both of them, but would go to her brother for advice. With thirty or so miles between them, Robert had a chance to finally focus on his life. He had a business to rebuild and run. And since returning Ohio was out of the question, he planned to make a go of it at the outpost. The money he carried and the bank note that bore both their names would get them started on a worthy adventure.

Meanwhile, René awoke for a restful sleep. She stretched to remove the kinks in her back and shoulders. It was the sunlight creeping through the small opening in the roof that had roused her. She gently ran her fingers through her hair, and a slight yawn escaped her lips. Her hair glistened with the ray shining in on her. Black Eagle had taken a moment to drink in the lovely view of the woman he adored. He had to stop himself from moment to moment, realizing that she was home and that she belonged to him. He quickly tossed a log into the pit where he had already started the morning meal. And quickly gazed back from time to time appreciating what he had.

"Good . . . I am glad you are awake," he said with a smile. He enjoyed the time when she slept as well. A pleasure he relished even more when she bared herself to the waist when she shifted from one side to the other. She didn't know how much she filled his heart with passion . . . with joy.

"Good morning!" she beamed. "Have you been up for every long?" she asked while taking her final stretch.

Nothing escaped Black Eagle's eyes. He had taken in every inch of her long and shapely body. He could hardly contain himself . . . but when a spark from the fire pit lit up the blanket covering his beauty, he sprung to her side and quickly doused the tiny flame. The spark helped to ignite the roaring flames in his heart. He became her blanket and he wrapped himself around her.

"Long enough, my love. Long enough," he said in her ear. Then he kissed her tender lips with a force of longing. His hidden passion unfolded before them. René felt his need for her and returned his love. At first, Black Eagle's hunger was insatiable. Each thrust brought her closer to fulfilling his desire. He loved her with every ounce of his being, and she loved him in return. The fear of not pleasing him no longer assailed her. She called his name freely as he suckled her breast.

"I . . . love you," she said breathlessly.

"Love! How much do you love me?" he asked while holding her tightly.

"I'll show you," she said and she did. She ran her finger through his jet black hair and then cradled his head in her arm. Her head began to spin with all the heat building between them, and soon Black Eagle brought her to a point of no return. He felt her body quake under the pressure of his, and she opened herself to all he administered.

"So beautiful," he said in her ear. "You make my heart glad. You make me feel strong . . . *like a bear!*"

Black Eagle kissed her again, but slowly. He wasn't about to let her slip away, not now. His arms tightened about her, and she submitted to his charms again and again. He was determined to reclaim her heart, wanting her to forget the past few days and to remember only the warmth they shared.

The day swiftly turned to night. While the people worked, the lovers played. No one seemed to mind that the young couple didn't join them in their daily chores. They all understood that the two were trying to rebuild their lives.

The couple slipped into the bearskin robe, too tired to eat. They stayed that way until the following morning, when they managed to join the others in the village in their daily routine of planting and maple tapping. The men busily patched up old canoes, while others built new ones. A few young would-be hunters had gone hunting to test their ability with the bow. One was lucky. He shot a rabbit. The others, ashamed and heads hanging low, hadn't even snared a field mouse. The young girls laughed at the accounts made of the hunt and then went about completing their chores. They enjoyed hearing of their future husbands' exploits and hoped that the next hunt would be profitable.

René's duties as the wife of a subchief gave her many privileges as well. She was given a space in the sewing circle with the important women of the tribe. There she learned how to use a quill, and she made a tunic for Black Eagle, between pricking her finger here and there. She was also being trained to use the bow, with which she struggled, but gave her full attention. After such a busy day, René headed for Robert's camp. She hadn't seen him in two days and she knew he was anxious to get back to the outpost. She couldn't wait to show him the tunic she had made. But when she arrived at the site, she found everything had been cleared away. Robert had left without so much as saying good-bye. She had become so used to having him there and felt secure knowing she could confide in him, like always.

René walked down the trail that led away from the village and tried to suppress the tears from flowing. She was so shaken that she didn't hear Black Eagle approaching her from behind. He knew she would eventually come to this place, and he knew what her reaction would be. "You are sad, Re-nea," he said softly, and placed his hands on her shoulders. "Your brother will return."

René didn't respond at first; she just continued down the path, hoping to catch a glimpse of Robert as he rode away. However, that wouldn't be the case. "He must have known . . . he must have known I wanted to see him off. He isn't one for long good-byes," she admitted painfully.

"We decided it would be best if he left as soon as possible," he added. "I wanted you to need me. Your brother understood why I wanted him to go. Now I need you to understand."

We decided? How can you make a decision for me like that?!" she asked angrily.

"I am your husband. I am the one who decides what is best for you and my son," he continued slowly. "I like your brother. He is a good man. But he made you think of home, and I did not want you to leave," he added, and then turned her around to face him.

Frustration was written all over her face. She sensed the men in her life were trying to control her rather than just protect her. Suddenly, without any forethought, René lashed out, "Just stop it! You . . . and Robert push my wants aside like they don't matter! If I did that to you, I would be wrong!"

Black Eagle witnessed her fury for the second time since their encounter. He was amazed at the manner upon which she projected her anger and made her point just as clear. It was quite obvious that she wanted to be treated with dignity, but he hadn't thought of it much, except the day he nearly lost her due to his callous behavior. And still, he knew that she would rebel against Robert's untimely departure. How could he reckon with such a strong-willed woman?

"He was right! He said you would be angry. But that changes nothing where my duties fall. I will protect what is mine. I will not allow you to come to harm as long as I am alive," he said sternly.

Later that evening, while they sat under the stars, Black Eagle decided he had had enough of her silence. The distance between them had grown, and their relationship was still very fragile. If he didn't handle it properly, he could lose the woman he wanted more than life. With hunting season approaching and the meat caches needing to be filled, he knew he would have little time to mend the way between them.

"You are still angry," Black Eagle stated calmly.

Although she hadn't responded, she remembered the days when she and Robert were at each other's throat. She recalled how Robert always had a way of turning things around to suit himself. He wasn't selfish, but he was most aggressive when he was set in his ways. He usually wound up winning the argument, or sometimes she would let him win just to shut him up. And now, Black Eagle had accomplished the same. All of the things she thought she had forgotten came flooding back. She was in a time warp, caught between what she was then and what she had become.

"No, I'm not angry anymore," René answered in a whisper.

Black Eagle decided to press on, hoping to make her release her hold on Robert. "Is your brother so important to you? Or have I lost you again?" he asked.

"I don't know . . . I mean . . . I don't know what I mean, not now!" she stammered. "I guess I wanted . . . .I wanted too much from the both of you. I wanted Robert to stay a little longer and I wanted you to understand that he . . . he was my best friend. You must have felt that way at one time," she reasoned.

For a moment Black Eagle felt a pang of jealousy attack his senses. He wanted René to think of him as more than just her husband. He wanted her to come to him when she was troubled for any reason. Yet, her words rang a sign of truth in his heart. For a time he was very close to his brother. There were days when they could never be separated, they were the best of friends. But those days ended when they reached the courting stage. He remembered how they rallied for the love of the same woman and how Running Bear always seemed to win out, sometimes out of trickery. But when it came to hunting and to war games, there was no contest: Black Eagle would win hands up.

It was as though the gods were smiling on Black Eagle the day he found René. It was a love that Running Bear could never tarnish. Yet, with all the competition aside, Black Eagle cared deeply for his brother and still felt the sting of death after finding his sister-in-law's lifeless body. His brother's painful loss made him realize how lucky he truly was.

"Yes, you are right. I do care for my brother in the same manner as you speak. But I will never let what I feel for my brother overshadow how I feel about you. He is my brother, like Robert is your brother. And they both must live their own lives, not ours," he answered carefully.

"But . . . you act as though Robert was trying to take you place. I'll admit he is an important part of my life, just as you have become and will always be. But Robert isn't just my brother . . . he is my friend, my confidant," she confirmed

Again Black Eagle was wounded by her words. She hadn't thought to include him. "I want to be just as important to you. I have been standing in the background long enough. Your brother understood. Now I want you to understand why it was necessary for him to go," he stated firmly. "Now we must rebuild our lives. We have lost so much, and it cannot be brought back even though we want it to. I need you."

Black Eagle had spoken and had taken charge of their lives again. He wanted his wife back, not as a woman led by her fears, but as a woman who made her desires and dreams known to him. Anxious to leave, he quickly rose from the ground. He offered his outstretched hand and waited for René to accept it. His heart softened as she gently placed her hand in his. Her eyes never left his as he helped her to her feet. "Home," he said gently as he gave a slight tug to hurry her along.

They walked back to the village slowly. It was time to revel in their own dreams and to prepare for the future. As far as they were concerned, the world outside wasn't important enough to dwell upon. However, as they neared the village, they could hear Jaewa and Walks Alone confronting one another. They were about to struggle when Black Eagle ordered, "Stop this nonsense and go back to your cabins!"

As if a mountain lion had roared, both Jaewa and Walks Alone nearly jumped out of their skin. The only thing both René and Black Eagle could see were their eyes peering through the darkness. Walks Alone quickly changed and turned her aggression toward René, who only stood a few feet away from her. Her eyes glistened with hatred as she stared at her nemesis with renewed courage.

"So, you finally came to face me," she said as she placed herself within inches of René. "I Walks Alone claim that you are a whore and that you willingly gave in to our enemies. It was you who brought them to our village. You are guilty . . . guilty of causing the death of your own children and of Running Bear's wife," she blatantly accused.

Jaewa was very weary of hearing the lies spoken by this wench. She was obsessed with destroying René in the eyes of the people who had come to love her. "I told this crazy woman that René had nothing to do with the raid on your village, but she continues to hurl these words to those who will listen," Jaewa interrupted sharply.

"No! You lie! You and that bitch, who thinks she's better than me . . . you both lie," Walks Alone yelled.

Now she was drawing the attention of a few passersby who waited patiently to see what the outcome would be. However, René grew tired of listening to such trifle and decided it wasn't worth creating a show at her expense. She continued to make her way home, but added as she passed the scornful woman, "I have been called worse than that. You however, seem to know what it's like to be a whore. Tell us, for goodness' sake. What's it like?" René asked with a mark of sarcasm, then she moved to leave.

But that wouldn't be the case. Walks Alone put herself in René's path, daring her to move around her. And still, she seemed overzealous, thinking that her behavior impressed Black Eagle, making it impossible to have a peaceful end. So rather than become the victim, René turned the tables and said, "Now that we have all gathered here, maybe you can tell us what really happened to the woman you brought into my cabin. She isn't in the burial ground, and her body isn't rotting out in the fields. And some of the women who remained in the village the day we were attacked say it was you who let the woman get away."

"You lie! You lie! That is not true. No one here dares to speak against me!" she retorted.

Fully charged and very angry with the accusation being hurled at her, René recanted. This time her words would sting with the truth. "You expect everyone to believe that I came back to the camp to help the woman escape and then, without considering my family, I betrayed them to the enemy. Well . . . we all know that isn't true! We know it was you, because Gray Wolf didn't get a chance to to speak to her. Not only that . . . you told her where the warriors had hidden their families. It just happened that they found *us!* But, *no* . . . it was you all the time. You betrayed your own people, for what? *For what?*"

All eyes were focused on Walks Alone. She had forced the issues only to get trapped in her own lies. She suddenly felt cornered as the people moved to close the circle around them. Then Walks Alone pushed by Black

Eagle and seized René by the hair. They both fell to the ground with a thud, wrestling for control. No one had dared confront her about the woman before. No one dare to point a finger at her, except René. And when it appeared that René was getting the best of her, Black Eagle pulled them apart. Both were breathing fast and hard, yet only one of them was telling the truth.

The last person known to be with the woman was René. However, Black Eagle had taken her away from the camp before they were attacked. He knew that the woman's injuries weren't serious enough to warrant much care, and yet Walks Alone said her wounds were deep, which meant that the woman wouldn't have been able to move from the cabin, no matter what the outcome.

Black Eagle interrupted, "You were seen leaving the village in the middle of the night. My warriors saw you. Are you calling them liars, too?"

"So . . . I left. Everyone has to relieve themselves at one time or another," she spat.

"And how is it that the Sauks hit us where our meat cache were located? Re-nea does not know where they are hidden. She has never known."

"That proves nothing. She has never been one of us. She stays in your cabin, eats your food, and maybe she serves you when you are home, but she has always remained separate from the women of the camp. You have seen this with your own eyes," Walks Alone added triumphantly.

Again René grew tired of having her character smeared in the eyes of the people. If she didn't try to clear her name, she would be shunned by them for the rest of her days—that is, if they allowed her to stay. And René had learned to be just as thrifty; after all, she survived another nightmare. She knew Walks Alone was lying, but it was a matter of proving it. René decided to ask, "Since I'm so clever, how did I get the woman out of the village?"

Walks Alone smiled, thinking she had won and thoroughly destroyed René's status with the clan. "You told her that there would be too much confusion when the fighting started and that they would not miss a woman captive," she stated strongly and feeling quite sure of herself. "Then I took her to the . . . I mean . . . I saw you and the woman leave that night." Walks Alone had blundered in her attempts to bury René. She was swallowed up in her own lies. Everyone heard her. She was as guilty as René was innocent.

"Well, well, well! It is truly amazing how you were able to do all of that and get away with it, too. You lie very well, but the truth always catches up with people like you. We all know it was you by your own words, don't we?" René said firmly. She was angry that she had been put through such a farce, one of jealousy and envy. "It's hard to believe that you would betray your own people just to get back at me."

"You know nothing! You come to our village, take my man, and have the children that should have been mine," she shouted. "They were supposed to kill you . . . that was the plan. They were supposed to take you away . . . far away! You are supposed to be dead!"

Walks Alone's voice had dwindled to a point of nothingness, and Black Eagle could only see her lips move with more lies. He watched her face distort as she continued, even after admitting that she was at fault. "Enough of this! Say no more, woman!" Black Eagle demanded. "Even now . . . you lie to yourself. Your tongue is that of a serpent. Evil! You betrayed your people and you betrayed yourself!" he roared.

Roughly, he snatched the woman up by her arm and led her to the center of the village. She struggled and tried to free herself, but discovered that she had no power over him. Fear streaked across her face as Black Eagle called to the people to join them in the circle.

The people slowly gathered in the center of the village where Black Eagle held the woman at bay. They had all heard the lies she told, and some had even believed them. However, this same woman was being forced to account for them. They hadn't considered that she was the one who had risked their lives and that of the one she accused.

"What say you now that you have the attention of all of our people? Where are your witnesses? Who will stand behind you and help spread more lies?" he demanded.

Walks Alone looked into the faces of the Ojibwa. There wasn't one there to offer her support in any way. They were angry. She had caused so much bloodshed. But she still refused to believe that an outsider would be accepted over her. "I did it for you, Black Eagle. I wanted you . . . I want . . . I love you. You have to believe me. I did it all for you!" she groveled.

Her audience heard the confession. Although much as some of them wanted to believe in the lies she spread, they were now faced with the proof of her betrayal. Too many lives were forfeited a woman scorned . . . now they must mourn the dead again, for their loss was great.

In his wisdom Gray Wolf couldn't believe that one of his people could act so thoughtlessly. The deed couldn't go unpunished. "In all my years as chief of the Ojibwa, I have never been faced with such a dilemma," he said slowly. "You lied . . . and you planned to blame your misdeeds on my daughter-in-law," he continued.

The people were silent. Fear. Anger. Betrayal. They seemed consumed with the thought of falling victim to a woman's envy toward another. The silence was finally broken when White Feather faced the woman who caused the death of her grandchildren. She joined René and Jaewa, who were still standing behind Black Eagle and Walks Alone. The other women began to taunt Walks Alone. They jeered at her and poked her in the ribs. One brave soul threw a stone and hit her square on the forehead. Soon blood tricked down her face and slowly dripped to the soft earth at her feet.

"Anyone who wants to throw another stone or cause injury to this woman before I pass judgment will suffer that same fate as she," Gray Wolf announced.

René wondered if the reaction of the people would have been even more harsh had she been on the receiving end of the punishment. Memories began to flood René's mind as she watched them taunt the woman and curse her. She remembered all that she had endured when the townspeople stormed her home and killed her parents, all because someone had spurred them on. Soon her head felt heavy with all those terrible memories crashing down upon her, and her stomach began to quake from nausea.

Black Eagle turned just in time to see her distressed and worried. Without consideration to Walks Alone, he immediately released her and clutched René close to him. Whatever the outcome, Walks Alone's punishment wouldn't be witnessed by René.

At home and away from the angry crowd, René was able to gather her senses. Black Eagle was confused with her behavior. He knew something . . . something from her past was bothering her. He wanted to inquire, but he wasn't sure where to begin or how she would respond if he did. Suddenly, the voices from the outside reached their ears. Walks Alone screamed, pleading for mercy. René quickly buried her head in her knees and prayed for these ungodly sounds to end.

Then, as suddenly as the screams began, they stopped. The people cheered as though someone had won a prize. They all had won. Walks Alone was banished from the tribe and her name was never to be spoken again. She was dead in their eyes. She was quickly ushered to the edge of the village, with one bladder filled with water and a small pouch of corn-meal. She was stripped of all valuables and wasn't permitted to take any of her belongings with her. She was, however, given more of a chance at life than she had given to her people. In many ways, she preferred death over banishment, but Gray Wolf had spoken. The lives of the brave warriors and his grandchildren would lay forfeit if he excused her crimes. It was better for her to suffer in the wilderness rather than take her life. The souls of the dead would be satisfied.

CHAPTER NINETEEN

TWO MONTHS HAD PASSED since Robert had returned to the outpost with his friends and Walks Alone had been banished from the tribe. René didn't know when she would see her brother again, even though he had promised her that he would see her before the winter season was over. September was quickly coming to a close, and the people were already storing the rice and dried meats in their winter caches. Most of the deer meat and fish were smoking in the smokehouse, and the deer and elk skins were being tanned. The people were preparing for the harvest ceremony, and the Ojibwa from the north, the east and the west would come from many miles away to celebrate with their southern brothers.

The Ojibwa tribe was considered the largest tribe in the northern Canadian territory and the most feared. Although peaceful in their intent for existence, they tarried to establish their power when a threat was near. They proved that when the Sauks attacked them. Many times they were called upon to be the middlemen when acts of trade were in session for their own tribe as well as the Miami, Ottawa, and the Sioux. It appeared that the tribes of the north would have to take notice of the strength and tenacity.

Ethan, followed by his entourage of mules laden with gun powder, rifles, tobacco, blankets, and scented oils, had joined in the festivities of the day. He had planned to make a big trade before heading for his winter camp near the French fort. At long last, he had ventured into the Ojibwa camp with the hopes of making amends for offending Black Eagle.

There were times where he found himself looking over his shoulder, hoping beyond hope that his friend hadn't heard of the mistake he made last winter. It would be a test of will to be sure that he wouldn't make the same mistake twice. However, in his passing from one camp to another, he heard of the beauty Black Eagle had captured and had taken for his wife. The rumors from the outpost had reached as far south as the Sioux territory and into the Plains region. Now he would get a better look at the treasure who warded him off many months ago. He wondered if this was the same beauty being sought by the American officer who chased a man and a woman from the Ohios.

Ethan was greeted by several elders who wanted to barter for the tobacco in his pack. They wouldn't be easily pacified with just a small amount this time. Gray Wolf and the shaman were the first to barter for the tobacco they wanted. Ethan was pleased with the trade. He received several beaver pelts and lynx skins in that one. As far as he was concerned, he had the better of the deal. He smiled as he ran his fingers through the fine furs.

"What luck! This is better than I'd expected," he said as he put his bounty away. "I better set up camp somewheres before all the space is taken."

With all the tribes coming together at this point, it could only mean one thing, trouble. Ethan felt the blood rushing to his head, because everywhere he turned he saw a Sioux or a Miami brave carrying a spear or a rifle. A major council meeting appeared to be going on in the Ojibwa village besides the harvest festivities. The war between the states was still underway, but when the Union enlisted the aid of the Indian brotherhood in conquering the South, it was inevitable that the tables would turn. The conquerors would fall victim to the ill-fated promises and the broken treaties. They wrote words on paper and sent their leaders, who were dressed in fine uniforms, to ask for the hunting grounds and the green meadows that stretched across an endless plain. Such word only transfixed the destruction of many tribes and many more to come. There would come a day of reckoning, when the Indians would fight back to preserve their own humanity and to protect the lands that would serve them well for many generations to come. The Sioux would be the worse affected by the broken treaties. The Fox, Choctaw, Miami, and Chippewa would soon feel the hunger from the loss of their staple food, the buffalo.

Ethan hadn't considered what part he played in the land-grab game. All he wanted was to hunt and to trade with the people who lived for the land.

In his musing over the coming events, he didn't hear Running Bear approaching from behind.

"So you have returned," said a stern voice from behind him. It nearly made him jump out of his skin, because he thought it was Black Eagle. Yet, when Ethan did turn to face the man, he was looking into the face of Running Bear, who warned him that leaving the village was better for his health.

Ethan sighed with relief and thanked his lucky stars that he had time to prepare for the real confrontation. "Yeah! Uh! I have . . . it is good to be back among friends," Ethan said, somewhat asking if it was safe for him to stay. "How is the little woman? I mean . . . your wife . . . Two Moons? I hear you are about to be a father."

Running Bear knew what was on the trapper's mind. He could see fear in the man's eyes. If Black Eagle had been here instead, the poor man would have collapsed. And Black Eagle wasn't the forgiving type when his family's life was in danger. "You hide behind your words, Ethan. You have to face the truth, just as I have had to. A man whose heart is shallow will always feel the sting of fear. Black Eagle knows it was you who attacked his woman," Running Bear stated. He had apparently learned that his self-ish ways were in fact the reason he had lost so much in the past.

"But I did not mean to hurt the woman. You know how it was. You said you would tell my side of it when I left, remember? You told, right? He know that I made a mistake, right?" Ethan clamored. He could feel his stomach tighten. The thought of being scalped made him sick.

"Ah! So you do fear the mighty Black Eagle. That is good," Running Bear continued.

"What is good, my brother?" Black Eagle asked as he approached them. He had only heard his brother using his name like a weapon. "What is good?" he asked again. Then he looked at the man with whom Running Bear seemed to be threatening. "Ethan, I have been waiting for you to return. What better time, when I am here," Black Eagle said distinctly.

"Well, well! It's my old friend, Black . . . uh . . . Eagle," Ethan stammered. His eyes passed from one brother to the other. It would be easy to make a mistake. How could he be certain that he hadn't revealed himself to the one he feared the most?

"You have found me. Now . . . you must tell me what you were doing in my home last winter," Black Eagle demanded without changing the tone in his voice. He knew that his anger would trigger some unforeseen action if he handled the matter with Ethan improperly. "And be sure . . . my wife has already told me everything."

Black Eagle and Running Bear walked Ethan to an unoccupied part of the village. The less people around to hear, the better. René's honor was at stake again, and the last thing Black Eagle wanted was to have her status jeopardized by the loose lips of Ethan Crane. He was a forty-five-year-old trapper, with no responsibilities himself. Yet, it seemed he had scheming ways and a deceitful manner about him. Somehow he was doomed to change that behavior, since he took it upon himself to take any unclaimed woman to his bed whenever he chose to visit the Ojibwa. He would leave when the woman wanted him to commit to her. Ethan had fathered at least five children; the eldest was now seven years old. He neither cared for his children nor did he support them.

The matter of his children and his trying to take advantage of René was the sole purpose of why Black Eagle escorted him to an undisclosed part of the camp. The man would have to ante up for all of his misdeeds. No sooner had the trio reached their destination, than Ethan suddenly began to whimper and beg for his life. The twins eyed their quarry with speculation and considered their options. They could humiliate the man further and ban him from their village forever, or they could force him into taking responsibility for his children. Besides, trade with Ethan was a good prospect and it opened other areas of trade for their people. The latter punishment appealed to them more. As far as his unwanted visit to Black Eagle's home, that matter wasn't negotiable.

The village was all abuzz with the chatter of women at the cook fire. There were tiny babes tied to their cradle boards and toddlers stretching their legs and testing their nerve at walking. The older children played tag and others danced to the music of the flutes being played by the elders. The smell of broiled venison reached the noses of the new-comers who quickly lightened their loads and tasted the tender meat.

Many of the women set up their blankets with trinkets, belts, and lots of finery to trade with their visitors. Then each man brought out their bows and arrows and prepared for the war games in the open field. In the center of the camp the older women cooked the food and prepared the large bonfire that would be set aflame as dusk appeared. The village came alive with the excitement of a country bazaar.

René', White Feather, Morning Star, and Jaewa set up their blankets with the items they had planned to trade. They had belts, blankets, and children's garments and the most decoratively beaded dress in the camp. From its delicate lines to its fringes, it was noticeable each had spent many hours on that piece alone. They all had hopes of getting a good price for that one. White Feather had her eyes on a cast iron pot, while the others waited to see the other wares being displayed.

After settling the problem with Ethan, Black Eagle and Running Bear headed for the open field to participate in the foot race. It seemed that no one had missed them at all. The foot race was one of the most arduous in the competitions to prepare for. Tall Elk had planned to arm wrestle , but decided to keep his arm intact when he saw his muscular opponent. All the events would prove to be a test of strength and endurance. And as it would be, Gray Wolf's sons would be in the center of it. Every subchief and warrior from each faction would endure this hardship for the honor of their village. Even though Gray Wolf had a lot to brag about, he would like to see the trophies of honor hanging on the wall of his lodge. His sons were strong and ready.

Before the first event took place, Black Eagle arranged a place for René to sit near the line where she could see him at his best. In turn, he would be able to keep a watchful eye on her as well. He took great pride in showing off his wife. She was well-dressed, wearing one of the beaded elkskin dresses with fringes that swayed as she walked. She caught the eye of many who sat in wonder, wanting to know who the delightful beauty belonged to. Whoever he was, he was truly the luckiest man in the village to have been blessed with such a gift.

Not only had she taken care of his son, she treated the baby as though he was her very own child. It was good to have such a woman. Those who knew Black Eagle truly envied him and made a point to stay where their view wouldn't be obstructed. The watched her rather than the games. Suddenly, the drums sounded for the men to make ready. Out of the corner of his eye, Black Eagle carefully watched over his wife and waited for the signal to be given, knowing that he would be rushing to her side at the finish of this event.

René was totally oblivious to the attention she was receiving. She was more concerned with keeping One Shoe happy, since he missed his nap and his last feeding. She held One Shoe up so that he could see his father, who quickly turned to give them a smile. Just then, the drums stopped and a war whoop was sounded. The men took off like a bolt of lightning, with Black Eagle in the lead.

"Look . . . that is your father," she said softly. The little one giggled as she tickled his chubby feet.

There was no doubt to those who saw them together that the babe was happy and well fed. One Shoe was about sixteen months old and was trying to walk. His eyes were always aglow when he was with René'. He enjoyed listening to her soft voice as she told him stories of kings and queens, when she was really talking about the chiefs and their wives. The little one was quite dependent upon her for many of his needs, and feeding time was one of them. The wet nurse wasn't always available to René since she had other babies to attend to. For René', it required a lot of strength to deal with a baby with teeth to suck on her tender nipples.

Seeing that she would have no other recourse but to put him to the breast, she spoke to him. "Okay, young man, I will feed you, but if you bite me just once, you will get no more," she said firmly to the wide-eyed babe. She quickly placed her tunic over his head, where he found what he wanted. One Shoe made himself very comfortable in her lap, molding René's arms to fit around him. He was so excited that he gripped her nipple between his teeth. René gasped from the pain he had inflicted, and her sudden movement made the little one release his hold. He knew he was about to be removed from his food source, but she smacked his leg instead. She warned him again, but this time her tone had changed. One Shoe understood what that meant and the feeding went along well. Before his father returned as the winner of the foot race, One Shoe was fast asleep and feeling quite pacified.

Black Eagle came in first out of thirty men. René was so excited that she cheered when Black Eagle received two eagle feathers and a shield with a painted figure of a giant bird in flight. He added another trophy to his father's collection, just as he had done every year. Now it was time for the ballgames to begin. It was played with a long, hook-shaped pole and a stuffed deerskin ball. Tall Elk and Running Bear were on Black Eagle's team. It seemed this game was the most dangerous of the others being played.

"Are you enjoying the games?" Black Eagle asked as he joined he wife on the blanket.

"Yes! I've never been a part of so much activity in my entire life!" René' exclaimed. "Is there more?"

Black Eagle nodded and said, "The best of all the games will be coming up soon. It is a game of strength. Sometimes it is very dangerous. Many men get hurt or even maimed."

"Dangerous! You could be maimed! Then, I don't want you to play this game!" René insisted.

But Black Eagle only laughed. He was moved by her concern, but he had no intention of sitting out this one. He and the others could easily beat their opponents, hands down. "There is nothing to worry about," he said gently Then he tied the eagle feathers to her braid.

There was a delay with the next event, so Black Eagle took time to sit quietly next to his wife. He was aware of the attention she had received, but he made sure all who were watching knew that she was spoken for. He played with his son's foot, hoping to wake the boy so that he might watch him play in the next event. But the boy didn't move. He slept in the comfort of René's arms and kept a constant vigil at nursing.

"He has become too attached to you, Re-nea. He is too rough on you," he said as he released the boy's grip on her. "I want him to be fed by the wet nurse from now on. You may care for his needs, but you will not take him to the breast," Black Eagle ordered softly.

René agreed with Black Eagle, even though she knew that the baby would feel cheated. He was such a handsome baby, and his nearness helped to calm the emptiness she felt. She had to accept that he wasn't truly hers to begin with. His needs were more than her body would be able to withstand.

"I understand that you care for him, but you are now with child. His sucking can injure you, and what good would come of it?" Black Eagle added. He read her thoughts just as clearly as if she had spoken aloud.

"I will do as you say, Black Eagle, but I won't like it," René said in a flutter.

Black Eagle lifted her chin so that he could look into her dark green eyes, and said gently, "In the time you have lived among my people, I have watched you adapt to the many things around you. You do not complain. You learned from them. Now you must learn what it means to care for yourself and for our unborn child. I want you to be well . . . happy . . . and safe."

"Since you have explained it so well, I will do as you say," René finished with a smile. It didn't take long for Black Eagle to touch her heart. e was warm and caring in his ways. He took her, a stranger, to his home, to his people, and loved her without regret. Such a man was worthy of being loved. "But . . . I think you have other ideas in mind, don't you?"

His silence only increased her curiosity. But the look in his eyes made all his intentions clear. Black Eagle was somewhat jealous of the attention she was giving to his son. He did want her all to himself. He would remedy that tonight, when they would finally be alone.

The game was played just as Black Eagle had stated. It was as violent as it was exciting. There was a lot of pushing and shoving. A few received injuries to the head and/or stomach. Just then, Black Eagle retrieved the deerskin ball and headed for their goal, which happened to be more than thirty yards or so. Tall Elk ran interference and he blocked the others from recapturing the ball. There were grunts from the men crashing into each other.

Throughout the game René would either scream when they came too close to Black Eagle or she would cover her eyes when they collided. She remembered the dangers her father and brother faced whenever they broke in a horse. But there was no comparison in this case. The dangers were there. After the game, which happened to be a winning event for Black Eagle's team, they all headed back to the main campsite. Black Eagle and René went to Gray Wolf's cabin to enjoy the company of family and friends.

The main meal was already prepared. White Feather made enough to feed an army. She had venison roasting on the spit, dripping with its own juices. She also made rice and cornbread, served with maple syrup. Water was plentiful, and all the cups were filled to the brim. Then White Feather topped off the meal with a hot darkened brew. It was bitter to the taste, and to René's delight, realized she was drinking coffee. She hadn't had the likes of such since she left home. She sweetened the dark liquid with the sugar Robert left behind and savored every drop.

The family spent the rest of the evening talking about their adventures and telling old stories from the past. Then they turned to René and asked her to share a story. Many of the things she remembered involved her family and the happy times she spent while growing up on the Bainbridge Estates. She suddenly realized how little her new family new about her.

René decided it was safe to share some of her secrets from the past, her childhood, and the many adventures she shared with her father. She recalled the times her father spent reading stories or sometimes surprising her with a new gift. She continued until Black Eagle asked how she happened to be in the outpost when he whisked her away. Her throat cracked, and her words wouldn't come forth. It was a very emotional time for her to remember. It pained her so that Black Eagle changed the subject. There was more to her sadness than she was willing to admit, and he wouldn't allow her to be pressed into disclosing more of her past.

While René and Black Eagle sat peacefully about the fire with the family, another group of trappers entered the camp. They, too, had mules in tow carrying many items for trade, but they didn't want to trade for pelts. One trapper in particular seemed to be the leader of the group. His tall stature and muscular build, defined by the way he ordered his men around, led a few warriors to believe he wasn't a man to trifle with.

Each man under his command had a common goal in mind. They planned to canvas the area for the white woman rumored to be in this village. Matt Wilson and Walter Cory had tagged along with the group since their fortune hunting went up in smoke. They were a pitiful sight to behold, for they cried every time they thought about the Bainbridge Estates burning to the ground.

"That old devil made sure we didn't get our hands on his money," Walter complained for the millionth time. He had his life all mapped out. He planned to live in New York and find a respectable woman of means in Society Hill and of course settle down. Matt, on the other hand, planned to invest his money, preferably in one of the larger banks in New York. He also planned to control the market and trade. He was sure that he would become the richest man on the East Coast within a year's time.

"You are always complaining about that money. What is lost . . . is lost. But, if we find the girl . . . maybe there is a chance to get something out of it," Matt said with a quick grin. "I'll bet my last dollar that her brother has a lot of money hidden somewhere."

That seemed to ease Walter's mind, for he put his gear away without causing a scene. The following morning, they would survey the grounds. They never saw the woman before, but how many white women were living among these savages? Yet, there were many tribes in the area as well. They would be lucky to escape with their scalps intact with what they intended to do on the morrow. They watched the sky as a few clouds rolled in, casting a blanket over the shimmering moon. There were no signs of light except from the campfires set by their companions.

On the other side of the trappers' camp, James stowed his saddle near the campfire. He found it hard to get comfortable with so many Indians around him. There were times when he felt he knew the one who clobbered him from behind, but that was over a year ago. He wondered if it was the same one who rode his horse carelessly through the outpost the day he arrived. However, he never really got a good look at his face.

"His hair was in the way. If I saw him now, I wouldn't know him," James admitted to himself, angry that someone dared to stop him. "And René', my little pretty, when I get my hands on your lovely half-breed body, you will enjoy dying in my arms."

Matt and Walter listened as they always had to his ravings, even after they rescued the captain from certain death in the outpost. They knew Captain Courtland's obsession with the girl wouldn't be satisfied until he had his hands around her neck. They hoped he would wait for them to collect the bounty or to extort a few healthy dollars from the brother first.

"The man is losing his mind," Walter said almost loud enough for James to hear. "He keeps talking about some Injun. Well, we have a lot of them to look at now. Look at him, he keeps talking to himself . . . making threats."

"Yeah! And when he finds the one he is looking for, he won't be able to do a thing with him," Matt added. "And, besides, if he kills the girl, we will lose everything . . . the bounty and the money from her brother. I don't know about you, but I'm going to keep an eye on him. He could spoil it for the both of us," Matt continued. His eyes narrowed when he looked in the captain's direction. "You keep an eye on him for a few hours, and then I'll take over. I want to get some sleep now, because tomorrow we are going hunting."

Walter agreed and quickly poured a cup of coffee. He had had money on his mind, and the bounty would definitely appease him after he lost thousands in a single night. As he leaned back on his saddlebag, a smile wisped the corner of his mouth. He would reach a point of satisfaction, money, women, and prestige.

In the main camp, René slept restlessly. She felt a hand grabbing her around her throat. She woke with a start, sweat dotting her forehead and neck. Even in the comfort of her own home, she felt something was desparately wrong. Black Eagle moved her closer, but it was too hot and her nerves were wreaking havoc on her stomach. René was showing signs of early pregnancy, the restlessness and the morning sickness seeming to attack at will.

Try as she may to keep cool, she found the heat of her cabin too unbearable. She couldn't stand feeling closed in any longer. Black Eagle sensed her urgency and took her for a brief walk toward the lake. With all the excitement of the day, it was a wonder that she would be able to get any rest. But the dream, and the hand on her throat, made her sick again. She needed more than just a walk in the night air.

René and Black Eagle walked through many campfire sites before reaching the lake. They noticed that each tribe made sure they could be recognized by their colorful plumage and finery. The Miami took pride in their gold and elk skins. The Sioux took pride in their buffalo hides, while the Ojibwa traded both with their pride in rice, maple syrup, corn, and potatoes.

Careful not to disturb their guests, Black Eagle and René went to a peaceful and secluded section of the lakeshore. When they arrived, Black Eagle scouted the area for intruders. Satisfied that the area was clear, he laid out the blanket for them to rest upon. It was good to see no campfires burning or to hear the voices of the restless, stirring in the background.

"Sit! The air will do you good," he said as he helped her to the blanket.

René did as her doting husband had commanded. She inhaled the sweet air as though it were from the nectar of a flower and soon felt the queasiness disappear. A soft breeze caressed her cheeks as she finally settled down. She rested her head on his broad shoulders and placed her hand on his chest. Black Eagle was right: The air did help. The air was cool, much cooler than it was in the confines of their cabin.

"It is good . . . you will sleep better," Black Eagle said soothingly. He always enjoyed sleeping under the stars or in the open field. He considered it a connection between him and the Great Spirits.

René couldn't help thinking that she was blessed to have him in her life. Their days and nights together were always special to her. There were times when she cried in silence, grieving for her children and her parents, and he would hold her until she fell asleep. She wanted so much for them to be alive and thriving, but she never disclosed her feelings about it. There were times she wished Black Eagle to say their names, but his beliefs were so strong and his customs couldn't be changed, not even for her.

Death was a matter Black Eagle never discussed with her. As a matter of fact, he never told her until they brought Dancing Wind's body home that they never speak of the dead . . . that their grief must be private. She had to hear it from someone else, someone who hated her with every fiber in her soul. Death and betrayal caused René to lose faith and sometimes to tie up her emotions. Yet, Black Eagle's strength, love, and devotion was most gratifying for René'. They shared more than just a cabin between the two of them. Their love was confirmed by the way they treated each other.

Feeling somewhat restless again, René asked, "Black Eagle . . . the people who come to our village . . . have they always been so friendly?"

For the first time René had included herself as one of them, and Black Eagle was proud. But instead of answering her question, he asked, "Why do you want to know such things? It is not important for a woman to know these things. It is our way." Then he said slowly, "You have much to learn, Re-nea. In time it will come to you."

René turned away from him, something he didn't enjoy. Many times he had tossed her words to the wind and the result was always the same. So, he answered, knowing that what she wanted was consideration and respect for her feelings, "The Sioux were once our enemies. But that was many winters ago. They took from us, and we took from them. We warred with each other until one of our tribesmen bargained a marriage with the chief of the Ojibwa. My mother, White Feather, is Sioux. She married Gray Wolf, my father, to put an end to the war between our two tribes. She is the reason there is peace between us."

René listened and tried to envision the wedding of the once young White Feather and Gray Wolf. She grew to understand the people she lived with, danced with, and gathered food with. They were in every sense of the word more civilized than the people she grew up with. She felt at home with these gentle people. At least that is how she felt after a year in hiding. She never felt that kind of closeness while growing up in the Ohio Valley. The only security and love she received came from her family. The people of Wilmot didn't treat her the same as her brother. She was envied by her schoolmates and they pretended to be her friend, only to come to her home to reap the benefits of her family's hospitality. She was forced to play hostess to the very ones who burned her home to the ground.

Rachel Bainbridge wanted so much for her daughter to have friends that she couldn't see that they were using her to get into society's graces. Instead, René could be found riding with her father and brother rather than playing with those who proclaimed to be her friend. René was truly a victim of the civilized world. She learned that she would eventually rise above their pettiness. She stopped caring and worrying about whether they would accept her. She was happy as long as her father loved her.

Then she met James Courtland, who in his own way tried to sweep her off her feet. However, René was too independent and self-reliant. At nineteen years of age, a young woman is usually married and planning a family. Her parents were eager for her to marry him since it seemed René would never meet a man on her own. James appeared to be the most likely candidate since he was a military academy graduate. They were sure he had potential when he received his captain's promotion in less than a year's time. He was the youngest man to hold such a rank at peacetime. René felt she could do worse. That's where it all started for her.

Then she told Black Eagle about her real mother and why she wound up in the outpost the day they met. Black Eagle listened to her words and, for the first time, he was able to understand the full danger she faced. René waited for a reaction from him. She had told him the truth. She told him the great secret that had haunted her from the day she was driven from her home."Now that you know the truth, do you still want me?" she asked carefully.

If her instincts told her anything, it told her to be aware of his temperament. He may love her with all his soul, but was it strong enough to survive? Was it a convenience for him to have someone who was perfect, flawless, and unmarked by shame? What more could she dare tell him? They had suffered greatly at the hands of the Sauks. And his silence was like an arrow, piercing her heart. Her life had changed so abruptly that she knew she could never return to the world she left behind.

"You ask much of me, Re-nea. But you do not see what is in my heart," Black Eagle said slowly. "You are a brave woman to have faced such sadness, such pain."

"No, I am not brave, Black Eagle. I am scared. The man you protected me from is still out there, searching for me. I believe he will find me and he will complete what he has set out to do," René said with certainty.

Black Eagle remembered the man as clearly as he remembered the Sauk who kidnapped René. He would never forget how the man stalked into the outpost and made his way into René's room. Then he remembered the vision he had of René running for her life from a man wearing strange clothing with bright buttons. That made him sit up, almost winded. He grabbed René and held her close. "If that day ever comes, he will die. I will not let him take what is mine. I swear it on the memory of my dead children and on the blood of my people," he exclaimed.

He had no intention of allowing James Courtland or any man to take his wife away. He had missed so much in the time they had spent apart. Now, everything that was important to him lay here in his arms, a thriving and compassionate woman. He had more than he ever dared by the joining of two people. He had professed with all sincerity that he loved her.

His very being was complete with her, and he would rather die than live without her.

Soon the night air finally cooled, and a light breeze filtered through the trees. Not far away, a beaver dragged a large branch to its lair. In another section of the wood, a rabbit scurried for its burrow, while a fox lay in its wake, waiting for the rabbit to reappear. It seemed the fox caught its supper when they heard a twig snap. Then there was silence in the stillness of the forest. The clouds had passed and allowed the stars to twinkle against its blackness.

"You still haven't answered my question," René stated coolly. She wanted to hear the words pass through his lips . . . to commit himself.

Black Eagle was caught up in her essence. René had put him in a position he wasn't ready for. He had no trouble telling his people that he loved her, but somehow the words hardly came when they were making love. She would be his beauty forever, but he could lose her by not expressing the few precious words.

He hesitated for a moment, thinking that he was a fool for saying what he already felt. "I do want you, Re-nea. I will always want you. Do you not feel that when I touch you?"

Black Eagle touched her in her most secret places. If anyone had the right to touch her, he most certainly was the one and he would kill anyone who tried in his place. It surprised her that he equated making love to her as the same as being in love. But when he did make love, she was able to forget the pain of yesterday. She felt him inside her even when they were apart. He always made sure that she was appeased in the time of their mating. Strangely enough, she began to feel foolish for questioning him.

"I feel . . . that . . . you . . . , " René tried to explain, but everywhere he touched, he made her catch her breath.

"You feel my touch. I want you to feel me when I make love to you. Your body is one with mine. Do you feel that, Re-nea?" he asked softly. Black Eagle gently eased his fingers down the hollow of her neck to the soft swell of her breasts. He could feel her heart pounding wildly as he removed the rest of her clothing.

René could only sigh in response to his request. Black Eagle had taken hold and made sure she knew that nothing, not even her past, would make him turn away from her. She fell right into his trap and was swallowed up in the abyss of his strength. She welcomed the solace of his arms. She wanted him to carry her away, to keep her and to sustain her need for him.

How could she ever doubt his love for her when he touched her that way?

René could barely contain herself, but answered, "Yes, my love . . . I feel you. I . . . love you."

"They are only words. I believe in showing how much I will love you, so that you never forget," Black Eagle proclaimed.

René was totally swept away and she was forever spellbound. Black Eagle's love for her was strong, far stronger than she ever imagined. Never in her wildest dreams had she ever expected to have someone's heart in the palms of her hands, beating with such fire. Then she remembered how her father described the unbridled love he felt for her mother. He must have truly loved Sarah Josephine, almost or even more than Black Eagle loved René herself. The night was theirs to do with as they pleased. They were two soaring eagles dancing in the night sky.

CHAPTER
TWENTY

THE LAST DAY OF the harvest celebration went on as scheduled. The Ojibwa, the Sioux, and the Miami danced until dawn. they sang the songs of the dead to wish them a merry journey. Food was plenty, for everyone had contributed their share to the merriment. Several couples were joined in marriage. Each couple gave an offering to mark a blessing for the following year. The shaman danced and bestowed the blessing of the Great Spirit as the bonfire was ignited.

This was the ceremony René missed. It also marked the first anniversary of their marriage. Black Eagle paid tribute to the shaman, who then presented René with a small medicine bag. He spoke loud and clear, so that the spirits would take notice. He asked for the spirits to watch over them and to protect the children they were expecting. He asked that the children be born strong and healthy. As he said these words, he touched René's belly with firm hands. At first she was stunned by his action, but realized that he was only acting out his prayer.

White Feather and Gray Wolf also joined in the tribute. They were sure another blessing would bring more grandchildren to fill the void of the lost ones. They were pleased that René was with child again. This time she would have the protection of the Great Spirit. She accepted the gifts of protection and said a prayer to her God and to theirs. For all she knew, they were one and the same.

The family was so absorbed in their prayer, they hadn't noticed the arrival of Subchief Thundercloud, who had whispered some unsettling news in Gray Wolf's ear. He jumped to his feet like a young warrior and headed toward the Sioux encampment with his escort. From the look on his face, Black Eagle and Running Bear knew that a serious matter had dragged him away. He wouldn't leave unless something was terribly wrong. They followed, mostly out of curiosity and to protect their father.

Black Eagle turned quickly to his wife and said, "Stay with Mother and Two Moons."

"Is something wrong, Black Eagle?" René asked softly.

"Do not worry," he offered. He didn't wait around to explain more. He and Running Bear just bolted off, leaving their women behind.

René watched him walk away until he was completely out of sight. She was still feeling ill at ease from the night before and could only hope that he would return soon. Although they had spent a wonderful evening together, there was still a sense of terror quaking in René's nerves. She had felt the strain coming on for several days, but never like that. Her nightmares were becoming real. At one point during the day she thought she saw James Courtland among the white traders in the camp. There were other sightings, but René was afraid she was losing her mind. She was too ashamed to tell Black Eagle, for fear he wouldn't believe her.

"What is wrong, my daughter? You seem so far away with your thought," White Feather inquired.

Two Moons agreed. René wasn't herself. The once vibrant and happy smile had turned sad and foreboding. She was forever looking, half expecting and half dreading the outcome of what she sought. In her heart, she knew James Courtland wouldn't stop pursuing her until she was dead. He promised her that she would know when death was near. He seemed so close to her, yet unseen.

Two Moons moaned and then leaned against the pile of moose skins that Tall Elk had traded for. The time for birthing a new babe was at hand. No longer thinking of herself, René rushed to Two Moons' side. She would worry about James Courtland later. But for now, Two Moons needed her.

James and his followers had come together to disclose what they had found. Each man said they had come to a dead end. But Walter Cory sat on his blanket smiling as though he had uncovered the lost Mayan treasures. He waited patiently for each man to give his report and watched the captain's reaction. It was his way of toying with the man's ego and he had succeeded.

"Damn it! Not one of you came up with the location of René

Bainbridge! Are you blind? You all know what she looks like," James snarled as he kicked the saddle at his feet.

Matt moved back and waited for the captain to explode in rage. He had many episodes while pursuing the girl and he had injured a few of his followers. Those under Captain Courtland's command were completely afraid to speak against him. He didn't have the respect of his men; only their fear of being hung for disobeying an officer helped him to maintain his control over them. Otherwise, they would have deserted him months ago.

"But, sir . . . the people here . . . they speak very little English. Those who are willing to talk to us say there is no white woman living here," Private Smith offered.

Courtland paced the dry ground like a caged animal. He was agitated beyond the realms of disgust. He visited every Indian village between the outpost and here and in every one of them he heard the same thing. The only time he seemed to lighten the burden on his men was the day an Indian woman wandered into their camp begging for food. Out of her gratitude, she told them of a woman who had come to her village over a year ago and had turned her people against her. She was the only glimmer of light to shine on the whereabouts of René Bainbridge.

"You blithering idiots! You will bring these people down around our necks!" he yelled sharply. When he finished, his voice could be heard echoing through the trees.

"You mean that you will bring these people down around our necks! It was you who had to come here in the first place! And it is you who is trying to destroy that godforsaken wench!" Walter said forcefully.

James was enraged by Walter's indignant behavior. He would hardly tolerate insubordination from his own men, and here was a civilian taking such a liberty. He stormed his views again, causing each man to turn around, with their hands on their weapons in preparation to fire at will. They were definitely outnumbered and outclassed by the tribes who were only yards away. They were only twenty facing at least five hundred or more. So far they were successful in making sure they were welcomed. But that could change at any moment, when they snatched the wrong woman from the Fox tribe. To complete the same act without bringing the entire network upon them would be a task of uncertainty.

Smith began to fumble with his hat and made one final pitch at making his captain happy. He had taken a walk in the forest late last night and had come across a couple near the lake. He would get into trouble, he thought, if he didn't say anything, especially since he wasn't able to complete any of the assignment he was given.

"Well, sir, I . . . might have seen . . . somethin' last night," he stammered. "I saw a man and a woman in the woods last night. They were . . . uh . . . you know . . . but I heard 'em talkin'. I could not see the woman, but I heard her real good. She sounded like the woman you brought to the fort. I am sure of it, cap'in, sir," Smith continued.

Somewhat amazed at the information Smith offered, James stopped short of knocking the boy down and listened for the proof he needed. If René was here, his search was finally over. He could exact his revenge, and no one would be the wiser for it.

Glad to have been reprieved from a thrashing, the boy continued. "She said your name . . . sir! She said somethin' 'bout livin' in a big house and bein' saved out ah marryin' you, sir."

That was the proof he wanted to hear. The Indian wench was right, and they killed her before she was able to tell them where her village was located. It took them several months to get to this point, and now René was only minutes away from her destiny.

"Very clever of her. She is smarter than I ever thought she would be," James said, flushing. "She was able to avoid me. All this time . . . damn it! It will be a pleasure to kill her slowly."

James walked quickly toward his saddlebags, which leaned neatly against his saddle. Everything in his area was neat and clean, including his sleeping area, while the others were quite slovenly about their belongings. He pulled out a map, which he unfolded and placed on the plush grassy spot near his bedroll. After he examined the map in silence, he called Walter and Matt to his side. The trio examine the map and began to argue. No matter what the other two wanted to do, it seemed Courtland had plans of his own.

Gray Wolf had been taken to the Sioux War Council, where Chief Bear Claw of the Sioux and Chief Chinock of the Miami were waiting. News from the South had come that the white man's war had taken a devastating turn. They were now coming into the Black Hill. It seemed the treaties that the white man had brought from the chief were not worth the paper they were printed on. The land was no longer the land of the Sioux. The white man had broken too many promises and killed many of their people. The voices of the young warriors could be heard, showing their discontentment. They wanted to fight, drive the white man out of their lands. They wanted him to suffer as they were made to.

"We have come to a crossroad, where war with the white man may mean the end of our way of life. There will be no turning back once the lance has been thrown. Our woman and our children will starve because their husbands and father will die to protect the land. The buffalo will no longer roam freely. The land that has served us and our fathers will be red with the blood of our people. This I believe will be the future for all our people," Chief Bear Claw stated to the council.

"If that is so, then the white man has already won. For he has not only come into your land, he has come into ours," Gray Wolf offered. He knew that a time such as this would one day affect the lives of his people. He wondered if the white men trading in his village had come as spies.

"You speak the truth, Gray Wolf, but the white man will have to fight the French and the British to get this land. I do not think they plan to come this far north. They want all the Lakota lands and all the land south thereafter," Bear Claw retorted quickly.

"Then what is your plan, Chief Bear Claw?" Gray Wolf asked.

The answer was clear before it was spoken. They would fight to protect their lands and their people. They would have preferred that the white man leave their lands and allow them to live as they saw fit and in peace, but that was not to be the case. "I call upon my brothers from the north and from the east and from the west to join in our struggle. I will declare war on the white man. He has raped our lands, killed our women and children. They shoot the buffalo for sport and let them rot under the sun. I saw the sacred White Buffalo in my dreams. It trampled the very grounds, which my brothers and I have hunted for many years. When the White Buffalo spoke, it was like thunder . . . thunder of guns, big guns; killing our people," Bear Claw proclaimed.

The vision was real. And at the same time it took the chief to disclose the inevitable premise, another plotted to disrupt the peaceful sanctity of the Ojibwa. A clash of two worlds was itching to unfold before them. The ideals of power and strength, glory and fortitude and the protection of the family would all be sacrificed in an instant. The medicine of the people must be great to withstand the pull of the white man's grip upon them. War touches the mighty and the weak. It stretches a man's soul to the heavens where he will meet and become part of the Great Spirit. The Indian Nation was supposed to prevail over all the injustices flailed upon them.

Black Eagle listened carefully, knowing that his father would call upon him and Running Bear to fight alongside their Sioux brothers. Then he whispered to his brother, "We are going to fight, Running Bear. Father has not given his word yet, but I think the answer is yes."

"How soon? Two Moons is ready, and I want to see my son before I leave for war," Running Bear stated quietly.

"I do not know. It is not my wish to leave my wife at this time. But from what the Chief says, we will not have a choice in the matter," Black Eagle answered quickly.

He was right. The issues being discussed were of a serious nature. Their livelihood was being threatened by an outside force . . . a force greater than they expected. They were determined to maintain their freedom at all costs. He could see the anger of his brother tribesmen growing while they waited for Gray Wolf to accept Bear Claw's hand in a gesture of friendship. It was their duty as warriors to protect the people.

"How say you, Gray Wolf, Chief of the Ojibwa and husband of my sister?" asked Chief Bear Claw. He had given Gray Wolf a chance to concede and acknowledge the facts as they were presented.

"I say this to you and to your people and to my people . . . I will stand by my brother in his time of need. My people are your people and your friends. Your enemies are our enemies. If you must fight to protect what is yours, our arrows will fly along with yours. It is right that we do this," Gray Wolf announced with great care.

The Ojibwa warriors along with the Sioux cheered as their two Chiefs smoked the peace pipe. It opened a new relationship between them. However, the Miami Chief felt slighted by his gesture. He wasn't asked to partake in the war against the white man. Even though his people were spread out in several reservations in the southernmost parts of the United States (Florida, South Carolina, and parts of Oklahoma), he felt assured that his people would break their bonds and join in the fight for freedom.

"I am sure that Chief Gray Wolf will do as you have asked of him. However, you have not asked me! I have pledged my honor amongst my people that I will keep the brotherhood of the Sioux and Ojibwa. It is my right to be part of this. The lands of the Miami were taken long before yours. The Ohios were our lands extended along to the lands of the Chippewa, your brother. We have lost more than you but we are not defeated. We will be defeated if you do not allow the Miami to take part," Chinock said sternly.

Many warriors agreed with Chinock's words. The fight with the white man couldn't be won without the aid of all the tribes banding together. Chief Sitting Bull, the great chief of all the Sioux Nation, would be pleased to know he had such allies at his side.

"So be it!" Gray Wolf said. "The Miami and the Ojibwa have pledged to come prepared for battle when the time nears. We will not be weakened by tears of sadness. We will be strengthened by the blood of our enemies."

On his last word, the drum started playing a loud and foreboding cadence. The warriors from all three tribes quickly rose to their feet to dance the war dance. In the main camp, the women began to pray, for they knew what the drums meant. Some cried, while other fell to their knees, holding their children. The drums caused an alarm in the trappers' camp. They began to scurry and pack up their mules. For all they knew, no white man was safe in this territory.

"What is that? What's going on here?" Courtland asked one of the trappers who managed to stow his gear.

The man was trembling from head to toe. He pulled on his mule, demanding that it follow. The mule tugged against him, and the trapper cursed him for delaying his departure. Then Courtland put himself in front of the man and demanded an explanation. "Tell me what goes here!"

"You'd better stow yer gear an' get the hell out o here. Them Injun are plannin' a wuh. You hear them drums. That means theys mad 'bout somethin'. Clear out whiles you got the chance," he said as he pushed Courtland out of his way. There was no way in hell he was going to stay in that village.

Courtland turned to his men and said, "The plans have changed! We will grab her tonight. With all this chaos, they won't be able to track us down. There will be too many trails leading out of here tonight."

Matt and Walter rushed to their mounts. It would be better if they got their hands on her first. At least she would be kept alive long enough to collect a ransom from the brother. No sooner had they mounted, the others, including Courtland, had taken to their mounts. Each man headed off in their own direction, hoping that they would find what they were looking for.

It was dark except where the light from the campfire glistened at the portals of each cabin. There were only a few women walking in the night air, Morning Star being one of them. She had planned to make her way to White Feather's cabin, when she saw a few men approaching fast on horseback. They appeared to be looking for someone and were in a great hurry, besides. They peered through several cabin doors, turning over pots, kicking the people's belongings out of their way. They started toward her, when someone yelled, "I found her!"

She saw a man roughly pulling René out of White Feather's cabin. When she was about to scream, they hit her square on the chin. She watched as the man tossed René's limp body over his shoulder and quickly carried her away to the horse waiting on the side. Then they disappeared into the darkness. It all happened so fast that Morning Star couldn't see the man's face. All she knew was that he was white.

White Feather came out of the cabin screaming. Two Moons had just given birth, when the man burst into the cabin. They weren't harmed because René pleaded with him to spare their lives.

"Help! Someone help us! A man . . . has taken my son's wife," White Feather cried. She was so shaken by the ordeal that she collapsed, holding her chest.

Morning Star finally gained the strength to move, and rushed to her side. Jaewa heard the commotion and made her way into the cabin, only to find Two Moons and her newborn huddled against the wall, too afraid to move.

"Where is Re-nea?" she asked, but received no answer. Then she remembered hearing White Feather's words. Jaewa's heart sank. Now that she had adopted Re-nea as her own, someone had taken her child away. "Someone has to tell Black Eagle before they get to far."

A young maid of thirteen was ordered to go, but her mother feared the men would come back. Then, as though a prayer had been answered, Running Bear approached. He was anxious to see his wife and hopefully his new son. But his happiness was turned to anger as he listened to the tearful account of what had taken place in their absence.

"White men did this? Black Eagle must be told,"he said as he ran to the council fire.

Courtland and his men were about five miles away when Running Bear reached Black Eagle with the news. They couldn't have planned it better. With all the men occupied, the women were left unprotected and unsuspecting. It was like stealing an apple from a child.

It was Walter Cory who found her. He took enjoyment out of her pleading for the lives of her family. He laughed at her when he pointed the gun at the old woman and then at the younger one. She could see they meant nothing to him. He had his prize and now he planned to protect it. It was strange at first. When he entered the cabin, René looked just like the rest of the Indian maids. She was dressed like them and even wore her hair like them. He had looked into many lodges, interrupting the feeding and the bedding of the young. She had adapted so well that her disguise nearly saved her. But it was her eyes . . . her dark green eyes gave her away. If she hadn't looked up when he entered, he would have passed her by.

René began to awaken from the dream world that had been forced upon her. Her chin throbbed from the abuse she had been dealt. Being thrown over a horse like a sack of flour wasn't comfortable at all. And her captor could care less if she were comfortable in the slightest. She knew from the way her assailant was riding that he wanted to put distance between him and her people. He pushed his horse into a full gallop and maintained that speed until they reached a clearing. There they were joined by several others, all of whom had one thing on their minds.

Cory dismounted from his horse very casually. He was pleased with himself since he was the one to find her. He then pulled her from the horse and eased her to the ground. His barbaric behavior had now turned to a more gentlemanlike manner. He handed her his canteen and tried to persuade her to drink, but René refused. She stayed where he placed her, without making a sound. Everywhere she looked, there were men with rifles. Some of which were the same men who killed her father and burned down the Bainbridge Estates. She had only a shadowy recollection of that day. There was so much hatred, she just closed her mind to it.

Matt Wilson made his way over while pushing Courtland's men out of the way. He wanted to make sure that his friend hadn't made a mistake and snatched the wrong girl. But there she was, the same beauty, the same green eyes. He could hear the others giving their appraisal as well. They, too, were caught up in her remarkable beauty. They were amazed that the wilderness hadn't tarnished her looks. The sun was kind to her. Her hair shone like fire under the moonlight, and her skin was like polished oak.

"I see we have what we came for," he said as he appraised her from head to toe. "You gave us quite a bit of trouble."

René looked at him, questioning his motives. "Trouble? What trouble have I caused you?"

"Never mind! You will be well taken care of . . . I promise you!" Matt said sheepishly.

His behavior puzzled René far more than she wanted to reveal. She shuddered to think that these men had tracked her to this point only to take care of her. How was the question? In the time she had spent with

Black Eagle and his people, she never suspected that someone other than her brother was searching for her She looked into the faces of the men who surrounded her. They seemed overly anxious at her presence, and their inane statements about her were quite uncomfortable.

"No wonder Captain Courtland came after her . . . she is a looker," one stated.

"Yeah, an' look at that body. I could do somethin' wid that . . . ha-ha!" another snickered.

"Shut up over there! You are scaring the poor thing out of her mind," Matt laughed. "And besides, the best is yet to come."

It was obvious to René that she would be compromised if something wasn't done to squelch their intentions. There seemed to be no end to the matter where men would take a woman's virtue and toss it aside like a used saddle when they were through with it. She had no weapons to protect herself. All she had was her wit, and at this point in time, her wit wouldn't deter them. They moved closer, hoping to get a better look and maybe touch the infamous beauty. With nowhere to run, René moved back against the tall steed that had blocked her way. Her captors were quite sure that they would be able to enjoy the delicacies that were hidden behind the beautifully decorated dress.

Just when it seemed they would attack, another group of men on horseback approached at full speed. René recognized one of the riders immediately. It pained her to see that the captain had keep his word. He had certainly found her and had spared no time doing so. She had avoided him for many months, sending him on false trails. In as much as she was safe in her husband's village, there always seemed to be a shadow pressing over her. And her heart nearly leaped in terror as he came near.

Then Courtland dismounted and, with quick and even strides, walked toward her. There was a glare in his eyes that signaled she was in more danger with him than with his men. He stopped short, within inches of her, and gave her the once over. He was so close to her that she could feel his hot breath on her forehead. She could sense the intensity of his hatred. But she stood her ground and never faltered. René held her head high and proud, as though she were facing a firing squad.

"Well, well, well! It seems we are back together, my dear. Back where we left off a year ago . . . or don't you remember that night? Hm?" Courtland asked forcefully.

"I remember very well. I remember that you are nothing but an animal.

You are the lowest thing on the face of the earth," René answered quickly. "How dare you— "

"Shut up, you little whore!" he snapped. He was pleased that his words shocked her. "Do you think I care how you feel right now?" Courtland bantered. "Do you think your Indian buck can save you? Now?" he asked as he grabbed her by the hair. He relished the pain he had caused her. To punish her further, he pressed his lips against her ear and said, "You have no rights. You must remember your place. So . . . you tried to hide the fact that your mother was black. Did you think I would never find out, bitch? Did you?"

"No! I didn't know about my mother until it was our wedding day! That was why I released you from your promise to marry me!" René admonished. She could feel her stomach quaking inside. "It's the truth!"

"Liar! You've lied to me for the last time! You were going to hide your secret by marrying me. Just think, I would have fathered little brown babies," James said sarcastically. "And you were going to let me believe they were mine."

"That's not true! I couldn't bring myself to hurt you. I cared for you!" René explained, but his grip tightened and made her gasp in pain as he yanked her head back.

With his ill treatment of the young woman, Courtland's men advanced on him when he appeared he would harm her, and yet with one glance he made them retreat. Walter Cory pulled his revolver, but Matt waved him off. The last thing they needed was gun play. If they were going to get anything out of this, the woman had to be kept alive, at least long enough for them to collect it.

"I'll break her neck if anyone interferes. Do I make myself clear?" Courtland demanded. he extended no mercy to the young woman except contempt.

Walter and Matt shook their heads to affirm his crazed statement. It wouldn't serve any purpose to try to weed her out of his hands now. They watched as Courtland escorted her to his horse and, without much care, he forced her to sit on his lap after he mounted. Then he ordered his men to get on their horses and to follow him. At least they were once again heading for Fort Wayne. Once there, maybe his madness would stop. They watched as he rode ahead and plotted their next move.

"We will have to kill him, Matt. He isn't in this for the money," Walter stated as he surveyed the distance between Courtland and himself.

"I agree . . . but we have to be careful not to make it look like one of us had anything to do with it," Matt answered quickly. "Remember, you and I made a deal to split everything, fifty-fifty. That doesn't include his men."

"I like the way you think, pal o' mine," Walter said, grinning.

They caught up with Courtland and maintained an even pace behind him and their bounty. They kept a watchful eye on the trail they left behind, hoping that they had put enough distance between them and the Indians in the encampment. If they were caught with the Bainbridge woman, they would certainly die. None of them had ever faced an Indian on the warpath before.

Black Eagle didn't take the news well at all. His first impulse was to follow the trail leading to his wife. The longer he delayed, the farther away she would be. There was no telling what these white men had on their minds when they had taken her, but it bothered him nonethesame. In his anger, he stormed away from the council meeting, which drew a lot of attention. Tall Elk and Running Bear were close behind, trying to calm him and allay his fears.

"Whoever this man is . . . he must die. He has taken what is mine and that I will not stand for," Black Eagle yelled as he pushed pass the warriors in his path. It was unlike him to be so brutish.

Running Bear could tell that his brother was plotting a coup. He felt obligated to go since Black Eagle had helped with the burial of his wife. And Tall Elk would do it out of friendship. They followed Black Eagle to his home, where he gathered his weapons and then donned his chest plate. Then he reached into the small pot, where René stored bear fat for medicinal purposes, and smeared it all over his body and then used the ash from the fire pit. Now he was ready to track them down.

As Black Eagle was about to depart, Gray Wolf entered. He became concerned when he saw his son storm out of the council meeting in anger. The troubled look on his son's face forced him to leave the council meeting prematurely. He and the other chiefs were about to document the agreement to declare war on the whites at the appropriate time and his son was about to wage his own war. He had to calm the anger generated in his son: If not curtailed, the loss to him would be great.

"My son, you are troubled by the misdeeds of the outsiders? You know this is not the way to take revenge. You are not thinking with the mind of a war chief. You are letting your heart lead you to destruction . . . not just for you, but for your wife," Gray Wolf said calmly. "Now you must tell me what you want to do and we will then work on saving your Re-nea."

It was hard for Black Eagle to maintain his emotions. If he weren't in love with René he would be able to think and rationalize the entire plan. However, he was very much in love and that clouded all his thoughts knowing that she was out there without him. She was carrying his child, and that meant they were all threatened. His whole world was at risk.

"The longer I stand here, the farther away they will be!" Black Eagle said in a rush.

"I understand, my son," gray Wolf said forcefully. "But, now, we must think of a way to get her back without causing the white man to seek her again."

Gray Wolf made Black Eagle sit down. The time for gathering strength had come. Then he ordered Tall Elk to bring Chief Bear Claw and Chief Chinock and all the subchiefs from each tribe, including their own. Tall Elk was off like a flash, while Running Bear stayed to console his brother.

To draw attention to his other son and to maintain a sense of sharing Gray Wolf asked, "And you, Running Bear, I am told that you have given me a fine grandson. That is good." Gray Wolf smiled and tried to bring some light into the darkness that prevailed.

"It is true, Father," Running Bear answered quickly. "But I have not seen him yet."

"Then go my son . . . your wife and child are waiting for you. Besides, I want to spend some time with your brother. He needs time to think," he continued.

At that same moment, René's route had changed. Instead of heading west as previously taken, they were now heading south. It was necessary to take the wide berth of the Ojibwa village so that they could get to the border without being stopped. From what René had learned about the land and its little secrets, she knew that her final destination would be Fort Wayne. James Courtland was a man of his word. He said it the night he was about to rape her. So there was no question she knew where she was headed.

"You are very quiet, René, " he said in her ear. "It isn't like you. You must be wondering what is in store for you . . . hmm!" James continued.

However, René held her tongue and said nothing that might provoke him because she imagined that if she did, he would harm her and the child she was carrying. She dallied over the prospects of telling him, but she feared he might become even more enraged. She had no choice but to keep silent and pray that Black Eagle was close behind.

"You don't wish to speak? That is well. After we get to Fort Wayne, I suspect you will have a lot to say," he said sharply.

They rode all night and all of the following day. James was totally in his element when it came to riding. He thought that everyone should be able to live on the saddle as he did. Private Jones and the other soldiers began to complain about their rumps. Some developed saddle sores, while others just felt dull aches in their backs.

Feeling nausea about to erupt, René asked, "Would you please stop! I feel ill."

"Ha! I don't believe you," James snapped, and continued on his course.

"Well, if you don't, your shiny boots will be ruined," René said as she held her stomach. "I do suggest you stop for a while."

He seemed surprised that she would become so defiant, but he was convinced she was serious. Even she was surprised at the tone in which she had addressed him. Her manner had changed. She was no longer the soft-spoken, mild-mannered young woman of last year.

"You have won this round, my dear. But the battle isn't over yet!" he said with certainty.

James pulled back on the reins and told his men, "Dis-mount!" He took a quick look and found a spot suitable for him and his guest to rest. he headed straight for it after leaving a few orders. Matt and Walter followed, but when they arrived, James kindly excused them to join the others. His plans for the day didb't include entertaining the riffraff.

"Gentlemen, as you can see, I wish to talk to the prisoner . . . alone! I know you will be comfortable in the main camp," Courtland said directly. "I understand your concern for her safety, so you will understand why I decided to keep her away from the others. She is perfectly safe in my care."

"It seems you have taken matters into your own hands. Maybe the young lady would like to have our company, instead. Right, Miss Bainbridge?" Walter asked coldly.

René wasn't given a chance to respond. She just closed her eyes and waited for the eruption from her stomach to occur. "I do believe I made it clear to you, gentlemen. She prefers to spend her days with me," he continued as he placed his hand on the revolver at his waist.

James was quick at the draw, quicker than the two of them put together. It would be necessary to take other measures to procure their property from his clutches. They had to wait for the right moment and then liberate her.

"All right, Captain Courtland. You win! But I believe you will slip up soon," Walter said arrogantly.

"Not before you do," James quipped. "I do take pleasure in making sure I get what I want. And since I am in charge here, I don't think you will want to question my authority again."

Walter hated to concede to James Courtland's position, but he was right. Rank definitely had its privileges. And James planned to oblige himself with the lovely creature's company all the way back to the fort. It seemed the battle over who was to ride with, care for, and share her blanket was an ongoing tiff among the trio. Yet, the captain would win out every time. René, however, made it impossible for him to get close to her. She feigned vomiting spells and fainted on numerous occasions to prevent the inevitable. She was so thoroughly disgusted with him and his wants that she used every means to create displeasure of her company. She envisioned the day she would be rid of him and his followers.

"She is giving him the business," Walter stated as he followed them.

"Yeah . . . looks like she is in control, not the infamous Captain Courtland."

Courtland could hear them snickering behind his back, which infuriated him even more. No longer did he assume that he had anything to fear from a possible attack from the Indians he had left behind. He had to watch out for the greedy duo who were keeping pace with him. They were now at least forty miles from a scalping, and he considered himself himself quite brave to have lived among the natives and outsmarted them with this farce. However, his prisoner wasn't impressed with him or any of his followers and he thought they were all cowards.

"It will do you no good to look for that Indian of yours. He is too far away to catch up now," Courtland stated as he pressed the horse on.

René remain silent for only a moment, then stated as clear and as strong as she could, "I'm not looking for him, because I know he will come. And when he does, you will feel his wrath. You will wish to die when he catches up with you."

Courtland was stunned by her brevity. She seemed unmoved by his constant badgering and relentless insults. She had taken everything he had dished out as he tried to force her to beg for her freedom. And when it seemed he would win, she would turn the tables.

CHAPTER
TWENTY-ONE

FOR FORTY-FIVE TEDIOUS AND unsavory days, René had to share James's saddle. He was brash at times and very annoying. There were days when he seemed unwilling to slow his pace, which he knew would cause her great discomfort. He cared little for her needs and made it a point to keep the others from helping her in their clumsy way. However, their motives weren't the same as his. Then there were days René wished that the sky would just open up and take her away. On the forty- sixth day they finally reached Fort Wayne. Tired, hungry, and weary, they dragged through the last leg of their journey until the fort's entrance was in full view. Even René was glad to end the ungodly trek.

The fort seemed almost uninhabited. There were only two men guarding the front gate. Both men had dozed off, so they didn't hear the captain and his party as they approached. Apparently guard duty had decreased, since most of the First Battalion had been sent to Fort Sumpter. That left only a few to guard and protect the supplies housed in the fort. The soldiers came to life when Courtland called out, "Get to your feet, soldiers!" He heard them scamper about. "Those bungling idiots!" he snapped.

One soldier yelled out, "Who goes there?" The men were tired. They hadn't slept in three days compared to last time they'd had to patrol the front gate.

"I am Captain Courtland of the First Battalion. My men and I have returned with one of the prisoners who escaped the Bainbridge Massacre," James said with authority. He felt René wince with his interpretation of the carnage that changed her life and that of her family. "Open the gate! I must report to Colonel Sheridan immediately," he demanded.

"He could be a spy. You know them rebels will do anything to get their hands on the powder kegs hidden in our storerooms," the young soldier said the other one.

"Yeah . . . but what if he is tellin' the truth? We could get thrown in the stockades," his partner stated quickly.

"I will take the stockades over that. I could sleep for ten years, you know?" he quickly added, hoping he wouldn't have to spend another second on the wall. "Let them in. They'd just better be on our side!"

The gate was opened slowly, then a few soldiers ran out of the fort fully armed. The men under James Courtland's command checked their rifles and handguns at the gate. Once inside, they passed several teepees that housed several Miami scouts and their wives. The smell of food cooking over an open flame and the women doting on their husbands was a pleasant sight for René. It was the first reminder of home since her abduction.

"What's happened here? There are usually five men on duty at a time. Where is the rest of your detail, soldier?" James asked in a roar. He was relieved to be inside the fort, but wondered whether there were enough men to protect it against a possible attack. He knew her man would be coming for her. It was just a matter of when.

The young soldier, Private Billy Stanhope, carefully walked up to the captain and said, "We are at war, sir. The First Battalion was sent to Fort Sumter one week after the fort was attacked by the Southern militia. We are expecting the Union to send for us, as well."

"We are at war and I didn't know it. How long has this been going on?" James asked as she steadied his horse.

Just then Walter came up from the rear of the column to make his demands known. "Why should you care?" he quipped. "You left your post to go after this wench and now you want to know about the war. Humph! I always knew you were a fool," he spat. His eyes gleamed with contempt for the man. When he thought he had a chance to kill Courtland, something got in the way. The man had the luck of the Irish on his side. Besides, he had no plans of getting himself killed over matters that didn't concern him. His concerns were with the woman and how much she was worth.

"I suggest you worry about getting back to Wilmot, Mr. Cory. It would be quite unhealthy for you and your partner to stay at the fort," Courtland retorted quickly. He grew tired of having to sleep with one eye open on the journey home. "Oh, and don't worry, I will take good care of Miss Bainbridge. She will want for nothing." Then he laughed as he turned to leave.

After being insulted and of course invited to leave as well, Walter reared his horse, startling the others and causing Courtland to grapple for control of his own. René's heart pounded wildly with fear of being thrown, but Courtland tightened up on the reins and locked his knees into the sides of the horse. What seemed like a millennium was in fact only a few seconds, yet, without aid from the other soldiers, Courtland got the horse back under control. "Now, inform the commanding officer of my return. I will be there shortly. Then he cut a god-awful stare at Walter Cory, who rode off without further acknowledgment.

Courtland wanted to get the formalities over with. His first priority was to get settled in his quarters, to bathe, and then change into a clean uniform. He had worn the same buckskin breeches for nearly a year. The touch of a woolen coat and starched cotton shirt would be a pleasant beginning to civilization. But first things first, he must report to the commanding officer of the fort before such luxuries could be enjoyed.

James quickly dismounted and handed the reins to Private Smith. "Don't let her out of your sight," he ordered rudely. Then without giving René a second glance, he stepped up to the platform and headed straight for Colonel Sheridan's office.

"Yes, sir!" Smith replied, and then mumbled something under his breath.

It was ten o'clock in the evening and the office was empty, except for a whiskey bottle lying on the desk and papers that had been carelessly thrown on the floor. He picked up the ones he could see and placed them neatly on the desk. Slowly, he moved around the desk to survey the shambled confines. He wondered about it, but then quickly decided not to waste much time worrying over the matter. He helped himself and poured a stiff drink from the bottle on the colonel's desk. With a quick jerk, the brown liquid passed his tongue and went down his throat. It burned as he swallowed, but he savored it all the same.

Private Stanhope entered suddenly and stated, "No one is allowed in the colonel's office without permission, sir." The boy swallowed hard after he saw the look on Courtland's face. He realized that the captain would be hard to reckon with. Yet, he held the door open and allowed the captain to take his leave.

"Tell Colonel Sheridan that I will report to him in the morning!" Courtland ordered as he pushed passed the boy.

"Yes, sir!" Stanhope said accompanied by a salute.

Courtland didn't return the gesture and quickly headed for the courtyard where his prisoner was waiting. He quickly issued orders to the others who couldn't wait to find a decent cot to rest upon. They quickly led their horses to the stables, tethered them, and then watered them down. With their chores out of the way, they were at liberty to head for the bunkhouse.

Meanwhile, Courtland escorted René to his quarters and quickly ushered her in. There were two large rooms, each containing a bed, a large chest with a mirror, a washbasin, and other meager furnishings. There were no curtains on the windows to liven up the place, only shutters. The beds were covered with thick woolen blankets. There were no sheets or soft covers to use instead. Dust could be seen everywhere, and cobwebs filled every corner. On the wall facing the entrance was a map of the occupied territory of the United States. The other walls were void of such luxuries.

It was, in René's opinion, a very sad room. It lacked heart and color. It was a room befitting the man who accompanied her. The cabin she shared with Black Eagle had character, it had love. She couldn't stay in a place like this for very long, especially with him. It had been over a year since René had walked on a hard wooden floor or heard the creaking of a door hinge or even caught a glimpse of herself in a looking glass. Long ago she would have treasured these things, but she no longer felt the need to have them.

René walked toward the window, anxiously. She couldn't wait for Black Eagle to free her. She had hoped in the forty-six-day trip that he would stop James Courtland's madness, but there were no signs of him. She almost started to believe that James was right. Black Eagle wouldn't be coming for her and he was sure to lose faith in her again. As difficult as it was, she started to believe that she had preserved her honor and protected the life of her unborn child for nothing.

James abruptly interrupted her most private thoughts and ordered, "You will take the interior room. It is far better than you deserve . . . better than being locked up in the stockades. Anyway, you will have little time to worry about other accommodations than these."

René only glanced his way. She had hardly spoken since his constant badgering and constantly berating of her for the forty-six long days. To share the confines of these walls and to be under his scrutiny wasn't the worse she had to face. She would be subjected to his constant harassment, and even rape was a possibility.

"Did you hear me?" he snapped again. "Take the lamp!"

René nodded and took the lamp from his hand, then slowly entered the room. She didn't turn to face him; she just heard the door slam close behind her, followed by a click. The door was locked, but from the outside. James took the key and placed it on his nightstand. She was at the mercy of the swine.

Finally, René sat on the edge of the bed and took a good look at her new surroundings. She blew the dust from the pillow and then snatched the blanket off the bed. Dust flew everywhere, and she choked as it engulfed her. She tried to open the windows, but the shutters were barred from the outside. She covered her face to protect herself from the whirlwind she had created. What she found was a tub under an old flannel blanket and a partition leaning against the wall.

When the dust finally settled, she went about sweeping the room with the blanket from the bed. She removed the dust from the chest and from the locker at the foot of the bed. Then she pushed all the dirt into an unoccupied corner and brought the chair closer to the bed. The lamp flickered with the new brightness in the room. She heard the door open from the other room and the voices of men, one sharper in manner than the others. She pressed her ear against the door, hoping to hear what James was planning, but at times it was muffled. She knew he was issuing orders, but for what?

On the other side of the door, James ordered young Stanhope to bring hot water, clean linen, and towels. The boy quickly left to complete the assignment, which left René alone with him again. The only reprieve she had was the door, but he was holding the key.

Within an hour's time, Private Stanhope came back with all the items James had ordered, including several men, each carrying two buckets of hot water. Suddenly, the door swung open, and James waltzed in without being acknowledged. He pointed to the tub and ordered the men to bring in the water . They entered quickly, stole a glance at her and then proceeded to pour the water into the tub. Suddenly, she was alone with him.

Even though she was covered with dust, René could feel the steam on her face. James returned to the room with a beautifully decorated bottle. He poured the powdery substance into the water and swirled it around with his hands. Then he picked up the towels and a bar of soap and demanded that she come to him. René backed away. His implied gesture was that he intended to bathe her. "Come here, René !" he commanded roughly. "I want to make you worthy of my needs."

"And how are you going to accomplish that?" René asked sourly.

"I'm going to wash the scent of your Indian lover off of your body. You won't mind it too much. After a while, you'll become accustomed to your new situation," he answered quickly. "Besides, we have some unfinished business . . . remember?" James continued as he advanced toward her. His grin was filled with devilment. It sent chills down her spine when he finally reached her and took her by the shoulders. In one jerk, he had torn her tunic and brought it down to her waist. He was taken by the beauty she had withheld from his view for over a month. His smile broadened as he removed the rest of her clothing. "Now. René, you have no choice. get into the tub! *Now!*" he yelled.

Like a spirited deer, René was in the water before he could blink. She covered herself with one of the towels draped over the side of the tub. The water was hotter than she expected, but she tolerated it. The scented salts he added to the water began to permeate her pores, forcing her to relax. The ache in her belly began to subside as well. She felt renewed. Her mind wandered, feeling Black Eagle's nearness. She could hear him say, *"I am coming for you, my love. You will be safe with our people again."*

But James's voice brought her back to reality again. He said things that didn't make sense to her. First he wanted to kill her. Then he was taking care of her. He seemed to think that they were married and that she adored only him. When James reached into the water for the soap and brushed her leg, she slapped him. He in turn slapped her back, hard. Every time he reached for her after that, she would flinch and would bring her knees closer to her body. She didn't want him in the same room, much less bathing her. But he went about soaping up the cloth, never once taking his eyes from her. René felt strange under his perusal and pulled another towel over her shoulders. But he felt he could see all and touch all that he wanted.

"I can wash myself," René said softly. Her cheek was burning from the slap. "Please! I would prefer to bathe alone!" she continued. But he was so painfully close and he wouldn't leave.

However, his temper started on the rise again when she not only dared to reject him but when she even put him out when he wanted to take her. "No! René, I won't be leaving!" he roared, and threw the washcloth into the tub. Water splashed on René's face and on the floor. James then marched to the other side of the room and grabbed the chair she had placed there. He returned and put the chair where he would have the full view of the tub and of her. There he sat, with no intentions of leaving at all. "Then bathe yourself! You are a prisoner of the Union Army," he quipped. "Which means, my dear, you are not to be left alone."

James crossed his legs and then folded his arms across his chest. He had been held off for the last time. But he behavior was abruptly ended when Private Stanhope knocked on his door again. The boy had brought a Miami Indian maid to attend to René's needs. When Courtland opened the door, the young woman walked past him without asking for permission to enter. She quickly surmised that the woman in question was in the other room and she quietly closed the door behind her as she entered. Since there was no key, she wedged her chair under the doorknob to jam it.

In the same manner she had entered the room, she spoke. "My name is Sky. I have come to help you." She was just as lovely as she was witty. She made it easy for René to relax with her kind smile. "I know who you are. The men in the fort talked about you and say how brave you are," she continued. René had been so accustomed to keeping her mouth closed that she found it hard to respond at first. She began to open up when the girl whispered, "Your man will come for you." It was the first sign of true happiness to stir in René's heart. It seemed too good to be true. How could he know where to find her? And if this were true, how could he free her from James Courtland now that he had her in a fortress.

"Brave? I'm not brave at all," René stated as quietly as she could. She didn't want another confrontation with James Courtland over a few words here and there, but she appreciated the friendly face. "I have to keep that man away from me . . . no matter what he says or does, I must not let him near me."

René settled into the water, which had finally cooled. She loosened her hair and washed it thoroughly. Sky placed a towel around René's head and squeezed the excess water from her hair. When René had cleaned the room earlier, a brush and a nightshirt had surfaced. Both had been tucked away in the back of the drawer with a few letters wrapped with red ribbon and other personal items belonging to young Lieutenant Gantry.

On the other side of the door, Courtland could be heard shuffling around. He would pause near the door, turn the knob, and then release it. He did that several times until someone knocked on his door again. It was Private Stanhope. This time he had been ordered to bring the captain to the officer in charge.

"Sir, Captain Birney requests your presence in his office, sir!" Stanhope stated officially. He and three other soldiers were there to escort the captain if he resisted in any way.

"Who is this Captain Birney? Well?" Courtland asked. He had been here for over two hours and he thought it strange that the commanding officer hadn't come to greet him. After all, he had been away for a long time.

Stanhope stepped back, giving the captain room to exit his quarters. "Captain Birney will explain when you join him, sir." Then he turned to his men. "Escort detail, forwaaaard ho!"

Stanhope and his men marched Courtland to the other side of the fort. He noticed that a new section to the fort had been added since his departure. There were new storehouses for munitions and food, and a stable large enough to accommodate fifty horses. Another stable was under construction and the inner walls to the fort were being fortified. There were large poles sharpened at the ends sticking out of the ground and ten cannons to each wall.

"A lot has happened in a year's time," Courtland said as he approached his destination.

"That is true, sir," Stanhope quickly responded. "Detaaail, halt!" he commanded, and waited for his men to comply. "At easeeeee!"

Courtland was instructed to enter the door at the end of the building. He entered cautiously. The room was bright, lit by oil lamps. A young man was seated at the desk with his hands folded. The desk was as neat as a pin. On each wall hung a map of the occupied territory, with flag points showing Union and Confederate victories. There were dark blue curtains covering the windows and the flag of the United States and the flag of the Union Army flanked the desk.

A curt voice came from the ma seated at the desk. "Come, Courtland. Please, be seated." Birney directed him to the chair sitting opposite his desk. It gave him a better vantage point, and he knew he was going to need it.

Courtland sat down, almost hesitantly. He wasn't sure what to expect from this young officer. He couldn't be more than twenty-one or so. How had he received his rank at such a young age, even younger than James himself?

"Good to see you again, Courtland," he said. James noticed that he had purposely misaddressed him. "You have missed a great deal while you were away. Our country is at war . . . I gather you know that by now. And now, it is important that you understand the true nature of the trouble you are in as well."

"First of all, Captain Birney, I outrank you by three years, and you have used my name in error. I must insist that you regard me correctly," Courtland demanded.

"But I have, Courtland. Or shall I say Lieutenant Courtland? As you can see, your absence from Fort Wayne was considered questionable. You and twelve men from the First Battalion and a posse of men from town went in pursuit of a young woman and her brother," Birney continued. "Well, it appears you found her, or have you?

Courtland didn't like the indignant manner with which he had been addressed, nor did he enjoy his sarcasm. Suddenly he asked almost out of sheer curiosity, "Under whose authority can you do this? It seems to me that you were after my position long before I even took that venture."

"You can believe what you like, Courtland, but the truth is quite evident. I am aware of the letter detailing a survey of the northern territory, but you abandoned your mission to pursue a woman. You are listed as a deserter, along with twelve men in your company. That is grounds for court martial, Lieutenant!" Birney stated as he stood over Courtland.

"Court martial? Are you seriously thinking that you have a case against me?" he asked.

Birney smiled. "Yes! I do! Not only will you be charged as a deserter, you will be charged with the murder of Lieutenant Gantry," he quipped. Birney had hit pay dirt. The astonished look on Courtland's face revealed that he had found the niche he was looking for. "You almost had me convinced that Gantry was following the trail left by Bainbridge. But you forgot that Gantry and I were assigned here at the same time. I knew him better than anyone, and he wouldn't take on such a task unless he had informed me. Even if you had ordered him to go, he would have taken time to let me know. Besides, Colonel Sheridan told us to turn over every rock and to look at every set of footprints on the estate. Your footprints and that of Gantry were found in the wood behind the stables. We found Gantry's body under a pile of leaves, his neck broken," Birney accused.

James was silent and unmoved for a while. He was caught and he didn't quite know how to deal with it. The accusations were real and true. He had done everything; he just hadn't expected to get caught right away.

"You know, I thought it kind of odd for Miss Bainbridge and her brother to just stick around while their home was being destroyed and maybe chance not being caught by the mob. You must have thought we were fools, Courtland. I can only imagine what Gantry saw or must have overheard . . . something that you didn't want to surface," he said as he moved around to the other side of the desk. "You know, Gantry died pointing a finger at you as well," Birney continued. He sensed worry in Courtland's eyes.

"How . . . how could a dead man point his finger at me? That's the most outrageous story I ever heard," Courtland retorted. "You're grabbing at straws. You have nothing to back up your accusations, and I know it!"

"Well, Lieutenant Courtland, we found a button in his hand matching those worn only by you. Your uniform, which is under lock and key, has a button ripped from it, with fragments of the material clinging to the threads. The button matched. It was only a matter of time before we found out who really killed him. So as you can see, we know René Bainbridge and her brother are innocent," Birney concluded.

James fumed at Captain Birney's interpretation. However accurate he was, James had no intention of selling himself out. His mind reeled at the prospect of being hanged. He didn't like that at all. He had to escape as soon as possible. With his career destroyed . . . how ironic that the letter said he would lose his rank and position. Yet, it was not caused by René's selfishness, but by his own foolhardiness.

Private Stanhope, take Lieutenant Courtland back to his quarters," Birney ordered. Then he turned to Courtland and said, "The young woman is under our protection. She is free to go whenever she pleases. But for now let her stay where she is."

Courtland smiled. "Why. thank you, Captain Birney! At least I won't die from boredom." He quickly rose from his seat and headed for the door to join Stanhope.

"Wait! Is there something I should know about this woman?" Birney asked.

Courtland had already exited his office without giving him an answer. The question of the woman's identity wasn't clear, but he would find out. "Soldier, make sure that Colonel Sheridan is informed of Courtland's return. And take him some fresh water. He's going to need it."

"Yes, sir!" was the final response as the door closed behind them.

Birney had never liked Courtland from the day he and Gantry had first been assigned to Fort Wayne. Now that he was a little older and more sure of himself, Courtland no longer seemed to be a threat. He promised himself to find Gantry's killer, and now the man had fallen right into his lap.

"Darling, are you coming to bed?" a gentle voice called from the inner room. "You spend too much time working, dear . . . come to bed," she cajoled.

The frown on Birney's face disappeared. The year had been good to him, even though he mourned the loss of a dear friend. He met and married Caroline Stewart when he was ordered back to Philadelphia. Bringing her here seemed to be the only thing to keep him going. He no longer felt the need for revenge, and he was able to enjoy life again. "I'm coming, dear," he said gently. "But first things first."

At the same time, Black Eagle and twenty-nine warriors had reached the outpost where Robert and his new bride had built a life for themselves. They had started a new business. Another rooming house had been built since he was there last. The place was active with new clientele, French and American. They had a larger stock of horses and a much better breed.

Black Eagle and his men traveled down the hill to the clearing where they set up camp for the night. They were too weary to travel any farther, but their goal was to return with René or die in trying. Tall Elk tethered their horses to a tree nearby, while Chief Chinock prepared the fire. Five braves led by Little Squirrel had gone ahead to follow the trail left by René's kidnappers.

Black Eagle dreaded the prospect of telling his brother-in-law that his sister had been taken again. He hated having failed to protect her from the evil that his vision had projected several month ago. She was his life . . . his strength. Now his whole world had been turned upside down. With an empty heart, he alone took the last leg of the journey to her brother's home.

Robert saw him coming and ran out to greet him with open arms. With the excitement of a family reunion, he introduced him to Lily. But his joy quickly turned to anger. He knew who had taken René. He had been told of a large group of men traveling in a peculiar manner several days ago. It never dawned on him that it was James Courtland. Black Eagle didn't have to ask for help. Robert grabbed his gear and headed for the door. Lily could only watch her husband ride off over the horizon. Now they were thirty-one strong.

Meanwhile, René had finally fallen asleep. She tried to stay awake, but her eyelids were heavy from fatigue. The bath was so soothing that it helped to induce the sleep she was trying to avoid. She didn't hear the door open to her room, nor did she sense that she wasn't alone. She needed rest, undisturbed rest.

James had locked the door and had wedged the chair under the doorknob to prevent entry. He sat quite gingerly on the side of the bed and removed his boots. Then he removed his clothing. Ever so quietly, he tiptoed his way to the tub. He put one foot in and shuddered from the icy feel of the water. It was his turn to bathe, but it wasn't the way he had planned it.

James kept his eye on the corner where René slumbered peacefully. He imagined that she had no past to keep them apart. Her share of the Bainbridge fortune would keep him in hot water for the rest of his life. The land alone would sell at a high rate, even though the house had been totally destroyed. If he could resign his commission before the court martial was issued, he could marry René and take her to Europe. There he could dispose of her quietly. But then, why do that? He could sell her to one of the dignitaries. They always kept their women under wraps. He would be able to claim her inheritance and travel the world as he always hoped.

Then he realized, there was no way for him to fulfill his dream with a war going on. He always wanted to be right in the front lines of the battle. It angered him that he wasn't here from the start. But he soon forgot about the war and became more concerned about himself again. He could lose everything if he were found guilty. The punishment for murder, especially the murder of a fellow officer, was death. There was no honor in dying a marked man. His body would be buried in potter's field without a headstone or marker. His name would be stricken from the record, and the mark of deserter and murderer would be his only epitaph.

"I don't plan on dying, especially now that I have so much to live for," James said aloud. His voice shattered René's peaceful sleep. She opened her eyes to find she was in the dark. Without moving from her bed, she searched the room, her eyes darting from one space to the next. When she heard the water in the tub splashing around, she held he breath, realizing she was no longer alone.

Trepidation filled her heart. This time, she wouldn't be able to ward him off. James would definitely have the advantage now. René heard him step out of the tub. He left a trail of water all the way to her bed, where he stood for what seemed the longest time. She could hear him breathing and she could smell the dampness of his skin. A droplet of water from his hair fell into the curve of her neck. René held her breath and tried to maintain the impression that she was still sleep. She thought he would go away, but he stood there, naked and desirous of her flesh next to his.

"Open your eyes, my dear. I want you to know what is about to take place, with or without your consent," James said tauntingly. He knew she was awake. Her hearing was remarkably uncanny, especially when he made advances toward her on their journey here. She avoided every tactical move he made. Now there was nothing to prevent him from taking her.

René remained very still. The slightest provocation would bring him to do unmentionable things. But he wouldn't be put off, not this time. James yanked the blanket away and slid onto the bed beside her. René moved away toward the foot of the bed, but she was trapped by the wall. His hand found her ankle, and he pulled her back where he could control her. "You can make this easy for the both of us . . . or . . . you can make it hard. You shouldn't fight the man who would make an honest woman of you," he laughed. "Besides, I want you to know *who* your master is," James said, and laughed again in her ear.

"Please! Don't do this!" René begged, but he pressed his lips hard against hers. She could feel his hand ripping at her nightgown. It was happening all over again. But this time Black Eagle wouldn't be there to stop him.

"It must be done. You know that, don't you?" James said in her ear. He enjoyed frightening her. "And besides, you owe me for the last time." The beast had been unleashed. He would have to kill her.

"I don't owe you anything," she spat, and then struggled to free herself.

Suddenly, like a jolt, the chair was forced away from the door. There was a flash of light followed by several footsteps. James was yanked from the bed, cursing and scuffling with his attackers. René heard the outer door close behind them. For some strange reason, for those few seconds, she didn't feel threatened. But her fears welled up once again when a gentle hand, from out of the darkness, caressed her head. As quickly as he entered, he then vanished, leaving her alone in the room.

The following morning, Sky returned and found René huddled in the corner. She held the medicine bags, her gifts, against her belly and prayed that the child within was safe. She was just entering her fourth month, and her body hadn't yet revealed the ripening fruit. Had it not been for the quick thinking of an honorable man, René would have been raped and the baby could have been lost. Sky helped René to her bed and wet a cloth to wipe her brow. There the young woman stayed, refusing to leave her charge's side.

"Are you better now?" Sky asked as she tucked René in, "I should not have left you last night," she added with concern.

When she saw René, she liked her right away, even though her brother had informed her that René was the woman Black Eagle had taken instead of her. For over a year she had hated this woman. But after meeting her and talking with her, there were mixed feelings.

"Yes, I am much better than I was last night. Someone stop him from . . . oh, God! . . . if he hadn't come!" René stammered.

Sky knew the one René spoke of. She had feelings for him as well, but had kept them secret since he had arrived with a wife of his own. She tried to maintain a strong composure whenever he came near her. "One day, I will have a man like the one you have. He will be pleased to have me, don't you think?" she asked.

"Of course, you will! You are lovely. A man would have to be blind not to notice you," René confessed. A tear fell, and she turned to her side, resting her head on the pillow. She hadn't slept since James had tried to take advantage of her, and now sleep was calling. René yawned and slowly closed her eyes and dreamed of her freedom and rescue from this place.

Colonel Sheridan slowly arose from his latest drunken stupor. He stretched, trying to pull the snarling aches and pains from his aging body. He was thoroughly out of touch with himself, and it was far from being over. He staggered to the washbasin and mirror. He grimaced and cursed at his own reflection. Then he washed his face with the stale water that had been in the basin for three days. He choked as some of the water managed to get into his mouth, and cursed again when his realized he didn't have a clean towel.

Three taps at the door and Colonel Sheridan no longer had the privacy of his quarters. The young private had entered his room with a bucket of fresh hot water just as he had been commanded. He was followed by Sergeant Wills, who informed the colonel, as was his duty, of the new arrivals. "Good morning, Colonel. I suspect you had a good evening, sir?" Will inquired while standing at attention.

"You know damned well what my nights have been like," Sergeant, Sheridan grumbled. "Let's not fool ourselves. I'm a drunk."

"Everyone has had a drink too many, sir. I suspect you have a lot on your mind, sir," Wills offered. For an entire year he had watched the colonel change.

Sheridan laughed and then leaned on the bedpost. His head was still pounding and throbbing. Then he reached the nightstand and pour himself another drink. He swallowed the golden liquid and shook his head as it burned on its way down. "Now, what brings you into my quarters so early, Sergeant?" Sheridan asked. He still felt the burn and produced a loud belch.

"Ah, sir, Captain Courtland had returned. He and the twelve men in his detail," Wills stated.

"Are you sure it is Courtland?" he asked as he looked out the window into the courtyard. The bugler had just played reveille, the flag was being raised, and then the cannon was primed . . . then fired. The sound of the cannon made him lean against the wall for support.

Wills gave him a hand and answered, "Yes, sir. There's no mistake. And . . . .ah, Captain Birney had him placed in the stockades last night. And, sir, he brought a prisoner. From the description, I think it's Miss Bainbridge." There were many times Wills had wished he had been sent to Fort Sumter with his battalion, but he just resigned himself to the terrible fact that he was on the same scale as his commander.

"What the hell is going on here? Why wasn't I informed of this?" Sheridan yelled as he pulled on his pants. He donned a wrinkled shirt and then headed out the door.

Wills followed and hoped he would be able to persuade him to go back into his quarters, at least until he was fit to be seen by his men. But the colonel made the situation all the more difficult when he entered Birney's office. He had burst in when the young officer and his wife were about to sit down to breakfast. The was a noticeable contrast between the two officers, but the command was still in the hands of Sheridan.

"Why wasn't I informed of Courtland's return, Captain?" Sheridan demanded. He had been waiting for this day to come and he act as though he had been cheated.

Captain Birney sent his wife into the next room and then asked the colonel to take a seat. Sheridan was still having trouble maintaining his composure. To this very day, it seemed he was no longer in command of this fort. The young captain had taken his authority away by countermanding his orders to his men.

"Damn it, boy, you young fool! I was leading a garrison when you were still in swaddlings, so don't undermine me!" he said sternly. He wanted to slap the boy, but that would be inappropriate and he wouldn't get what he came for.

Birney stood at attention, realizing that his commander was serious. The very idea of his trying to take over Sheridan's position was far from being right. "Colonel Sheridan, I sent word to you this morning that Courtland had returned. Last night you were somewhat indisposed. I felt it was my duty to handle this matter as quickly as possible," Birney answered directly. "If I hadn't acted as quickly as I did, the young woman he brought back would have been compromised."

The colonel cleared his throat and asked,"You mean, Miss Bainbridge don't you?

"Yes, sir, it was necessary to put Courtland in the stockades. He proved to be a threat to her well-being," Birney continued as he watched the colonel lean against the table. He apparently became unstable while on his feet.

George Sheridan had to face the man whose life he had disrupted. And then there was René Bainbridge: What could he possible tell her? No one knew he had written the letters that had caused so much pain. James Courtland would indeed endure a court martial. However, he wasn't sure what the outcome would be for René. She was considered a fugitive from the law in Wilmot. He wasn't sure whether to keep her locked or to set her free: a decision that had plagued him with guilt. He had pined over the death of Rachel, his only love, for over a year. Now that her daughter was back to twist the knife in his heart he began to laugh uncontrollably, to a point of hysterics. Then he fell to his knees and begged for deliverance.

"Colonel Sheridan! Sir, are you all right?" Birney asked. He never knew the full reason for the colonel's drinking. He attributed it to a woman, but not until this very moment did he know what woman would bring a man so low. There was no fight left in his soul. There was just the shattered shell of a man. "Caroline, bring some coffee!" he insisted. Then he turned to the sergeant who stood quietly by, but in a state of shock. The man he thought was iron clad was just as weak as a crying babe. Sergeant Wills, what you have witnessed here stays here," Birney ordered. "It is imperative that this incident stays inside these walls. Do you understand?" he demanded.

"Of course, I mean, yes, sir." he answered with bewilderment. "My lips are sealed."

Later on that day, René received a visit from Mrs. Birney. She held her head high as she entered the room and seemed somewhat taken by surprise when she found René resting in bed with an Indian maid in attendance. It was noon, midday, and no woman in the fort would be found sleeping after the stroke of seven. But René wasn't one of the many wives in the fort and was surely not planning to be one. With a sudden chill in her tone, she directed Sky to wake René.

"Well, young lady . . . I'm waiting," she said sternly.

Sky read the tone very clearly and she wasn't mistaken in the way the Birney woman had addressed her. Caroline was aware of Sky's feelings toward her husband, even though they went unanswered and unnoticed by the young captain. But Sky cared, anyway, and Caroline felt a twinge of jealousy when there was nothing for her to worry about. Sky stood her ground and took control of the situation, leading the woman straight into the anteroom by her elbow. "The woman is very tired. She has traveled far with no rest," she said softly, so not to waken René. "When she awakens, I will send word to you."

Not knowing how to respond to such impudence, Caroline waved her off, "You do that. Oh! And don't forget, you have another house to clean. I do suggest you hurry about getting your chores done before the colonel misses you. You know how he hates not having his breakfast ready when he awakens."

Without another word, she flitted out the door, opened her parasol, and sashayed toward her quarters. She didn't like being ignored or treated like one of the poor folks in town. If she could hobnob with the rich for a day or so, she would be the envy of all of the other wives in the fort. She had heard about the rich and beautiful René Bainbridge and wanted to spend some time gossiping and maybe spreading a few tidbits about what she had overheard between her husband and James Courtland. She was growing bored hearing the same old stories and seeing the same old faces at the fort. The few women who stayed with their men were slowly showing signs of age, and it frightened Caroline. She didn't want to be like them.

Sky gave a sudden sigh of relief and quickly closed the door to allow René to sleep undisturbed. It wasn't easy for her to help the woman she should be hating, but René made it impossible to dislike her. She treated Sky as an equal and spoke to her in her own language. And still, there was the matter of her stolen life.

CHAPTER
TWENTY-TWO

IN THE YEAR THAT passed, many changes had taken place in Wilmot. The streets were now paved in cobblestone. The telegraph had expanded through and into the next state. The state of Ohio had also joined the Union. They had also participated in the underground railroad and had housed and fed many runaway slaves. All of this occurred after the Bainbridge incident.

The people of Wilmot had learned to be more tolerant rather than setting themselves as judges against the helpless. In all the years of claiming to be a just and civilized town, they had resorted to violence and mayhem. They destroyed the lives of the Bainbridge family as well as their own. Some were still recovering from their losses, since entire families were involved.

With the war going on and most of the menfolk gone, the town was virtually empty, except for the few who wandered into Wilmot. Now they had a new sheriff, Chester Snow, whose first objective was to set the record straight with all newcomers. Unlike Sheriff McDaniels, he had established a strong relationship with the people, and with their help he was able to close down the saloon at midnight. The curfew enabled him to maintain order. And since the gun law had been passed, no guns were pass the town line. Anyone carrying a firearm had to check it in or face incarceration.

Walter and Matt had come when the sheriff was on duty. He eyed the shabby and unkempt men as they approached with their pack mules loaded with ammunition and pelts. He knew that they would need watching. He directed three deputies to bring them over. "Do you know them?" he asked.

One of the deputies stated, "I am not sure, sheriff. But one of them looks familiar."

"They are definitely packing," Chester said calmly. "In this line of work you meet all kinds. We will keep a close watch on them," he said with confidence.

Matt wanted a hot bath, at least two bottles of whiskey to wash down the trail dust, and a warm bed. He had already planned how he was going to spend his day, but was sidetracked by the young voice behind him. "Excuse me, mister, the sheriff wants you and your friend to come to his office," the boy stated calmly.

The boy had been well-schooled, but he had not been taught how to handle men like there. The other deputies stood on either side of the men with their hands on the six-shooters." You say the sheriff wants us? Why? We just rode into town. How about letting us get settled first?" Walter asked with a tightened lip.

"First you will see the sheriff, and then you can go about your business," the boy continued. He could feel a sharp pain growing in his throat. He knew that the one doing the talking would be the first to show his hand and he was right.

Walter had put his hand on his gun, but he heard a familiar sound. The click of a double-barrel shotgun hammer being pulled back made him freeze. "My deputy I wanted to see you. Why are you making it difficult for him to do his job?" Chester asked sternly. Walter raised his arms above his head, while Matt just shook his head with disgust.

"It seems you boys have something I want," he stated. "The sooner you check in your firearms, the sooner you can get settled." Chester and his men escorted the two to his office. There they unloaded a keg of powder and several shells and casings. There was a small arsenal between the two of them. "How long are you planning to stay, gentlemen?" Chester asked. He was concerned about the bad element in his town and didn't want any more to follow.

Matt spoke up quickly. "We have business with Captain Cortland. I am sure we will be moving on as soon as we have completed our transaction."

The sheriff was puzzled, but accepted his explanation. It didn't matter to him that these two souls were involved, but he hoped it would not affect the peace in his town. Since these men were just passing through, he would give them the regular warning. "Gentlemen, I trust that you will stay out of trouble," he said as an intended threat. "If you slip up in any way, you will spend your days in our jail. Do you understand? No guns are allowed in this town, and the saloon is closed after midnight. That means, gentlemen, you must be in your rooms no later than a quarter past."

"You must be kidding," Walter snapped. "I plan to have a helluvah good time! And that means drinking until daybreak," he continued. "I have had nothing but charred meat, dried beans, and stale water for over a year," he bellowed. Chester could see that he would be a problem, more so than the other. However, he made his point clear to Walter and his friend that there was room in his jail for anyone who broke the law. "I will not warn you again. You will spend a lot of time in my jail. One offense is all you need," he offered coolly.

As soon as they completed the business at hand, Walter immediately headed for the saloon for the drink he had promised himself for many months. Matt just tagged along, hoping that they would be able to discuss the matter of their funds, which weRe-nearly exhausted. There was only enough for three nights in the hotel or a month in the rooming house down the street. Anything was better than spending another night on a bumpy road. With Walter planning to spend the money on drinking, the luxury of a warm bed would be gone within minutes.

"Hold it, Walter. I think I have a right to decide how our money is going to be spent," Matt said as he followed his friend.

Walter didn't care. With the Bainbridge woman in the hands of Captain Courtland, he needed to drown his feelings in a bottle. "Shut up! I want a drink and I'm going to get one. Now!" Walter said forcefully. He walked into the saloon uninterrupted and undaunted by his friend. He was looking for whiskey and, better yet, a fight. Matt stayed outside and waited for the show to begin.

Black Eagle and Robert rode into town late about four nights later, much like the others. They decided to follow the trail leading to the town first, with anticipation of the ones who had taken René. Robert knew that the other trail, which led to the fort, would be their next stop, only if they came to a dead end. Without saying much about their business, they gave up their weapons and headed for the saloon.

It was Black Eagle's first time being in a place like Wilmot. Life here was very different from the life he led in his village. Many of the people he encountered worked to maintain their own property, rather than working together as a whole. He sensed indifference and hatred, mostly thwarted toward him. The general behavior of the people made him wonder why they called this civilization. He could see why René always felt at home with his people.

"Your people are a frightened lot. They trust no one and fear everyone," Black Eagle remarked as they walked down the street. The feel of the cobblestones beneath his feet felt like slippery rocks. He made every effort not to fall as he continued on his way. It amazed Black Eagle to see the women cross the street to avoid him. Several men stood with their hands on their hips. Some wished they had their guns, while others ran to the sheriff's office to get theirs, only to be thrown into the jail.

Chester knew when he saw them that the night would be an interesting one. He sent for his deputies. If there was going to be trouble, he needed all the help he could get. In the meantime he would join these strangers. "I want you to be ready when trouble breaks out. The Indian and his friend are here for a reason. Let's make sure it is a peaceful meeting," Chester stated to each boy. "Take one of those rifles over there, and you take this revolver. You will not shoot unless I tell you to. Do you understand, Albert, Tommy, and Pete?" he asked each one. These boys were young, too young for the army and too young to make decisions of life and death, but they agreed. Then the headstrong lads followed Chester toward the saloon, each taking a place that would best conceal them when trouble erupted. Albert hid behind the livery stable, Pete took to the roof of the hotel, and Tommy staked out the supply store just across the street. The street was well-lit, with the new streetlights that were installed last year. The boys were able to see the sheriff and inside the saloon without much of a strain.

It was quiet in the saloon. Sam Finkel had just poured Walter another drink. He swallowed hard when Walter grabbed his arm and said, "I'll keep the bottle." Then she entered and took a seat at a table across from the new arrivals, who also watched Walter guzzle down the bitter liquid and then poured himself another. Chester his hands by his holster. It was clear to him that these men had business to settle with the other. They waited until Walter had taken several drinks before Robert approached him. Chester eased forward to take one of them out if a fight should erupt.

"You must not interfere!" Black Eagle said straight away. He had been watching Chester from the time he entered and sat down. Chester was angry a mere savage would tell him what to do. So he disregarded his words and headed for the two standing at the bar.

Robert had just poured himself a drink when Chester put his hand on his shoulder and forced him to turn around. Robert had spilled his drink on the floor. It didn't matter to him about the drink so much; it mattered that the sheriff had taken leave of his senses. He looked at the sheriff scornfully and said, "If you wanted a drink, all you had to do was ask." Then he turned to Sam, who was startled because he finally recognized the young man behind the beard and said, "Give us another glass. I want to pour a drink for the sheriff here."

Sam handed him a glass with shaking hands. It was as though he was staring into the face of a ghost. When he overheard Old Cap and Captain Courtland plotting against the Bainbridge family, he felt shamefully coward-like for not having warned them. He had refused to get involved and had lost a dear friend in the process. There were times when he thought he would never get the chance to redeem himself. How could he ask Robert for forgiveness when he couldn't forgive himself?

"Here . . . you . . . are, sir!" Sam choked while staring into the light green eyes of Robert Bainbridge. Robert winked at him and gave a quick grin. For some reason Sam knew that he still had a friend. "Will there be anything else, sir?" he asked as he wiped the counter.

"No, I think we have everything we need right here" Robert said as he nodded thanks. Sam's silence was the only thing he really wanted at that moment. Sam then busied himself in the supply room. If Robert needed an escape route, the back door would be opened.

Black Eagle walked toward the bar to join them. Walter had had so much that he didn't realize the Indian had taken the spot right next to him. Robert offered him a drink, but Black Eagle declined. He had never developed a taste for the white man's whiskey. He had seen the consequences of drinking the bitter brew often enough to know that it meant no good. Instead, it was time to get answers.

Like a streak of lightning, Black Eagle lifted Walter from the floor by his collar. Robert quickly relieved Chester of his revolver and directed him to sit on the other side of the saloon away from the door. Then he eased toward the door to keep the area clear. "Go ahead, make him talk," Robert insisted.

"Why are you letting this Indian question a white man like that? He has no right to do that!" Chester yelled?

"Shut up, or I'll let him rip your tongue out!" Robert spat. "There is a reason for everything, and his reason is far greater than that man's honor. So keep still and listen!"

Black Eagle had not slacked up his hold on Walter. The man was hanging at least two feet off the floor. Black Eagle wanted him to taste the same fear that his wife had endured. He shook him until Walter had begun to whimper and blubber uncontrollably. Black Eagle maintained his stranglehold and demanded, "Where is my wife?" Where is Re-nea?" He asked this over and over again until Walter couldn't take it anymore. "Tell me, or I will split you in two like a gutted deer."

Walter had never faced a man like this before, and his worst fears had come to pass when he was confronted with his misdeeds. He was alone. Matt had taken his pack aide to the edge of town to set up camp. With no money for a room or food, he resigned himself to hunger and to sleepless nights on the hard ground.

"I don't know where Re-nea is! I just got into town myself a few days ago. I haven't had time to check out the ladies here. Ha-ha . . . us! You know what . . . I mean!" he squealed. Black Eagle knew he was the one. The description given by Morning Star fit him. Robert even recognized him from the meetings he had had with his father and posse. It was not a mistake. "You lie!" Black Eagle said as he tightened his grip. "You came to my village. You took my wife and child away. Now, tell the truth. Where is Re-nea?" he demanded.

Walter's mind was out of focus, but he knew the woman in question was bewildered about the child. René was his passport to Society Hill. But at this moment she was the only thing keeping him alive, and he so desperately wanted to live, at least long enough to see if he could collect a reward or something for his troubles. "Okay, okay! I know where she is. But it will cost you," Walter said. Black Eagle eased up on his neck. "I know where she is," Walter repeated.

Chester couldn't believe his ears. He had let two kidnappers enter his town with a war party on their trails. The safety of the town was at stake. With only a few young boys acting as his deputies, there was no way in hell for them to protect the town. And with the fort being more than fifty miles away, there was no chance of getting help in time. "Are you going to attack Wilmot?" he asked anxiously. "You can't bring savages down on us! With no men to protect the women and children, we will be at their mercy."

Robert laughed. It amused him to no end that this sheriff was as singleminded as the people who, without provocation, attacked his home and then killed his parents. "Are you so stupid that you can't see what is going on here?" Robert asked angrily. "Will sheriff . . . I will explain as much as I think you should know." He paused for a brief moment. For the first time in over a year, he was standing in a place that, in his mind, he wanted to forget. He gazed at the sheriff and continued. "The man you seem so eager to call a savage is my brother-in-law. He is my sister's husband and I honor his judgment. Whatever he plans to do, I will stand beside him, especially where my sister is concerned. The man he has by the throat kidnapped her. He and a few others, including the captain at Fort Wayne, are involved. We have come to take her back."

"Then you're the one they told me about. Some of the uptown have not been able to live with themselves after that horrible night. I tell you that they are sorry about what they did. But, I can't sit here and let that Indian hurt a white man over a squaw," Chester said with indifference toward Black Eagle.

"Squaw?" Robert snapped. "Her name is René. She's not just any woman, either. So, believe it when I say I will let him kill that bastard. If necessary, I'll let him kill you. We don't have a quarrel with you or this town. We just want René. When we get her back, we will leave," Robert stated.

Black Eagle still hadn't released Walter, not until he heard the truth. "This man took my wife and our unborn child. I want her back and I want her now!" he said in Walter's face.

Walter lost control and began to cry, "I don't want to die. Please, don't kill me!" He realized that his life meant nothing to this man. He reached up with both hands to ease the pain around his neck. If he wanted to live he had to talk. He had to tell. He had to give up the money that he dreamed would be his. So much to lose. "I'll talk . . . I'll tell you anything you want to know. Just . . . please . . . don't kill me!"

"You cry like a woman," Black Eagle said harshly. "Did you make Renea cry? Did you touch her?" Walter choked as he shook his head. "Where is she?" he berated as he released him and Walter hit the floor with a loud thud. He was relieved when he found that his throat was still intact. "Now talk!" Black Eagle insisted. "Okay, okay! She's at the fort. The captain has her," Walter said as he darted back and forth from Black Eagle to Robert. Then he decided to put a little extra into the tale he was going to describe. He would be able to kill birds with one stone. "Yes, and she didn't seem to mind riding all the way here with the captain. Yep, she use is a pretty young filly. I don't blame the captain one bit for keeping her all to himself."

Black Eagle didn't let him finish. He had grabbed Walter by the throat again with the intent of sending him to the other world. He heard him gasp and jerk as he tightened his grip around his neck again. He couldn't stand the thought of his wife being with another man. His anger had escalated to a point of no return.

Robert rushed over and said, "Don't believe it!" He wants you to act stupidly. Think! You know that she loves only you. She is waiting for you! Don't let this fool bring mistrust in your heart!" Black Eagle heard Robert. Robert turned to the sheriff and ordered, "Call off your men! We have what we came for, and no one's been hurt. Do it!"

Chester eased his way out of the chair and walked to the swinging doors. He felt powerless and in some way he felt he had failed to uphold the law. He had let an Indian dictate his movements. He had watched a white man confess his wrongdoings to the same man. In his heart he knew he was wrong. He could see that the boys still had their weapons trained on the entrance. Either the boys were real loyal or they wanted blood. He could let them shoot it out with these intruders and would have to deal with their crying mothers or he could send them home. He chose the latter. "Pete, Tommy, Albert, go home!" Everything is under control," he said with a shaky voice. He waited for them to move or to respond, but they stayed in their place. "I mean it! Go home!" The boys wavered for a moment. Then Pete asked, "Are you sure, Sheriff?" No matter what he wanted at the moment, he was under the scrutiny of both men, whose patience had been worn. However, they wanted information and nothing else.

"Yes," Chester answered. "I can handle things here. I'll see you in the morning." He watched as the boys left their hiding places. They would have wiped out the whole lot of them had they received Chester's signal. They marched off disappointed that they had not been able to prove themselves as men. But for now, they were alive and would be able to tell of their close call with an actual gunfight.

The fort had become extra busy in the past few days. With one under lock and key and the other being placed under guard, the small company had its hands full. Each soldier was supposed to sleep in four-hour intervals and to stand guard duty for another four. They were supposed to remain on alert until they received orders from the battle front.

The men who had accompanied Courtland on his trek were given quick trials sitting depositions into the character of their leader. All of whom were put back on act, without pay for six months. The Union needed its men and it was the only sentence the government could impose while the war was still a major factor. Courtland's fate, however, had to be judged differently. There were mitigating circumstances surrounding the death of Lieutenant Gantry. His trial would have to be held in Philadelphia.

As to the matter surrounding René, she was to be set free. There was no evidence to prove that she had conspired in any way in Gantry's death or that she had incited the riot that destroyed her home and her family. Everything pointed to James Courtland.

Colonel Sheridan waited until after the men had disclosed their actions to visit with René Bainbridge. She had refused to have any visitors for several days. He assumed it was due to the fatigue and weariness of the travel. Yet, she had allowed Captain Birney to call. She had also allowed the Indian woman to enter as she pleased, but no others were permitted to grace her. He felt a twinge of anger build in his brow. "How dare she refuse me. She has no choice in the matter," he said as he burst through his office door. It was time to break down the wall she used to shield herself. She was the only link to his beloved Rachel, and of course she was Devon's daughter.

Sky had put the finishing touches on René's long hair. She received a single decorated leather strip intertwined in her hair. René was pleased with the effects of her new-found friend's attentions. Not only had she had gained some strength, she had regained the belief that Black Eagle would be there soon. She finally felt refreshed and at ease. The threat of James Courtland had been taken away, thanks to the young captain. He removed the thorn that had been a constant pain in her side for over a year.

"You have done wonders with my hair. Thank you!" René said gratefully. "Please . . . sit down . . . talk with me for a while. I miss having that pleasure."

"You miss him," she offered. This young woman had suffered greatly. There was sadness in her voice when she spoke of the people she had grown to love.

René nodded. It was hard to speak of him. Somehow she knew that he would feel betrayed. She couldn't bear having him doubt her fidelity, her loyalty again. This time was enough for her. "Yes, I miss him very much. I only hope he gets here soon," she said softly. "I can't stay among these people much longer. I fear what they will do if they find out that I am here."

"But no one knows. My brother has told me," Sky answered quickly. Her friend needed consoling She would say anything to ease her mind, which included lying.

There had been much talk going thorough the fort and most of it was damaging to René. Sky had overheard one soldier saying that he was going to pay her friend a visit sometime in the near future. His remarks were very suggestive and they were talking about the way she betrayed her people by turning Indian. They seemed angry that René had found happiness with people who didn't judge her for who she was. sometimes Sky wound up running to Captain Birney's office in order to have him escort her to René's quarters. She couldn't bring herself to tell René of the goings-on in the fort. It would kill her.

"Now, my friend, you must rest. You must think of your child," Sky said gently. Even though it was still daylight, she made René get into bed. She closed the shutters to minimize the light and then sat in the chair beside her to guard her from the evil around.

René was tired and quickly fell into a deep sleep. All her thoughts were about her son and Black Eagle. She could see them, but as hard as she tried she couldn't reach them. She became agitated and had awakened with a start, to find that Sky had been replaced by Colonel Sheridan.

René pulled the covers around her. "What are you doing here?" she asked. She was noticeably shaken by his presence. Even though he was once a friend of the family, she had never really liked or trusted him. He always seemed to find a reason to come when her father was away. Yet, she never told her father of her suspicions.

"Well, well, well! I never thought I would ever see you again," he said slyly. "It's been a long time, don't you think? I mean, I was sure that you were among the dead, like your poor mother and father. James Courtland turned the wilderness upside find you. I must commend him for his efforts," he continued, only to be faced with contempt from René. "I understand your anger, my girl, but it was necessary for James to fulfill his need for revenge as it was for me to fulfill my need for revenge against your father."

René was confused. What did her father have to do with Colonel Sheridan? Had he seemed so crass when he spoke of her father? "I don't understand. You talk as if he did something to you. And now, you feel justified with what James Courtland has done to me?" she asked without showing any fear. Even as he got up from the chair and opened the window, he appeared to be menacing. But René held on to the hope that he could be reasoned with.

"Yes . . . with Courtland's help, I was able to destroy the perfect family . . . the Bainbridges. My only regret is that my beloved Rachel got caught up in such ugliness," he said. "My lovely Rachel . . . my dear sweet Rachel. You look nothing like her, although you have her manner. But you are nothing like her at all," Sheridan said as he reached over to caress René's cheek, only to receive an icy stare.

"My mother never gave you the idea that she was interested in you. You act as though she offered you more than a mutual friendship. You who sat at my father's table and proclaimed undying friendship to him and to his family. You did nothing but stab my father in the back. It was you, wasn't it? Wasn't it ?!" René shouted. "And it was you who sent the letter. Of all things to do, you deliberately set out to hurt my father. You were the only who could have done it."

René didn't know how right she was. Accusation after accusation, she hurled them like a champion. The colonel absorbed each one she threw, knowing that eventually she would determine the reason behind his behavior. "Get out!" René screamed. "Just . . . get out!"

"I'm sorry you feel that way, my dear. You see, if Devon Bainbridge hadn't come into the picture, I could have been your father. Your mother would be alive today, and there wouldn't be a question about your birth. Think about that!" he said grimly. Then he opened the window further to allow more air to filter in. She watched every move he made and pulled the covers closer to her. "This life would have agreed with your mother. I do miss her. But, we both know the truth, don't we? You and he made it necessary for me to write that letter. Yes, your father thought that the truth died with the midwife and that old slave, but I was there. I was there when you were born, René Alexandra Bainbridge."

René was in shock. The only other person who knew her secret, besides Robert, was James. Now this man was telling her life's story as though he had written a daily diary. She wrapped the blanket around her and climbed out of bed. René opened the door and said, "Please leave. You have said your piece. You have nothing to fear from me, Colonel Sheridan, but your own guilt will be the death of you. Now, if you don't mind, I need to get some rest."

"Yes, get all the rest you can. You will be quite busy in the next few days. You see, I need a housekeeper, someone to keep up with my laundry and things. So, get your rest, my dear," he said with a terrible grin. He gently caressed her hand.

The windows facing the wall of the fort were her first choice. Quietly René slipped the window nearest her bed. Sky whispered, "You cannot climb over the fort yourself. I will get my brother to meet you over there." She pointed to the building next door. It was up to René to get there without being seen. As she inched her way to the building she found a pickax lying on the ground within view of the soldiers passing by. They apparently didn't care, because after several passes, no one bothered to pick it up. Their laziness allowed René to get her hands on it and quickly move

Within minutes, René was joined by Lame Fox and Sky. He wasn't pleased to be helping in an escape attempt, which could jeopardize his standing. He figured he could get even with Black Eagle for walking on his promise to marry his sister. He directed the women to follow him to a ladder that just happened to be resting against the wall.

Everything seemed to be so easy, until they reached the roof. The lights in the fort were flickering brightly. Some created shadows, which seemed to move as they moved, or was it their imagination working against them?

Lame Fox pulled the ladder up and put it over the wall, then he directed René to go over the wall and climb down. She was going alone. There was no argument whether he would put his reputation on the line for Black Eagle's woman. The only reason he was helping this woman was because his sister had asked him to. In fact, he should be hauling this woman to the colonel's office instead of aiding in her escape.

Sky handed René a small bundle. It was her way of saying farewell. René climbed down the ladder; to the east there were trees to shield her, and to the west there was nothing but open field for miles. She decided to take to the cover of the trees and work her way north.

Meanwhile, James plotted his escape as well. He needed a way of getting past the front gate. And later, he would work on getting a horse and some supplies. He didn't like having his freedom taken away, when René was given free reign of the fort grounds. It infuriated him even more to know that she was thirty feet away from his cell and the only thing in his way was a few inches of cell door.

Private Stanhope had entered James's cell with a tray of food. He wasn't used to dealing with a man like him. James could tell that the boy's nerves were on edge, while Stanhope tried to give the impression of being strong and brave. Yet, in the presence of this man, he felt weak and uncertain.

The soldier tried to place the tray into James's hands, but his rifle inhibited his movements. He placed his rifle on the floor near the door and then placed the tray on the captain's cot. His mistake was to turn his back on the captain. Courtland landed a blow to the back of Stanhope's neck, knocking him out.

Courtland was surprised that the boy had come alone without an armed escort. He eased the door opened and found the grounds empty except for a few standing watch at the front gate. Like a shot he dashed toward the stables, and what luck: There were twelve horses tied in the stalls.

Private Smith entered the stables to water the horses and to smoke his homegrown cigarettes. He dropped the water bucket while trying to light it with the oil lamp. James couldn't believe how inept this soldier was. And yet, he was the most loyal of all the soldiers who had followed him. He waited for the soldier to complete his duties. But unlike most soldiers, Smith had a knack of taking too long. Impatient and tired of waiting, James slipped up behind Smith and covered his mouth. Smith was so startled, he wet his pants. "Listen carefully, Smith," James said. "I want you to saddle a horse for me . . . now." He looked around to make sure that the coast was clear, then said, "I want you to create a diversion . . . something that will bring those soldiers over here. Now do it!"

Smith shook his head. The sooner he did as he was told, the better. He saddled the horse while James kept watch. It wouldn't make his day to be interrupted again. Then James gave him one final order. "Now, go to Miss Bainbridge's quarters and tell her that her horse was brought in. Bring her to this stable. Do you understand me, boy?"

The boy nodded and did as he was told. Courtland waited impatiently and paced the hay-filled stall. For what seemed like an eternity was only a few minutes. Smith had returned, but without René. "She is not in her room, sir," Smith offered quickly. He ducked when James raised his hand, as though to strike him.

"What do you mean she is not in her room? I have had her room in my sight all night. The only people to come and go were the colonel, the captain, and that Indian wench. "What about the soldier guarding her room?" James asked finally. But Smith only shrugged. He was in charge of the horses and that was all he could account for.

"You're lying. You blithering idiot! Bring her to me. Now," James ordered.

And the boy stated again, "She ain't in the room, sir. I even looked under the bed. She ain't there."

James was infuriated. The last thing he wanted to do was leave without the woman who had caused all his troubles. If it hadn't been for her, he would be receiving honors instead of a court martial. "She just refused to come, right, soldier?" he asked.

"No, sir! I looked. The room is as empty as a coon's patch in huntin' season," Smith continued. "Ah think the gal's done run off."

"Damn it! Birney should have kept her under his watchful eye," he said with contempt. "He and that infernal drunken Colonel Sheridan! But I'll get her. If it's the last thing I do, I'll get her!" James continued, consumed with determination. James had no choice but to take the word of the half-wit who stood before him. He was running out of time. Soon the soldier he knocked out would be missed, and that meant the fort would be searched. He would never get out once that had begun. "Now," he stated slowly, "I need you to distract the guards at the gate. Do anything you have to. But get me out of here. Don't fail me, boy!" James ordered.

Smith, like a mindless child, again did as he was ordered to do. He released all of the horses from their stalls. Then he lit a match and dropped it into the pile of hay near the middle of the stables. Once the flames got out of hand, the horses started to rush toward the entrance. The door burst open, and Smith watched all of his charges rush out, whinnying and kicking in all directions. One kicked over the water trough, and another jumped the fence and ran toward the family quarters. It ran aimlessly through Mrs. Birney's flower garden. Several horses, accompanied by an unseen rider, galloped out of the open gate and into the field. The confused soldiers who were on guard were too busy trying to calm the frightened beasts to even notice him.

Black Eagle and Robert wasted no time leaving Wilmot after getting what they wanted. They were sure that the sheriff would not interfere in their quest. He seemed quite subdued, even though he claimed to be a man of action. Yet, he let himself get caught up in a struggle to preserve a family, and his only response was as savage as that of the man he verbally attacked. And who, without showing any savagery, let the man who stole his wife live. The least he could do was put Walter Cory under wraps until they reached Fort Wayne.

Just before their departure Walter received a message from the Ojibwa, which was also carried by the Sioux and the Miami. He was banned from ever entering the northern wilderness. He and his friends were now marked men. Their scalps were considered a bounty worth collecting. Walter took heed of the warning, wanting very much to keep his scalp intact. The best way to do that was to work his way east to New York or to Pennsylvania. At least there he would know what was coming. So, he settled for the cot in his jail cell and the rotten food he would receive in the morning. Anything would do now that he had his life. And yet, he was happy that he wasn't in the captain's shoes.

After their visit into the town, Black Eagle added another notch to his spear to indicate the number of days he and René had been separated. In his heart he wanted to believe that René would fight to stay alive, but in his mind, he saw the ever-looming threat of her nemesis. He was a menace, something that needed to be destroyed, before he destroyed her.

However, Black Eagle knew that René was strong-willed and that she would prevail. She had said as much when they were together, and he wanted so much for it to be that way. And then there were times when he felt the danger that hung over her. But that would not stop him from trying to find her, to release her from the bonds that kept them apart. Walter Cory had ignited a flame of suspicion for which only René had the power to put out.

Black Eagle and Robert traveled most of the night until they joined up with Chief Chinock and his party. They were about to sit down to roasted venison and capons. And yet, they waited for the duo to tether their horses and join them before they partook in their meal.

"What news do you bring from the white man's world?" Chinock asked as he gave a solemn greeting and noted that they had returned emptyhanded.

The news he had to share wasn't pleasant, especially for him. Black Eagle reached for a piece of roasted capon and handed it to Robert. *"a, wi -wi ssenik!"* ("Come on . . . eat!") he said strongly.

Robert gave his brother-in-law a strange look and then accepted what was offered. "Thanks, brother!" he said through his ragged beard. He heard the worry in his voice and decided not to press him, but offered, "We'll get her back!"

So many days had passed, and the only glimmer of hope came from a man whose greed was his only companion. "I can only hope that you are right," Black Eagle stated. "What kind of man hunts a woman and shows her no mercy?"

"James Courtland . . . was never a man." Robert stated coldly. "He only wants one thing, and that is René's inheritance. If he could, he would have mined a well. James Courtland . . . I should have killed him when I had the chance. I curse the day he walked into our lives."

Agitated by what he had just heard, Black Eagle quickly got to his feet and headed for his horse. Too much time was spent on talk, and René was still in his hands. The longer he waited, the less likely he would be able to get her back and he knew it. But Chinock quickly added as he reached Black Eagle's side, "No matter what you feel at this moment, my son, you will have to show mercy to this man. He has done a great injustice to you and to your wife. But if you kill him . . . you will not be able to free your soul from the hate that is welling up inside you."

"I do not understand," Black Eagle said questionably. "He does not deserve to have mercy. His scalp will hang from my shield. The white man will know what it means to fear."

"They already fear you, my son. They fear us. They fear the unknown, and they are afraid to keep their word. You have seen them . . . they live behind high walls made of wood. They bring their guns to our lands and they take what they want without asking. And we fight back with our arrows and spears."

"That is true," Black Eagle responded, his eyes narrowing as he returned to the circle. "Re-nea and the life of our unborn child must come first. But I will do what needs to be done, no matter what! One way or another, the man will die!"

With that, Black Eagle closed himself off from everyone, including Robert. He would have to come to terms with the entire matter in his own way. It was his wife and child who were in danger, and the others were there just to support him. If it came down to a contest of will, he would have to act on his own. The night air became cool, and everyone pulled their blankets or their robes around their shoulders. However, Black Eagle faced the cold, and held on to the hope of bringing his family home again.

CHAPTER TWENTY-THREE

RENÉ WALKED AS FAST as she could to get as much distance between her and the fort. The extra weight she was carrying added another burden besides not knowing where to go first. If she was sure of one thing, it was to protect her unborn child. And even though she was out of their range, she was sure that someone would notice that she was gone. Colonel Sheridan made her feel unclean and insecure. His arrogance and callousness forced her to take this route. She knew he wouldn't allow her to go back to Black Eagle. And since his behavior dictated that point, she ran. Each step brought her closer to home and closer to her loved ones.

The moonlight slowly dimmed, and she could barely see two feet in front of her. However, even with that obstacle she continued on her way. Going home was a pleasant thought. It made her smile knowing that somewhere in this vast forest she would find her home and her family. She imagined that the village was only a few steps away and that White Feather and Jaewa were just beyond the trees to greet her.

So many days had passed since her abduction, and she wondered whether Black Eagle knew where to look for her. He would be in unfamiliar territory. The people wouldn't be willing to answer questions, much less answer the questions of an Indian. "I won't let it bother me. I'll find them," she said to herself as she continued north. "Eventually someone is bound to come this way," she added, almost praying.

René was at least two hours or better from the fort, and her confidence grew with each step. How she longed to be in Black Eagle's embrace, safe and warm. She wanted to cuddle her son, One Shoe, and even worried about the food she would have stored away for the winter months. By now everyone had received their share, everyone but her. But for now, she was happy. She was finally free . . . free to be herself again.

She wasn't surprised by her own musings. From time to time she remembered the home she was forced to leave behind. She didn't long to return to Wilmot or to come anywheRe-near it. She no longer relished to be apart from the life she had grown to love and respect. Even in its simplicity, her life was fruitful and quite satisfying. She had grown up in a way that her father would have been proud of. Even the mother who bore her would have been proud. René dropped to her knees in prayer and thanked God for giving her life back to her.

Suddenly she heard a rumble coming up fast from behind her. She imagined the worst, wondering who could have known she was traveling this way. "They told—Sky and her brother betrayed me," she cried as she tried to find a hiding place. Even the shield of the darkness wouldn't be enough to conceal her. She appeared to be surrounded with nowhere to run.

There were horses, several horses with no riders. Some still wore their bridles, while others were bare and running free. One horse got tangled up with the branches of a fallen tree and struggled to free himself. If she could just get close enough, without startling him, she would have transportation home. At least with the horse, travel would be easier and faster. But the horse tugged on the leather strap connected to its bridle and yanked himself free. As if jumping in triumph, he leaped over the fallen tree and made his way into the clearing and right out in the open, which was vibrantly lit by the crystal moon. There he stood, nervously, but seemingly awaiting her approach. His breathing was labored, yet he appeared to be able to run another ten or twenty miles without stopping. Then his eyes flashed. He reacted to another beast approaching. René heard it, too, and rushed for cover.

René couldn't believe her luck. She thought that she had control over her own outcome, but as always, James managed to rip away any shred of hope she had. She recognized his tall muscular form as he drew nearer. And she knew her situation had changed from bad to inconceivably worse within seconds. She held her breath and prayed that he would just pass her by, but he could hear her terrified breathing just as sure as he could hear his own. He quickly dismounted with his rifle in hand and tried to survey the area she was located.

"You there! Come out where I can see you!" he demanded. René couldn't move. Her knees were paralyzed. All she could do was lean up against the tree and hope he wouldn't detect her presence there. "I know someone is here. I can hear you! Now come into the light where I can see you," he stated bluntly. She watched as he aimed the rifle in her direction and then pull back on the trigger. "I'll give you to the count of three! One, two, thr—" click.

The rifle wasn't loaded, and he cursed the owner of the weapon. Relief washed through René as he bantered on about the weapon. Then she took a chance, while he was distracted, to ease her way to the other side of the tree. She had to run for it or get caught up in James's fury. Quickly she darted for the next tree, taking care not to get into the light. The last thing she needed was another delay, but her quick movements through the forest startled the horse she sorely needed. She tried to calm him, but he reared and snorted loudly. In great haste, René slung herself onto his back and took to the open meadow. That got James's attention. He saw her hair flowing in a trail behind her as she fled.

James mounted quickly and within seconds was within arm's reach of her. René tightened her grip on the reins and directed the horse to zigzag, which kicked up grass and sod into her pursuer's face. That alone made him more angry and more determined to catch her. René was fine until she looked back to see where he was. That was her mistake, because she panicked and lost her rhythm with the horse when she loosened her grip on his reins. James was able to grab her firmly about the waist and whisk her away from the tired mount.

He cursed in her ear as he came to a sudden stop and then quickly surveyed the space he had traveled. They were both out in the open, vulnerable and unarmed. He could barely see the lights gleaming from the fort, which seemed like a child's toy in the distance. Feeling certain that he hadn't exposed himself, he turned to René and gave her a walloping slap across the face. She went crashing to the ground, stunned and shaken by his intrusion on her person.

"You stupid little bitch!" he yelled. "If you run or move in any way, I'll kill you! Do you understand?" he demanded. "Do you?" he yelled again, pointing his finger at her with each word spoken. René shook her head, too afraid to speak. "I didn't hear you, René!"

René didn't want to respond to him. The fewer words she shared with him, the better. It was bad enough that he touched her, but she saw no way out of this one. "Yes! I understand you!" she yelled back. The sting to her face brought back everything he had done and said to her in the past. She wished him dead and hoped that he would drop his guard long enough for her to slit his throat.

He was in power again and liked every minute of it. He knew what she was thinking, before she was able to formulate it in her own mind. "I know what you are thinking my dear. Don't try anything. I'm better than you at killing. Mark my word, I won't feel any guilt when I'm done with you. Besides, we have unfinished business to attend to. You can thank your lucky stars that I just happened along," he said laughingly.

It appeared his treachery would win over at every turn. He had outsmarted everyone, including her. It was shameful that two men, James Courtland and his counterpart, George Sheridan, wanted to dominate her at will. There was no place on the green earth where she would be able to go without having to fend off some would-be threat as long as they lived.

"How did you find me? How did you know?" she asked in anger. He had disrupted her life from the time she left Wilmot and even to this very moment. Always on her trail, hunting her, like an animal is hunted. Always calculating how he would kill her once he found her. No matter what, she was plagued by his incessant hatred and greed for her fortune. She couldn't take his constant insults or his probing eyes invading her private world. James was a thorn, and he needed to be removed. *If I were a man, I would be rid of you,* she thought to herself, knowing that if he heard her say it, it would be another means for him to abuse her.

"It doesn't matter how I found you," he said as he pulled her to her feet. "I have to give it to you, you are a clever woman . . . clever indeed," James put in her ear. He was too close, much closer than she could tolerate. She struggled with him to release her, at least to get his hands off of her. But that was a losing battle. He held her tightly to maintain his power over her. He was determined to keep her for whatever spurred him on. "You may as well stop fighting the inevitable. I have you now and I will decide what to do with you when the time comes," he stated bluntly.

Then he mounted his stolen horse and, without much effort, he lifted René to his lap. He was heading west toward the Illinois territory. He was sure that he wouldn't run into the Union army unless they considered that a possible threat from the Confederacy. There would be enough time for him to disguise himself and to find another means of survival. Meanwhile, they would ride until . . .

The following morning Black Eagle and Robert had finally reached Fort Wayne with the intention of getting René out their clutches. They had traveled through the open fields with grass as high as a man's waist and as blue green as the waters of the Pacific. It was good land . . . good land for farming and raising fat cows and horses. There was plenty of fishing and hunting in this land of many promises. It was the land that had once sustained many tribes with food and shelter for many seasons, but no longer.

"You are very quiet, my brother," Robert said with concern. He was right as always: His brother-in-law was troubled. He was troubled and concerned. He sensed Black Eagle's doubts upon his return to the campsite even more after they disclosed what they learned about René and her whereabouts. Walter Cory had fed him a bitter pill, and Black Eagle was unable to swallow it. Black Eagle nodded, for words were useless at this point. Nothing could fill the emptiness he felt. Only the sheer knowledge that he may regain his family pushed him ever onward toward the walled structure in their wake.

A soldier on watch yelled, "Who goes there? Stop and state your business."

Robert identified himself quickly. "I am Robert Bainbridge. I was told that my sister was being held—"

Before he could finish, the gate opened and several soldiers rushed out fully armed. They surrounded the two men and escorted them inside to the officer who awaited their presence. Chief Chinock was right about the welcoming they would receive from the soldiers in blue. It was his idea to hold the remaining warriors out of range of the fort, but within a pace in order to advance when the time would arise. As Black Eagle and Robert entered the fort, they passed several tepees, which Black Eagle identified as Miami. Then he saw a familiar face, Lame Fox, who seemed nervous and refused to acknowledge him. Sky, his sister, was standing by his side. She was lovely and appeared to be nineteen or twenty years old. She, too, seemed quite upset with his presence as well. Their eyes locked, and Black Eagle knew he would be meeting with them later. But for now, their attention was on the man standing with his arms folded in front of him, commanding and in charge.

"Bring . . . those two . . . into my office, soldier!" the old man demanded. He had aged at least ten years since Robert last saw him. His temples were gray, and his hair was dry and stringy. he uniform was unkempt and wrinkled. The smell of whiskey was in the air. His speech was slurred and inhibited and worse yet, Robert knew the man recognized him.

When they entered his domain, Colonel Sheridan was already seated. "Well, my boy! It seems . . . you have come at an opportune time," he said as he cleared his throat.

Robert raised a brow and said, "I have only one concern, and that is the well-being of my sister. I was told that she was being held here."

"That is true, but there is the matter of the young lady standing trial for murder," Sheridan stated freely. He was sure that he had covered all aspects of René s involvement with Lieutenant Gantry's death.

"Murder! René didn't kill anyone," Robert insisted.

Sheridan waited for a brief moment. If he could, he would twist the story and make it appear just as he said it had. He had no intention of letting René leave the fort. He had plans for her. He had envisioned having her as his own personal slave, such a lovely one at that. She intrigued him, just like Rachel sparked a fire in him.

"She is charged with the murder of one of my officers. It will not be possible for me to release her until after her trial, and that won't take place for months," he stated quickly as he eyed the tall Indian, who appeared quite shaken by the news.

Robert knew that René hadn't been out of his sight except when Black Eagle took her away, and then of course, James Courtland. "When did this killing take place?" Robert inquired. He wanted to get to the bottom of the truth and get René out of here.

"That's a matter for the court to decide. She will have a fair trial. Meanwhile, she must remain under guard," he continued. He smiled as though he had won a poker hand. Yet, he knew that Robert was as thrifty as his father, the infamous, Devon Bainbridge. The boy wouldn't leave unless he was thoroughly convinced that there was nothing he could do. "Who is this?" he said, turning his attention to Black Eagle.

"I'm sorry . . . let me introduce you to Black Eagle. He is the son of Chief Gray Wolf, and he is also René's husband. So, before telling me anything else, you had better tell him that she is well and that he can see her. Otherwise, you have made an act of war on his people. His people are strong and have many tribes to support them. I know . . . I have seen them," Robert indicated sternly.

"What do you mean, her husband? You . . . let your sister live among these savages?" Sheridan asked with a mark of sarcasm.

Black Eagle moved over to the door to secure it and said, "The only savage my Re-nea has come to know is the one who stole her away. She, who is my wife, lives among my people in peace. She does not fear for her life. She has had a good life . . . with me."

George Sheridan was stunned at Black Eagle's impertinence. He dared to imply that his people were civilized. He was appalled that René Bainbridge was a squaw, the wife of this savage. He turned away for a moment, trying to think of a way to avoid any carnage and to maintain control over the Bainbridge woman. He decided to let one of them see her. At least that might pacify them for a while.

"Uh, I will let you see her, but under one condition," he said to Robert. "I can only let you see her. I am sure that you want this matter cleared up just as much as I do," the colonel continued as he addressed Robert. He was in control and rallied at the thought that he could maintain it. "So . . . you, Robert Bainbridge, not the Indian, will see her. I can't afford *this one* trying to take her out of here when she has charges to face."

This matter definitely wasn't over. Colonel Sheridan may have pulled one over them, but that wasn't going to last for long. Robert knew the colonel was lying for some reason or another. René was no doubt under the impression that she was being blamed for everything—from the riot to the lieutenants death. It had to be frustrating for her with the evidence pointing at her.

"Soldier!" he yelled through the door. "Take Mr. Bainbridge to his sister. In the meantime, Mr. Eagle can wait in the anteroom." Sheridan pointed to the room adjoining his office. Then he posted a guard with orders to shoot if Black Eagle even poked his head out of the door.

Robert was taken to René's quarters. From what he saw, apparently she hadn't been mistreated. Her accommodations were clean, and she was given the privacy she hadn't received under the scrutiny of Courtland. He called her as he entered the first room. Then he knocked on the second door, thinking that she was still sleeping. When there was no response, he opened the door to find the bed empty. The room was empty, and there was a soldier standing guard outside her door. The soldier suddenly became nervous, since he had been on duty all night.

"Where is she?" Robert asked as he eyed the soldier. "Is this some kind of a joke?" Robert insisted as walked through her room.

"I don't know, sir! She was here last night! Honest, sir, she was!" he said with concern, but it was mostly for himself. He had really slipped up.

It was the first time he had ever been assigned to guard a woman. How hard could it be? She seemed too refined, too ladylike to run off like that.

Then Colonel Sheridan entered the room more or less to gloat over her captivity. He thought he had gained the upper hand and wanted very much to show his enjoyment in their present troubles. But when he saw that René was nowhere in sight, the smile he bore changed to undeniable anger. He beat his fist into the wall and cursed René for cheating him. Robert watched in wonder as Colonel Sheridan continued his outbursts, ranting and raving over what she had done to him. Maybe René found her own way out or she had help, but it was better than her having to face the likes of this. Or, maybe the colonel was trying to keep her out of sight, away from him.

"You have her hidden somewhere, don't you?" Robert snapped. "If I don't see her in the next few minutes, I won't be able to help you. By now the fort has been surrounded. Every man in this fort will have ten warriors against him," Robert confirmed.

The colonel was set back on his heals. This boy dared to threaten the fort and indicated that he had the power of control over him and every man in the fort. "Do you expect me to believe that?" Sheridan asked. He just knew the boy was bluffing.

However, Captain Birney entered with news as Robert was about to answer his question. He was wearing his full-dress uniform, with his ceremonial saber and sash. To compare the two, Birney was the true soldier, where Colonel Sheridan just wore the title. "Colonel Sheridan! There is a large band of Indians approaching the fort from the east. I counted at least fifty or so. There may be more," Birney exclaimed. "There is plenty of powder and casings. I also ordered the men to make ready for battle, sir."

Colonel Sheridan turned to face Robert, realizing that this wasn't a mere boy standing before him, but a man. He was his father's son through and through. "You said that if you didn't see your sister, these Indians would attack, is that right?" Sheridan asked. "Well, I don't want any blood shed over a woman. The charges have been dropped."

"What charges are you speaking of, colonel?" Birney asked quickly. "She is free to leave the fort anytime, don't you remember?"

Sheridan turned away to conceal his guilt. "That is utter nonsense. I knew nothing of the sort!" he exclaimed.

But Robert saw through his lies. The young honorable captain had exposed him for what he was. "You were planning to keep her here against her will, weren't you?" Robert asked. "You are no better than the slime who killed our parents. You and the whole lot of you can go to hell!" Robert yelled as he walked through the door. Then he asked the captain who was close on his heels and who had the only honest face in the room, "If she's not here, then where is she?"

Captain Birney was at his wit's end. He couldn't for the life of him think where the young woman had gotten off to. Then he remembered the Indian woman who had attended René when she'd arrived several days ago. They had developed a close bond, a friendship, so to speak. "I can't answer your questions, but maybe, just maybe I know someone who can," he said anxiously. "Come with me! There isn't a moment to lose!"

Sky had just prepared the noon meal for her brother. She assumed that he would be entertaining the handsome Black Eagle and his companion, so she tidied up the the tepee and placed her brother's pipe where he could reach it. She was pleased with her handiwork and knew that her brother would be proud. Then she sat quietly, waiting for Lame Fox and his guest to arrive.

All was well until Captain Birney burst in. Sky could tell that he was upset and she hoped it didn't have to do with her. *Maybe they were here about the missing horses,* she thought to herself. But the questions that were directed toward her were not about the horses, they were all about René. She shied away, trying not to implicate herself in any way with the missing woman. She continued to clean her home, until Robert made his plea.

"I need your help. Black Eagle and I both need your help. We are searching for my sister, Black Eagle's wife. She was taken by force by the man who brought her here. I know you understand. I know that you helped her," Robert said softly, but his words fell on deaf ears. She said nothing to him at all.

Suddenly, Private Stanhope came staggering out of the cell that once detained James Courtland. He had a hefty bruise on the back of his head, and his neck was swollen from the blow he received. He could barely walk, but he headed straight for Captain Birney as he left Robert and Sky in the tepee. Stanhope's weapons were missing, which gave him cause to be alarmed about Courtland's escape.

While the captain was occupied with the injured soldier, Sky took that moment to make her peace with Robert. She told him how she and her brother had helped René to escape. She feared the punishment she would receive from the colonel more than she feared anything else. And with her admission for helping in the escape, her life could be in danger next. The colonel had threatened her with a gun the night she promised René she wouldn't leave her side. He could care less about her well being, including that of René. She was soft spoken, and her gentle manner would be used against her. Robert observed much in the little time they had. Was she lying? He didn't know for sure. But she had told him things that only René would have divulged. She told him everything she thought he wanted to hear without being goaded into answering.

Then she offered, "She has been gone since nightfall. I saw her run for cover under the trees. She has some food and a small blanket to keep her warm. I wanted to do more, but my brother was against it."

Robert was confused with all he had heard. "What made her leave so abruptly? I mean, why did she want to leave a place where she was safe?" Robert asked quickly.

Sky explained, saying almost in detail the threats she had overheard. She remembered how frantic René was after the colonel left. How she paced around the room trying to decide what to do. "Your sister asked me for help. She didn't explain why, but I knew. She was upset after the colonel left," she offered gently. She walked to the door and checked for would-be intruders. Satisfied that Captain Birney wasn't within earshot, she gave Robert René's knife. "She forgot to take this when she left."

"That isn't good . . . not good at all," he retorted. He threw the basket she had been weaving against the wall. "I'm . . . I'm sorry. I don't mean to take my anger out on you," he said apologetically. He quickly retrieved the basket and placed it in her hands. Even though he didn't want to hear any more, Robert listened as Sky continued to explain what she could understand. She was his only link to René's whereabouts, and from what he had been told, she was better off out of Sheridan's reach. Yet, he couldn't help but worry that René was out there alone with no weapon to fend off the wilds of the land. If only she could have waited a little longer.

Robert became anxious and quickly thanked her before rushing off for Colonel Sheridan's office where Black Eagle was being held under guard. He was there in a flash, angry to see that Black Eagle had been treated so poorly. "You can put that gun away now," he insisted as he pushed the barrel of the rifle away from the door. He opened the door, never once giving any consideration to the soldier who had been given orders to keep Black Eagle locked away. "Black Eagle, I have news. But we have to get out of here," he said as he pushed the soldier aside again. "The fewer ears, the better René's chances of being located."

Black Eagle was puzzled at first. He thought René was somewhere in the fort. "You must tell me everything . . . quickly!" he insisted. "Where is Re-nea?" he inquired, searching Robert's eyes for some light of hope. But Robert hesitated and the feeling of hopelessness attacked him again. "I want to see her . . . now!" he insisted, and headed for the door. But Robert stopped him from leaving. There were things he had to say, and he was having difficulty putting them into words.

"It's about René. Black Eagle . . . she . . . is not here. Something happened last night that made it necessary for her to run away. She is out there somewhere, with no weapons," he said as he handed her knife to his brother-in-law. There was so much anguish in his face that it nearly brought Robert to tears.

"Then we must go . . . now!" Black Eagle insisted. "He can not get far on foot."

Black Eagle was anxious, just as anxious as Robert to leave the fort. He was out for blood, and he wouldn't be satisfied until his thirst had been quenched. For too long he and René had had to put up with someone else's wants and demands, never once were they truly allowed to think of themselves. They weren't trying to be selfish, they wanted to be with each other . . . to raise their family in peace and to love one another openly, with regard. It seemed that they were on a judgment block, waiting to be tried and sentenced for just loving each other. However, Captain Birney reentered the colonel's office, on the premise that the news he was about to give would tax the demeanor of an already impatient Indian. What could he say to lighten the load or to ease the tremendous gravity that would weigh upon a man who waited for word, any word, about his wife? He had been treated like a prisoner of sorts and wasn't offered the grand gesture of a man of rank or position. And that was going to end.

"You will tell me if Captain Courtland is here! Tell me!" Black Eagle ordered as he neared the officer.

Captain Birney backed himself into the wall, but he answered Black Eagle without delay or inquiry. "Captain Courtland . . . I mean, Lieutenant Courtland escaped during the night. I think he was the one who caused the confusion, where all our horses from the main stable had gotten lose. Right now there are five horses, and one saddle missing," he continued. "I have also been informed that he is carrying several weapons. I am very sorry!" Birney said to Black Eagle, acknowledging his importance. "I didn't know about it until a moment ago. He attacked one of my soldiers last night and took all of his weapons."

"What kind of place are you running here?" Robert interrupted angrily. "My sister is missing . . . Courtland is on the loose and is armed. If anything happens to her, I will hold everyone here responsible!" Robert exclaimed harshly. "And tell the jackass of a commander that I'll see him in hell before he threatens my sister again!" Robert could feel the blood boiling in his veins. One thought on his mind and he knew his was the echo of Black Eagle: "Find René!"

Black Eagle, however, was silently enraged. He was the first one to leave the compound even with the threat of death looming over him. It didn't matter if they shot him down; they wouldn't be alive to tell the story later. Before Robert could catch up with him, he had already sent out a scouting party in the last known direction René could have traveled. The others scattered into the four winds, looking for any clues they could find.

Birney watched from the sentry post as they rode out of sight. They knew more than they had led him to believe. "Sergeant Wills! I wanted you to get a small detail together, fully armed and with a five-day supply of rations. I want them ready in less than half an hour," he ordered. Then he headed for Colonel Sheridan's, where the old man was drinking himself into a stupor.

René had finally fallen asleep in James's arms since she had no choice in the matter. They had traveled all night, stopping once to let the horse rest. They must have covered at least fifty miles or more in the ten or twelve hours of their passage through the wood. James took this time to allow himself a little sleep, since René wasn't up and about making trouble for him. He dismounted and gently brought René to a soft grassy section just beyond the clearing. He amazed himself at the care he had taken with her. He stroked the cheek he had abused so quickly the night before. He wondered why he never noticed her beauty before this. In the year he spent courting her, he never really paid her much mind. All he was concerned with was her fortune. He then gently adjusted his bedroll under her head and caressed her cheek again, placing himself where he could reach her if she decided to run.

James had had at least two hours' sleep. He was able to take short naps here and there and still give one hundred percent to his duties. He was pleased to see that René was still sleeping in the spot he had placed her in earlier. She hadn't moved at all. Yet, the quiet rhythm of her breathing made him look at her in a new light. For some strange reason, he felt a twinge in his stomach whenever he gazed upon her. It wasn't enough to look at her' he had to touch her, to possess her in every way. So consumed in his own thoughts, he brought her closer and wrapped the blanket around her shoulders.

René sensed the tremendous warmth afforded to her and stayed in the cradle of his arms, thinking of Black Eagle all the while. James brought his face closer to hers and examined the curl of her lashes, her nose, and even the fullness of her lips, which enticed and thrilled him. She had innocently parted her lips only to take a breath and release a gentle sigh. His mind worked against him, wanting to kiss her lips, and that he did. He planted a hearty kiss upon them. His passion had awakened René, who in turn was startled and angry to find that it was James, not Black Eagle, kissing her in a full embrace. She had let her guard down and had relaxed when it wasn't safe.

René pushed him away and beat upon his chest until he finally released her. Her heart was racing as she flew from where they had shared a sleeping space. She didn't like him being so close to her, much less touching her. And yet he seemed to enjoy her reaction, her discomfort. The memory of her softness wouldn't be enough to calm the beast she had awakened in him. He wanted her and it didn't matter that she didn't want him.

"Stop! Stay where you are!" René demanded when she saw him edge toward her. But all she could see was passion in his eyes. She turned to run, but James was too fast for her. He just reached out and brought her down to the plush blanket of grass. He held her fast and hard, squeezing his fingers into her flesh. He said things that weren't fit for any woman to hear, and he knew it frightened her.

"I was deprived of your comely beauty once. Now you are mine. I have the right to take you, with or without your consent! Don't forget that, René !" he said hungrily in her ear.

René's heart was pounding wildly in her chest. She knew she didn't have the strength to stop him, but she hoped that she could appeal to his sympathy or his reason. "Please, don't do this! This is wrong!" she said with urgency. Never was it so clear that she was nothing but a toy or an object to be played with whenever the whim struck him. *"Please!"* she begged as the glare in his eyes intensified. Instead of listening to her pleas,

James snatched off all her clothing and sent it flying in all directions. Then he unleashed all his wanton lust upon her, making sure he enjoyed every bit of the sweet morsel in his arms. He was pleased with himself and had already made plans to keep her busy filling his nights.

When he had finished with René , he ordered her to get dressed and ready to leave. At first she lay trembling on the ground, wondering how a man could be so cruel, so uncaring. She didn't deserve to be treated like the dirt beneath his feet. Yet she dared not say anything to rebuke his manhood. She feared for the child she carried and feared any outburst on his physical part would cause her to lose it. She couldn't stand being raped again.

René dressed very slowly, keeping her back to him, all the while checking on the baby's movements. She was grateful that his manliness wasn't as great as his need to humiliate her. "What is taking you so long?" he demanded while coming toward her. "Get a move on! I don't want to lose the daylight!"

"Where are we going?" she asked. She almost smiled when the baby moved again, giving her a tiny flutter in her belly. She wrapped the blanket around her shoulders to conceal the small swelling that seemed to appear overnight. Then she looked at him when he seemed to have appeared to ignore her question.

"Don't concern yourself with where. When we get there, you will know . . . I promise you, you will know!" he said sharply as he swept her up and then mounted the horse himself. His behavior had changed to impatience, although now, his manner was less harsh.

Black Eagle and Robert followed René's trail from the fort, which led them to believe she was heading northeast. In another section of the woods, they found the hoofprints of the horses known to have run this way. Only one set seemed to stand out more clearly than the others. They knew René had to run into the party riding the horse and now her direction had changed. She was now going west.

"She has been taken again!" Black Eagle exclaimed. He was at the end of his rope. The longer they were apart, the more their relationship was in danger. He didn't count on this, not one bit. He walked through the trees where René had been and touched the soil where she had tread. He only felt the emptiness creeping into his soul. He had no one to blame but himself. He should have known that the man would do everything in his power to hurt her. That night he took her away, he should have killed James on the spot. But he allowed the man to live. He could only wonder why.

Chief Chinock, a man wise beyond his years said, "You are too emotional, my son. She is still alive or else we would have found her by now. You have great pride in the woman you chose to be your wife. Think! She has left you a sign. And soon, you will find her."

"I hear your words, Great One," Black Eagle said with respect. "I know she is alive. I can feel it . . . here," he said as he pointed to his heart.

The chief knew a man's heart was always afoul when he was in love. A man shouldn't become so attached to his woman. She is here to serve the man and to satisfy his needs. Yet, this young man treated his woman with respect. He valued her thoughts and felt lost without her. He wondered what kind of woman would make a man act this way. He was determined to meet her. At least then, he could decide for himself whether or not she was worth all the trouble.

Meanwhile, Captain Birney, accompanied by a small detail and Lame Fox, followed the same trail as their predecessors. He planned to make sure that James Courtland stood trial for his friend's murder. Not far behind, they, too, were being followed, by Sky. She didn't want to be left behind, especially now that her brother was leaving.

Lame Fox had a score to settle with Black Eagle, since he had broken his promise. Black Eagle was betrothed to Sky, according to Lame Fox, even though a formal ceremony hadn't been given, in his mind, Black Eagle had promised to marry his sister. The gift of beaver pelts and elk skins was a sign of marriage that would have united both tribes. However, Black Eagle was just making a fair and even trade to pacify him after he won the gray roan.

Lame Fox had vowed to make it right if it was the last thing he did. He wasn't happy about helping the woman who cheated Sky out of a good life. He knew that one day Black Eagle would be chief, and his sister should be the one to reap the benefits, not the woman. That alone would give his family a status of importance, which he had failed to do thusfar. At thirty winters, he couldn't risk making another error in judgment where his sister's future was concerned. He felt a need to get rid of the woman who caused all of his problems in the first place.

Meanwhile, the ever-cautious James had to double back to cover his tracks. He had learned a lot since he had lost René's trail so many times before. They had traveled three long days without stopping. They traveled to an old fort, which appeared to be falling apart at its rafters. The entire structure could have easily been ignited by the strike of a match. And yet there was shelter and maybe some food hidden in the storage areas. The fort was dark and deserted, a place where the smallest creatures refused to dwell.

Apparently James had plans to make his way here all along when he escaped. He quickly surveyed the fort, checking for anything that moved. When he was satisfied that they were alone, he dismounted and headed for the main building. He left René unattended and untied.

René thought, "He's in the building. I can escape now!" She grabbed the reins and turn the horse toward the entrance. She had her path set before her and was ready to make her move. However, she was pulled roughly from the saddle.

"Thinking of leaving, were you?" he asked sharply. "Answer me, you little fool!" he continued, and shook her wildly by the shoulders.

"Yes! Yes! I want to leave. I can't stand you or this stupid game you're playing!" René snapped. She was surprised that she had so much to say. "Take you filthy hands off of me!" She yanked her arm away, not quite sensing how quickly he would retaliate.

"So . . . there's still some fire in the well. That is good. It will serve to keep you warm. However, I am going to have a nice hot meal and a warm bed to sleep in. This is your bed," he said while pointing to the ground. Then he grabbed her wrist and dragged her to the entrance of the building. René resisted and pulled against him. She knew that angered him more than her trying to escape. When she wouldn't relent, he quickly tied her to the hitching post. "When you are ready to act like a gentle woman, let me know. You had better hope that I hear you," he said roughly. Then he walked away, laughing.

It was getting colder by each day, and the blanket René had draped over her shoulders wasn't enough to calm the chill. All the way there she trembled from the chilly winds. Yet here she was, sitting on a hard, cold ground, her bed. At least she didn't have to contend with him nor was she going to give him the satisfaction of hearing her beg. She had done that once and had gotten attacked for it, giving James the upper hand.

Later on, René could smell food cooking in the structure. She could feel some of the warmth coming from the fireplace, which helped to ward off some of the chill. Suddenly, René's arms began to feel numb and heavy. She could feel tiny needles prickling at her fingers. She tried to loosen the rope with her teeth, but the rope was too thick and it was cutting into her skin. Fatigued and angry, René drifted off to sleep, sometimes waking to the sound of rustling noises or the cold breeze touching her senses, forcing her to the brink of tears.

The following morning René found herself lying on a small cot in front of the fireplace. She still suffered from bouts with the cold, but the numbness in her arms and hands were gone, and she could feel her fingers again. She heard the door open abruptly and felt the cold air rush in. She wasn't sure if it was late October or early November, but she could tell that the snow had come. The air had a definite bite, which was enough to chill the bone.

Wake up!" James ordered. I have a rabbit and a few fowl that need to be cooked right away," he continued as he placed them on the table. Then he crossed the room and joined her by the fireplace. He placed another log on the flames and watched it spark new life. "Here!" he said, handing René the very dress she thought she was still wearing. She eyed him suspiciously, wondering if undressing her was all he had done. "No need to hide. Are you still awfully shy?" he asked mockingly. "Shouldn't I have had this privilege long ago, my dear?" he asked as he reached over and removed the blanket to reveal her naked beauty for his pleasure. She was a sight to behold, and he drank in every inch of her lovely form.

To his delight, René was unable to maintain her composure. "Please! If you don't mind, I would like some privacy," she stressed calmly but quickly as she covered herself. His mood swings were unpredictable, and she didn't want to chance making him angry again. The hitching post wasn't the greatest place to be in this weather. She was determined not to make trouble for herself, although it appeared that trouble was aching to find her at every cross. Her trouble was leaning leisurely against the mantle with his arms crossed. He had no intention of being robbed of the wonders she had hidden from view. Further more, to her dismay, James had taken too many liberties with her. She knew he would only make remarks that she couldn't bear to hear. So she put it out of her mind and dressed quickly to prevent another onslaught of his unwanted lust.

Without saying a word, René headed for the door. James instinctively sensed that she was trying to run away again and took several giant steps to block her path, putting himself between her and the door. René was forced to explain the obvious. "I need to refresh myself. As you can see, I can't go very far." She pointed to her feet, which happened to be bare. "I won't run away, I promise!" she said as she walked around him. In her mind, though, she calculated every step she would use to get away from him.

"Make sure you stay where I can hear you!" James ordered while he watched her walk behind the cabin structure for privacy.

They had traveled to the first Fort Wayne, which was built at the turn of the century. The small cabin was the only structure left standing after the fort had been deserted over twenty years ago. James was glad he remembered his readings into the former establishment. The last known use for this fort was to maintain contact with the missionaries in the area, who serviced the Miami and Blackfoot tribes. Now it lay abandoned. The protective walls had all but lost their strength and had fallen to the ground. Only one building remained standing among the ruins, as if held up by a shear breath. It was dying slowly, becoming one with the earth again.

The old cannon with its broken wheel was corroded and rusted inside and out. A tiny bird had made its nest in the large hollow of its barrel. It was, in its way, the last remnant of the once powerful post in the territory. Then there were the hidden caches, which housed supplies from canned rations to ammunition. All were marked with flagged poles near each decaying building.

James located five of such caches earlier and now he was canvassing the area for a pickax and a shovel. There was no need in tying René up before he went about his work; she had slept through the entire time he was away. As far as James was concerned, he had the best of both worlds.

While he busied himself with the cache, Rene ventured to the other side of the cabin. She had been out of his sight for at least five minutes. Periodically, she would make sure he could hear her by creating some noise, or just moving about. It was long enough for her to check out the area for a good hiding place. She was about to give up when she spied what appeared to be a small cave just beyond the tall and plush evergreen trees. She hoped it was empty, at least empty long enough for her to hide out.

CHAPTER
TWENTY-FOUR

IT WASN'T UNCOMMON TO see snow during this time of year with winter being so close. The weather had become quite crisp of late and the soil that was once soft and yielding had become hard and refused to give up its secrets. The trail Black Eagle and the others had been following had ceased to exist. They had traveled both day and night, sometimes without stopping to rest. For three long days and four horrid nights they trudged through the forest, turning over every shred of material that lay on the ground or was caught in a branch.

Frustrated, angry, and cold, Black Eagle conceded to his loss. At one time, he felt sure he would find his love, but throughout his long and fruitless journey, he would always come to a dead end. He had come to the realization that René was gone for good. In his heart, he still felt she was alive and thriving, yet he had to face reality: She was gone. Or maybe she just didn't want to be found. He couldn't help thinking that Walter Cory might have been telling the truth. The words kept ringing in his head, over and over again. He was torn by his own thoughts and torn between his love for René and his honor as a man.

He had to make a decision: Leave now—and lose the respect of his people—or stay and keep up with the search. If he returned without her, his people would wonder in silence. They would never ask, but the questions would still be there. To have dragged so many men away from their homes in a quest that he alone should have made caused his ire to rise. Black Eagle stopped short and turned his horse around to face the many who had followed him thusfar. Pride swelled in his chest as they continued to follow him . . . faithfully, without question.

In a solemn motion, he raised his hand to stop them from going any further. "Stop! We will stop here for a spell. You must rest!" he directed, still offering his strength. Then he dismounted and wrapped the bearskin robe around his shoulders. "We must keep on the lookout for Little Squirrel."

Confused and quite weary, they did as they were told. They could tell something was bothering him by the way he had spoken to them. He had changed. He had become a shell of a man, empty and void of any chance for happiness. Ever since he and Robert had returned from the white man's village, he had been acting strangely. So they waited, waited for the man they knew to come back to life. It would be a matter of time, so they thought, that they would resume their journey. However, Black Eagle had other plans for them.

"Chief Chinock . . . Tall Elk and Robert, you have all come a long way. You have left your homes and your families to help me find my wife. Well, I must send you home. You must go back . . . .back to your families," Black Eagle insisted. "I am proud that you have come all this way. But it is not fair to you or your families for you to continue in this way. I am not . . ."

Robert and Tall Elk were quick to disagree with him and stated, "We are staying."

However, Chief Chinock agreed that it would be in his best interest to get back to his village. It was time for his people to move to their winter camp. He and his warriors mount their ponies and, with a final gesture of friendship, Chief Chinock spoke: "Your heart is good, my son. And the woman you seek is worth all the trouble. When you find her, treat her well. Be her strength, for all she has seen is treachery."

They were about to leave when Captain Birney and his patrol came bursting through the thicket. They had been following the band's every movement from the time they left the fort. The snow had masked their approach for many miles, even though Black Eagle was aware of them from the start. And since he was deadlocked as to which direction to go, it seemed futile to avoid any confrontation with the captain and his men.

"Whoa! Whoa!" Captain Birney called out as he pulled back on the reins. He stopped within two feet of Black Eagle, who at this point had his rifle trained on him. The captain had to think fast. He was the intruder here, but he was most anxious to capture James Courtland. "Black Eagle, sir! I offer to assist you in your search. You are a man of honor. I believe that you and your brother-in-law have been treated unjustly," he continued firmly while trying to entreat a symbolic means of calming the tension that was brewing between them. He had hoped it was enough to impress the young warrior that he was on the level.

"The white man does not help the red man without getting something in return. You must want something," Black Eagle stated coldly.

Captain Birney realized the intelligence of this man was far greater than he had expected. If he could only tie the knot of friendship or even build some trust, he would not only be aiding Black Eagle in his search for his wife, he would be able to fulfill his duty as an officer. "Yes, my friend, I do want something. I want justice!"

Birney answered quickly. "And you deserve to have justice."

"Justice! What kind of justice can you offer a savage?" asked a familiar voice from the rear of the detachment. "If there is going to be any justice served, it will be served when I kill all of these damned savages!" he yelled as he advanced forward. Colonel Sheridan had spoken, and his antics were just as foolhardy as Captain Courtland's. However, he spoke so freely due to his fondness for the taste of whiskey. He had brought his own supply with him when he embarked on Birney's trail. He and Sky had kept a constant pace in following the small unit to this point, and now he was barking, throwing verbal threats toward Black Eagle and his company. Sheridan took another drink, wavered, and then joined Captain Birney at the point.

Shocked and embarrassed, Birney quipped, "Pay him no mind. He is a drunk and has been for a long time." He hoped that his explanation would be enough to satisfy the big Indian and take his attention away from the colonel and his insulting remarks. Yet, the colonel was persistent and the captain's attempts, although well noted, would go unchanged.

Colonel Sheridan yelled a few more insults, hurling them in Black Eagle's direction. What began as a peaceful meeting had turned into bedlam. Sheridan fired his revolver, shouting, "Kill them all . . . the vermin." He shot once in the air and then he shot at anyone within his range. Chief Chinock was the first to be mortally wounded in the melee of gunfire. Another young warrior, about nineteen, lay in a pool of blood, and Tall Elk had received a minor wound to his upper arm.

The colonel then wielded his gun in Black Eagle's direction and smiled as he pulled back on the hammer. "I'll give your wife your most humble apology," he said, then wobbled a bit before regaining his aim. But he was too late. Black Eagle had already fired, killing Colonel Sheridan instantly. He watched Sheridan fall lifelessly to the ground. Then without wavering Black Eagle pulled his knife, the only weapon he had left, to defend his ground from the rest.

Captain Birney was unprepared for this type of diplomacy. No hand-written treaties could calm the wave of violence that was doomed to follow. He panicked and called his men to arms, but Robert yelled, "I would-n't do that if I were you. Drop your weapons . . . now!"

The small detail was heavily surrounded, with no avenue open for escape. At that point, Captain Birney was forced to resign himself to do as he was told. He ordered his men to do the same. He was too shaken to try anything. Their weapons were quickly gathered and placed out of their reach. Then he wondered if he should dare approach Black Eagle about his reasons for following him in the first place. The colonel had made it almost impossible for them to communicate with respect. Without seeming to presume the matter was closed, he dismounted and took his chances with Black Eagle again.

They had already surveyed the damage and had begun the burial rites of the chief. One of the warriors began to sing the song of the dead. Soon the others joined in as they lifted the body of Chief Chinock and that of the young brave. Birney was touched by how they cared for their dead, treating them with respect and bestowing their blessings upon them in their journey to the hereafter. The young captain felt helpless indeed, especially when he didn't feel or want to grant an honorable burial for the colonel.

He ordered his men to prepare a grave for the colonel, without the formalities. "Make it quick men! I don't know what they have in store for us." Yet, he knew that the big Indian had acted only in self-defense. If it had been an-all out attack, they would all be dead.

"But, sir, we can't dig a grave. We did not bring anything to dig with," one stated without hesitation.

"Then use your hands, soldier! Use you hands!" Birney ordered, and then stiffly walked away. His nerves were totally on edge. The stories he had been told of the savages and their brutal scalpings just made his skin crawl. "And soldier, tell the others to do as they are told or we may be digging their graves next."

René had prepared a hearty breakfast consisting of beans, salted pork, and sourdough biscuits. The table was set, and all she had to do was call him in. James had been standing watch just outside the door ever since he had heard gunfire. He wondered whether he had covered his tracks well enough. Then again, they may not be tracking him after all.

"Your breakfast is getting cold," she said coolly. She didn't care whether he starved or not. She had completed her task; now it was up to him.

Seeing how unconcerned she was about his stomach, he ordered, "Bring it to me!"

However, René didn't move at his command. He was quick to order her again, but René felt she was within her rights not to comply. She sat down and prepared her own plate. Upon his third demand, he was standing by her side glowering down at her as she bit into the soft biscuit. James arrogantly snatch up her plate and tossed it into the fire. "Now, bring me my breakfast!" he snapped.

Angry that he had tossed her meal into the flames, she defiantly threw his plate in with hers. "There! Then nobody eats!" she yelled. She had grown tired of being ordered around and of being forced to wait on him. The colonel wanted her for the same thing, to enslave her. And René refused to be a slave to either one of them.

She had pressed every nerve, causing James to go berserk. He wickedly snatched her up by her arm and harshly led her to the stove where he jammed the frying pan into her hands. She knew that he would tear her apart if she didn't do as she was told. Regardless of the way he was acting toward her, he knew that his continued cruelty would make her less likely to sway in his favor. He put his temper in check, but firmly ordered, "Now, fix my breakfast and when you're done, bring it to me. Or else I will make you regret ever having been born. Do you understand, René?"

The changed tone he used had succeeded in frightening her. René shook her head and quickly went about preparing another meal. She threw more wood into the fire and poked at it with another piece. The stove was ablaze, and the smoke seeped out of the chimney leaving the remnant of a black cloud hovering over the cabin. She molded the biscuits with her hands and then placed them onto the flat tin. After which she cut strips of bacon and tossed them into the hot frying pan.

It wasn't long before she had another batch of biscuits ready to be eaten. She slapped them and the bacon onto the last remaining plate on the table and then handed them to James. He quickly gobbled down everything and then looked at her for more. There were two biscuits remaining in the tin with one slice of bacon. He knew René hadn't eaten, but he felt his hunger was greater.

"I'm still hungry," he stated dryly, and held out his plate for her to fill it again. René's stomach rumbled loudly. She knew James could hear it, but he didn't care. "Hurry up!" he yelled, and René promptly served him and then rushed over to the fireplace to stay out of his way. At least there she had the warmth of the fire. Her stomach, however, would have to remain empty for a while longer.

Behind the tree that René had determined was an escape haven a lone scout had taken cover. He was drawn in by the smell of food cooking. The scent enticed him so much that he dared get closer to the cabin. Silently, without so much as breaking a twig, he slipped up to where James was sitting and enjoying his food. Right next to the door was an open window and he took a quick peek inside. He heard the man ordering, "Get me some water. I need to wash these biscuits down! Do as I say!"

The young brave pressed his body against the wall and quietly looked in. There she was as he had last seen her, only a bit thinner. The glow that was once in her face was gone. She seemed overly tired and quite hungry. He watched as she brought the man the water he demanded and how he in turn snatched it out of her hands. The scout waited, keeping one eye on the man and the other on her. He wanted her to see him. He prayed that she would recognize him. It was all he could do to let her know that Black Eagle was near.

"Will that be . . . all?" René asked, almost stammering on her words. The shadow in the window had gotten her attention and had become bigger than life. She looked at James, hoping that he didn't see the expression on her face. Excitement welled up in her belly like never before. She knew that face in the window, her husband's loyal friend. She could barely contain her fear of giving in to the possibility that he wasn't real at all. But he signaled for her to remain silent and not to give him away, "Oh, God!" she murmured softly as he disappeared.

"What did you say?" James snapped. He glanced at her, questioningly. René had paled and tried to conceal her happiness. She no longer felt she was at his mercy. She almost laughed out of sheer pleasure knowing that Black Eagle would be here and that James would be unprepared for him.

"Nothing, nothing at all," she answered, and headed back for the seclusion of her mat. Even though Little Squirrel's presence had helped her regain some hope, she knew she was in for a long wait.

It took the scout less than three hours to ride through the densely wooded forest to Black Eagle's campsite. He had one thing on his mind, and that was to give his friend the news he had long waited to hear. Behind him, the smoke from the stove filled the sky. It was her beacon, her signal to freedom. Upon his arrival, the final burial rites had been given for Chief Chinock and the young brave. The tone of the men who stayed behind had changed, yet that didn't stop him from feeling elation at the news. "I have found her, Black Eagle! I have found her!" he exclaimed. Little Squirrel had definitely found something. He was so excited that he gathered up their supplies and pushed them to their horses.

Black Eagle looked at him in disbelief. After having missed her so many times before, it was hard to accept his word on it. "Are you sure that it is my Re-nea?"

Little Squirrel practically burst, but her understood why Black Eagle had asked the question. "I was so close to her, I could almost touch her. She saw me. She is alive, but . . . she is . . . we must go for her now," he insisted, trying not to cause too much concern as he leaped upon his horse.

"What about them?" Robert asked, referring to the soldiers, Lame Fox and his sister Sky.

They had just buried the colonel in a shallow grave. They were lucky to be alive themselves. In their own way, some of them cursed the colonel for putting them in jeopardy. He was so gullible, so headstrong, that no one could sway him; not even the captain had the power to outwit such a man. Now the colonel was dead, but only by his own accord.

"Bring them along, but no guns!" Black Eagle stated as he mounted his horse. "They are a dangerous people . . . with no discipline and no purpose."

Robert couldn't agree more, even though the people he was accounting for were his own. The people he had left behind had shown him their talons again. He was able to appreciate the fairness of the people, and especially the man who had adopted his sister. "We will be better off without them tagging along," he offered.

"That won't serve us, now that his leader is dead," Black Eagle stated as he eyed the captain.

"You mean we have to take them with us? Why?" Robert asked angrily.

"They'll just be in the way . . . another problem for us to deal with."

"Maybe that is so, but I may have use for the decorated one," he said as he and Robert rode toward the young captain and his men.

Birney and his men had just completed the burial rites of Colonel Sheridan, such that it was. There was no ceremony of honor and no one offered a prayer for the belligerent old man, except the captain, who stated with a solemn tone, "Rest in peace."

"You mean, may the colonel rot in . . . " one soldier spoke out of the heat of the moment. Suddenly, he bowed his head in shame as the others stonefaced him. If he made it back to the fort, he could be brought up on charges for his brashness.

However, Captain Birney quickly disciplined him, "Soldier! That will be all! Your duty is to follow orders, my orders! Do you understand?" He knew that all the men under his command felt the same way. Yet it wouldn't serve to act or say anything irrationally, especially since they were unarmed and outmanned.

"That will be quite enough!" Robert said firmly. "We are leaving . . . now. Black Eagle feels it would be in his best interest if you came along. However, I beg to differ in that area."

"What about our guns?" Birney asked quickly. "You can't expect us to go into God knows where without our guns."

"No guns! Get to your horses and follow Black Eagle. If you try to escape, you will be shot," Robert said dryly. It didn't matter anymore to him whether they lived or died. "That includes you," he said as he directed his attention to Lame Fox and Sky.

"But I am Lame Fox, his friend," he stated as if it meant anything to Robert.

"I don't care who you are. I do appreciate knowing that you helped René to escape, but there still is the matter of what you and your sister want out of this. I don't know what it is, but I will soon find out. You, on the other hand, better hope we find René alive." Then he turned to the rest of those who lagged behind and ordered, "Now . . . all of you, move out."

Birney and his men had no other choice but to follow him and his friend. Robert soon took up the rear of the column, holding his shotgun on those who tried to escape or lag behind. Lame Fox and his sister rode with the captain, since their status hadn't yet been determined. Black Eagle was in his rights to be suspicious of them. The larger unit, most of them Miami, had started for home, leaving their prayers with Black Eagle. They trudged away in single file, holding their new weapons and a new sense of pride.

It seemed as though days had passed instead of hours since Little Squirrel had departed. René stared at the door, almost willing it to open, hoping that Black Eagle would come through it. She was so consumed with her own thoughts that she didn't hear James calling her. She didn't even see him close in on her. The only time she became aware of his presence was the moment he jerked her to her feet. "Let go of me!" she screamed. She could feel her heart pulsating through her ears.

James had grown weary of her constant rebellion. There were times when he wanted to bring her to her knees. He was convinced in time she would accept him and her plight, even with his brutish behavior. He could be sitting in the lap of luxury, rather than in this squalor. "You want me to let you go? Ha! I have had nothing but trouble from you. Nothing! You don't follow orders . . . not without being threatened. What do you expect?" he asked sharply while holding her by her arms.

René struggled to free herself and turned to run, practically dragging him with her. With her inability to tolerate his nearness, James became so angry that he couldn't stop himself. He grabbed René even more firmly about her middle, holding her tighter than he had before. With his hands pressed hard against her belly, he managed to stop her from fleeing. Suddenly, René stopped fighting and an intense sense of fear washed through her. She could feel the baby moving, stretching, and demanding. As if repelled by his touch, a small knot from within pushed at his hand. It was so apparent, he couldn't have even if he had been mistaken about what he had felt. René's secret was finally exposed, and she knew by the look in his eyes that he would explode.

He reacted just as she had predicted, but she wasn't prepared for the outcome. He pushed her hard, until her body slammed into the wall. She could barely keep her balance as she bounced off the wall, bumping her head in the process. Her legs wobbled and she slid to the floor stunned, but still protecting her child as best she could. "How long did you think you could keep this from me?" he demanded as he dragged her by the hair across the floor. He flung her toward the mats by the fireplace. He still maintained his hold on her hair, yanking her from side to side as he spoke. "You . . . little . . . slut! I should . . . kill . . . you!" he yelled as he forcefully released her.

Each time he yelled, René felt it deep within her soul. He was angry at this new discovery. He threw his chair against the wall and toppled the table, sending the flour and salted bacon to the floor. And if that wasn't enough, he broke the only working window in the cabin, which brought in the winter chill. She knew that in his present state of mind he was more dangerous to her and to her unborn child. She tearfully, but gently caressed her belly and prayed that his wrath was over.

"I should have known! That's why . . . now I understand why you wouldn't let me touch you. You *are* clever!" he said as he walked toward her again. He was going to force her to talk. "That red bastard will be coming after you, won't he? We . . . he may just find you . . . and when he does . . . "

As suddenly as James began his rendition of what he planned to do to her, he grew silent. René was grateful for that. It seemed something outside had distracted him. He was no longer standing over her or pulling on her hair. She watched him as he cautiously peeked out of the broken window where he had placed the few rifles he had acquired. She hadn't noticed them before. Apparently he had accomplished a lot while she was asleep.

He stood there scanning the brush for any movement. It was getting dark and it was hard to tell if the bush in the small patch of snow had moved. James turned to René and said, "I think you had better move from that spot. If any shooting starts, I won't protect you. You are on you own, my dear. Ha-ha! Maybe I should put you out of your misery. Hmmmm?!" He laughed again, then aimed the rifle at her and feigned to release the hammer.

"Why not?" René said blandly. "But only one of your problems will be gone. You will still have to face Black Eagle. And, knowing how he feels about you at this moment, I would say that you should be very scared. Your head will be meeting with his ax very soon," she offered bravely. Her head still hurt, and her body ached, but she felt sure that somewhere in this vastness, Black Eagle was coming or he was here.

"Shut up! I doubt very much that your so-called husband can do anything to me, much less find you!" James snapped. Then he went back to the window and found that the scenery had changed slightly; yet when he blinked, everything appeared to be back to normal, which he passed off as fatigue.

René sat silently on the floor and began to wonder if James was correct in his assumption. By now, Black Eagle must have given up on her and their child. She wouldn't blame him if he had. A lot of time had passed since Little Squirrel had departed. Maybe she imagined him being at the window. Maybe everything that was happening to her was just a nightmare. Was she going mad? She wanted to cry out, yell, scream, anything to wake up from this madness.

However, she knew it was all too real. Her pain and all the abuse she was forced to endure, including his horrible mannerisms, were not a dream. The real world of pain was hers and hers alone. From the moment her father had told her the truth, she had all but faced her true self. From the countless times James had maligned her and tried to destroy her sense of dignity, she had deemed it futile to fight back, to hold on and hope that soon she would be liberated from the evil one who had cursed her. And since rescue was too long in coming, René decided to bide her time, waiting for an opportunity to escape on her own.

René was right to wait. James had become so distracted with the activity outside that she was able to ease her way to the other side of the room. She snatched a few crumbs and a knife without being noticed. She used the table for cover and pulled it closer to the windows that flanked her on both sides. She took the window to her left, which faced the west and the cave.

Quietly, while James kept a vigil at the front door, René slipped out and dropped to the ground in silence. Resting her back against the cabin's rough wall, she waited. She heard him swear aloud, angry that he was the hunted, rather than the hunter. He didn't even notice that she was gone. Then she drew in a deep breath and ran toward the cave. The distance hadn't seemed so great before, but it was far greater than she had first anticipated. The cave was only minutes away, but the cold, hard ground made it difficult for her to run. She didn't care about that anymore, because the farther she ran, the more secure she felt.

The security left her when she noticed out of the corner of her eye that a shadow, or what appeared to be a shadow, was following her every move. He moved when she moved and stopped when she stopped. Renés heart began to race again, but she was determined not to surrender to her fears. And yet, she couldn't help feeling that she had walked into another trap. However, this time she had something to fight with, and never again would she be caught vulnerable. She held the knife tightly in her hand and continued toward the cave. If she had to fight, she would do so in a place of her choosing.

A shot rang out and whizzed passed James's head. The shooter wanted him to know that he could have been killed instantly. James quickly grabbed one of his rifles and took aim, but there was no target, nothing for him to aim at. Next, an arrow pierced the door frame just above his head, forcing him to duck for cover. Then the wall was sprayed with arrows, coming in three and four at a time. They were carefully aimed in his direction, pinning him to the floor.

A sudden barrage of gunfire and a wave of arrows followed simultaneously. James was unable to return fire. It would have been one bullet to ten or even twenty. He was definitely outnumbered and quite open for attack from any angle, which wasn't to his liking. The fire in the fireplace was dying, and the cabin became dark and cold around him. Then silence, the unyielding silence, attacked his senses. He checked the three remaining corners of the cabin, but René was nowhere to be seen. She had taken her leave of him just as she had promised. He had to admire her will to survive. Then he realized that he no longer held the person who would keep Black Eagle in his place. An uncontrollable laughter passed through him as he was on the brink of insanity. Death was near, and he could taste it.

James snapped back to reality when a voice he knew and hated came from the forest, calling out, "You in there . . . James Courtland . . . drop your weapons and come out with you hands up." He knew that voice belonged to none other than Robert Bainbridge. He, too, was just as clever, or even more cunning than he. James crawled to the other side of the room, thinking that René was hiding behind the table he had over turned. He poked the rifle through the opening, hoping to frighten her enough to bring her out into the open. To his disappointment, she wasn't to be had. "Damn it!" he snapped. And then another wave of arrows sprayed the cabin. He knew he was going die. However, he was robbed of the pleasure of taking René with him.

"James Courtland, this is your last chance! Don't be a fool," Robert yelled again. He had the window in his sight and had planned to shoot regardless.

"Ha!" James retort loudly. "I'll kill her! Come in and get me if you dare and I'll slit her throat!" he said, hoping that he had sounded convincing enough to delay their attack. And for a short while, he heard nothing from the ranks hidden within the forest.

René heard the gunfire and continued to run. She realized that the form following her wasn't James after all. If it had been James, he would have made himself known. This one stalked her and played with her nerves. He maintained his distance, always keeping her in his view.

She entered the dark cave and stayed against the wall, feeling her way to safety. The cave was damp and cold inside. Water dripped from curved rocks that jutted from the ceiling. Everywhere she stepped, she found a puddle or thick, sticky mud. Her moccasins were nearly pulled off of her feet as she pushed her way further into the darkness of the cave. She was sure that the one following her would stay outside, but she heard his footsteps quicken and then stop at the entrance. She hoped that the darkness would be her haven.

He seemed to know where she was instantly and made no pretext in his pursuit. He was tall like her husband, but he lacked the muscular build. He seemed angry that she had bothered to hide from him. He called her name as he entered the cave, "Re-nea . . . do not hide. I have no gun . . . no weapon." But he lied. He was brandishing a large hunting knife in his hand. There was no mistaking a gleam like that anywhere. The moon cast a reflection that flashed as he entered the cave.

René remained silent and held her breath as he was within inches of finding her. She knew the voice that was hidden by the darkness. How could he help her escape and later try to kill her? Her eyes widened as he walked past her, heading for the inner depths of the cave. Then another person had entered the cave and called out, "Lame Fox . . . Lame Fox, it is me, Sky. Please do not hurt her."

"Shush! You will spoil everything!" Lame Fox whispered heavily as he reached her side. "Black Eagle was to be your husband . . . not hers."

Sky knew that her brother was trying to gain his honor back by marrying her off. But Black Eagle had only one woman in his heart. There wasn't room for another, not unless that woman was dead. The thought did cross her mind once or twice. Then, Black Eagle would have no choice. He would have to honor Lame Fox's tribe and family by marrying Sky as he had originally promised. The thought of being the wife of a chief made her heart swell, but she knew that Black Eagle wouldn't want her under those circumstances.

"If you kill her, you will have to kill me as well, my brother. You speak of honor . . . what honor will there be in a lie? You kill to give me happiness . . . bah! I will not have it!" Sky yelled.

"Say no more, sister! You know nothing in the ways of honor. She must die! She must die so that you will have your rightful place in Black Eagle's lodge. Soon he will be chief. He will have the support of his people, who will welcome you with open arms. This woman is not of our people. She is not of his people. It is better that she die here and now, where no one can find her," he said without a care.

René heard and understood him well. He had cornered her where Black Eagle and the others wouldn't be able to hear her screams for help. She knew there was no way out but through him and Sky. She squeezed the knife and kept it secure in her palm. She kept her body pressed against the wall of the cave so as not to lose her balance. Then a wave of nausea attacked her, but she refused to give in to her weakness. The baby had to be protected and she wasn't going to give in to death, not now or ever.

Black Eagle and Captain Birney were both crouched behind a tree, listening to James's shallow threats. There were too many threats. However, no pleas could be heard from René. "The man is bluffing. Give me a gun! I want him just as much as you do!" Birney demanded. For a moment, Black Eagle ignored him, but Captain Birney forced him to look at him. They glared into each other's eyes, daring the other to make a move. "Give me a gun," he said again while holding out his hand. "You need my help. I want to help you get your wife back. Let me help . . . please!" he offered, hoping to gain Black Eagle's confidence. "What can I do to convince you that I am honorable?" he asked calmly, noting how he changed his tone.

Hearing those words brought Black Eagle back to the day he had first heard them from his beloved. His ire had finally softened a bit, and he began to sense that the man facing him was indeed a man of honor. If he wanted his wife back, he would have to trust him. Hesitantly, Black Eagle placed a rifle in Birney's hands and gave him powder and shot. Again, he said nothing to the captain. His attention went back to the cabin and to the man who held René against her will.

The cabin shed no light as the sky darkened around them. They had to rely on the moon to light the way, but the forest was quite dense around the abandoned fort. Black Eagle ordered Little Squirrel and Robert to circle the cabin and to check for any signs of activity. As Little Squirrel headed out, he noticed that Lame Fox and his sister weren't where they were supposed to be. They were careless enough to leave a trail, which he in turn followed. He surmised that they were following something or someone with a great deal of interest.

The trail came extremely close to the cabin. He heard the man inside moving things around, as though looking for something. He seemed frustrated and angry that he couldn't find it. Then, Little Squirrel dared to look inside, only to find that James was alone. René had run off, leaving the man with nothing to bargain with. She, however, left her footprints in the snow, and Lame Fox and Sky knew just where she had gone. From the way Lame Fox had been acting toward his friend, he knew that René was the target. He quickly signaled Black Eagle to come, and by the way he delivered the message, Black Eagle knew that he was serious.

The door to freedom had been blocked, and René realized she would have to kill or be killed. Desperation and the powerful need to escape pressed her to confront the very soul who denied her passage. She had to turn the tables on her stalker. Lame Fox, on the other hand, didn't know where to begin looking for her in this cave. The darkness was a great cover, and she had learned well how to use it to her advantage. As he passed her again, never once suspecting that she would ever attack him like a wildcat, she slashed him. In quick movement, she slashed his back and his chest, then quickly disappeared into the darkness of the cave. René knew she had done major damage when he cried out in agony.

"Sky, help me! *Sky!*" He cried, and staggered from the cave, trying to hold his life's force within him. Sky couldn't help him. She could only cradle his head as he collapsed.

While he lay on the ground somewhat helpless, René drummed up enough courage to leave the cave. She had to face the other one who had planned to destroy her as well. Lame Fox was still alive and was still holding the knife he was planning to use on her. His actions had thrown her off and he made no attempts to defend his motives. He thought he was justified in his means for protecting his sister's future.

"Why did you do this?" Sky asked. It seemed she wanted answers from both of them from they way she gazed at René and then her brother. René offered nothing. She felt no need to explain why she wanted to preserve her life. It was her life or his. He was in the same league and was no better than James Courtland as far as she was concerned. "We helped you to escape from the fort. And this is how you repay a debt!" she screamed.

"That much I owe you, but I don't owe you my life, and I don't owe you my husband!" René snapped quickly. "Do you expect me to just stand still and let him kill me? You and your brother are no better than the man who captured me. What you want can't be given or taken lightly," she stated calmly.

Sky only hear what she wanted to hear. She didn't care how wrong her brother was. It was enough that he was the only one who cared enough to fight for her. She had never really appreciated his efforts before on her behalf. But now, it meant everything. "And you think this is over?" she asked as she lifted the knife from her brother's hand.

René caught the gleam of the blade in the darkness that surrounded them. "If this is what you want . . . we both may die. I'm no longer afraid. I assure you, I won't die easily," she quipped as she wielded the weapon between her fingers.

As Black Eagle and Little Squirrel neared, they heard the two women as they readied themselves for battle. Sky removed her brother's head from her lap as René had taken to the snow, away from the rocks and the solid ground. She wanted a cushion in case she fell. That was the wisest move she made. It gave her the advantage she needed over the angry young woman confronting her.

Without thinking, Sky lunged at René, losing her footing and slipping in the wet snow. She had become ensnared in the low-hanging pine branches. In her struggle to free herself, she became more entangled and lost the knife she so willfully tried to use against her friend. But that wasn't enough to keep her still, and she became enraged with the whole matter. When she finally managed to free herself, she rushed René again, only to fall into a slippery mud puddle.

Frustrated and upset that she, too, had failed to bring some dignity to her family, she began to cry. She never imagined that she would put her life and the life of another on the line for her own gain. She was further humiliated when she witnessed the happy reunion between René and Black Eagle. Sky had failed, just as her brother had failed, and a sudden chill wracked her soul as she watched with utter sorrow, the tenderness the mighty Black Eagle had bestowed upon his gentle wife.

In her haste to bring some recognition to her claim, Sky asked, "You would take her over a woman such as me?"

Both René and Black Eagle stared at her, revealing their contempt for her and for Lame Fox. If anything, the siblings had thrown away any trust that was once there. Black Eagle was puzzled with her question and asked, "Where did you get the idea that I wanted you?"

Sky looked at her brother, who groveled in pain and offered no excuse for his own actions. Then Sky quipped, like a puppet mimicking what her brother had said moments before, "She is not of your world . . . she will never be! You will soon be chief of your great tribe and you need a woman who knows the ways of your people. This one knows nothing!" she continued while pointing at René.

Black Eagle was about to speak up on René's behalf, but the ever-headstrong René, still angry that her life was jeopardized yet again by another, had interrupted. "The world you speak of has many faces. You just haven't taken time to look. You can't see the truth when you cover your eyes and you can't hear the truth when you cover your ears. You take so little pride in your own womanhood . . . so little care that you would hurt me and my child."

Black Eagle was angry at first by René's sudden outburst, taking his power away again. She still had a lot to learn about the ways of his people and what she, his wife, was expected to be. Yet, her words rang true the values she had in fact learned while adapting to his ways. His anger soon passed and turned to approval, which was witnessed by all except René. Her desire to live was far greater than Sky had ever expected, and she was swept by the revelation that there was no room for her in Black Eagle's life. Nor would there ever be. Her brother had promised her the life of an Ojibwa princess. This promise and more made her daily chores at the fort more bearable. It sickened her to no end that her brother had put her in the middle, hoping that Black Eagle would honor a one-sided pledge made over a year ago.

Before René could say another word, Black Eagle gently touched her shoulder, silencing her. "Re-nea speaks very strong, but she does not say what is in my heart," he said sternly. "When I have completed my quest, I will settle the matter."

Sky then rushed to her brother's side, only to find him cold, withdrawn and mostly ashamed. Both were swallowed by pride and besieged by guilt, waiting patiently for their punishment. They both hoped that the blow would be swift. However, they were truly mistaken about Black Eagle and his fairness. The only thing they heard was the gentle caress in his voice, rejoicing at being reunited with his wife.

"I thought I had lost you forever," he said softly, "You are alive! And our child is alive!" He held her tightly, as if for the first time. The madness that had once assaulted his reasoning had finally passed.

René was speechless and overcome with the realization of him actually being there, holding her. She let her fingers glide over his features, which he had hidden under war paint, and prayed that this moment would last forever.

"Soon you will be home," he said gently. Come . . . rest here," he direct-ed as he removed the blanket from his shoulders and placed it around hers. Then he eased her to the soft mound of spruce fir, pausing momentarily to adjust her blanket, assuring himself that she was safe. With great difficul-ty he spoke again, but this time to Little Squirrel. This time he was deter-mined to right the wrong that had been unjustly waged against them. "Take care of Re-nea," he said abruptly, and then headed back toward the cabin.

"Wait! Not now!" René called after him. But it was too late. The only thing left of him were his footprints in the snow. She knew where he was going. She knew that he had unfinished business with James Courtland. "God only knows what James Courtland is capable of. Dear God in heav-en, please bring Black Eagle back to me."

CHAPTER
TWENTY-FIVE

WITH EVERY SECOND THAT went by, René remembered the cruelty she had endured. The more she remembered, the more she feared for her husband. It rallied in her mind that James would be the victor and that he would carry her off again. Her fears were well established. James had a resilience that wouldn't quit even when the odds were stacked against him. He had caused so much pain. How could one man be so evil, so cunning?

Little Squirrel touched her shoulder and tried to put her mind at ease. He knew what his friend had planned to do all along. He had never seen a man so obsessed with finding a woman. But then, he had never been in love, either. He wondered if he would ever feel this way toward a woman. Women are too much trouble, he thought to himself as he gazed at Sky and her wounded brother.

In her fight to stay alive, René had forgotten how cold it was. A chill passed through her body and was suddenly squelched by the warmth of a fire that Little Squirrel had quickly set. She pulled several pieces of dried deer meat from his pouch and warmed them over the flame. He handed them to René and directed her to eat. He seemed to have little time for words. However, his gentle manner made up for that. She was grateful to him for finding her and for bringing Black Eagle to her. She couldn't thank him enough. And yet, he knew how she felt and managed a quick smile in response to hers.

Suddenly the silence of the forest was interrupted by an explosion, followed by a flash and the gunfire. War whoops and battle cries penetrated the darkness. René stood up, hoping to catch a glimpse of what was transpiring, maybe catch a glimpse of Black Eagle. But Little Squirrel forced her back behind the trees. The shots that missed the cabin had whizzed by, missing them by a hair. "Stay here! It is not safe in the open!" he said cautiously as he used his body to shield her.

More bullets showered through the trees. Then the sky was aglow with a bright yellow and orange light. "Black Eagle! I must find him!" René fussed as she tried to push pass him.

"He will return . . . soon!" Little Squirrel tried to assure her. "There is much danger! You must stay here!" He hated having to force her to stay, but he had been ordered by his leader to protect her.

But René would hear none of that. As far as she was concerned, her husband was in danger. She wasn't worried about herself anymore, and she had had enough. For almost two months she had prayed for him to find her and when he finally did, it seemed he would be taken away from her. The prospects of losing him made her shiver. She knew James would take great pleasure in killing him, and knowing that she would be affected by it would make him the victor. She had suffered enough under that despicable man. She feared him and what he could do when pushed.

"I want to go to him. Let me go!" she cried, but Little Squirrel was just as stubborn as she. With her last outburst came silence. The melee of bullets had ceased. The quiet was so intense that even Sky and Lame Fox took notice of the change.

Black Eagle had finally slipped into the cabin, unnoticed by James, who was seated on the floor across from the door with his rifle primed and ready to take out anyone who dared to show his head. Those who were on the other side of the door remained where they were until they received a signal from their leader. Black Eagle watched and waited in silence for the right moment to make his move.

"I should have killed her," James muttered as if he knew Black Eagle was within earshot of hearing him. "She's been nothing but trouble for me since I met her. Damn her . . . damn the whole misbegotten family!"

As if cued by those words, Black Eagle rushed James as he placed the rifle against the wall. He didn't have a chance to regroup when Black Eagle slammed into him. James tried to grapple for some control, but he couldn't move. He was getting the same treatment he had dished out to René, only worse.

Black Eagle pressed the length of the barrel against his neck, choking James and making him weak. He could smell his own sweat pouring from his brow as the large hands lifted him without much effort and tossed him aside. "Oh, my God," James cried out. "Please don't kill me! Please don't kill me! Have mercy, please!" he begged.

But Black Eagle was unmoved by his pleas. He could only imagine the pain James had inflicted upon René and their unborn child. "No mercy!" Black Eagle retorted. "You did not show any mercy to Re-nea! You took what is mine and you will pay with your life!" Then Black Eagle brandished René's knife. It was suiting that James would die by her weapon and end the torment he had caused once and for all. Justice would be served in two worlds.

A sharp, agonizing cry ripped through the still air and echoed deep into the darkness. It was heart-wrenching and frightening all at the same time. So frightening that René immediately thought it belonged to her beloved. Now, more than ever, she wanted to be with him. "That could be Black Eagle! You must let me go to him!" she yelled.

However, Little Squirrel stood fast behind his orders. He knew Black Eagle would never cry out even when death was near. "No!" he said firmly. "You will wait for your husband. He will come!"

For some reason René believed him. He spoke with such conviction, such faith, that she had no choice but to believe. If anyone was going to die tonight, it certainly wouldn't be Black Eagle. The Spirits were protecting him. "I will wait. But not for long!" she replied quickly, and waited impatiently for Black Eagle to return to her.

Meanwhile, the only remaining shelter was engulfed in flames. The last of the cabin's foundation exploded, spewing ash and debris in all directions. The few who remained behind watched silently. Their hopes for a warm night out of the cold was burning recklessly before them. Even Tall Elk felt a strong need to come in out of the cold.

Robert wrapped his coat tightly about him and quickly scanned the area for his sister. He could only hope that René wasn't trapped in the burning cabin. He turned to Tall Elk, who seemed to know every move his friend made, even without seeing him. Tall Elk in turn knew what Robert wanted to know and silently directed his attention to the far end of the burning structure.

No more than ten feet away from the burning mass lay a man whimpering and huddled in a ball. He appeared to have been to hell and back.

He suffered major burns on his face, hands, and feet. He had been stripped of all his senses and reasoning. He screamed, "Go away! Goooo awaaay!"

Robert, Tall Elk, and Captain Birney made their way to him, thinking that one of the men in their party had been injured. But as they approached, they recognized the man through all his injuries: James Courtland, no longer the tyrant but the whimpering child before them. In agony, he cried out again. He could only see the face of one man: Black Eagle. He never considered what would drive a man to undergo such lengths as to hunt him down in this manner. Now he was cowering in front of the men he once led. He had been treated like an animal, worse than he had treated René.

"What the hell happened to him? He's gone mad!" Birney demanded.

"It seems he got a taste of what he dealt René," Robert answered. "Justice is served!"

"Justice! What man deserves to be treated like that?" Birney asked.

Something quickly dawned on Robert before he answered. Something Chief Chinock had said to Black Eagle several days ago. "It's called humanity!" Robert spat. "Black Eagle gave him more than James ever dealt to René or anyone else as a matter of fact. And I know it's tearing him apart knowing that he could have ended Renés nightmares here and now. But he let the bastard live." Then it dawned on him again, René was nowhere to be seen. She could be lying dead somewhere.

James cried out again in fear or from his wounds, but there was no pity in the faces glaring at him. "Stop blubbering! You brought this on yourself!" Captain Birney said without remorse. It surprised him that the big fellow had bothered to spare Courtland's life.

"Black Eagle should have killed you! You got better than you deserve . . . better than you gave my sister!" Robert spat. The pain of not knowing whether René was alive or dead forced him to attack James as he lay helpless.

The captain pulled him away, saying, "That won't help your sister any. And if you kill him, I'll be forced to arrest you. Let me take him back."

"And what good will that do? My sister may be dead, for all we know. That bastard doesn't deserve to live!" Robert retorted. Recklessly, he grabbed for the gun in the captain's holster, but he was jarred from behind with a stiff blow to the back of the neck. It was so swift, he never knew what hit him.

Tall Elk had taken it upon himself to keep Robert out of trouble. "He will rest now. When Black Eagle returns, he will know the truth."

The captain acknowledged him with respect. To his surprise, both

Black Eagle and Tall Elk had acted within the realms of civility. He wondered how such people could show humanity when it wasn't introduced by the white man. He witnessed this and more in the short time he had spent in their company. Even after the colonel had attempted to spoil any chance of communication between them, they still offered their friendship.

"You are right," Birney answered quickly. Then he quickly issued orders for his men to set up camp. At least they wouldn't have to face the cold without shelter. If Colonel Sheridan had had his way, they would have frozen to death. Since the men had lain the colonel to rest, they were more at ease. The pressure of not meeting his expectations and fearing the consequences was no longer a threat. They went about their chores with a sense of commitment, almost happy to do as they were told. The temporary camp was built, and the fire from the burning cabin supplied the heat to warm them.

Robert flinched and then grabbed the back of his neck, cursing as he rubbed the pained area. Still dazed, and angry that he had acted so impulsively, he sat up and demanded, "My sister . . . is she alive?" He rubbed his neck again, grateful that someone had stopped him from committing murder. James's death wouldn't have solved anything, except to delay the inevitable. "Whoever hit me . . . sure knocked some sense into me. I could have killed him, not that he doesn't deserve to die," he said, hoping to satisfy the guilt that rushed through him. Tall Elk nodded his head in agreement, also accepting the acknowledgment for his deed.

For René, Black Eagle had been away forever. Her only thoughts were of him and her unborn child. "I can't bear another minute . . . not knowing . . . not seeing him!" she stammered.

No sooner had she completed her last statement, she noticed a strong aroma. It was coming from the cave where she had fended off Lame Fox earlier. Now something pleasant was coming from its confines. The light from within was like a beacon, and the warmth just seemed to caress her bare ankles. She felt the pang of hunger assault her senses again, and she swallowed to keep the bile from escaping . . . remembering that she hadn't had a decent meal in several days.

René wasn't the only one captured by the aroma. Little Squirrel and Sky were both caught by the warmth coming from the cave. Now that the fighting appeared to be over, the cave was the only haven away from all the elements surrounding them. Each in their own way wanted to put a wall between the weather and themselves. But no one dared to move.

The entrance to the cave was suddenly blocked by the tall, dark figure of a man . . . almost menacing. But René pushed by Little Squirrel and ran into the waiting arms of the dark stranger. Those who remained behind were astonished. But René knew. For a brief moment, Little Squirrel felt as though he had let his friend down. But when Black Eagle spoke, he felt a surge of relief. "Come . . . come in out of the cold. Warm yourselves by the fire."

The cave was no longer dank and smelly. The strong aroma of pine and spruce, as well as the meat cooking over the fire, completely changed the interior. Black Eagle had arranged several areas where each could sleep and had separated his sleeping area from the others with a large bearskin robe. It was suitable for the moment. He had accomplished much in the little time since his return.

While the others examined their new surroundings, René examined her husband's wounds. There was blood on his brow and a slash on his fore-arm that he apparently tried to clean up earlier. He wasn't surprised at her reaction when she became fussy over him. *Nothing escapes her,* he thought to himself. Yet, his eyes gave a glint of approval. They never left her. He memorized every touched of her fingertips as she glided them over his flesh.

Little Squirrel used a small metal pot to melt clean snow, and Renéscooped up a handful and placed it on Black Eagle's brow and then applied it to his arm. The coolness of the snow squelched the stinging pain. He had tried so hard not to let her see he had been wounded, but she was too quick. The slash to his arm was quite deep and needed tending to.

René applied pressure to the wound and kept the bleeding under con-trol. Even though he didn't complain, he was weak from the loss of blood and tired from the battle with James Courtland. An hour had lapsed before René felt sure that the bleeding had completely stopped. "Rest now," she said softly as she sat down beside him. "It's my turn to look after you."

"My heart . . . will not let me rest. You have been here," he said, point-ing to his heart. It pained him so that he had once again thought that she was gone forever. He could smell her hair in the breeze and swore that she was with him. He sensed her nearness as he slept, but nearly lost faith. Doubt and anger clouded his mind, but his love for her . . . his need for her was stronger than time itself.

"And you have been here," René added as she swallowed her fears. "I don't know how you and Little Squirrel found me, but I 'm glad."

He smiled and slowly closed his eyes, still keeping her image sealed in his memory. René watched as he slept, something she had missed for so long. Her mind was finally at ease, yet she still remembered the pain. She remembered the last time they were separated and how his ego nearly destroyed any chance of healing the wounds they both had suffered. She knew that it would only be a matter of time before he asked her what transpired between her and James. She hoped that he would trust her love rather than the word of the monster who had stolen her away.

And he wondered silently, fearing that she may never be the same. To be kidnapped from the people who loved her and to have suffered under the brutal hands of the enemy, he could only hope that René was still his. So much time had passed and she was still the strong, ever-vibrant woman he had fallen in love with. He had to admit many times that she had clouded his thoughts and filled his waking moment and his dreams. She had bewitched him, had stolen his heart and captured his soul with her smile. But Black Eagle felt the pains that only a man could feel when love is threatened.

Black Eagle and René remained undisturbed behind the cover of the bearskin while Sky and Lame Fox shared an untimely meal and were quickly ushered off to bed. They were placed on the far side of the cave, where they couldn't make another attempt on René's life. However clumsy the attempt, it was clear that the siblings needed to be watched. They seemed to be desperately trying to make a claim, a means to save their own existence.

Black Eagle hadn't forgotten that he had convinced Lame Fox that he needed a wife. However, he hadn't bargained for his sister, not in any way. To his recollection, Lame Fox had only casually mentioned his sister in passing, saying what a good wife she would make. Still, there was nothing to indicate a marriage agreement. He had only offered his friendship when he gave Lame Fox the pelts. That was the day he collided with his lovely Re-nea. That was a day he would never forget, a day he found the one and only thing to fill the empty void in his heart.

Later that evening, Black Eagle approached Lame Fox, who appeared quite embarrassed by the wounds inflicted by a mere woman. "I am remembering the day when you and I wrestled for the right to a horse . . . the silver roan. That was also the day I told you about my quest to find a wife. Do you remember that day?" Black Eagle requested.

Lame Fox listened, but didn't acknowledge Black Eagle. And yet he, too, recalled the day as if it were yesterday. He remembered losing to the fast-footed Black Eagle and how he'd appeased him with furs of lynx and beaver.

"I believe you do. I knew when you lost the match to me that you lost more than a horse . . . you lost your honor. That was why I presented you with my best furs. I was not asking for your sister's hand. I gave you the price of the horse I had won," Black Eagle stated. "I had no intention of bargaining for your sister then or at any time."

"You gave me a bride price," Lame Fox lamented in agony. His behavior had suddenly changed from stern to sullen.

"That is where our customs end. I thought it was a fair trade for your loss, and you thought it was a bride price. I cannot change what has been done. I remain true to my vision, and my vision included the woman who is now my wife. I will not choose another over her," Black Eagle continued.

Lame Fox held his breath for a moment, then gazed in the direction where René slept quietly behind the barrier. He could only imagine what spell she had cast over the young would-be chief. His final gaze fell upon his sister, who rested near the fire. He felt he had failed her and had failed to do right by his people. Had he completed what he had set out to do, their lives would have had a better outcome. But now, that would not be so. He had settled for an easy life under the watchful eye of the white man. He had betrayed his people by throwing out their teachings and beliefs. Black Eagle, on the other hand, was living every bit the way of the traditions of his people. He respected them and he respected his family . . . his wife.

"It is not over! You gave a bride price according to the ways of my people. That, you must honor, and I do not care about your visions or the woman you claim to be a part of them. You owe me," Lame Fox yelled

"No, brother, Black Eagle does not owe you anything and he does not owe me anything," Sky stated in a curt manner. "You speak of honor, but you show no honor to a man who is telling you the truth." Then she turned slowly to Black Eagle, her eyes cast low, and said, "I do not expect you to honor my brother's claim. He does not understand the heart of a man since he has no heart to begin with."

"Cut me no more with your words, sister. I am your brother and will not accept what you deem fair!" Lame Fox yelled angrily. "You toss your desires to the wind. That is not what I wanted for you."

"It is not meant to hurt you, Lame Fox. It is meant to show you another path," Black Eagle interrupted.

"How do you know these things?" he asked. "She is but a mere woman, of no importance. What wise tale can she present to me?"

Black Eagle had to weigh all the factors surrounding their two cultures. What Lame Fox wanted was far more than Black Eagle was willing to give. He didn't want his life dictated by an outsider, much less one from another tribe. He understood the plight of the two tormented souls and wanted to make amends for the misunderstanding. But knew he hadn't mistreated them. He had been fair with Lame Fox from the beginning.

"You have much to learn about my clan, just as I have much to learn about yours. It would not be fair to your sister to make an idle promise . . . something I cannot keep. She is aware of that," Black Eagle stated. "She understands that I will not give up my wife for anyone."

"Then how can I keep peace between our tribes?" Lame Fox asked, thinking that if a threat of war could be ensued, he would gain the upper hand again.

"That is something for you to think about while you nurse your wounds. Peace or war—over a bride price—when in fact it wasn't meant to be. You decided without asking me if I agreed. Remember, a bride price is offered when the intended bride has been seen by the groom. I did not have the pleasure."

Angry that he had been outwitted, Lame Fox retorted harshly, "That changes nothing. It is a matter of your word against mine. Your people will know what I say is true."

"By rights, I should kill you. You tried to harm my Re-nea! You are lucky to have escaped with these wounds!" Black Eagle stated with force. He had grown weary listening to him banter on and on about what should have been. There was never a bargain, and he wasn't planning to become part of a lie, especially in this matter.

"Enough of this talk!" Sky yelled. She had had all she could take of the yelling, the broken promises, and the loss of a friend. "Black Eagle is right! He is a good man, and I believe him when he says that you misunderstood his act of kindness. You wanted to trick him into a marriage. And when it did not go the way you had planned it, you decided to clean up the mess you had created. You tried to kill my friend. And I was stupid enough to follow you."

"I only wanted you to have a good life. Soon he will be chief, and the wife of the chief would be in good standing among the people. You know that," he stated quickly, forgetting that his motives were now out in the open.

But Black Eagle and Sky were sure that he had other reasons besides wanting a better life for her. His motive for wanting Black Eagle as a brother-in-law was under the guise of selfish greed. "From this day forward, I will . . . I will be the one to choose the man who will be my husband. You have done all you can to destroy my life . . . control my life. Well . . . it is my decision." Then she turned to Black Eagle, embarrassed and ashamed. "I do not expect you to honor a marriage promise you did not make. My brother is thrifty and lies well when it suits him. You and Re-nea . . . belong together."

Lame Fox tried to stop Sky from closing the door on his good fortune, but she had already released any hold on Black Eagle. The sudden quiet of the cave was only disturbed by a soft sigh of relief. Little Squirrel sat up, awakened by the conversation and waited for Lame Fox to recant. But for some reason, he no longer had an argument. The matter appeared to have been settled.

The following morning the inhabitants of the cave made their way to the main campsite. There René was reunited with her brother. She was so happy to see him, she had forgotten her appearance. She was thin, weak, and fatigued. But even in her disheveled appearance, she was happy being around the ones she loved. That alone helped to overshadow her sunken cheeks and her frailness.

"You are a sight to behold," Robert said as he gave her a massive hug. "I'm so glad . . . so glad," he continued as he squeezed her in a strong embrace. He tried to hold back the tears as he greeted her. She would never know how much he wanted to find her. And in doing so he had pushed all of her guilt away.

Both he and Black Eagle said she had nothing to be ashamed of. She had expected them both to blame her for the insane behavior of James Courtland, who had been her tormentor for so long. She wasn't expecting any understanding whatsoever. Yet, to her surprise, Black Eagle and Robert had opened their hearts to her again, ready to shield her. She could only think how lucky she was to have men in her life such as these.

There was still one matter to deal with: James Courtland. He was still alive. To her regret, he was only injured and half insane. She heard his wretched moans, but felt no pity for him. She thought, maybe hoped, that he had died painfully. However, Black Eagle had spared him, though for what she wasn't sure. And her heart sank as she began to relive the terror all over again.

When James heard her voice, he made many claims upon her, demanding that she face him. He swore revenge as well as claimed the child she was carrying was his. And those who were within the small circle whispered among themselves as they turned away to keep her from noticing their stares.

Black Eagle quickly ushered her away, knowing that he would have to kill the man before they reached Fort Wayne, if his threats continued. The fact that he had let the man live to face the charges against him wasn't enough to soothe the pain James had caused. And yet, Black Eagle himself began to wonder what liberties he had taken during his flight from the Canadian territory to this abandoned fort.

"I can't believe it! That animal is still alive!" Renésaid with conviction. She spoke as though she had been disappointed or even betrayed. The tone, no matter how it was misinterpreted, depicted fear. She knew what James Courtland was capable of doing and as long as he was still breathing, she would be in danger, always be preyed upon.

Captain Birney seemed amused by her statement, even though she wasn't the only one who wanted to see him dead. However, he unwittingly tried to put her mind to rest. "I understand how you must be feeling . . . uh . . . Miss Bainbridge, or is it Mrs. Eagle? I assure you, he won't trouble you any longer," he said with a slight grin.

"Trouble? Do you call kidnapping me from my home 'trouble'?" René blurted. "He had no right to do that. That monster lives to torment me and he's not through . . . I know it!"

"Don't be silly, woman! He can't do you or anyone else any harm. He's mad! Look at him!" he ordered. "He's not going to get within two feet of you."

Upon hearing that, René retreated. In her mind, she was certain that James Courtland would loosen his bonds and come after her again. No matter what the captain said, James would do his utmost to make his promise a reality. "It's not over until he dies," René said sharply, and without remorse.

René had looked at the man and had seen nothing to entreat any sympathy toward him. Even Robert was shocked at his sister's sudden declaration. And then there was the question of her virtue and the child she was carrying. Having spent so much time in the company of one man, how could she have fended him off for so long?

How ever silent Black Eagle had become, he had no doubts about the child being his. But René's behavior put him in a mood that needed calming. She soon realized that Black Eagle had given her more ground on which to stand. She was standing alone without his support. She watched him as he walked back toward the cave, and not once did he look back at her. He felt overwhelmed with anger and hate, and he felt consumed by it as well. In having her for his wife, he had endured the journey of ridicule at the amusement of one white man, one he hated with intensity.

"René, you know that I have only had your best interest at heart, don't you?" Robert asked sternly. René nodded her head, expecting that gesture would be sufficient. But it wasn't enough. She had crossed the line. She had taken Black Eagle's power and thrown it to the four winds. "I don't think you really understand what you have done to him, René," he interjected. "I'll wager everything I own that Black Eagle feels he has let you down. You said so . . . in so many words."

René wasn't aware how Black Eagle felt, or maybe she just wasn't paying attention to his needs. She could only feel the fury burning in her soul when she found out that James had lived through it all. "But I didn't mean for it to sound that way. I was angry. No! I'm still angry. That brute did things to me that I can't bring myself to tell Black Eagle. I've been shamed in his eyes. I want revenge. Can't you understand that?" she stated as calmly as she could.

"And in the need for revenge, you have told your husband that he did nothing to protect you. You stand your ground very well!" Robert stated sarcastically. "You don't know what he has been through in these past few months, looking for you. As a matter of fact, I'm surprised he even bothered."

René turned to face her brother in disbelief and said, "How can you say such things to me? You know I could never hurt him!" But she was only met with silence. The door to her reality had been closed in order for her to recognize the sacrifice given by the man who loved her. She never realized how hard it was for him to spare the life of a man he despised above all else. Again, she had to swallow her pride and listen.

"You could lose him with this pride of yours," Robert offered with concern. "You know, the day I first found you after Black Eagle had taken you away, I hated him. I wanted to kill him for taking you away. But, you see, that husband of yours has taught me the value of love."

René stood quietly by as Robert talked on. She didn't know how hard it was for him to come into this land that was once her home. He had given up so much, just to come after her. "I didn't know . . . I just didn't know," she said softly. "I'm going to him," she said as she ran in the same direction Black Eagle had gone.

Black Eagle had covered a lot of territory when he departed from the camp. He wrapped the bearskin robe tightly around his shoulders and turned periodically to the sound of scurrying creatures in his path. There were times he hoped to see René coming through the thick spruce and he would curse when he could only see the mist from his own breath. He remembered the moments they had shared and the times he had wrestled with his mind, tormented by the thoughts of losing her. He needed her to depend on him. He needed her to leave her world behind, but it seemed she was destined to be a part of it no matter what. She was so consumed with handling her own affairs that she had forgotten the code of his people. How could he deal with her independent ways?

It was no sooner that he had come to the small clearing than he turned sharply with his weapons ready, only yo find René running in his direction. She had followed his tracks like a hunter. It pleased him to see her, but he maintained his distance until she reached a point where he felt satisfied. There, surrounded by the columns of trees, near the opening of the cave, Black Eagle forced his spear into the ground.

The air was still quite brisk, even though the snow had stopped. Every inch of the ground was covered with the white fluffy mass, which made it difficult for René to maneuver as she ran toward him. When she finally reached him, she was quite winded and very upset that he had made her run this far. She had barely caught her breath when he asked, "What do you want from me?"

René recognized the manner in which he had presented himself. He had put up a barricade, and now it was her turn to break it down. No matter how hard she thought she needed her independence, she needed his support even more. She approached him as though she had stepped on delicate egg shells, trying not to crack them. "I need you to understand how I feel. I am scared," she said softly. She trembled, nearly quaking, as she continued. "I don't want to live in fear. I can't be the silent woman you want me to be."

Black Eagle folded his arms against his chest, placing another barrier for her to cross. Only his heart melted when he saw the tears building in her eyes. She had never lied to him. But he needed to take charge of the situation that had ruled their very existence. He reached out and touched René's shoulder, bringing her close to him. He couldn't shut her out now.

"I understand more than you know," he said calmly, even though her behavior had set him back. "I cannot protect you when you choose to do it for yourself. I am your husband," he said, almost questioning. "It is my right to defend my family and my home when threatened. Or, are you—"

She interrupted him, trying to assure him as well as convince him that he was the only important factor in her life. "I had to speak up. It was the only way I could keep from losing my mind. When I saw that he was still alive, I lost all hope," she stammered. "I want to be able to live a good life with you . . . not spend my days and nights worrying whether he will find me again."

Each time she spoke, she moved closer to him, and Black Eagle could no longer avoid looking into those dark green depths that made him think of his passion for her and his home . . . and his family. René was now standing a hairsbreadth away from him, and he couldn't resist taking her in his arms. He could feel her quiet sobs as she tried to hold on to him for the strength she lacked. He looked up and gave a silent prayer to the Great Spirits, thanking them again for her safe return.

CHAPTER
TWENTY-SIX

THE JOURNEY BACK TO the fort was going to be slow, since the snow had made an untimely arrival. The entire search party slowly made their way to Fort Wayne. They rode in single file, the Ojibwa and the soldiers had joined rank, and had maintained some kind of civility. Tired from the trek and chilled from the cold, they continued to press onward, leaving behind the mottled grave of Colonel Sheridan, who never received so much as a kind word of remembrance, not even from the fair-minded Captain Birney. Each man kept to their own needs and grumbled periodically when a chilling wind brushed their faces.

Black Eagle and Renérode ahead of the entourage and basked in the warmth of his large bearskin robe. If it was cold, they never paid it much mind. As far as they were concerned, it was as warm as a spring day. Robert and Tall Elk kept a constant watch on the pair who rode just ahead of them. Sky and her brother, on the other hand, were not allowed to ride with the foursome. They were under the watchful eye of Little Squirrel. Captains Birney and Courtland closed up the rear of the column with two men in tow. Twenty, forty, sixty miles they traveled.

They arrived at the fort late in the evening of the following day. As Fort Wayne came alive with their return, Captain Birney immediately issued orders for full armed guards by the stockades. "Private! I want four men on watch and two men here to guard the prisoner," he stated quickly.

"Yes, sir!" the private replied, and hurried his salute, then rushed off toward the barracks to get more men. He passed Sergeant Wills, who approached the captain uneasily. The others hustled as he ordered them to clean the guest quarters for Renéand her party. They may have been tired but they dared not complain about it in his presence.

"Excuse me . . . sir, uh . . . Captain Birney . . . we have a visitor in the fort. He . . . uh, arrived almost at the moment you and Colonel Sheridan left. . . . A General Wallingsford. He is waiting in the quartermaster's office. He seems a mite angry, sir," Will pressed.

"General Wallingsford!" Birney snapped. "That's all I need . . . another brass ass to deal with."

But before he could say another word, General Wallingsford was making his way toward them. He walked as though he had been born in the gold brass decorating his uniform. The brass buttons on his uniform glistened, even though the sun was hidden by the clouds. He wore a neatly trimmed beard, which was graying on the sides. He seemed to dare the wind to move his hair out of place. He was in every way a model of military brass just out of Washington.

Birney wasn't happy with the new turn of events. He considered the arrival of such a high-ranking officer another obstacle for him to overcome after finally being rid of Colonel Sheridan and his biased behavior. Under the circumstances of the pending trial, he would consider RenéBainbridge's standing as a witness against Courtland and wondered whether this officer would prove to be another ploy to prevent him from arriving at the truth.

"Harrumph! You! You there . . . captain . . . where is Colonel Sheridan?" he asked indignantly. "I must say, this is not they way to run a fort in times of war."

"Indeed, you are correct, sir. However, there was due cause for my absence from the fort," Birney answered quickly. "It was necessary to bring in a prisoner who has admitted to the killing of a fellow officer . . . and friend," he continued. He could feel his throat giving way to the pain of mentioning his loss.

"I understand why you weren't here, but where the hell is Colonel Sheridan? I can't believe he would leave this fort in the hands of half-wits," he stated, and glared at Sergeant Wills, who quickly saluted and took his leave.

Captain Birney decided he couldn't break the news of the colonel's death tactfully. If it had been under different circumstances, he would have dealt with the general's coming in a more ceremonious way. And yet, he had demanded to know of the colonel's whereabouts. "Colonel Sheridan is dead, sir," the captain answered, and waited for the finality of the matter to sink in. "Yes sir, he is dead. He was killed while in the pursuit of Captain Courtland, who escaped several days ago. As a matter of fact, sir, I was about to write the incident in my report and then send it to Washington."

The general's reaction was as the captain had predicted. The general's shoulders were no longer broad and straight, and he appeared to lose the power of his demanding stature. However, he was only momentarily stunned and quickly reorganized his thoughts. "If that is the case, Captain Birney, then it is my duty to inform you that a garrison will be arriving in the next few days for supplies and that you will assign as many men as you can spare to accompany them to the front lines," he said almost apologetically. "The South is getting weaker, but they have spies everywhere. Our supply lines have been cut, and we have to attempt another supply route to Raleigh and then to Wilmington and finally to Fort Fisher."

The young captain listened intensively as Wallingsford explained the details of the war. Excitement welled up in the captain's chest as he thought of accompanying the garrison to Raleigh. However, Wallingsford didn't include him. Now that the colonel was dead, the duty for commanding the fort fell on him. He suddenly felt cheated, for he longed to be a part of the war. He had to settle for commanding Fort Wayne. It wasn't supposed to be like this. The colonel had been in his own world, and he had been as incompetent as he had been drunk. He had died by his own carelessness and, to further add insult to injury, he'd had to deal with a man who had committed crimes so heinous against the innocent that he should be hung for three times over for them. Maybe it wasn't the battle-front, but it would be his first full command.

"General Wallingsford," he said with some familiarity, but was careful not to exceed his bounds. "If I understand you properly, I am to stay here at Fort Wayne. But, the war, sir."

"That is correct, young man. You don't seem to realize the importance of what you have here. It is your duty to keep our men supplied. It is you duty to make sure that the Confederacy doesn't spread to this point," Wallingsford stated with great intensity, totally understanding the captain's disappointment. "Think of Generals Sherman, Grant, and McClellan, all of them strong warriors and leaders, but they all have to follow orders, as well as give them," he continued.

Captain Birney tried not to show his disappointment again and swallowed his pride. He knew there would be no chance of changing the general's mind. The old gent definitely stood by his word, something the young captain respected above all else. Besides, General Wallingsford had no desire to be the bearer of bad news. Before arriving at Fort Wayne, he had to come through Gettysburg, which was one of the bloodiest scenes he had ever witnessed while in command. The bodies of the dead and the shattered lives of the wounded still bore a massive twinge of agony on his brow. He had been granted the privilege of writing the letters to the mothers and wives of the fallen soldiers, men no older than Captain Birney himself. It didn't appeal to him, this job, but someone had to do it. Never having had children of his own, he tried to harden his heart. But under the circumstances of war, he became a sort of father figure and friend to those he had once led into battle.

Then his attention was drawn to the people standing on the porch across from the stockades. He noticed how protective the three Indians were of the young woman who stood in the shadows. He was also puzzled at the attention they received from the soldiers. It could be conceived as royal treatment. He watched as the soldiers rushed to bring in fresh linen and water. They only stopped momentarily to ask if the party was satisfied with everything. Then, without pausing, they took the horses to the stables, brushed them down, watered, and fed them.

"And now, Captain Birney . . . who are they?" he asked. "Are you planning to open relations with the Indians as well? And who is that young woman?"

Captain Birney had forgotten momentarily about his guests. As a result of the new circumstances surrounding them and his new command, everything was happening much to quickly. He knew he would have some explaining to do. It was considered unusual for Indians to be housed in the main quarters of the fort. But he felt he could justify his reasons. "They are witnesses to one of the crimes committed by James Courtland, sir," he stated quickly.

"And what crime is it that allows Indians to be housed in the fort? They are savages. They can't be trusted," the general pressed.

"But I beg to differ . . . sir!" Birney announced. "In the past few days, I learned about these people. They are no more savage than we are," he said almost mockingly. They were under the protection of the fort, and Captain Birney felt it was his duty to treat therm with all the courtesy befitting honored guests. Since the command was his, he could do as he saw fit. "Sir, it is because I gave my word, as a gentleman, that the young woman came here to testify against Courtland. She is the daughter of Devon Bainbridge, and the man to her immediate right is his son," Birney stated carefully.

"So why are they in the company of heathens? A well bred young woman like her . . . I knew her father well!" he exclaimed.

"Sir, if you please, I would rather you refrain from calling them heathens. That young woman has been through hell. Beg your pardon, sir. She has put everything on the line to be here. She has vowed that this is no longer her home, and to be honest . . . I don't blame her for not wanting to come back here," Birney stated with certainty.

The general eyed him questionably because Birney wasn't speaking out of anger. He seemed to sense the young woman's need for stability and home, which was something she apparently hadn't found here with her own people. "I must speak to this young woman. Invite her and her party to supper," he stressed with great interest.

"Supper! I don't know—" the captain could barely complete his statement when he was interrupted.

"That's an order, Captain Birney! I plan to hear this most intriguing story and I want to hear it from her own lips," he grunted.

The captain dared not argue. General Wallingsford had proven to be quite demanding and set in his ways. He wasn't given the chance to keep his promise to René. He had a job to do, which was more than he had intended to do even when he had started out after Courtland two and a half days ago.

With that he saluted and quickly turned to join Renéand her husband. He knew she wouldn't rally at the thought of being the subject of a dinner conversation. The general's demands were unwarranted, but Birney was the junior officer in this case, and his career would be on the line if he disobeyed a direct order. He rehearsed each word, hoping to make his guests uncomfortable with the new arrangements.

Captain Birney was still talking to himself when he reached them, and soon realized that they overheard everything. "I'm sorry," he said, trying not to seem overly concerned. "But I am doing what I have been ordered to do." Their stares bothered him more than their silence, but he continued. "General Wallingsford wants to talk to all of you at supper. It is not a request . . . it is an order," he pressed.

Black Eagle broke the silence, and the anger in his voice was enough to still Birney's blood. "No! You will tell your gen-er-al . . . we will talk tomorrow. Tell him!" he demanded as he escorted Renéinto their quarters. He refused to be ordered, especially when his wife needed to rest. She hadn't had a moment to take a breath, and now someone else was making demands on her.

The young captain was stunned by Black Eagle's sudden outburst. He hadn't expected him to refuse so harshly. But Black Eagle had set the terms, and Renédidn't interfere. She didn't appear to be the same woman who had openly defended her honor a day ago. And it did surprise him that she didn't speak up before Black Eagle whisked her away. Furthermore, Robert made no effort to persuade him otherwise.

"I don't know what to say," Captain Birney said to Black Eagle's back. "The general is most anxious to talk to her."

"Re-nea will not play puppet to your friend!" Black Eagle stated firmly. "No more talk!"

Then Birney turned to Robert, who listened but cared little for what the general wanted. Too many people were making demands upon his sister without a care for her feelings. "What did you expect, Captain Birney?" A lovely civilized supper . . . with my sister as the main course to entertain your precious general?" Robert said snidely. "My God, man, don't you think she has been through enough?"

"I know, I know, but, I'm not the one demanding her presence," Birney answered coarsely. "If there was any other way, I never would have asked. The whole matter surrounding this entire situation would be closed. Even I will extend your apologies to General Wallingsford." He knew General Wallingsford wouldn't enjoy being put off so brashly, especially by an Indian.

In the next few days, the fort became very active with the preparations for the court martial. General Wallingsford had sent word to the town of Wilmot that he was in need of civilians to act as jurists, since the soldiers weren't impartial to the case. Later, he found that the people of Wilmot were just as unacceptable,because of their involvement in the Bainbridge massacre. Finally, without much choice in the matter, he was forced to elect Captain Birney and Sergeant Wills. It was futile to consider any other solution, when Renéand her husband planned to leave within a week, no matter what the outcome.

The day of the court martial came, and Courtland was escorted to the courthouse, chained and shackled to the wagon transporting him. His ride through the fort was quite the opposite of what he picture upon his return. He never expected such a reception, with the soldiers' wives glaring at him with disgust. There was a time when he would have made them blush or even cower from his glance.

Upon his arrival into the dimly lit courtroom, James marched boldly down the aisle until he reached the chair in the center of the room. His chains were removed, and he rubbed his wrists with the palms of his sweaty hands. Then calmly he sat and waited, with his arrogance surrounding for all to see.

General Wallingsford entered the courtroom, drawing the attention away from James. Everyone grew silent. The general had hoped the inspector general would arrive on time, but he had been detained in Raleigh. Slowly he raised then hit the mallet, calling the court to order. A slow hush came over the people, who waited anxiously for things to begin. There James heard the first of the many charges filed against him.

"Lieutenant James Courtland, you are charged with the murder of Lieutenant Joshua Gantry, on the twenty-fifth day of July, eighteen hundred sixty. How do you plea?" Wallingsford asked without emotion. He soon pressed the quill pen into the paper to record Courtland's response.

For a few seconds James remained silent, almost as though he had to determine whether he was guilty or not, and the courtroom spectators waited, nearly bursting with the intensity he instilled. Then he spoke, arrogantly, *"Not guilty, sir!"*

Wallingsford wasn't at all pleased with Courtland's brash manner. He wasn't used to hearing such a tone coming from a junior officer, treating his rank of general as if it were of no consequence. "You are also charged with conspiracy to riotous behavior and desertion, and furthermore, the charges of kidnapping, rape, and unlawful endangerment of the well-being of a civilian," Wallingsford stated directly.

Courtland stood with his head high, and said again, "Not guilty, sir! Not guilty to all charges."

If he could, Wallingford would prolong the trial and keep René from leaving the compound. He was grabbing at straws and he hoped to build a defense since he was completely and utterly on his own. But Wallingsford assigned the charges according to their importance, calling the kidnapping charge first, since the victim and the witnesses were ready and able to testify.

"Now that we have heard all the charges, we will take the case, Bainbridge verses Courtland," Wallingsford stated as he pounded the gavel.

Shock and disbelief shone on Courtland's face. He thought sure that this case wouldn't be heard for a while. With his behavior still fresh in everyone's mind, he began to show his darker side. René's testimony would seal his fate, and he knew he wouldn't have a chance for freedom. But it was still better than having his throat cut by Black Eagle.

Then came the moment when Renéwould have her day in court. She walked into the courtroom wearing the beaded dress she and her friends had made. Her hair was adorned with a single eagle feather drawn into a long braid, which swayed as she walked. She maintained her composure as she made her way to the witness box, which was opposite that of James Courtland. Although it was a bright and sunny day, the room appeared to be swallowed by darkness, and all she could see was his angry face.

She kept her eyes straight ahead and tried to concentrate on what she had to say as she gave an account of her innocence in Lieutenant Gantry's death. There was silence in the courtroom as she spoke. Soon the courtroom was abuzz with whispers from the wives and curses from the soldiers who were allowed to attend. The men were appalled, throwing angry stares in James's direction, and the women, out of sympathy for René, wept. James wasn't pleased with the emotion Renéhad generated. They finally understood the pain suffered by this poor woman, how she must have felt to have had her world torn apart by the two men.

Stunned, speechless, and taken completely by surprise at the horrors inflicted upon the young woman, Wallingsford didn't press her with any further questions. He felt sure she had stated her case and dismissed her from the witness chair. But Renédidn't move, forcing him to ask, "Have you anything further you wish to add?"

Renélooked around the room, which had finally come into focus, seeing all the faces of those who had come to see her and to hear how she had been ravaged and degraded. She finally cleared her mind of all the fears she had built up inside, and spoke. Her voice was tender and gentle to the ear, even though what she was about to say would make them despise her. "Yes, General Wallingsford, I do have something to add," she answered slowly. Then she turned back to the people and gave them her full scrutiny, saying, "In the year since I was forced to leave Wilmot, I have learned many things. One thing I have learned is that I am still RenéBainbridge. I know now that in order for me to live a happy life, I cannot live here. You have proven that by not accepting me for who I am. It is true, my mother was a black woman, not a slave, but a free woman. So my secret, as you might call it, is out and I will not disgrace myself by denying it. And I know had she lived to see me now, she would be proud. I am sorry I never had the pleasure of knowing her, of holding her hand, or of even saying the words a daughter says to her mother. But I will say them now, with you, the people of Wilmot, as witness to them. *I love you, Sarah Josephine. I am proud your blood courses through my veins. I am proud to end the torment and shame, because there is no shame in being a part of you. You were free once, and now you are free again through me and my children.*

A strange hush came over the crowd of spectators, many of whom had come to watch with enthusiasm and now for the first time were stricken with the shame of the carnage in which they had participated. They were facing the same young and very gentle woman whose heart had been broken by their acts of hatred and of Jamess' act of vengeance. What was worse, they were finally seeing their own evil sides and were quite shaken by it.

"You speak as though you haven't forgiven the good people of Wilmot. Is that the legacy you intend to leave behind?" Wallingsford asked.

"The good people of Wilmot never thought of anyone but themselves. Look at them! Ask them why, and you will find nothing but another lie to cover the first. I knew nothing of my birth until my wedding day. I lost everything in one night of *hate*. The *good people of Wilmot* have nothing to fear from me, and I want nothing from them or anyone else," René stated harshly as she directed her statement toward the prisoner.

Suddenly, James, fearful that she had damned him in the eyes of the people, stood up to be recognized. He eyed René with contempt as he moved from his seat and headed for the witness box where she was seated. "General Wallingsford, I beg of you, let me question this witness. She has made several statements that have damaged my good name. Surely you will allow me a chance to clear myself," he said as he closed the distance between them.

"Surely you would rather have your defender represent you in the face of the evidence that has been given," Wallingsford stated, though he seemed almost to be asking.

"As you can see, General Wallingsford, I have no one to represent me. I am therefore my own council and I must make things right by getting to the truth," Courtland stated, and continued toward the witness.

"Well, then, proceed, Lieutenant Courtland. However, I must remind you that you will conduct yourself as a gentleman," the general stressed with caution as he watched Courtland approach the young woman mockingly. It was against his better judgment to allow the prisoner near the witness. But James Courtland was, by his right, able to defend himself, and that meant putting RenéBainbridge within his reach.

James smiled at Renéwith contempt, feeling quite pleased with himself for winning over the old goat of a general. His manner was most threatening, causing Renéto sit back in her chair. She knew very well what he was capable of doing, even with a room full of spectators. James had no bonds to curtail his movements, and it appeared he was free to advance on her at will. Without warning, James had René's hand clasped in his, assuring her and himself that she had nowhere to run. "Now, René, let us hear the real truth, which seems to be far from your lips," he stated carefully, still holding her hand tightly.

Renéyanked her hand away from him and recoiled. "You mean that the truth is something foreign to you. You seem to fear what I have already stated, all of which is fact."

"You have said a lot, but is it the truth?" he asked sharply. "You and your family hid the truth about your birth from everyone, including me. How did you expect me to react?" Suddenly there was a wave of agreement on his behalf as the spectators confirmed his argument. "You would have married me if the truth hadn't come out on that day, wouldn't you? If you had succeeded, I would have been the the fool."

Renéhad grown tired of hearing of victimization when, in fact, *she* was the only one on the receiving end of his treachery. "If that is what you wish to believe, then be my guest," she said without remorse.

"So, it is true that you and your father planned to pass you off for white and marry you off to the first man who would have you." From the gaping looks of the spectators' faces to the smirk of triumph on James Courtland's, Renéknew he had turned the tables in his favor.

"If you are trying to switch the blame of what actually took place, you have failed to do so," Renéresponded sharply.

"Have I? I beg to differ. And I suppose you didn't beg me to take you away from those savages?"

"That's not true! You hunted me down for months. I never would have come back here if it hadn't been for you and your meddling. I was happy where I was!" René recanted, angry that he had brought her to this point.

"You call being happy living among the savages and wearing animal skins? What a life you have chosen for yourself!"

"Yes, it is a far better life than what I would have had with you! Besides, you wanted to kill me. You thought I had planned to trap you, when I only released you from your pledge when I learned the truth. It is a shame my father couldn't be here to tell you that himself. I have to thank you and the people of Wilmot for making sure of that," she continued with anger. "I'm sure he would appreciate everyone knowing the real truth of the whole matter: that you only planned to marry me for my share of the estate. And that your only reason for hunting me down was to punish me for cheating you out of a fortune. That's the only truth, isn't it?!" Renédemanded.

James paced the floor, angry that she had such a lethal tongue. Even in her weakened state, she was sharper than ever and had gotten the best of him. Not only had she rekindled the sympathy of the crowd, she had slapped him with the unmistakable truth of his own greed. If she had wielded a knife, she would have split him wide open for all to see.

James was noticeably agitated and began to moved toward her with great speed with his hands reaching for René's throat. She was totally at his mercy, even though Black Eagle wasn't permitted in the courtroom. And in front of witnesses, James would fulfill his quest by killing her. "*Noooo! Damn you!*" he yelled as he reached over the barrier that separated them.

There was no place for Renéto run. The soldiers who were guarding James were all too stunned to move when he lunged into full attack. General Wallingsford's eyes gaped open in disbelief, as he reached for Courtland's arm, trying to sway his assault. Captain Birney struggled to release the safety on his revolver, hoping to fire in time.

The courtroom was alive with the terrible screams of the spectators. As a result of his own cunning, Black Eagle made sure he wasn't far away. He was in the anteroom, waiting escort Renéback to their quarters. He heard the commotion and, out of concern for Renés safety, he entered the courtroom. Everyone gasped, including General Wallingsford, at the sight of him. But Black Eagle refused to change his course, for only a few feet away Renéstruggled to escape James's clutches.

James saw his adversary out of the corner of his eye and stopped dead in his tracks. He was, without a doubt, guilty of the charges levied against him. He cowered in front of Black Eagle and the witnesses in the courtroom, crying as though he had been wounded. "Don't kill me, pleaseee! Don't kill me! I'll do anything, pleaseee! I'll tell the truth. I caused it all: the lies, the riot, everything. I admit it, I killed Gantry and made it look like Renéand her brother did it! I did it all! But I had a right to the money, and she. . . ." James babbled on and on, telling how he had plotted to destroy the Bainbridge family for cutting him off. No one, not even the starchy young captain expected him to disclose the true facts surrounding the deaths of Devon and Rachel Bainbridge or Lieutenant Gantry.

James was a sight, groveling before Black Eagle while his peers and their wives looked on. No one moved to help him and they considered it justice if James Courtland could be put out of his misery. But Black Eagle contained his anger. His only regret was having allowed this man to live in the first place. He could have easily killed him a few days ago. And yet, James was a simpering coward, weeping like a woman and begging for mercy. Something he had not extended toward René. Black Eagle no longer tasted hate, and he refused to allow it to swallow him up again. His wife was only a few feet away and she had endured enough of the savagery of this so-called civilized man and of a people whose hearts were weak with fear. He was sure of only one thing: In order for Renéto have a good life, they must leave this land soon.

Captain Birney had truly blundered, despite the fact that he had promised Renéthat James wouldn't be allowed to get close to her. He had compromised her safety to satisfy his own need for justice. He knew he was wrong in doing so, but in his eyes, it had to be done. "Soldier, put that man back in irons," he ordered, and watched as the shackles were closed around James's wrists and ankles. Then the young captain turned to René, who could barely stand on her own, and asked, "Are you injured? May I assist you in any way, Miss Bainbridge?"

"No!" Black Eagle yelled. "You and your kind have helped enough. We will go now."

"But the trial . . . it's not over," Wallingsford stated slowly.

"Oh, but it is for her," Captain Birney disclosed. "She has done all that we asked of her . . . all that there needs to be done, General. Let her go. Let them both go." Reluctantly, Wallingsford agreed, even though it was against his better judgment. The chief witness to this court martial was slipping through his fingers.

Black Eagle extended a hand to his wife. With that gesture, she rose from the chair and made the painful walk back to the place where she felt secure, to her husband and to the warmth he had to offer. Never once did she look back into the faces of those whose prejudice once clouded their very existence.

Finally, with the door closed behind them, the courtroom exploded with the excitement and anger of a barroom brawl. James was doomed by his own actions. He had confessed in front of everyone. The hangman's rope had been securely tightened around his neck. Renéhad closed all chances of his reaching her again. Her life in this fort and in Wilmot was completely over. She was free to leave.

One final task needed to be attended to before she closed the door forever on her past. Renéhad to return home for the last time and say goodbye to her loved ones.

The Bainbridge Estates still possessed the most beautiful land in the territory. The richness of the soil had yielded a bounty of tall grass that swayed in the breeze. In the distance, a few horses and their foals raced through the upper meadow, periodically taking time to graze. It was a sight that both Renéand Robert longed to behold, and yet, they shuddered when they remembered that fateful night, fore in their wake lay the ruins of what used to be home. The last remnants of their happy existence was gone.

Far out, just above the rise and surrounded by a whitewashed fence, were two gravestones. They were like two beacons, calling out to them. Without realizing what she was doing, Renéforced Black Eagle to release his hold and she made her way up the hill alone. This was something she needed to do for herself, and he in turn didn't want to intrude on her grief. This was another barrier he would have to chip away at to keep from losing her again.

CHAPTER
TWENTY-SEVEN

IT WAS MID-DECEMBER WHEN the rescue party entered the outpost with René in tow. They had traveled long, not waiting or wanting to hear the outcome of the trial. Too much time away from home had lapsed, and winter was serving up its worst, but they were forced to push on. There were many instances when Black Eagle would stop just to allow René to catch her breath or even stretch her legs. Few would doubt that he cared deeply for her if they witnessed the tender treatment he so gladly bestowed on her.

Yet, Black Eagle's heart ached, knowing that he may have to leave René behind, even if they did arrive at the outpost before the heavy snow. He had to consider a lot of things when it came to her ability to travel and to her needs. In as much as he didn't want to succumb to the realization, she would only slow them down or even hinder their attempts at getting home before the big freeze across the lake. This weighed heavily on his mind as he rode toward the outpost. He valued his time with her and hoped that he had filled these past few weeks with enough memories to last until his return.

The outpost was a welcome sight, and the band were greeted warmly as they entered the post. A few well-wishers touched the weary couple as they passed. Gray Wolf and a few of his followers were also there to greet them. Black Eagle felt a sudden rush as his father signaled for him to join him. He quickly acknowledged Gray Wolf and followed Robert into the trading post and up the stairs with René in his arms.

René hardly had a chance to question his reason for rushing her like that. Everything had happened too fast. And she sensed something was bothering him, as he hurried off without an explanation. She decided to wait until his return, rather than worry over something that may be unimportant. So she enjoyed the warmth billowing from the large fireplace and basked in the sheer luxury of being in a safe haven for a while.

The room itself was spacious and well-furnished, with enough room for at least ten people to sleep comfortably. Someone had been very busy making preparations for their arrival and spared nothing to make her feel at home. In the far corner to her right was a large window with dainty white curtains. The room had just been aired out and freshened. The scent of pine and rosewater caressed her senses. She was amazed at how much the room resembled her old one, with a huge feather mattress and a canopy. There were also soft white sheets to rest upon, and a fluffy patchwork quilt draped over the edge of the bed.

René finally walked around the room, testing her balance and absorbing the finery lavished upon her, when Black Eagle and his father entered abruptly. She greeted them both with a smile and slowly walked toward her father-in-law to embrace him. But she was stopped cold by Black Eagle's somber glances and Gray Wolf's stern lip.

Neither René nor Black Eagle had expected Gray Wolf to make the long journey during this season. Yet, here he was, as bold as ever, acting as the leader of his people and not the father of the young man standing beside him. The silence between them forced René to pose the question, "Is something bothering you?" She glanced periodically from son to father and from father to son, hoping that one of them would break their silence.

Immediately, before Black Eagle could explain, Gray Wolf answered, "There is my child. There are many things that concern me."

Confused, René decided it would be better for her to sit down, rather than face what he had to say head-on. She sat on the edge of the bed and waited for Gray Wolf to disclose the matter on his mind. "Re-nea, you have lived among my people for only a short time. And in that time, you have been taken twice. The first time was by a red man, who took the lives of your children. My son proved that he loved you by bringing you and the wife of his best friend home again. And then, you were taken by white men, who are now a threat to the safety of my people," he said slowly but directly. "I fear these white men will return in search of you, dear child, now that they know where we dwell."

René said nothing, but gave him her full attention. She remembered all too well how she was whisked away, helpless against the lot of them. But she wasn't the cause. These men acted on their own. Gray Wolf believed that she brought the harmful element into their domain.

Black Eagle held her close as Gray Wolf determined her fate. He was a fair man when it came to matters of the heart, and it seemed the current circumstances surrounding her abduction bothered him greatly. He and his people would have to uproot themselves and move to parts unknown. No matter what he declared, he knew that Black Eagle wouldn't be pleased with his decision.

"You, my child, must understand why I feel you should not return with us. You must stay here, with your own kind," Gray Wolf said gently, trying to spare her any further discomfort. "I cannot risk having the white man return to our village in search of you when our Sioux brothers may need our aid," he added.

With that, René swallowed her pride, to keep hidden down the truth only Black Eagle and her brother knew. It had been a long and difficult time and now she had to deal with nonacceptance all over again. And she wasn't really sure what to believe since Black Eagle wasn't responding. As a result of his ruling, she knew Gray Wolf wouldn't reconsider. Gray Wolf was probably right about his assumption. She was bad medicine for his people. René pulled away from Black Eagle, feeling betrayed, as Gray Wolf's words cut into her soul. She was never to return to the village she called home.

Finally, Black Eagle spoke, asking, "What about our children? Are they to be banished as well?" He hoped that the bringing of a new life to the village would prompt Gray Wolf to change his mind.

But Gray Wolf hadn't considered the child at all. And, what with everything centering around his decision, he would have to show it mercy. He paced the floor for a moment, without looking at either one of them. Then he came to an abrupt stop, clutching the small medicine bag around his neck. "My grandchildren have not committed any crimes against my people," he said sternly. "Black Eagle will return in the spring to fetch the child home. I will have my grandchild around me," he continued.

René was stunned. He would accept her children and yet have nothing to do with her. She became infuriated with his continued reference to his grandchildren and spoke quite brashly. " I won't let you take them from me! They are mine, just as much as they are Black Eagle's. You can't take them from me. I won't let you!" René said angrily.

"Don't be silly, child! What can you offer them?" Gray Wolf asked without hesitation.

"I . . . don't know what you mean," she answered.

"They will not be accepted by your world, just as you have not been accepted. You can offer them nothing but a horrible existence." he responded quickly.

Stunned again by his abruptness, René was forced to say the only thing that would hurt the one she loved more than anything. "So when you come back in the spring, I won't be here. The children and I will be gone. You will never take my babies from me."

"You are not thinking of the children. You are only thinking of yourself," Gray Wolf snapped. "It would not be wise for you to keep something that is not yours to begin with."

"I can't believe what you are saying. I can't believe that you would do this to me! You call yourself a fair man, but you're not!" René quickly retorted. "And you," she directed her anger toward Black Eagle, "You brought me back here . . . for what? This? I will never believe another word you say . . . ever!"

She had said more than she had planned, and severed any kind of communication between her and Black Eagle. They had decided her fate, had planned to take her children and leave her with nothing. Without giving them a second glance, she opened the door and commanded them both to leave. Gray Wolf was unaccustomed to being treated in such a manner, and left in a huff. Black Eagle stayed. He refused to give in so easily.

"I have nothing more to say to you, Black Eagle!" she said harshly.

Black Eagle didn't like her tone, but he attributed it to the shock of what his father had declared as law. He was hurt by the decision—even more than she. What was he to do? "I have much to say to you," he said strongly as he removed her hand from the door and closed it behind his father. "In time . . . I would have convinced my father that you were not a threat to our people. But you spoke too soon. He is old, but he is a wise man. He would have seen the error in his judgment, but I fear your manner has angered him greatly."

"You expect me to believe that you would have changed his mind? I remember Walks Alone and how she was banished. Now it has happened to me, with a few simple words. And you were planning to leave without me, weren't you? Was that your plan all along? You never intended to take me home. I won't give up my babies!" René yelled again.

"You silly woman," Black Eagle said, echoing his father. "Do you believe I really planned all this?"

"Yes, I do. I can't stop you from leaving me behind. You and your father have already decided my fate. You even tricked me into believing that you came for me, when you actually came for the child I bear," she said quickly.

"That is not true! You speak foolishly!" he roared. "I did come for you. I cannot say it in any other way. And my father, he thinks much about our people. He is thinking about you and the well-being of our children. You must believe that he cares for you."

René said nothing. She felt she had been thrown away without any regard for her feelings. She had lost the man she loved and whom she thought loved her. She was alone again, and this time James Courtland wasn't in the picture. Everything was completely out of control.

Black Eagle realized that he couldn't reach her. He had chipped away at the wall she had put between them, but to no avail; he was blocked at every turn. She neither heard him say he loved her or even that he would come back for her. She could only see him exit the room with her heart.

In the same manner René had responded to him, Black Eagle responded to his father. He traveled the journey to their home in silence, holding up the rear of the column while his father led the way. He had no idea how he would convince his father that René was an important factor in his life. He couldn't imagine being without her, and felt a threatening urge to return to the outpost. Even though he had asked Robert to keep her from leaving, he could only wonder if he would honor his request. René's reaction to the possibility of losing her child would only add fuel to the flame he had already ignited. René would run off. And the distance he had put between them made the threat even greater.

Gray Wolf didn't understand the pressure he had placed on his son, forcing him to relinquish the only woman who had loved Black Eagle unconditionally. He realized that Black Eagle would not forego a hardship as long as he could have his precious wife. Black Eagle was bound by honor to follow his father back to their homeland.

After ten weeks they finally reached their homeland, laden with many furs and meats from the vast forest. Everyone had headed home, to the warmth of their cabin and to their families, while Black Eagle headed for his dark, cold, and empty cell. Gray Wolf watched his son enter and close the door behind him. He hadn't taken any meat for himself, nor had he taken any of the furs.

"It is good to have you home, husband," White Feather said as she approached her husband from behind. "I see our son has come home, as well . . . but he is sad."

"Yes, that is true, dear woman. His heart is heavy. I fear I may have acted too hastily," he said slowly. "But what I have passed down is law. It cannot be changed," he added as he turned to greet his wife.

White Feather listened to her husband's words. He had suffered greatly from his son's loss and he felt the same pain when Black Eagle's young Re-nea was taken. He couldn't bring himself to put her in any more jeopardy, knowing that the white man would come again, seeking his revenge on her. As much as he wanted his son's happiness, he didn't want his people to be in danger. Black Eagle would just have to find another woman to fill the emptiness in his heart.

"Husband, put yourself in your son's place. If it had been me taken by force, away from the people that I have come to love, would you not want to bring me back?" she asked carefully. "Re-nea is our daughter. She loves us like she loved her parents. She carries our grandchild in her body. And you speak of laws, my husband! You are the one who makes the laws to help us. Are they not meant to protect Re-nea as well?"

Gray Wolf listened with an open heart. His wife had spoken with wisdom. Yet, she made him understand why René had reacted the way she had and why Black Eagle suffered without her. They were truly one in the body and mind. His decision lay forfeit in the four winds, but that was better than losing his son's loyalty.

"You are right, dear woman. Black Eagle must go back for her. Re-nea will be welcomed here for the rest of her days," he said slowly. "But I hope we will not live to regret this."

"Then you must tell your son. You will make his heart rejoice with such news," White Feather offered with excitement.

"Tomorrow, White Feather. He needs to rest."

But White Feather wouldn't let him off so easily. She wanted Black Eagle to know now. Tomorrow may be too late. "No, my husband, you must tell him now," she said as she walked toward Black Eagle's cabin.

When they arrived, they found Black Eagle sitting in the dark. He didn't answer when they called his name. In his mind, his father had issued the worst punishment given to any man. And he had been forced to abandon his wife, leaving her in the hands of her brother. What was worse, she had threatened to leave before the spring. He worried that he wouldn't arrive in time to stop her. And what about the child? How could he look upon it without seeing her face?

Gray Wolf cleared his throat and waited for his son to acknowledge his presence. But he was in Black Eagle's home and he was compelled to ask permission to enter. With a slight gesture of his hand, Black Eagle bade him to enter, but made no effort to light a fire to warm the place. It was as cold a welcome as it was cold in his home.

White Feather quickly lit the kindling and started a fire roaring in the pit. She placed more wood on the flames as it began to pick up, and then prompted Gray Wolf to disclose why he had come. He was reluctant at first, but then the words began to spill from his lips like water over the falls. "I may have acted too hastily when I banished Re-nea. She has done no harm to our people, but I foresee more trouble ahead. Black Eagle nodded, but said nothing. He had said all he could before they arrived, and his father had not responded. It was Gray Wolf who had to make amends now that René and Black Eagle were separated. "I cannot blame her for the behavior of outsiders. And since she is not to blame for what they do, she will be allowed to return to our village."

Black Eagle didn't like the implications around that and stated, "She will be allowed to return. Then you do not consider Re-nea as one of the people. She will be cast out if she makes a mistake!"

"It is all I can do to keep my son home. I fear I will lose you to this woman. You, my son, are destined to be chief. You are a good leader and a fair one," Gray Wolf added.

Black Eagle thought about everything his father had said. He was destined to be chief. It was a position of honor, one he thought he wanted more than anything. But he'd found his niche. He'd found René was the one thing he wanted most. It wasn't enough that she be allowed to stay; she had earned the right to be here. "I will not be chief to a people who exile the woman I have chosen as my mate. They must accept her," Black Eagle stressed. "She is my life as mother is yours."

Gray Wolf couldn't argue with that. He would rather die than spend the rest of his life without his wife. Black Eagle had married for life, just as he had done.

Meanwhile, René had made several attempts to leave the outpost, trying to outwit her brother at every turn. On her last try, she had persuaded one of the priests to take her to the French fort. She had a twenty-mile lead when Robert caught up to her, bringing her back, and locking her in her room. She tried not to run away, but the ensuing threat of losing her children outweighed everything else.

"I can't understand it! René has been acting very strange lately You would think that James Courtland's hanging would have calmed her down by now. But, I just can't seem to put my finger on what is bothering her," Robert stated as he folded the last of the pelts and placed it on the pile with the others.

"Well, for one thing, you can't keep her locked in her room forever," Lily stressed as she prepared a tray of food for René.

"I'll stop locking her in her room when she stops running away."

"But, Robert, have you looked at her lately? She hardly eats, and she's so pale. She just sits in the chair by the window. looking at nothing and saying nothing. I don't like it," Lily said with urgency.

Robert hadn't been paying attention to his sister since he brought her back and he was forced to take notice of what Lily actually meant. His sister had changed . . . greatly. And he had failed to see that even as he dragged her back to the outpost. She obviously felt threatened, so much so that she was felt to run. He was more concerned with the life he and Lily were trying to build rather than dealing with his sister's situation.

"I haven't noticed anything. I just don't understand why she keeps running off," he said softly. "If she weren't my sister . . . well . . . I don't know what I would do!"

"She is your sister, and you have been neglecting her," Lily stressed again. "Have you asked her why she keeps running?"

"No! But she has no excuse!"

"That's where you're wrong," Lily stated, almost angrily. "She 's been served nothing but treachery, and to be honest I don't blame her in the slightest for any of her actions."

"Whose side are you on, anyway?" Robert asked as he placed the fine lynx furs on the pile marked for transport. He marveled momentarily at their softness while Lily fumed from the small kitchen.

"I'm on her side, if you must know. She has more to lose than either one of us, or didn't you realize that? And until you hear her side of it, you will never understand the why of it," she snapped, and headed for the stairs. Lily was angry and quite flustered with her husband's lack of heart. "She'll run again once she gets the chance. I'm just afraid she'll get hurt the next time she tries," she warned.

Lily was right and she had finally gotten his full attention. Something was wrong, and Renéwasn't saying anything. There were no clues to guide him on this one. The only lead he had came from his wife, and she only opened the door to other possibilities. Yet, in these past few months, he hadn't given René the attention she was due. He was suddenly assailed with guilt. To further add to his guilt, he had become what he had promised that he wouldn't: true businessman who was even more absorbed in his work than he was with his family. It was true; in fact, Robert's trading post had become so popular that he bought up Denver's share of the business. This allowed Denver to take up with Mrs. Graham in her rooming house, something he'd always wanted to do. Robert kept the business up with prime stock in horses, flour, and other trade goods, bringing in new prospects from miles around. He even opened the line of trade to the French and hoped to set up a trade agreement with the United States once the war was over.

"Wait! Lily, let me take it to her," he said as he rushed up the stairs. "You're right, I need to talk to her."

Lily gently handed the tray to her husband and then walked toward their bedroom. She had done her job for the day, now it was his turn. She heard him fumble with the lock before opening the door. Then she heard the door close gently behind him. "At least now you will hear her side. Listen well, my darling."

René was now well into her eighth month and showing every sign that motherhood was approaching. She didn't like being trapped and vowed she would be free of this mess soon. If she had the chance to flee again, she would definitely take it. She wanted to avoid being caught here with her guard down, which above all else left her anxious and totally vulnerable. She had only wished she had been successful in getting away with Father Lucas the first time she ran away. By now, Black Eagle would be well on his way here. And with her being locked in her room, there would be no chance for escape again. She was riding on blind faith, hoping that the weather would keep him away from the outpost a while longer.

"René, René," Robert interrupted. "I've brought your supper."

René heard her brother, but said nothing, not even a small greeting. It seemed futile for her to speak when no one was listening to her in the first place. She was about to lose everything she held dear, her child and her home. She already knew she had lost her husband as a result of her unwillingness to listen, but most of that was attributed to his father's pride. Sometimes, when she really thought about it, she had seemed overly defiant when she recalled her reaction to his ruling. But Robert didn't realize that he too was partly to blame for some of her troubles. She couldn't even bring herself to scream at him, knowing full well that he wouldn't understand her anger if she had.

When René didn't respond to him, Robert quickly marched in and then placed the tray on the table beside her. Next, he pulled up a chair and placed it next to her. It didn't take long for him to notice the change Lily had mentioned. René had paled, and the healthy, lively glow she once had was now gone from her lovely face. She appeared to have given up.

"I brought you a wonderful meal. Lily thought you might like to try some pheasant and small potatoes. Look!" he said as he removed the napkin and placed it over her lap. "It looks wonderful. She spent a lot of time preparing this for you," he continued.

Again and again René remained silent, refusing to allow him to break down the protective wall she had built. Robert's patience was wearing thin. He had tried everything he could think of, but René said nothing and didn't acknowledge his presence. Even his clumsy attempt to put a spoonful of food into her mouth became frustrating. As a last resort, he took a bite himself, hoping to draw her attention. "Ummm . . . tastes really good!"

No matter what he said, she refused to give in. He was at a loss on how to get her out of the depression that was taking its toll on her. "I'm sorry, René," he said while placing the fork on the tray. "I'm so very sorry. I hurt you and I haven't been here for you at all. I know, I haven't been listening and I should have. Everything has changed . . . you . . . me and Lily. If you could only help me understand why . . . why you kept running away. Please, René," he offered softly.

That was the start of a wave of anguish that poured from his sister's lips. He was totally devastated by what he heard, and he allowed her to release everything she had bottled up inside for these past few months since Black Eagle and his father had gone. He understood why she continued to run even when her pregnancy was making it difficult for her to get around. She was in pain, a far greater pain than he could ever imagined.

I didn't know, sis. I really didn't know!"

"Of course you knew? Black Eagle is your friend. You would do anything to please him," René offered coolly.

"But I should have understood . . . I should have seen what was coming."

"No, you wouldn't have noticed anything, anyway. You are a man. You think like a man. This child is all I have left of any happiness I once had. When Black Eagle comes, it won't be mine anymore," she said sadly, and gently placed her hand on her belly. "It will never know me. It will never know how much I love it."

"I can't let you suffer like this! What can I do? I don't know where to begin,"Robert said softly. His heart was breaking for her.

"Suffer? That seems to be the only thing I have to look forward to. I can't break the chain from Wilmot or from Black Eagle any more than I can break the vice that hovers over me now. I wanted so much, but all I have to show for it is . . . helplessness. And I don't have the strength to fight anymore."

Robert heard her painful declaration. She needed his support, but all he had given her was a room with a key that locked her in. She had been put into another prison of sorts, but this time her jailer was her own brother. He couldn't make amends for this no matter how hard he tried.

"How could I have been so stupid . . . so blind?" he asked as he touched her hand. "Why didn't you tell me?"

"I panicked after I heard you promise Black Eagle you would keep me here. After all, he is your friend," she said as she pulled her hand away. She sensed betrayal from all directions and wanted no part of it. "There is only one thing I will ever ask of you and that will be the last. Please send for Father Lucas. I need him here," she implored, almost bringing Robert to tears.

"Why? What can he do for you?" he asked, hurt that she didn't want his help.

"I don't know . . . but at least I won't be alone when my time comes," she said finally.

"But, but you're not alone, René. Lily and I will be here for you like always."

"No!" René snapped. "You have your own life . . . .you and Lily both have your own family to deal with. I can't come between you two, ever."

Robert didn't hear her clearly and quickly stated, "You're making things difficult for me, René."

"How, Robert? How am I making things difficult for you?" she asked slowly. "I've got more to lose just sitting here waiting for Black Eagle to come for my baby. And when he comes, I don't want to see him," she snapped. "I can't deal with all the madness around me. Now, please . . . ask Father Lucas to come. He's the only true friend I have left. At least with him nearby, I won't lose my mind."

Robert realized that René had nothing further to say to him. She had made her peace with him and now she expected him to honor her request. So much was at stake and he couldn't fathom or even share in her pain. In his quest for friendship with his brother-in-law, he had denied René the right to decide to do for herself. All he could see at the time was Black Eagle's point of view. And that was no excuse for the way he had treated his own flesh and blood. He went over her words again: *You and Lily have your own family . . .* " He was beset with confusion, and then with a spark of revelation, he realized that Lily, *his* Lily was carrying his child.

CHAPTER
TWENTY-EIGHT

IN ALL THE TIME he had spent away from his beloved Re-nea, Black Eagle could only wonder whether he would return in time. He had great news, and it was important that she hear it from his own lips. He hadn't been this happy since she had first agreed to be his bride, and now . . . she would be with him forever. He continued to make his way there, traveling over the frozen lake and through the snow-covered lands toward the outpost. Each day brought him closer to mending the wounds inflicted by his father and by his unwillingness to speak up for her. With only a few miles separating them, he hurried to the outpost, hoping.

The outpost was alive with the new arrivals ready to barter their skins, while others were trying their hand at cards, hoping to get a stake before the snow came again. Robert sent for Father Lucas, and René seemed more at ease and at peace with each passing day. Meanwhile, the good father enlightened his subject with many stories of his adventures with the Blackfoot and Cree tribes and of his travels to the great blue oceans. He never seemed to tire, usually finding time to read to René from his journals or a passage from the Bible. Every waking moment was spent preparing her for the time when her husband would come.

"You seem cheerful today, my child," Father Lucas remarked as he studied her expression while she read. She had color in her cheeks, and her eyes sparkled with new life when she smiled.

"It's been a lovely day, Father Lucas. I haven't had much to smile about lately, but . . . it's been a lot better since you came," René stated as though she had taken a breath of fresh air.

"Is that so? Is that so?" he asked with a chuckle, but suddenly his manner became serious. "Then, my child, you must tell me what you plan to do when your husband finally comes to the outpost. You have avoided talking about him for many weeks. What you feel . . . will not go away. You must face it, even if you are frightened by the outcome."

"There is nothing to say," René responded. If only she could change the path of his train of thought. However, Father Lucas was a persistent old man, and very much like her father when he wanted her to face the truth.

"Is that so?" he asked again. This time he held a stern, but gentle grip on her hand. He wanted her to draw her attention to her own pressing needs and that of the children she carried.

"Don't trouble yourself, Father Lucas. I don't want to think about him right now. Besides, the snow hasn't melted, and he won't be here for another few months," she said.

"From what your brother has told me about Black Eagle, the snow won't keep him away," he said. "Well, my child, I can't help you until you are willing to face the facts. Black Eagle will be here before you know it."

René's eyes widened when she realized that her semihappy little world could in fact be shadowed by Black Eagle's untimely arrival. Again she felt overwhelmingly threatened and had the uncontrollable urge to run. "I know he's coming and there nothing I can do about it," she offered.

That moment finally arrived one snowy evening. It seemed it might be the last snow of the season. The spruce and maple trees were beginning to show buds. Black Eagle rode past everything and headed straight for the trading post, sparing no time to tether his horse or even to dust the snow from his clothing. He rushed in only to be greeted somberly by Robert and his wife. It had been a long spell since their last encounter, and he knew from their lack of enthusiasm that his situation had changed.

"What say you, brother-in-law?" Black Eagle asked as he extended his hand in greeting.

Robert took his hand, but his heart wasn't in it. He couldn't help but feel that he was still betraying René with this gesture of friendship. "I know why you are here, Black Eagle. And I can't say that I am pleased."

"You are angry that I have returned so soon?" Black Eagle inquired. "Or . . . have things changed between us, brother?"

"You could say that . . . René told me all about what your father said before you both left. Did you think I would let you hurt her like that?" Robert demanded.

"I came to bring my family home," Black Eagle stated quickly, realizing that Robert was upset with him and the mess that had been created upon his leaving.

"You mean . . . your child, don't you?" Robert demanded again.

Black Eagle was stunned by his tone, but answered calmly, "No, I have come for Re-nea. For me, Re-nea comes first. My father did not understand. I will not live in my homeland without her. But now my father understands that Re-nea is my life."

"You mean . . . you don't plan to take her child away from her?"

"The child is everything, but I will be nothing without Re-nea. She means more to me," Black Eagle offered slowly.

While her brother and husband spoke downstairs, René began to panic. Seeing Black Eagle as he passed through the gate and headed straight for the store pushed her to move carelessly. Her time was up, and the contentment she once felt diminished within those few seconds. There would be no escape for her now.

In her panic, she bumped into the large chair by the window, causing her pains to start prematurely. It was the most horrifying moment she had ever experienced. Yet, with all the pain she suffered, she never uttered a word, nor did she cry out for help. She hurriedly walked toward the bed, only to be caught by another sharp pain and a sudden wetness at her feet. Her water had broken, and she knew there was nothing to stop the baby from coming. It wanted to be born, and they chosen to come on the very day Black Eagle arrived.

The pain passed as quickly as it had come. René quickly changed her gown and used the soiled one to clean up the floor. Time appeared to be on her side for the moment. She was able to complete her task and to get into bed before the next wave of pain hit. There she stayed until a knock intruded on her silent cries. Quickly she wiped away the tears and answered, "Come in!"

Black Eagle entered first, carrying two cradle boards and a small bundle in his arms. His excitement didn't outweigh the fact that she felt enraged by his intrusion. And he had no idea what he was walking into. He was followed by Robert, who waited for any inkling or hint that René was uncomfortable with the company. Another wave assaulted her, letting her know that she wouldn't be going anywhere anytime soon.

René didn't welcome him or give her usual greetings. But she watched every move he made. Suddenly the little bundle began to move and squirm, forcing Black Eagle to place it on the bed. Inside the bundle revealed the handsome little tyke René had left behind. And Black Eagle thought it appropriate to bring little One Shoe, who struggled to free himself of the bearskin wrapped around him. He wanted out and he wanted to see where he was. He fussed when he didn't see his father, and he buried his face into the quilt.

"You see . . . I told you I would come for you. And I brought One Shoe with me. He misses his mother," Black Eagle offered gently.

René wanted to hug the little babe, but the pain of her contraction wouldn't permit her. "Please . . . this . . . is not the . . . time!" René stammered.

Upon hearing her voice, the toddler moved toward her, giving René a huge hug. He remembered her. As young as he was, he remembered his mother and called to her. But René couldn't give him the attention he needed. At first Black Eagle was upset at his reception, but he later noticed how René bit her lip, holding back the tears.

"You are right . . . it is not the time," he responded, and quickly removed One Shoe from the bed. Then he placed his hand upon her belly and felt the tightness from the contractions that were attacking her. "Your time has come . . . and you said nothing."

René couldn't answer for fear of crying. It hurt more than she wanted to admit. When the pain suddenly subsided, she begged, "Please . . . Father Lucas . . . Get him!"

Robert was out of the room like a shot, leaving René and Black Eagle in each other's company. She could barely hold back the screams that caught in her throat.

Black Eagle put all his feelings aside and grabbed her hand and held it, as if for dear life. She tried to remove it, but he wouldn't let go. "If you must . . . scream!" he said sternly. One Shoe grabbed her other hand as well, calling her name to a point it seemed he begged for her to hold on.

Nonetheless, Black Eagle's manner confused her even more than it had before he had left. But she didn't have time to worry about such things. Her attention was elsewhere. When the pain was over, she was finally able to focus. The issue at hand that bothered her the most was her child. "I can't let you take it from me!" she said strongly.

And he answered without waiting, "I did not come to take the child away. I came to get my family. You and the child . . . Re-nea."

But she didn't respond to him. She could hardly hold on to the light as it faded out around her. She heard him say her name, calling, beseeching, "Re-nea . . . Re-nea . . . ,"until nothing. She lay unconscious.

Minutes later, Father Lucas and Robert rushed into the room. He carried blankets and a small bag with medicine and herbs. "And who is this?" he asked as he checked René s pulse.

"I am Black Eagle," he said proudly. He watched as the priest removed the covers, checking her contractions.

She had not responded to his voice as he entered, he knew that she was in trouble. "Then you are the one she has told me so much about. Come with me," he said as he walked to the other side of the room. He didn't want René to hear him even in her unconscious state. "Do you want her to live, my son?"

Black Eagle didn't understand why he would ask such a question, but he answered, "Yes . . . I do want her to live."

"Then you must tell her that you want her. You must convince her that she will be going home with you, even if it is a lie," Father Lucas stated calmly.

"A Lie? Black Eagle does not lie . . . not ever!"

"Well, you had better be very convincing, my son. She has lost faith in you. If you truly want her to live, you will tell her. Tell her . . . now."

Black Eagle looked back at the woman he loved, who lay peacefully still in her bed. He had come all this way to bring her news of home, and now this. She wanted to die. He could feel it. He had failed her again, and the Great Spirits were waiting to take her and the child where no one could hurt them ever again. But he wasn't willing to part with her. He considered untimely death a way of cheating life. They had too much to do together, to see and to learn from each other. They were still learning how to communicate. How could he let her go now?

"I will do what I must to save her," Black Eagle stated quickly, and then went back to René s bedside.

There he stayed all through the night and into the wee hours of the morning. He held her hand, speaking softly in her ear. He said many times he loved her, and he told her of the many antics One Shoe had played while en route to the outpost. There was still so much that he wanted to tell her. All he could do was hope that she would hear his pleas.

The following morning she appeared to have gained more color in her cheeks. The contractions started up again, and her eyes opened with a flash. She was surprised to see so many people standing around the bed, from the smallest who ran to her side, smiling, to the one who had talked to her throughout the night. Black Eagle was visibly tired, but he stayed by her side. And when the time came for her to bear down, he helped her. In any other circumstance, he would be standing on the other side of the door, waiting for the sounds of new life to greet him. However, today he was there following every lead Father Lucas gave him up to the point where the sounds of glory entered his ears. The first came yelling at the top of his lungs. Then the second, crying in wee tones.

To all who were witness to the birth of the twins, a sudden relief overcame them and they were washed with pride. Father Lucas extended his blessings over the young and then congratulated the proud father, who had never dreamed he would ever behold such an event. He would never forget the pain or the thrill of their birth. His chest swelled with pride as he was ready to mark this a day of celebration.

"*Onijishin!*" he exclaimed. "It is a great thing she has done!"

Father Lucas was quite moved by Black Eagle's elation over the event. In the many years he had served in the ministries, he had witnessed many births. But he'd never had the pleasure of witnessing the father taking part in it. It was considered bad medicine for the man to be near the woman during a birth. He hoped to enter this event in his journals as he saw a new side to the red man and his ways.

"You are pleased, Black Eagle?" Father Lucas asked.

"Yes! I am more than pleased. She has honored me," Black Eagle announced proudly.

"But what have you done for her?" Robert asked. "She is still afraid. Can't you see that?"

Black Eagle saw more than he knew. He wasn't going to leave her side, not until she understood the reason why he had returned so quickly. He couldn't let her go on thinking of him as a man of no heart or love for her. "I will make her understand. She is my wife. That has not changed."

As Black Eagle tried to bring mutual understanding between Re-nea and himself, his parents and Jaewa were on their way into the outpost. They had planned to surprise their children by bringing gifts and other tributes to make amends. They had left one month after Black Eagle and One Shoe had departed. In Black Eagle's absence, he was given the chiefhood as his loyalty to his people was always outstanding. They felt sure that he and René would want to return to the village once they heard the news. But they could only hope that their children had patched up their differences and had begun anew.

Their arrival into the outpost brought a great deal of commotion. White Feather and Jaewa had built a small cabin beside the store and had nearly completed working on the second when Robert finally took notice. They had acquired a good portion of his land, a piece he had set aside for Lily's spring garden. Then they had put up a barrier to protect the confines of the shelter. The trio had taken the smaller cabin for themselves, leaving the larger one for Black Eagle and hopefully for René .

"Greetings, my son," Gray Wolf said as Robert approached in question.

"Greetings to you, Gray Wolf. What brings you and your lovely wife to Lorraine?" he inquired. "And you, Jaewa, it is good to see you again."

The women nodded briefly and then went about their work, leaving the men to talk. "We have come for our grandchild," Gray Wolf stated quickly. "Has it been born?"

Robert wasn't sure whether it was his place to answer. He couldn't bring himself to betray his sister a second time, noticing that they hadn't asked about her at all. However, that matter was quickly settled for him. Black Eagle and One Shoe had come to greet their family.

"Greetings . . . Father . . . Mother!" Black Eagle exclaimed.

"It is good to see you, son," Gray Wolf offered. "And how is my daughter-in-law?"

"She is well. She is very well, Father."

"And the child?" White Feather inquired most anxiously.

Black Eagle waited for a moment, then said, "*They* are well and growing fast."

It seemed they were appeased by the news and they waited patiently for their invitation to visit with the newborns. Gray Wolf wasn't sure of the reception he would receive from René, since his last encounter with her hadn't been favorable. He had hoped that time would heal her wounds. However, after he pondered over that, he patted his son on the back to congratulate him.

"You will see them later. But for now, rest and tell me the news from home," Black Eagle stated quickly.

"No time to rest. We must finish your cabin before nightfall," White Feather insisted. "It would not be appropriate for you, the chief of the Ojibwa, to live in the house of his brother-in-law. You must have your own home," she continued.

As the shock of what his mother said finally sunk in, Black Eagle moved away to clear his mind. He was chief. That meant only one thing: He had to return home, and soon. And as chief, his wife would hold the same rank as White Feather. She would be of importance to the people. Now he had to convince René that he was truly there for her. She had blocked every attempt he had made this month, and he was slowly losing his ground, although there seemed to be one person pulling for him, Father Lucas, who advised him to take his time. She was still very fragile and couldn't be pushed into making decisions. And yet, his mother was right: He needed his own home, a place where he and René could mend their differences.

"I will help you," Black Eagle stated quickly, and began weaving the heavy straw through the poles. White Feather put the final touches around the cabin by packing mud and straw around the base. It would be enough to weatherproof it when the rains came. Lastly, Jaewa put in the spruce and evergreen branches to cover the floor. Everything was ready for the young couple and their little family. However, it would be a matter of time before René felt she belonged again.

Soon days turned into weeks before René made her way out of her room. White Feather and Jaewa had paid her a visit several times and were received warmly. However, Gray Wolf and Black Eagle were still in the shadows, gradually opening the door. They tried not to crowd her or force her to accept them. They knew it would take time to mend the damage they had caused.

The following morning, White Feather and Jaewa pushed René out of the house. She needed to feel the cool breeze against her skin and to allow the sun to add some color to her cheeks. "You will take some time to yourself. Don't fret! We will watch the babes for you," Jaewa gently scolded. She quickly grabbed her shawl and placed it around René's shoulders and then walked René to the the door. "You need to get out for a while, my child. Now, go . . . the babes will be fine."

Reluctantly, René made her way out of doors. The sky was bright, and the sun was shining warmly over everything. René was glad to be out and almost felt guilty for ignoring her favorite season. The air was sweet, just as Jaewa had said, and the sky was the bluest of blue. René never imagined a day could be so beautiful. Then she moved quickly off the porch like a deer and headed for the clearing just beyond the gate. From the clearing she could hear the whispering waters of the small brook.

René had missed so much being shut in. There was so much to see and so many places to explore. Even in her musings, she took great care not to wander too far away from the outpost. But that was the least of her concerns. And since she believed there was no threat to her well-being , she stretched her self going further and deeper into the forest. However, unknown to her, she had a armed escort covering every move she made.

The crystal-clear waters were refreshing to the touch, and it pleasured her to feel the coolness of the water streaming through her fingers and toes. She hadn't had such pleasure since Black Eagle had taken her to the waterfall in his homeland. But that thought brought back painful memories of things they shared ages ago. Those days were now gone, and she had to look to the future.

She knew she had to consider moving on with her life, now that Black Eagle and his family were there. She needed to forget the past. In as much as she wanted to forget, she was still faced with her love for Black Eagle and could feel that her future plans were meshed around him and her family. As time passed, she had gathered enough strength from all the attention she received from Jaewa and White Feather. In many ways she was happy that they had come. Eventually, however, she would have to face Gray Wolf, since she hadn't given him much of a chance. He had sent for her several times, but she refused to come or would fain to be ill.

"I see you are well enough the wander into the woods," Gray Wolf stated bluntly. "I wish to talk to you . . . daughter."

René was noticeably startled and moved to run, but he put up his hand and commanded her to stop. René obeyed, standing true to her ground as he approached. He had waited long enough, and she had evaded and ignored him far too long. He wanted an audience with her and he expected her to honor his request.

"You have been avoiding me, my child. It is not like you to act so," he continued.

René remained silent for a moment, and then decided she had nothing further to lose by speaking up for herself. "Yes, I have been avoiding you. It was my way of keeping my sanity."

"I do not understand . . . sanity," he remarked. "I do not understand. Is it important to you?"

"In many ways it is, Gray Wolf. When I last saw you, I wasn't given a chance to decide what I wanted to do. You and Black Eagle made those decisions for me. Yet . . . it was my life . . . my choice."

Gray Wolf listened for a moment and then put his hand up to silence her again. "It is true . . . it is your life. And it was not my desire to hurt you," he answered quickly. "I had to think of my people. I feared that the one who took you away would come back for you. I saw death . . . and it would have been the death of my people that would have haunted me until the end of my days."

"I thought I had earned the right to be one of the people you speak of. But in your own words . . . you have told me that I am not," she stated calmly. "Yes, I wanted to be a part of a people who saw beyond my color, but that isn't so. I am to be forever caught between a world of hate and a world of doubt," René continued, feeling that she destined to be alone for the rest of her days.

"I do not understand your words, my child."

"You never really understood why your son brought me to your village in the first place, and sometimes even I am quite amazed at the reason myself. But . . . if I had to do it all over again, I would gladly have accepted Black Eagle as my husband. And . . . I remember how you welcomed me as a member of your family. I had a home again, something no one could take away from me. And then . . . you banished me."

Again, she had Gray Wolf caught in the mainstream of his own words. He had welcomed her and then tossed her aside when it suited him. And Black Eagle, in his attempts to convince him that René was no longer in danger, gave up everything to be with her. "But you are Black Eagle's wife and you are my daughter-in-law. That makes you a member of my clan, my tribe."

"Does it?" she asked almost sarcastically.

"It is true. And my son has told me about the man who took you away. He told me that he has been punished by his own kind. He told me that he will no longer be a threat to you . . . or to my people."

That was news to René. In all the time she had spent with her brother, he had never mentioned that to her. Suddenly, she felt dizzy with relief. Lost was the sting of vengeance she once felt when she thought of James Courtland or remembered the trauma he had caused her. Finally, she would had been released from the prisonlike cell of her own fear. She was free to go as she pleased and she wondered where this new freedom would take her.

Gray Wolf noticed the change in her behavior. He hadn't planned for her to take the news like this. And from the looks of things, she was thinking of other places . . . of places that didn't include his son. The reaction she gave definitely made him worry. "Where are you planning to go, my child?" he asked quickly.

"I don't really know right now," she answered softly. "It doesn't matter anymore. I have no plans at the moment, but the thought of travel and having the freedom to go anywhere I please does interest me. There is nothing to keep me here."

Gray Wolf could see that. He had to make her understand that he had made an error in judgment. From the way she had spoken just now, he appeared to have little time, if any, in convincing her to stay with his son. "What about my son? He has spent much time with you. Is he not reason enough to stay?" he asked as he placed his hand on her shoulder. "He cares very much for you. He has sacrificed much to be here with you."

The sky reflected in her eyes as she tried to balance what Gray Wolf said and what he actually meant. She had been approached many times by Black Eagle, who tried to encourage her to stay. He appeared sincere at times, not putting too much pressure on her. And yet, all she could remember was the day he left her behind and how Gray Wolf's words continued to ring in her ears. She felt she wasn't important enough to be to be a part of his clan or his world. She had finally reconciled herself to a life without him when he returned to take her heart again.

"Not this time," she said. "If Black Eagle ever wanted me . . . he never would have left. He was my whole world, and now . . . I have to go, but this time on my own." It hurt for her to say these things when in truth she still loved her husband deeply. She wanted to belong, to share in his life, but that wasn't to be the case.

In the moment she made that statement, Black Eagle had joined them. He heard everything and wasn't sure how he could make a difference when she was so distant from him. If he only the chance, he would snatch her away and keep her prisoner. But she had been in a prison far too long. Her jailer was long dead and gone. The only threat hovering over them both like a cloud was loneliness.

"Re-nea . . . I want you. I have said as much and more, but you do not hear me," Black Eagle interrupted.

Stunned and uneasy by his sudden presence, René turned to face him. His appearance was that of man in pain. He had reached out to her, but she only pushed him away. He then placed in her hands his prized bow and arrow and said, "Aim it! Point it at my heart, Re-nea, and let it go. I will not stop you from leaving. But I will not live without you, either. It will put an end to our misery."

René closed her eyes. Could he have been telling her the truth all along, or was this another ploy to keep her off guard? "The only thing to come of this will be more anger and . . . more vengeance," she stated as calmly as she could.

"No! But it will bring about the end of our torment, my love. We have suffered long enough, pulling away from each other. Do you wish to spend the rest of your life not knowing that . . . I truly love you? Do you know that?" he pleaded.

René shook her head. It was no use. He had snared her once again. This time, he had placed his life in her hands and had given her a chance to decide what to do. It would be a life with him, or he would die without her. What could she say when she ached for him, loved him? There was no denying how she felt, and yet she couldn't allow another day to go by when she would see his face in her waking dreams.

"I can't think about such things right now," she said as she tried to walk past him. "Besides . . ."

"I will never let you go, Re-nea!" he interrupted, almost demanding.

"Why are you doing this to me?" she asked as she tried to walk pass him again. "Can't you see . . . it won't work for us."

That wasn't the end, at least not in Black Eagle's eyes. He blocked her path and quickly grabbed her by the hands, forcing her to face him. He was a hairsbreadth away, and she could feel his warm breath upon her forehead. Before she knew it, he had wrapped his arms around her, holding her securely in his embrace.

"I want you in my life, Re-nea. I am nothing without you. I am nothing without you. Nothing . . . "

Gray Wolf was witness to his son's proclamation and waited for René to respond. Her tears flowed down her cheeks, and she was soon overwhelmed by all Black Eagle possessed. She had seen this side of him, one of total urgency and of complete defeat. And he couldn't bring himself to press her again if she refused him. He simply released her and walked away, again hoping.

EPILOGUE

THE WAR BETWEEN THE States was over, and therein lay a new enemy of the United States government. His skin was red, and he lived by simple means: from the land. Since he wasn't of their so-called "civilized world," he was, from their point of view, considered a parasite. Thus, the greed of the white man for the long meadows and the deep valleys pushed the red man further into the wilderness and away from the land his ancestors had known for centuries. This time the white man used cannons and guns that fired seemingly without end.

The white man had come to take more than land in the Americas, forcing the Sioux to migrate north and then east, into the lands of the Ojibwa. It had been three years, and the prophesy of the white man's invasion had come to pass. They had slaughtered many, taking scalps and dismembering men, women, and children. The only chance for survival was to move the people as far north as possible. Long lost would be the buffalo and the sweet earth that once gave them life. Long lost would be the sacred burial grounds, no longer sacred, but tainted with the whites pillaging the land for gold.

What good is the land when it is raped of its richness and the carcasses of the vast herds of buffalo lay rotting under the sun? It was a sad thing to be witness to the defiling of such beauty and yet, they came. They came without asking. They took what they wanted, leaving little or nothing behind for the Sioux to live on.

So the Sioux went north and settled in the land of their brother, the

Ojibwa. There they lived peacefully, although they missed their homeland. They had to begin anew in a land they weren't familiar with. Yet, the land was good, though sometimes cruel when the winters came; but, still, the land produced for everyone.

There were many children playing in the field, while the men prepared for the hunt. Word had come that many deer and moose were traveling westward. In addition to the sighting of the large herds, the Ojibwa were planning to celebrate the joining of two tribes. It would mark a time that they were brothers for life. The old and the young made preparation, gathering berries and tapping maple sap for the feasts. Soon the chiefs of both tribes would come to the center of the village to proclaim they were one in blood and body. It would be marked a proud moment in history. The Ojibwa and the Teton Sioux would live together in peace in the northern territory, vowing to protect one and all who asked.

Black Eagle sat in council with the new chief of the Sioux, Thundercloud. Their worlds had come together to share in the vastness of the territory. The land as they knew it was quite plentiful, and both chiefs felt sure that their people could and would be able to live as one. The drums sounded when Black Eagle handed the pipe over to Thundercloud. The ritual was continued until the subchiefs of both tribes had their turn at the pipe. Finally, the Shaman gave a great whoop to indicate that the deal had been set and the drums sounded again.

"It is good that our people will live together in peace," Black Eagle offered. Thundercloud was openly in agreement as he signaled to his warriors for the celebration to begin. Black Eagle complied as well with a brief nod of his head and then watched as their warriors joined together in song and dance. *"A petik nenka ni ma ca"* ("I must go now"), Black Eagle said directly to Chief Thundercloud. "I have much to attend to," he continued.

"I understand," Thundercloud answered. "One must take care of home as it is the center of one's heart."

"It is good to know one's heart," Black Eagle responded quickly as he rose to his feet.

"That is true, and I must take care of my own as well," Thundercloud proclaimed and joined his friend in their walk toward home.

Both men departed from the circle, pleased that they had come to terms with the needs of the other. While the celebration went into full cadence, Black Eagle made his way home. The winter would be long and harsh this season and he had every desire to spend it at home. The celebration could wait until his return. His interests were elsewhere. Suddenly, One Shoe leaped out from behind the cabin, calling One Feather and Falling Leaf. They giggled as they tackled Black Eagle by the entrance and then ran away in the same manner. They were all under Jaewa's watchful eye, who followed the trio into their secret hiding place. Black Eagle smiled, seeing how well and how happy his children had grown.

Black Eagle had pledged all he had to make this day a reality. And by the Great Spirits, he had been given the ultimate gift any man would be proud to receive. He had everything a man could ever want. He entered his cabin, still happy and fulfilled, and was welcomed by the loving smile of his wife. No other man could be so rich . . . so blessed.

"I see the children found you. They have been planning this all day," she said as she dusted him off. He was covered from his shoulders down to his ankles with dirt and grass.

"Indeed so! Then it is only fair that I wrestle with you," he responded, and snatched her up into his arms. The feelings were the same. He still felt the passion boiling for her, and she wanted him as well. It was destiny that brought them together, and he held her tightly, never to let her go.

"You have no time for this," she said softly. "You are chief . . . and the people are expecting you to celebrate with them."

Black Eagle had all he wanted. The day had just begun, and the people would just have to wait. Besides, the celebration would be right unless she was there to enjoy it with him. "The day is young, Re-nea. They will celebrate whether I am there or not. Besides, since I am chief, I should have what I want. Is that not true?"

"And what do you want, my love?" René' asked. She closed her eyes and waited. She was happy and had found the place where she belonged.

"I want you, my love," he offered, and carried her to their bed. He kissed her gently, yearning for her and keeping her close to his heart. "You are forever in my heart and forever to be mine," he said as he kissed her tenderly, drinking in the softness she had to give.

They lay together basking in each other's warmth and feeling renewed with each waking moment they shared. They had everything: a home, three frisky and loving children, and of course . . . they had each other

One Feather, My Father
By Kathryn and Amber Williams-Platt

He gave me one feather,
An eagle feather,
One of strength and power.

He said, "This is me,
I am but one . . ."
But I did not understand.

He said again, "This is me,
I am but one."
And . . . I felt drawn to know more.

This time I listened when he said,
"This is me,
I am but one feather.
I am the warrior.
I am but one . . .
Of many feathers
Take it and be strong.

But when the feather passed through my hands
and drew closer to the ground as lost from the
eagle who once owned it . . . I cried.

For all I have left of my father is one feather
and a memory . . . his legacy.

We will always remember you with love, Dad.